# STEPBROTHER GAMES COLLECTION

A.K ROSE

*This wildly popular dark stepbrother romance was previously published on Radish as a serial and is now compiled into a collection.*

I grew up with Jared since I was a kid. For years I've been subjected to his ridicule, and his taunts. I thought I was safe when he drove off to Harvard in his father's birthday gift—a black Maserati. Now he's back and determined to have me. I can't give into his games, no matter how much I want to. And, God, I want to.

**Content warning**
This series is a dark MFM romance, which means it includes dub-con situations that some readers might find disturbing

Volume One

# Chapter One



"I ALWAYS DID LOVE THE MOUSY ONES."

I slapped Jared's hand from my face and pushed the hair out of my eyes. "I'm not mousy. If you touch me one more time, I'm telling Dad."

He chuckled. The sound made me cringe. I didn't like my stepbrother and I knew he didn't like me. We were worlds apart. He was an Ivy League brat with more money than I could count, and I just wanted to be left alone. I glanced back to Dad in his tuxedo and Connie in her wedding dress. Even though we'd lived together over six years, but less than seven. Now we were supposed to be a family. College couldn't come soon enough.

"Four weeks of just you and me. By the end of their honeymoon, we'll be an old married couple. Just like them."

I yanked my gaze back. "You're not staying for the entire four weeks."

Jared took a long draw of his scotch. "Sure I am. Didn't your daddy tell you? He wanted me to keep an eye on you.

Something about a young girl in this city alone could be trouble, and this time I tend to agree with him. An innocent young girl like you left to your own devices, who knows what could happen?"

His words were slippery like ice. I shuddered. The cat-and-mouse game Jared played was relentless. It started six years ago, when Dad and I moved into their house and, continued ever since. Even leaving for Harvard hadn't curbed his cruelty. If anything, the torment was getting worse. I held his stare as he ran his hand through his blond hair, the movement hiding a wink. He'd turned from a pimply brat into an asshole. There was no way I was spending my last four weeks before college with him.

"I'll talk to Dad before they leave tonight. I don't want you at the house."

People clapped and cheered as our parents cut the wedding cake. I turned at the sound of camera shutters snapping. Flashes sparked like an electrical storm as the knife sliced through the marzipan flowers. Dad leaned in for a kiss, Connie started the clichéd wrestle, ending with Dad wearing cream on his nose. He looked happy. I hoped he was happy. Mom would've wanted him to be happy.

The orchestra started to play. I crossed my arms over my body and gripped my elbows, blinking back tears as memories of my old life flooded me. Mom and Dad smiled, huddled around a campfire. We'd been broke half the time, but we'd been a tight family, until cancer took Mom away.

Now, my life was full of false smiles and broken promises. The pretense was more than I could bear. I had four weeks until I left for campus. I planned on spending them on my own, watching re-runs and packing my bags. I wasn't about to let anyone ruin that.

Jared tapped me on the shoulder and held out his hand. "It's our turn."

I glanced at the guests watching us. The dance. I'd forgotten all about it. I swallowed hard and took Jared's hand, trying not to flinch at the connection.

"Smile, April. Is touching me really that bad?" He muttered leading me onto the dance floor.

I wanted to answer honestly, but Jared could be cruel. The last thing I needed was a scene, especially here. Dad and Connie swayed in each others arms, eyes only on each other. My hand felt hot in Jared's grip as he spun me to face him and stepped closer. I tried to focus on the music and not the two hundred people staring at us.

My gold satin dress slipped against my body as I moved. The cut was tight, hugging my plump thighs before flaring. I worked the bust line upwards with one hand. At least I could walk in the damned thing. Jared's hand strayed down my back. Splayed fingers pushed me against him as we moved. *Please let this night be over soon.*

The heat from his gaze burned. A bead of sweat trickled down my back as I kept pace. "Stop looking at me like that."

"You've filled out a little since I saw you last. Bigger around the ass, although your tits haven't fared as well."

Heat rushed to my face. I shifted my gaze toward Dad. My salvation may as well have been miles away, wrapped up in the arms of another. Dad laughed and twirled Connie around. No one was coming to rescue me. I had to take care of myself. "I see the millions your daddy threw at Harvard hasn't improved your personality. You've always been an insufferable bastard."

"Insufferable? What have you been reading? Pride and Prejudice?" Jared chuckled, smiling for the audience and wrenched me harder against him.

His hard body rubbed mine in places it shouldn't. Long strides kept me off balance. Each pace was longer. His groin brushed against my sex. His hand on my back left me nowhere to move. I couldn't tilt my hips away from his. Each rub made me more aware of his erection. I clamped my teeth shut and hissed through frozen lips as his thigh stroked mine. Jared spun me around the room. I clung onto his jacket as he thrust his hips, his bulge gouging into my body.

The heat from my face traveled lower as the applause broke out in the crowded room. Everyone's eyes were on us and the walls seemed to close in. Couldn't they see what he was doing? Jared's grip was unyielding. His body was lean and powerful. I was helpless against him as we spun. My stomach rolled. His seductive cologne, mingled with the thrust, made my skin feel tight. This was my stepbrother.

The guests climbed to their feet with their ovation, the thunderous sound deafening. My hand clung tight to his to stop from falling, the other gripped his jacket. My heaving breaths rubbed my breasts against him , trying to keep his pace. His strides were too long. I stumbled, making two steps of my own, and in the process, treading on his shoe. His hand tightened around mine. A groan escaped his lips and I couldn't help but smile. The bastard deserved a little pain. Every guest's attention was on us, but Jared's stare was the one I felt the most. Pins and needles scattered across my face. The thudding of my heart spiked an ache that settled between my thighs.

I stared at his chest and searched for the closest doorway from the corner of my eye, praying this song would end. One hard stroke from his erection and I felt my panties grow damp. My legs shook as the violin drew out one bittersweet final note. I shook with relief and tried to pull away, but Jared refused to let me go. "Bow for our audience, April."

His hand entwined in mine as he stepped to the side and dropped at the waist. I refused to bend. I didn't think my legs could hold me for long. The guests blurred as I yanked, trying to break his hold. I could feel tears running in silky lines down my face. Jared's fingers were cruel as he pulled me close in one final hug and a pat on my ass. "Thanks for that, little mouse."

His sickening leer stayed with me as I stumbled toward the door. I needed air. I needed to get away from Jared. Most of all, I needed to get away from this wedding. This day felt like the final nail in mom's coffin. No matter how many years had passed, I hurt like she'd only died only yesterday.

I gripped the hem of my dress and stumbled down the steps to the garden, taking refuge behind thick hedges and thorny roses. The music from the orchestra faded while my tears flowed. How could he do that to me? His own sister?

---

"WE MISSED YOU AFTER THE CEREMONY," Dad muttered as he loaded his suitcases into the car.

"I'm sorry I left. I couldn't stay there any longer. Dad, there's something you need to know about Jared."

He stilled after wrestling an overstuffed back in the already cramped trunk. His sigh cut through me. "I understand perfectly, April. You're angry and you have every right to be."

I fought the panic rising inside as Dad straightened and turned to face me. He held out his arms and, one minute I was an adult demanding justice, and the next I was ten years old all over again. I stepped into his arms and felt the comfort of his embrace. "But your mother is gone, April. She's gone, and there's not a damn thing I can do about that.

I shook my head. He didn't understand. This wasn't about Mom dying. "Dad, this is about Jared."

His chest rose and then fell with a sigh. "I already know. He told me everything."

My hands gripped his crisp white shirt. Connie's perfume lingered on the fine cotton. Would she tell Jared to leave? Would Dad threaten to punch him if he came near me again? "I'm sorry Dad. I'm sorry for Connie, too."

"We understand you're under an enormous amount of strain, honey, with college, this wedding. It's natural for a young woman to act out, but Jared is your brother now, and inappropriate contact like you forced on him tonight isn't acceptable."

I let his shirt go and stumbled backward. "What are you talking about, Dad? It was Jared who touched me."

He shook his head and raised his hand. "This is what he thought you'd say. He's not upset April. None of us are. We just need to understand that we're a family. Connie said sometimes these things happen when a mixed family grows up together."

The tone in Dad's voice told me there was no point arguing. It was the same tone he used to ground me for fighting at school a week after I was told about Mom's diagnosis. Still, I had to try.

"That's not what happened, Dad. Please believe me. Jared was the one who touched me, for Christ's sake."

"April, that's enough. You know Connie doesn't like language like that."

"I don't give a fuck what Connie likes. This is me, Dad, your daughter. You have to believe me."

Anger flared in his eyes. This wasn't the father I knew. His raised voice shattered the night. "Connie is my wife now April, and I'll not have you disrespect her again. You need to learn some damn manners!"

*Me, manners?* I tried to swallow the lump in the back of my throat. I hated how my lower lip trembled. I could see how it was now. Jared spun them a mouthful of lies to make himself the innocent—just as he always had.

Would my life always be like this? Serving my sadistic stepbrother while he had the best of everything? How could I have expected anything different? His father was worth billions, while I was the poor sister—the afterthought.

I lifted my gaze, searching for an ounce of understanding and finding none, as Dad repeated. "He's your brother and wants only the best for you. We all do."

"*Step.* Brother." My tone was as icy as I could make it. "I don't want him here, Dad. I don't want him anywhere near me while you and Connie are gone."

"Oh for Christ's sake, April. He's not staying here. I've asked him to look in on you from time to time. Anyone would think you hate the young man. He's trying to help you. You could do a lot worse for a brother than Jared."

"Stepbrother," I snarled as I backed away. An ache spread in my chest as I finally comprehended—I'd get no help here. Connie stepped out onto the front porch with the last of her bags. I could see her scowl from where I stood. "Enjoy your honeymoon, Dad. Your new wife is waiting."

## Chapter Two

MY CHEST STILL ACHED WHEN I WOKE THE NEXT DAY. AT first, my brain was fuzzy, until the pieces of the puzzle fell into place: the wedding, the dance, and my confrontation with Dad. How had things gone so wrong last night? I'd be lucky if he wanted to speak to me again after that. I groaned and rolled over, wincing at the sunlight streaming through the cracks of my curtains.

Had I blown last night out of proportion? The swell of Jared's erection came back to me. I felt the hot shaft against my thigh like a ghostly brand. *I always did love the mousy ones.* My breathing quickened. I could feel the familiar panic rising, sweeping me away whenever he was near. I yanked back the covers and slid from the bed. Lying here thinking about him was only making my anxiety worse. I needed a shower, then a fresh set of pajamas for my hectic day of watching re-runs.

I stepped out of my room, listening for the sweet sound of silence. Dad and Connie wouldn't be back for four glorious weeks. Their absence would give me enough time to pack my bags. Maybe I could even leave for Geraldton a little earlier and bypass the awkward goodbyes. I couldn't wait for college. Freedom was calling and I was desperate to answer.

I stumbled down the hallway toward the other end of the house. My room was hidden behind the library, away from the other bedrooms. I didn't care to be near the bed Dad shared with Connie, much less near Jared's. The location only inflamed my love of old books. My aching bladder was the only downside to the morning trek to the bathroom. I passed the library and two guest rooms, spying the door to Jared's bedroom two doors down from the bathroom. Maybe after last night, he'd stay away. Maybe his only goal was to get his rocks off by causing a rift between me and my father, just to fuck with me.

I hit the lever for the shower, waiting for the water to run hot while I used the toilet. With any luck, Jared would be too busy to harass me. He always seemed to travel in a pack with his rich friends, in their Maseratis and Lamborghinis. I flushed the toilet and stepped into the shower, letting hot water run over my hair. The shampoo was a thick lather when I rubbed it through the strands of my hair and dropped my hands to my breasts.

They were small, perky. My nipples swollen and pink. I lightly pinched the smooth flesh, rolling the tips under my fingers until they hardened. My one clumsy attempt at sex had been disastrous. Ben Smalls had been nothing more than a horny rabbit with a very small penis. I blame myself. Why'd I choose someone with a name like that? *Because I'm desperate.* His frenzied thrusts had taken me by surprise until he collapsed seconds later. Even now, I had doubts whether or not I was still a virgin. There had been no pain, and there sure as hell had been no pleasure. I shuddered under the piercing spray. I didn't want to go through that again.

I conditioned my hair and finished washing, then turned off the shower. Maybe I'd be lucky and meet someone at Geraldton. Someone tall, handsome, who loved books and was prepared to take his time with me. I slid on my robe and tied the belt as my stomach rumbled. Pancakes and popcorn sounded like the perfect meal. I'd eat it in the den. To hell with Connie's rules.

***

THE DAY PASSED PLEASANTLY, continuing watching Ned Stark evade the wrath of Cersei. This was the third time I'd watched *Game of Thrones* and every time was like the first. I hid behind my pillow, then threw the damn thing at the screen. Horrified by the brutality and swept away by the raw beauty. By the end of the day, I'd watched the last half of season two. Wrapped up in the on-screen drama, I forgot all about my own. When I finally surfaced, I looked around to see packets of popcorn and used tissues strewn over the leather couch. My mouth was dry from the salt and my cheeks were still wet from the tears. I needed food—and to clean this place up. Unlike Jared I refused to be waited on by a maid.

I climbed from the couch and grabbed the litter before making my way to the kitchen. I looked out to the patio and was drawn to the sparkling lights in the pool. The clock on the oven said almost ten o'clock. I rubbed my eyes and looked again, surely it couldn't be that late? The grandfather clock was the only thing we had of our old house. Connie detested it, banishing the tall oak case to the games room where Dad's pride and joy sat in the middle of the massive room.

The ornate billiard 'able gleamed as I hit the lights. Blue felt covered the surface, the color Dad's only request. I trailed my hand along the black walnut frame, slowing to caress the engraved scripture. *To behold a thing of beauty is a joy forever.* It was a gift from Jared's father on Connie and Dad's engagement three years ago. Our old clock looked out of place in this room. I stepped closer, straining to hear the tick, tick, tick, but there was none.

The hands, stuck on two, didn't move. How long ago had Dad stopped bothering to wind the mechanism? A weight settled in my chest. I headed back to the kitchen, the last reminder of my old life now silent.

I opened the window, feeling the cool evening air wash over me. A swim sounded nice. The water was heated, but Arya Stark and the Hound called. I'd already watched two episodes of the last season and the rest waited for me. I stretched, working movement back into stiff muscles and yanked open the fridge.

My meals for the next three days were in stacks, neatly marked. The calorie count displayed. My new stepmother had been dropping not-so-subtle hints about my weight for the last ten months. A gym membership had become my annual Christmas gift. For my last birthday, Connie gave me a pedometer rather than conversation. I slammed the door closed. Pizza was what I wanted and she could shove her damn fitness bullshit up her ass. I grabbed the phone and dialed the pizza parlor. I wanted a Meatlover's pizza with the works and a bottle of cola to go with it. My chest swelled and I smiled as I hung up the phone. "A toast to my damn freedom."

I showered and changed into fresh pajamas. At this rate I'd run out of my sleepwear in three days. I piled my hair on top of my head and fastened it with a tie. Episode three was already half over as the doorbell rang. I hurried for the foyer, gripping a twenty. The bell cut through the house once more. Did no one have time for me? I reached for the handle, snarling. "Impatient much?"

The giggles greeted me as I opened the door. The woman in the doorway was struggling to stay upright. Her barely-there dress revealed a lot more than I wanted to see. She gripped Jared's arm, moving close to rub her body against his side. The smell of alcohol assaulted me, even in the night breeze. I turned to my stepbrother. He merely gripped the door frame with one hand

and grabbed the woman's ass with the other. His navy shirt was open at the collar, his black slacks immaculate, as always. His eyelids lowered, scanning my thin cotton shirt. The hairs on my arms stood and my body tightened and puckered in places it shouldn't. I dropped my hand from the door and folded my arms a'ross my chest. "What are you doing here?"

He shrugg'd and pulled the woman tighter against him. "I forgot my key."

For the last few hours, I'd forgotten about the dance and the lies. But now his manipulation came crashing back. My hand tightened on the money in my hand. Jared's eyes shifted to my grip. "What do you have there, little mouse?"

Lights washed over us as the pizza delivery car pulled up in the driveway and parked behind Jared's jet black Maserati. The sleek machine reminded me of a jaguar, poised, ready to pounce, an expensive jaguar at that. Jared shifted to look over his shoulder. The faded sign of Papa's Pizza was crooked on the wreck of a car. He shook his head and turned back to me. I could already hear the judgment I was about to receive. "I see you're sticking to Mom's strict calorie-controlled menu. Never mind. I won't tell, if you don't."

His wink made me cringe. Somehow " didn't f'el like pizza anym're. "I don't want you here. Leave."

"Now, you know your father demanded I come and keep you company. So, here I am, and I bought along a little company of my own." He patted the woman's ass, earning a giggle.

My stomach rolled as the delivery guy strode up the sidewalk behind them. It was either stand to the side, or leave the driver waiting in line behind them. Defeated, I stepped to the side.

Jared leaned down, giving me a peck on the cheek as he passed. "Thanks, sis."

His date shot me a hate-filled gaze as she passed. Jesus, the rich were in class of their own. I knew a gold digger when I saw one. Jared's business was his own. I just hoped he stayed out of mine.

"One Meatlover's and a cola?" The driver muttered.

I nodded, handing him the scrunched note in my hand. "Keep the change."

One smell of the greasy pizza and I wished I'd heated the dinner in the fridge. I gripped the box with one hand and took the Coke in the other. Jared was sure to tell Connie the first chance he got. Lying little snitch. I closed the door, turning toward the cackle coming out of the kitchen. My cheeks burned as I walked in, pizza and coke in hand.

Jared leaned against his date's back, reaching one hand under her dress. One of the containers was out of the refrigerator. The label—Garlic, Turkey and Broccoli Stir Fry, two hundred and thirteen calories—stared at me.

Jared picked at the food, hand-feeding the bitch who sniggered and looked my way. She dipped in to take his finger into her mouth and sucked. I wasn't waiting around to watch the display. I was going to eat the damn pizza, even if was going to kill me. I walked over to the cabinet and grabbed a glass, filling it with Coke.

"Angela and I are going to stay the night. I hope you don't mind a little noise. I think this one's going to be a screamer."

I caught movement from Jared as he yanked his hand from between her thighs and slapped her ass. The sound cracked through the kitchen, followed by a moan. I shoved the cola into the fridge, slammed the door shut, and ran for the den. Enduring his presence was one thing, but subjecting myself to his version of foreplay was another.

The glass hit the coffee table hard, spilling the cola on Connie's expensive furniture. I cursed, bending forward to mop the mess up with the end of my shirt. My hand trembled as I stabbed the remote. I prayed the music would drown out the noises in the kitchen and flipped open the cardboard box. The pizza looked delicious, piled high with meat. Grease dripped from the cheese as I pulled a slice free. But as I stared at the glistening slice, I knew I couldn't eat it. I threw the wedge of dough into the box and flipped the lid down.

I forced myself to stare at the television. But no matter how hard I tried, I couldn't shut them out. The clatter of ice from the tray had me turning toward the kitchen. The sound of his shoes echoed seconds later, heading this way. I snapped my gaze back to the screen, tracking his steps into the den. The sound stopped when he stood behind me.

"Game of Thrones, eh? You know there are more incestuous relationships in that show than there are normal ones. You like that kind of thing, little mouse?"

I felt fingers slide through my hair. I wrenched forward, shaking off his touch, and spat. "No, that's disgusting."

"Pity. I guess it will be just me and Stephanie then."

"Angela." I reminded him. "Your date's name is Angela."

"Right, Angela. Stephanie's the one I fucked earlier."

I clenched my jaw until pain radiated into my neck, spreading out along the base of my skull. *Please, just leave me alone.* My throat worked, trying to swallow my humiliation. Why was he always doing this to me?

"Why did you lie to my father? You told him I was the one who touched you. Now he thinks I'm either upset over the wedding, or some kind of degenerate."

He wound his fingers through my hair once more. I tried to pull away, but his hold was unforgiving, pinning me in place. "Maybe a degenerate is exactly what you need to be? Look at you. Sitting here with your stained clothes, your greasy food, and this damn TV for company. You think college is going to be any different for you? You'll be shunned and shoved to the back of the class with all the other little mice."

He yanked my hair. My vision bl"rred. Tears spilled from my eyes. "Get away from me, Jared. Stop it, just stop."

He leaned over, jerking my head to one side, evelled me with his eyes while my scalp burned. "You know what happens to little mice who get fat and just sit in one spot all day?"

I shook my head.

His brown eyes sparkled with malice. "They become a meal."

He jerked my hair so hard I arched backwards over the couch. My feeble slaps hit leather and the back of his hand. Still, he didn't let me go. I was used to the cruelty from him. The slaps on my ass. The pinches under the table when no one was looking. Nothing to leave a bruise—except on my self-esteem. But this was different.

He clasped his hand over my breast. His fingers kneading, taking what he shouldn't. The cotton was so thin I felt the heat of his hand. His fingers found my nipple. Pain flared, sending shocks through my body. Despite my tears, I felt heat flare between my thighs. I clamped my knees shut as the sound of giggles drifted to my ears. I clawed at his hand, trying to pull free. "Jared, stop. Stop or—"

"Or what, April? You gonna tell Daddy I was a bad brother? You gonna tell him I came home to find you eating grease all over mom's expensive leather sofa? How you screamed at me and threatened to cry rape?" He waited, one eyebrow raised. His voice turned icy. "Because, that's the version I'll be giving."

His hand left my breast and the other let go of my hair. I slid down the cushions as he turned and walked away with Angela. Sniggers followed their every step as they climbed the stairs. My tears flowed, spilling down my cheeks. I pulled my knees to my chest, staring blankly at the screen. Cersei was screaming under Jamie thrusts in front of her son's coffin, her feeble blows as useless as my own had been. My body shuddered, choked sobs tore from my mouth as I watched Jamie ravage his own sister.

Jared's words hurt. His cold assessment of me was vindictive, forcing me to the back of the class where he said I belonged. But what hurt the most, what filled me with a fear so dark I felt torn apart, was the yearning between my legs. The desire I had for Jared to slide his hand lower, to take from me what he wanted. Jared triggered a ferocious need inside me. A need unfulfilled.

# Chapter Three

I HUGGED MY KNEES AND STARED BLANKLY AT THE SCREEN. I still felt the pinch of his fingers and the sting of his words. For the last five years I'd been in denial. Pretending I was wanted here, when it was clear I wasn't. *Little mouse.* Those words were different now when he said them. I used to think the term was his special name for me. That it was somehow endearing. Now, I knew different.

I shuddered. I tightened my grip, still feeling the warmth between my thighs, knowing this desire was wrong. He was my brother, for God's sake. I rubbed my eyes. They felt raw and gritty. Sleep was what I needed. Tomorrow would be better. I'd hide in my damn bedroom with the door closed if I had to.

I hit the remote and the screen went black. The pizza and cola sat on the table. How was it that an hour ago I'd felt so different? I grabbed the box and glass before heading into the kitchen. Now food was the last thing I wanted. I shoved the pizza into the fridge and poured the cola down the sink, rinsing the glass before switching off the lights.

Their voices drifted toward me as I climbed the stairs. A squeal made my heart race, followed by a moan that slowed my steps. My hand lingered on the banister as I stepped onto the landing. Jared's bedroom was in the same wing as mine, but closer to the stairs. I'd have to walk past to get to the bathroom and my own bedroom, further down the hall.

The flutter in my chest quickened as her moan filtered through the door. I stepped closer, keeping to the opposite wall, unable to take my eyes off the grain. The bannister was smooth under my touch. My fingers dug, stopping my steps as a slap stilled her delight. I waited for a scream, or the sound of crying. Was he hurting her?

Drawn by my need to know, I moved closer. Inch by inch I crept, straining to hear the sounds Jared's lover made. I reached for the smooth doorframe, gripping the edges as I heard her grunt. "Fuck me, you dirty little rich boy."

I swallowed. The sensation of his hand on my breast still felt so real. The image of Cersei under Jamie was vibrant in my mind. How would it feel to be taken like that, without restraint? Grunts echoed all round me. My mouth felt arid. I licked my lips, listening to their flesh smack together.

"Fucking bitch. Does this hurt?"

Her whimpers were the only answer I heard. They turned into noises so guttural they made my breath catch.

I pressed my ear against the door, hearing her utter. "More. Harder."

My hand trembled as I reached for my breast. I closed my eyes. In my mind it was Jared's hand that gripped me, pinching my flesh, taking what he wanted. So help me God, in that moment, brother or no brother, I would've given my innocence to him. I squeezed my flesh, but the cotton was too much of a barrier. I dropped my hand lower, under the hem to slide along my stomach and cup the peak.

Her moans inside the room became my moans. His thrusts forcing my thighs apart, sliding his cock into me, working his way in deep. I shoved the shame aside as my body tingled. His low grunts were for me. I wanted to hurt him, just as he hurt me. I wanted to fuck him, just as he fucked me. I wanted to dig my nails into his back. I wanted him to spread me wide and forced himself inside.

I dug my nails into the wood as the image came to life. I dropped my hand to slide it between my legs. Through the fabric of my pajamas, I felt the heat of my desire, slick, ready. One sweep of my hand was all I could take. My heart battered my chest as I stumbled to the bathroom. Jared's cruel eyes stayed with me as I hit the doorway and swept the door closed. His voice inside my head drowned out the click as it closed. I wasn't listening to anything else but his words as he asked me, *does this hurt?*

My body quivered, needing release. With Ja'ed's taunting voice racing through my head, I slammed the toilet seat down and fumbled with my pants. I probed deep as I kicked free of the flannel and spread my legs wide. The feel of my own hand was so familiar. I knew crease, every pressure point to find the end I craved. I closed my eyes, picturing him over me. His dirty blond hair falling across his face as he pounded into me. *Does this hurt?* I nodded, slipping my finger over to skirt the hood around my clit. Round and round, lightly at first, until my senses tingled. I slipped one finger in, to spread the slickness through my folds.

*My brother. He's my brother.* Images of Cersei and Jamie spun inside my head. I moved my fingers faster, gliding inside, then slipping out to circle my nub. I was so wet and hot. I moaned and bit my lip as I raced toward the end.

*Does this hurt?* Jared asked and inside my head I whimpered. *No,* I whispered, *I want more.* My brother pounded my opening, forcing me wide. Jared... Jamie. Both wanted me and I was ready to give.

My hips jerked. Tiny jolts of electricity shot through my body and I slowed my hand, waiting for my breaths to follow suit. I opened my eyes to see the door ajar. Jared stood in the doorway in nothing but his boxers, his erection straining the fabric. His gaze was on me. He took his time moving from the crease between my legs to my eyes. Then he smiled and I knew, this was what he wanted—to use my desire against me.

The room seemed to spin as I snapped my legs closed and lunged for my pants, snagging them from the floor. My legs refused to work as I raced for the door. I hit the basin with my hip. Pain flared. Still I kept moving, stopping when he refused to budge from the doorway. I clutched the fabric, hiding my body. I could do nothing about my shame. I hardly recognized my husky squeak. "Just let me out."

"Why stop? I was enjoying the show."

The rush of heat to my face took my breath. I shoved past him as I ran bare-assed down the hall.

"You know, if you wanted to join us, all you had to do was ask."

I barged through my bedroom door and then slammed it shut, locking out his voice and my humiliation. The skin of my ass stuck to the door as I slid to the floor. What the hell was happening to me? Jared called out to me from behind the door. I clapped my hands over my ears, trying to stifle his words. But it didn't stop the ridicule inside. God, I was disgusting. How could I have been so stupid? I clenched a fist and hit the side of my head. *What have you done?* The blow revived the ache at the base of my neck. Each pulse drove the pain deeper.

I'd crossed the line and there was no going back. I should just leave. Pack my bags and drive away. I could sleep in my car, wait for college to start. I'd be letting Dad down. He depended on me to look after the house when they were gone. *Yeah and Connie depended on you not to seduce your own brother.* I pulled my knees up and hung my head. Tears welled in my eyes. I brushed them away with the back of my hand. I couldn't leave, even if I wanted to. Even as I sat here, I knew I'd reached the point of no return.

It wasn't just the fact Jared saw 'e naked, touching myself. I'd never been so wet. Even though I had release, I wanted more. It wasn't just sex that I wanted. I wanted to be possessed and I wanted Jared to possess me.

# Chapter Four

I tossed and turned, replaying what had happened in my head, until the thumping of my heart turned savage. The nerve at the base of my neck pulsed with a life of its own, clawing my thoughts until they were warped and strange. I shoved back the covers and climbed for the bed. The room spun as my feet hit the soft pile. I need something to dull the pain and sleep. Maybe then, my life wouldn't look like a disaster.

What if they're still here? What if Jared's out there waiting for me? The nerve sent shards of agony that pulled me from the sheets hours later. The constant ridicule playing in my head had turned the ache into a migraine. I gripped the door handle, praying Jared and his companion were either asleep or gone. The door squealed as it opened. I gripped the frame, easing it open an inch at a time and listened.

The normal creaks of the house were all that filled the hallway. I yanked the handle and stepped outside. Each step drove that shard deeper into my head as I made for the bathroom. Even in the dark, I sought out his bedroom, straining to hear any noise from across the hall as my feet hit the cold tile.

The overhead lights flickered on. The glare was blinding. I raised my hand, shielding my eyes and pushed against the base of the mirror. A click sounded before the mirror swung open. Bottles lined the wall, everything from antibiotics to vitamins. I squinted, searching for something strong enough to dull the pain and found tablets Connie had given me for a migraine before.

I twisted the lid and shook two pills out, shoving them into my mouth as I replaced the bottle. A noise snatched my attention. Was that footsteps? I slammed the cabinet, ran the water into my cupped hand and took a gulp. The noise came again. Was it Jared coming for me? I hit the lights, plunging the hallway into darkness and stumbled over the threshold. *Little mouse.*

I skirted the wall with my fingers as I hurried into the sanctity of my room and closed the door. I couldn't live like this, running and hiding. Not for a day, not for the next four weeks. I slipped under the covers. My body hummed so, it seemed I felt each silky thread against my skin. Minutes slowly slid by as I closed my eyes and waited for the pain reliever to take hold. The dull thud against my skull softened. My thoughts slipped as my breathing deepened. Oblivion waited, and as the darkness moved in to wrap around me, I felt the soft brush of a hand and the sweet whisper of words hot against my ear. "Goodnight little mouse. Sleep well. You're gonna need the rest."

---

I SURFACED, my thoughts were slow to return. I reached for the base of my neck and massaged the muscles, now soft and supple. The ache was gone, leaving me with the aftertaste of the pills. Scattered memories came back. Pizza, the pain from my hair as Jared pulled me backward over the couch. The way his hand felt on my breast. The sounds of sex in his bedroom. Then, the shame when I opened my eyes, seeing him standing there, watching me pleasure myself as I thought of him.

The pillow couldn't hide my shame as I buried my face. How could I possibly fix this? *Goodnight little mouse.* His voice echoed back to me and something in my stomach tightened in warning. Did I dream those words? I reached for my face, running a hand down my temple.

I shook the memory off and reached for my phone. Ten a.m. More *sleep*, my body urged. I rolled over, but the thoughts of last night hounded me like a rapid dog. Could I face Jared? Ask him to forget the last twenty-four hours... more like *beg*. I had to try.

I slid from the bed and opened my closet. I never wanted him to see me in pajamas again. I selected jeans and a soft pink cashmere sweater, underwear, and a lacy bra before I made for the door. A quick shower and I'd face the music. Maybe in the light of day, we could all agree to move on. Maybe this accident would force us to get along?

This time I made sure the door was locked before I dropped my pants. I waited for the shower to warm and stepped in. Working fast I washed my hair and lathered my body. I hit the lever, shutting off the spray and toweled dry and slipped on my underwear. The full-length mirror reflected the pink lace against my pale skin. I gripped my dimpled thighs and ran my hand over my stomach. Why do you care what you look like?

*Because, I want him to see me as something other than the little mouse.*

The thought stilled my hand. I lifted my gaze, catching my own dark eyes in the mirror. My dark brown hair was plastered against my shoulders, the trickle running over the curve of my breast to soak into the lace. I turned away from the mirror and the dark need in my eyes. No matter how hard I tried, I couldn't undo the humiliating desire inside me. I yanked on my jeans and sweater. I trembled at the thought of his hand on my breast. Taking what he wanted without remorse.

Something had changed in me. A switch had been tripped that couldn't be undone. I opened the bathroom and stepped into the hall. Drawn by a force I didn't understand, I made my way to his bedroom. I clenched my fist and raised it to the wood. I'd only been in Jared's room once before when I was younger. Kept away by his steely glare and the dangerous tone I'd never ventured inside again. I knocked, then stepped back and waited.

I shifted from one foot to another and picked lint from my sleeve. The seconds felt like hours, still there was no answer. I stepped forward, thumping the door one more time before I turned the handle and entered.

Jared's bedroom was larger than mine, leaving me to fumble in the dark. Sunlight peeked from underneath the dark drapes. I reached for the wall, listening for soft snores, and crept deeper into the room. Courage was in short supply. I gathered what I had and whispered. "Jared, are you awake? I need to talk to you."

My foot tangled in something as I stepped, tipping me off balance. I sprawled forward, catching my upper body on the end of the bed, feeling the outline of someone under the covers. Jesus. I recoiled, scrambling backwards, stopping only when I hit the curtains. *What was that?*

The heavy fabric parted, light reached across the floor, turning night into a soft hue. A pillow lay lengthways under the cover, giving me the impression of a body, but the bed was empty. I shoved the curtains aside, staring around the empty room. A bookcase lined the far wall. I climbed to my feet and made my way across the floor. Embossed spines sparkled with gold leaf. I ran my fingers across the expensive volumes. Thick law journals crowded the top shelf. On the middle shelf was a single photo of an older man shaking hands with Bill Clinton. I'd never met Jared's father, but one look at the image and I could tell straight away who the man with the former President was. Both shared the same hard gaze, the same fit physique; both were predators in every sense of the word.

I dropped my gaze to a collection of thumb drives. Thick black pen scribbled across each one: Step 1 Gym, Step 2 Carpark, Step 3 Nightclub, Step 4 TBA. I gripped the USB, TBA: to be announced? What did that mean? Was it some kind of formula for his studies at Harvard? I picked up one thumb drive. They looked brand new. I turned the device over in my hand, then placed it back on the shelf and turned to the bed.

The covers were strewn beside the bed, left for Marielle to make fresh when she came today. I made my way over to the side. The sheets were crumpled on both sides. Had Angela stayed the night? Or had they had their fun and left? I lowered myself to the edge of the mattress, trailing my fingers along the sheets as their noises replayed inside my head. *Does this hurt?*

My body came to life, blooming in a dangerous way. *Stop it. This is wrong.* I wrenched my hand away and stood. There was nothing I could do to change what'd been done. Something on the floor caught my eye. A card peeked from under the bed. I bent, grabbing it from the floor. The satin-black card had one name embossed on the front, Riptide. I turned it over to a white back which read, Be Swept Away. In a neat scrawl were the words, door code: Billionaire Brats.

I turned the card over. I'd never head of Riptide before. Was this some kind of club? Excitement buzzed through my veins as I strode from his room, the card in my hand. I hurried to my room and grabbed my laptop from my dresser. I hit the power button and waited for the screen to come to life before punching the name into the search engine.

There were hundreds of hits. I narrowed down the list by adding nightclub and Boston and waited. I scrolled through the first three returns—all for male strippers—and clicked on the fourth. Riptide, for the elite. I nodded. Rich boys with plenty of money, this was exactly where they'd go. I scribbled down the address and closed the computer. Was I actually thinking of going? I stared at the name, then the words printed on the back. Billionaire Brats. Gripping the card, I walked out of my room and headed downstairs.

I stared at the damn thing all day. One minute, the idea of searching out my own brother at some expensive-yet-seedy club horrified me, and the next I was burning with the desire to find out what this place was. My mind kept returning to the drives in his room. Something about them nagged me. I shoved off the couch. Maybe I could get one and see what was on it? A click of a key in the lock had me spinning. Marielle stepped inside and closed the door. I smiled as she made her way toward me with a bucket brimming with bottles and rags in one hand, her house key in the other. I was thankful for the intrusion. Searching through someone else's things was wrong. No matter how big of a jerk he was.

Marielle was a small, timid woman who hunched when she walked. But she kept the house immaculate. I'd never seen glass shine as bright as it did when she was finished. She smiled as she walked through the room, making small talk before disappearing. This small act broke me out of my mindless rut. I wasn't the timid little mouse that Jared made me feel I was. I was someone worthwhile, just as Marielle was.

His father's bank account separated Jared from the rest of us. But that was all. I wasn't less of a person and I sure as hell wasn't a mouse.

I APPLIED a sheer gloss to my lips before checking my appearance one last time. To turn up in jeans and a sweater would surely get me kicked out, even if I gave the password and got through the front door. I found the black dress shoved at the back of my closet, an unwanted gift at the time, one that would serve its purpose now. It was a little shorter than I liked. I yanked down the hem, hoping to hide my thighs and the only set of nice underwear I owned. The extra sheer panties had been last year's embarrassing birthday gift that I shoved to the back of my drawer. I was thankful for them now.

I slid the card into my purse and grabbed my keys from the foyer, hitting the garage door opener. My tiny Corolla was far from new, a gift from Dad when I was accepted to Geraldton. Much to Connie's disgust, I loved the blue beast. I slid into the driver's seat and started the engine. A cloud of gray smoke wafted into the garage before I put the car into reverse and backed out. Riptide was somewhere downtown. I had a rough idea where I was heading. The map on my phone would see me the rest of the way.

The tiny car hugged the streets as I drove from the Range Road. I hit the stereo and my usual playlist blared. Five seconds later, I couldn't stand the sound. What was wrong with me? My body felt hot. My skin itched, like I was shedding the old April to make way for the new. Gone was the girl in sweat pants and the stained shirt. Now, I felt different. I kept my hands on the wheel, but my mind was racing. The city lights sparkled, capturing my gaze as I passed. Strip parlors beckoned with red neon thumping music.

I checked the clock on the dashboard. It was just after eleven. If I could get in no one would notice me. Just a look, that was all I wanted. One drink and I'd leave. I slowed as I hit the strip, parking the car in front of security cameras. I straightened my dress and hit the remote to lock, praying this wasn't going to end with me in jail. I had no one else to call if it did. Would Jared come for me?

I crossed the street and made my way along the sidewalk, avoiding hostile stares and the catcalls from those inside the packed bars. I gripped my purse and hurried, slowing at the blue neon sign. A long line of people waited to enter. The bouncer at the front pointed at the back of the line as I slowed. Should I show him the card? Should I ask if Jared was here? Would he even tell me? I inhaled and muttered, "Billionaire Brats."

One nod and he stepped to the side, allowing me to enter. I stepped through the black-tinted doors and breathed a sigh of relief. The club was busy, but not overly packed. There were more women than men, which accounted for the long line of frustrated males out front. The bartender nodded as I sidled up to the bar and took a seat. The music was nothing exciting, not what I'd been expecting.

"What can I get you?"

"She's with us." I spun at the sound, eyeing a gorgeous hunk in black slacks and a white collared shirt. "April, right? You're Jared's sister."

"Stepsister." I corrected, spying the bartender move off.

"Sure. You want a drink? We've got better stuff out back. Jared was hoping you'd turn up."

His comment was like a punch to my stomach. "He was?"

He moved closer, sliding his gaze down my dress. "Didn't you get the card?"

*Card?* I gripped my purse tight. The business card. He knew I'd come looking for him. He'd planned this whole thing. He knew I'd try to make things right after what happened last night. He knew I'd go into his room. Did he know I'd find the drives too? "The UBS sticks in Jared's room, what do they mean?"

I thought Jared's friend flinched, or it could've been an illusion caused by the strobing lights. "I don't know anything about USBs."

I nodded. Did I want to make things right? I tried to think this through. The music became too loud. The walls seemed too close and my thoughts were a mess.

"I'm Heath, by the way. Jared forgot to mention how pretty you are." He smiled and held out his hand. Just like a gentleman would.

My stepbrother might an asshole, but he was still my brother. Family was important to my father. He loved Connie. It might not be the same love he had for my mother, but it was still a commitment. Now I had to make a commitment. Did I try to make this right, or leave? I looked to the door and thought of home. The greasy pizza was still in the box. My life of re-runs waited patiently.

Excitement ran through my veins like a low hum. I slid from the stool and took Heath's hand. His eyes lit up. His hold tightened around my fingers as he led me along the dance floor. We passed the roped barriers marked *private* and pushed through the hallway doors. Was this what money bought? A backstage pass to everywhere? No questions, no comments? Freedom raced through my veins like a drug as Heath stopped at a door and punched numbers into the keypad lock.

The door swung open. Music blared, dark tones that swept me away with a hungry beat. Soft, white light lit up the room, until the bar was plunged in darkness. Blue lights illuminated the counter, lined with filled shot glasses. No one knew they were back here. No one cared. In this room money reigned supreme. Judging by the hungry gazes on me as I stepped inside, I was guessing it was more money than I could count. Private. That's what this room was. I searched the floor, finding Jared sitting in a lounge, legs crossed, staring at me as I entered. Knowing he watched me sent shivers along my arms.

Heath leaned close, brushing my shoulder. "Let's get you a proper drink, eh? That crap out the front is mostly water anyway. We've got some nice stuff in here."

I nodded, not really listening. I followed his steps, unable to take my eyes off my brother. One guy bent to a table. I followed the movement, watching as he sniffed something white laid out in lines, and straightened. *That's cocaine.* My heart pounded. I tried not to stare. Did Jared do that too?

"Try this, you're gonna like it." Heath handed me a shot glass. Clear liquid sparkled under the soft blue light.

I lifted my gaze to Heath. "What is it?"

"It's only white rum, it's not heavy. You'll be fine. Trust me."

His hand tightened on mine. I nodded and lifted the glass to my lips. The liquid burned. I coughed and spluttered. One hard slap to my back forced the fire all the way down.

"The second one will be better." Heath handed me another.

I shook my head and yelled over the music. "I can't, I'm driving."

His grin widened, but the smile didn't quite reach his eyes. "It's all good, we have it sorted."

My stomach dropped. "What do you mean sorted?"

"Lighten up, April. We were just gonna have your car towed back to your house, so you don't have to worry. Here, take this. It's a card for my driver, call him anytime you want to leave and he'll drive you home. No pressure, okay?"

Heath held out the card, giving me a slight nudge. I reached for the card, glimpsing the number. Maybe I was wound a little tight. He passed another drink along the counter. "You're Jared's little sister. We just wanted to show you a good time."

He reached for another glass, waiting for me to follow. One more drink couldn't hurt. I unzipped my purse and slipped the card inside, feeling like a fool. The second drink spread a delicious warmth through my body. Heath was right, the drink tasted a little sweet this time. My tension melted.

"Grab another and I'll introduce you to the others. Everyone's been waiting to meet you."

I needed little convincing this time. I was floating in the seductive taste of white rum. I grabbed another shot, following Heath's lead. Jared was laughing, joking with the one who inhaled the line of cocaine. He lifted his eyes, meeting mine.

Surprise held me as Jared pushed from the couch to tower over me. "Nice to see you here, April. I've been telling everyone how much I love my little sister."

Something sparkled in his eyes. The seductive warmth from the alcohol spread. "Stepsister."

He laughed and nodded. "Stepsister. This is Maurie and Jed. Over there is Connor and Kyle and it looks like you've already met Heath."

Heath turned to give me a wink as he pushed through the others. God, these men could've come from a model shoot. They were all tanned, fit, and drop dead gorgeous. I felt swept away by strong jawlines and wicked smiles. Only three women were in the room. Naturally, they were stunning.

Each one of Jared's friends greeted me. Some raised their glass, others stepped forward to clasp my hand. I managed to mutter. "Nice to meet you all."

Jared raised his glass. "Drink up, April. I thought it was about time you were introduced to my friends. A toast, to getting to know each other."

"Getting to know each other." The others chorused.

All eyes were on me. I raised my glass, draining the contents, and felt the warmth fill my stomach. The music seemed to echo through my body. Heath handed me another glass and motioned to the couch. I didn't know if it was Maurie, or Jed who moved. But one of them made room for me, sitting directly opposite Jared.

One of them patted the leather cushion. Heath tugged my hand, leading me through the muddle of splayed legs, and waited for me to take a seat. Smiles and glassy stares surrounded me. *You know what happens to little mice who get fat and just sit there all day? They become a meal.* I felt, like one fat, easy meal.

My heart raced. I was already floating from what I drank. The tiny glasses seemed never ending as I swallowed another. Movement to my left dragged my gaze. Maurie massaged his crotch. The small bulge seemed to grow as I stared.

"You know, I was telling the boys about what happened last night. About how I feel so bad that I accidentally walked in on you." I wrenched my gaze back from Maurie's hand to see Jared leaning toward me.

I nodded. A bead of sweat ran down my neck to my chest. One of the women danced in middle of the sofas, off to the right. She rubbed her hands down her thighs, then moved up, drawing her skirt over the back of sheer black panties. I'd never seen anything so erotic.

She spread her legs, then bent at the waist. Her muscles flexed and I ran my eyes up her silky flesh. Jed leaned forward, slapping her ass. Her thighs jiggled. One tiny squeal cut through the room, then she shifted backwards.

"April. Did you hear what I said?" Jared called. "They way you touched yourself was the hottest thing I've seen in ages. I almost came in my fucking boxers."

His smooth voice tugged something deep inside me. The dancer turned around, moving against Jed as he sat on the lounge. She lifted one leg, bracing herself against the armrest while she ground her hips a breath away from his face.

Jed placed his hand on my leg. I jumped at the touch, but I was absorbed by the sight of his hand against her skin and the way it dipped under the fabric. One tug and the skirt ripped and was gone, leaving her in only panties.

I'd never seen a woman like this, other than on TV. Jared massaged my thigh, his other hand slipped between the dancer's legs to cup her sex. One finger snagged the edge of her panties, pulling the sheer material aside to expose her slit. A pathetic sound escaped my lips. My body burned from the alcohol. But the heat between my legs was the worst.

"I want to see it again, April. We all do." Jared said, moving to kneel between my legs. His hand slid over Jared's, helping him massage my thigh, drawing up the hem of my dress. My pale thighs drew my own gaze. Jared's hand moved over my skin. A soft moan pulled me away from the motion. Jed's fingers were deep inside the dancer. Her pink flesh, so close. All I had to do was reach out to touch her.

"Do it. She wants you to touch her."

Jared's husky voice was more than I could take. The woman angled her hips toward me. Jared's hand reached for mine, guiding me against her folds. Jared pushed against my thighs, spreading them apart. "My beautiful little sister. Serve me. Show me you know what it means to be a good girl."

My finger slipped in. She was warm, wet. Just like my own body. Jared swept his hand down my crease and I shuddered. I pulled my finger out to grip the sofa as Jared reached inside my sheer panties. I opened my legs wider, desperately needing to feel his fingers inside me. Elastic pulled taught, the thin material useless under the force of his fingers. My hips jerked, the elastic burned as it cut into my skin as he punched a hole through my underwear to tear the crotch. "Open wide, April. Open for your big brother."

Cool air teased my pussy before my hand slipped between my folds. I was past caring who watched now. The alcohol and the vision of Jed's finger slipping inside the dancer heightened the need inside me. I spread myself wide, exposing my channel for Jared's gaze. "Oh yeah, baby. That's a good little girl."

I worked the silky flesh with hard hands, circling my clit before sinking in deep. The sound of a zipper drew my eye. The smooth, pink flesh of Maurie's cock bobbed as his hand gripped the shaft, working the skin all the way to the tip, before sliding back down. Jared's hands on my thighs spread me wider. I dipped my fingers inside and moaned.

All eyes were on my ruined panties, but mine were on Jared. He kept me locked into his gaze. Electricity singed my nerves. "You want to serve me, April? You want me to fuck you?"

I nodded. I'd never wanted anything so much in my life. Each muscle of my body screamed for release as the fire licked deep. Jared moved to grip me by my hair, twisting it cruelly, like he'd always done. He gripped my wrist, moving my own hand as I worked my pussy. He plunged his in deep, pushing against my own touch, parting my folds. His touch was possessive. His demands dangerous. "Then this cunt is mine. You will fuck when I tell you to fuck. You will fuck who I tell you to fuck, and no one else."

His grip was painful, both in my hair and inside my body as he thrust. I cried out, tears filled my eyes and still, I couldn't spread my legs enough. I pumped my hips, wanting more.

"Yes." I blubbered.

"Yes, *brother*." He corrected.

Flames exploded, ripping me apart from the inside as I came. "Yes, brother."

His hold on my hair relaxed, but his slick fingers remained. "Good girl. Go with Harmony and get cleaned up. Take care of my pussy now. Tomorrow you get to serve all of us. How does that sound?"

He smiled and licked his lips. I knew in that moment what he said was true. This fat little mouse was about to become the meal.

## Chapter Five

I stared at my ruined panties. The perfect print of a man's shoe stamped the torn crotch, if I pulled the pieces back together. I could still feel Jared's fingers punch through the sheer fabric. I could still feel the heat of my body when he was cruel, and the need inside for him to be sweet. Our relationship would never change. I'd always want the Jared underneath the mask. I wanted something he wasn't prepared to give. Now he wanted to take something I shouldn't be giving him—my innocence.

I reached for my purse and shoved my underwear inside. The stark white lights of the ladies bathroom revealed every dirty little secret. My face was flushed. Red marks from Jared's fingers marred my face. I shifted my messy hair and touched my scalp, which still burned from his grip, then dipped my hand between my legs to cup my mound. My pussy ached from his fingers, and from their absence. Everyone in the room had seen what happened. Had they also seen how much I liked it? I gripped the basin and stared into my glassy eyes. "What have I done?"

The dancer, Harmony, eyed me in the bathroom mirror. "You did well, sugar. Was this your first time with them?"

I nodded and gripped the basin, as the room spun.

"It will get easier. Just make sure you do exactly what they tell you. I swear these rich boys have a thing for family, eh?"

I glanced up, catching her gaze in the mirror. "What do you mean?"

Her smile looked more like a grimace. She handed me my purse. "Nothing. Let's get you cleaned up and back home."

"Home?" I tried to remember. My car, something about my car. "I can't drive. Not like this."

"It's fine, we'll get you a driver." Her hand massaged my back. "You really are a pretty little thing, aren't you?"

I shook my head. No one had ever called me pretty. Fat, or a problem, yes. But pretty, never. Pain flared between my legs. I sucked in my breath, riding the sting.

"Did he hurt you?"

I shook my head. "I don't think so. It's just... I'm...."

Her hand on my back stilled. Her dark eyes narrowed behind chocolate bangs. "Wait. You're not a virgin, are you?"

The bathroom became stifling. I reached for the tap, turning on the water. The cool water trickled into my cupped hand and I splashed my face to avoid her gaze.

"Jesus Christ. The virgin stepsister. Honey, a bit of advice. Keep a little of yourself out of the big, dark hole you're about to sink into. Jared's cruel. That's for sure, but he's not the worst of them. You can always say no, you know that right? Run away, find some sexy guy and hole up at his place until this whole thing blows over."

My laugh ripped through the stalls and bounced off the walls. "Look at me. Do you honestly think I have guys lining up to provide a refuge from my shitty life? My stepbrother might have a cruel way of showing it, but I think deep down, he cares."

"Jesus, don't tell me you're in love with him? "Harmony gripped my arm until pain flared.

My silence was all she needed.

"I might be a whore who peddles my ass for a living, but brother and sister? That's fucked up." She chuckled.

I flinched at her words. "Stepbrother. Jared's my stepbrother."

I tried not to hear the words I deserved , but they stung. I deserved them, no matter how hard they were to hear. The bathroom door flew open, ending with a bang against the tiles that made me jump. Harmony jerked her gaze up at the sound. Heath strode in, flashing me a smile in the mirror. "Is everything okay in here, ladies?"

I nodded, feeling her hand leave my back. "Sure is, honey. Heath, can I talk to you for a moment?"

He flashed me one quick look, then turned to Harmony and growled. "Outside."

The cool water on the back of my neck felt soothing. I switched off the taps, following the pair's movement though the door and into the hallway from the mirror. Harmony's voice was a growl through the door, so I slipped off my heels and padded over, pressing my ear against the door. "Did you know this kid is a virgin, Heath?"

I strained to hear his answer. There was none.

"Jesus Christ. She has no idea what she's in for. You're gonna break her. You do know that, don't you?"

"She's Jared's conquest and none of your damn business. We pay you to keep your mouth shut and take care of them, Harmony. Do your fucking job, or I'll have to report this to Kyle."

"You know what?" She snarled. I pressed until my ear ached. "You can go fuck yourself, and you tell that to Kyle, too."

I stumbled to the basin, mind spinning, trying to make sense of what was happening. Something wasn't right here. There was more to this than I could understand. What did this have to do with Jared, or me? Maybe Harmony was right, I should just leave. But I had nowhere to go.

The heat spread from between my thighs. This dangerous game Jared and I played excited me. All these years I'd been hating him in the open and wanting him in secret. Now Jared wanted me, but what did Heath mean by *them*? The door opened and Harmony strode in. "Okay, honey. Are you ready to go?"

"Sure. Everything okay?"

"Of course." She grinned and nodded. "Why wouldn't it be?"

An uneasy feeling settled in my stomach, swirling with the remnants of the alcohol to make a dangerous combination. This Harmony was colder than the one who rubbed my back seconds before. This version made me feel vulnerable. I stepped into my heels and muttered. "No reason."

Harmony reached for my hand, leading me into the hallway. An eerie silence filled the room now. The music had died, along with the rest of the party in this private room. As I stepped out into the room, I realized why. Everyone was gone. Jared and the others left us behind. Was that why Heath checked in on us?

I followed her past the bar, now filled with empty glasses, marred with finger and lipstick prints under the harsh overhead light. The bartender cleaned the counter, lifting his head as I passed. There was no smile, no nod of the head—only silence followed as we left the room.

*This cunt is mine. You will fuck when I tell you to fuck. You will fuck who I tell you to, and no one else.* Jared's words replayed inside my head, although in my fantasy he spoke softer, with just as much desire as I felt for him. And, instead of an audience, there was only me and him.

I shuddered as Harmony closed the door behind us to the private room. The main nightclub was still pumping. The beat from the music shook the walls of the hallway as we exited onto the dance floor. It felt like days since I arrived here with good intentions to set things straight between me and my brother— now, there was only a bigger mess to clean. I caught movement from the corner of my vision. A knock to my side had me stumbling sideways. I clawed for a hold, gripping the nearest man, and felt his arms wrap around me.

"Hands off, Romeo. This one's taken." Harmony snarled, pulling me free. Somehow, we made it through the crushing crowd to the front door.

The cold air hit me as soon as we stepped outside. The sleek black limousine waited for me, door open. Harmony pulled me down the steps, nodding to the driver as we slid into the backseat.

The thud of the driver's door reached through the glass barrier before the car eased forward. I sobered quickly in the cool night air, leaving a dirty aftertaste. "What have I done?"

Harmony patted my hand. "Don't you fuss over it now, honey. If you didn't come to him, he would've gone to you. Either way, Jared's determined to have you. Now just go home, take a nice hot shower and sleep. Leave tomorrow for another day."

The rest of the ride passed in silence as I replayed her words over in my mind. *Jared's determined to have you. I swear these rich boys have a thing for family....* The cold seeped in and I wrapped my arms around my chest.

Harmony's hand left mine to dip into her purse. "Here, take one of these tomorrow, before the party. It will help you relax."

I stared at the tiny plastic bag she pressed into my hand. The bottom held small round pills. I'd never done drugs in my life. This night was crazy enough without starting a habit. I shook my head and pushed the bag into her hand. "I don't do drugs."

"They're prescribed. Just take one tomorrow night. You don't want to be meeting these guys sober. Take my word on it."

I looked up into her eyes. In the soft blue hue of the interior lights of the limousine, they looked kind and sad. She'd taken care of me tonight, even if Jared had forced her to look after me, he couldn't force her to be nice. I took the bag from her hand, squeezing her fingers, and slumped against the seat as I felt the familiar climb and the car slowed moments later.

"Take care of yourself, April. Remember to take the pills, honey. No more than two, okay?"

"Sure, thanks."

I shoved open the door and climbed out. My little blue car sat in the driveway. I sighed with relief and fumbled for the keys in my purse as the driver waited. I snagged the cold metal and shoved the key into lock. The door swung open and I crept across the threshold, the little mouse, home again.

# Chapter Six

THE INSISTENT BLEATING OF MY PHONE WOKE ME. My head felt thick, memories hazy, as I slapped my dresser, finding the vibration and swiped the screen. "Hello?"

"It's about time you answered. Be ready at six. Wear something nice. Skirt or dress only, no pants. You'll have others turn up at five. Let them in and don't ask questions. Do you understand what I'm saying, little mouse?"

"Yes." My mouth felt dry.

Jared's voice slapped me awake. "I'll expect you waiting for me at the door. This time, I better have a nicer reception than the last."

I hesitated for a moment. I could hear his heavy breath through the phone. "Jared, I just want to say that I'm not sure what this is, between us. But I've never really loved you as a brother. It's okay if you don't feel the same. I don't need you to. But ever since I was old enough to know the difference, I wanted you to see me as something more than a snotty-nosed kid who was always in your way."

"April," he snapped. I waited for him to laugh, or say something cruel. His heavy breath was loud through the phone, it took a long time before he spoke. "I've never seen you like that. I... oh shit. *Shit....*"His voice broke and torment came flooding though. "Tell me to fuck off. Tell me you'll call the police. Tell me tonight in front of everyone. I... I can't say any more, but there are things in play that I can't get out of. They'll hurt me, April. They'll hurt you too, if they find out I told you anything."

My heart thundered. I couldn't comprehend what he was saying. All I thought of was my own selfish reasons. It was as though the real Jared was here, the one I desperately wanted—the one I hoped who wanted me. "It doesn't matter, any more. If you're in trouble and there's something I can do, I'll do it. Use me if you have to, Jared. Just please, tell me I'm not alone in this. Tell me that you at least feel something."

"Of course I feel something," he snapped. "Why do you think I wanted to leave for Harvard? Why do you think I was cruel and hurtful? Because I wanted you to hate me. It would be easier if you hated me."

The room was spinning out of control. I gripped the handset until my knuckles burned. "I'll never hate you, Jared. Whatever happens with us, I'll never hate you."

His voice turned cold. "Then I guess I'll have to try harder."

I stared blankly at the blank screen as he hung up. Jared's harsh tone triggered something other than anger or resentment. I was swallowed by a dark urgency, waiting for him to notice me, for him to want me. And he did want me. This proved what I'd felt all along. Why did it have to be Jared? *Brother, sister....* I was dancing along the line of indecency. The thought made me shiver and my heart race. I wanted what I shouldn't.

And now he wanted me.

I fought the sheets, dragging myself from bed. I raked through my drawers, searching for panties and a bra. Dress or skirt, those were Jared's demands. The only dress I had lay in a heap on my bedroom floor. Connie was almost the same size, a little thinner around the ass. A skirt would fit well enough. I could have it cleaned and replaced without her ever knowing.

Jared was in trouble, that was as much as I knew. Who he was scared of, I couldn't tell, but he needed me and I had to be there for him—no matter what.

Steam filled the shower stall as I hit the taps. I stepped into the water and grabbed the loofah. My body felt fine, although my sense of decency was tattered and torn. I touched my pussy, gently prodding my slit. There was no tenderness, even though Jared had been anything but. Would he show me a different side tonight?

My stepbrother brought out a desire I never knew existed. The heady rush of being owned swept me away. How many times had I sat, watching television, and wished for my own fantasy? How many times had Jared found his way into those fantasies? Too many times to count.

I switched off the spray and wrapped myself in a towel. Time was ticking. In a little over two hours, people would be arriving, then Jared would be here.

I raced for Connie and Dad's room. The door swung in and I walked into their bedroom. The room felt strange without Dad or Connie being here. I was an invader, poking about in places I shouldn't. I shoved the feeling aside and walked into their closet.

The overhead lights made me flinch until my eyes adjusted. One side of the room was filled with slacks, sweaters, and three-piece suits. The other sparkled with gold, blue, and silver fabrics. I ran my hand over the dresses, searching for anything black and plain, and spied the soft pleated skirt toward the end of the rack.

The cut was a little short for my liking. There was no way I could hide my thighs in this. I had no other choice. Jared's demands were undeniable. They triggered a need in me to obey.

I stepped into the skirt and worked the waist up to close the zipper and button. Connie's tops were too revealing. I had an off-white number that would look better. I hit the light switch, plunging the walk-in wardrobe into darkness before heading to my own.

I fingered the satin and lace, tugging the top into place and sliding the hem into the waistband of the skirt. *Sex.* The thought sent chills down my spine and sweat prickled my armpits. Would Jared and I have sex tonight? I slipped my feet into my heels. The thought of lying naked with my stepbrother heightened the chills. I brushed my hair, spying the bag of tiny tablets beside my dresser. Harmony said they were something to relax me and God knew, I needed to relax tonight.

I palmed the bag before heading downstairs. Intent on thoughts of Jared, I almost ran into Marielle.

"You look nice, Miss. You going out?" Marielle asked, eyeing me up and down as I entered the kitchen.

I swallowed and nodded. "Just to a friend's house."

"Well, you look the part, that's for sure."

I burned under her scrutiny. Did I have slut written all over my face? I busied myself with a drink, watching the clock, waiting for Marielle to leave. When she finally said goodbye, I sighed with relief.

I kept glancing to the clock. Jared's friends would be here any minute. I walked to the front of the house and peeked through the sheers. What kind of reception did Jared want from me? Would he expect me to kiss him? I raised my hand to touch my lips. How would he taste? Would his lips be soft? Or hard, like his love?

A sound roused me from my reverie. A car pulled into the driveway and stopped. My hand trembled. I gripped the door handle, waiting. I didn't have to wait long. A hard knock made the door shudder. I twisted and took a step to the side to open the door. A young man stood on the doorstep, holding a black bag.

The splash of red between his crisp black trousers and jacket drew my eye to his shirt. I lifted my gaze, searching his face. He had sensual lips for a man, dark hair that was brushed back off his forehead, and dark eyes that glinted in the afternoon sun. Parts of last night were still a blur, but he seemed familiar. He held out his hand. "April, it's nice to formally meet you. I'm Kyle."

I gripped his hand as my palms broke out in a clammy sweat. "Hi."

"Jared asked me to come early and make sure you're taken care of."

There was something about the way he looked at me. His eyes were cold, calculating. Jared did say that others would be coming.

But he didn't say Kyle, to be exact. I held the door, keeping his friend waiting. "Does Jared know you're here?"

One eyebrow rose. His lip curled into a sneer. "Of course. Who do you think sent me?"

I couldn't make him wait outside. My instinct was as silent as the grave. *Make a decision.* I gritted my teeth and stepped to the side, allowing him to pass. Kyle stopped in front of me and pierced me with his gaze. "You do want to be taken care of, don't you, April?"

I wanted to nod, but fear pinned me to the floor. My heart sped until my chest throbbed. Jared's panicked voice echoed in my head. I licked my lips. "If this is what Jared needs, then yes."

He nodded. "Good. That's what I was hoping you'd say."

I closed the door and followed him into the games room. Kyle sauntered over to the wall and switched on the lights. Dad's billiard table gleamed, freshly buffed. I hung back, watching Kyle as he placed his bag on the end of the table and wondering when he'd become so familiar with my home.

The harsh snarl of a zipper cut through the room. I stepped closer as he pulled black evell straps out and something that looked like a whip. I tried to peer inside the bag, but he closed it before I could get a good look. The throbbing of my heart increased, eying the whip. "What's that for?"

Kyle turned toward me. Those dark eyes held a mystery I'm scared to solve. "It's a surprise."

I shift in my heels. Should I go, or stay? I felt like a fish out of water, helplessly flapping on the ground. "Can I get you a drink?"

One shake of his head answered my question. "Come here."

I obeyed, making my way toward him, but stopped just out of reach. My disobedience seemed to excite him. A smile crept along those perfect lips. "Do I frighten you, April?"

I froze, trying to weigh my answer, sensing any answer I gave wouldn't be the right one. I opened my mouth and prayed my voice held. "Yes and no."

He nodded and turned on me. One step, and he'd be within reach. "You have good reason to be. I could fuck you right now and no one could stop me."

My breath caught at those crude words. I stared into bottomless eyes, eyes that gleamed when he spoke. "I could rip that pretty lace from your body and mark your breasts with my teeth."

Visions of bruises and blood filled my mind. I gripped the edge of the billiard table.

"I could hike up that skirt and tear off your panties. I'd be inside you before you could scream. Would you like to be filled, April? Would you like that pretty little cunt of yours stretched wide?"

Kyle took a small step toward me. I couldn't move. Pinned by the seductive tone of his voice and his terrifying words, I was helpless.

"You're a virgin, isn't that right, April?"

A pathetic sound escaped from my lips as he moved closer. He dropped a hand to reach for his crotch. What he gripped was enormous. His cock lay across his groin, one hand unable to encase the girth.

Fear made me stumble backward. My insides clenched tight.

"I fucking love virgins. I love watching them buck and scream as I slide in. Do you want to feel that?"

I swallowed and shook my head. Is this what Jared had planned? Is this why the sudden honesty about his feelings? I could still hear the words I whispered to him and the cold words before he ended the call. *Whatever happens with us, Jared, I'll never hate you.*

*"Then I'll have to try harder."*

"Come closer." Kyle murmured, reaching for my hand. His body blurred under the shimmer of tears. If Jared wanted me to hate him, then this was a perfect act of cruelty. To make me care for him and make me think he cared for me, then send Kyle in his place.

Kyle's grip was too strong. My tears slipped silently from my eyes as Kyle steered my palm to encircle his member.

His other hand cupped my breast, kneading and pinching, until my body responded. I closed my eyes, but darkness only heightened the sensation. His thick muscle under my hand swelled and tightened. I hissed as pain flared through my breast. I looked down to see Kyle roll my nipple between his fingers. The heat streaked through my body to settle between my thighs. I swallowed hard, unable to stop my body from responding.

"You like a little pain?"

Unable to answer, he took my silence as a yes as he pinched and rubbed. "Let's see how much, then?"

He moved from my breast to my skirt so fast I barely caught the movement. Kyle moved, pushing me against the edge of the table, until I couldn't move. One hand reached under my knee to jerk my legs wide. "Open up, you dirty little fucking slut."

My breath caught. Anger flared for a second before he shoved aside my panties. His greedy fingers slipped inside. I clamped my jaw shut as the slick rush of desire tore through me. "Dirty little fucking slut. Wanting to fuck your own brother. You're nothing but a whore. A cunt for me to ride until I come. I'm going to shove my dick so far up inside your cunt, you're gonna split in two."

Desire mingled with disgust at his words. I moved my hips against his grip, grinding my body as the need took over. His words never stopped... *dirty... fuck your own brother.*

I opened my eyes, holding Kyle's gaze as his fingers rode my body. His dark eyes were endless pools that sucked me in, just like Jared's. "Your brother and I are gonna take turns fucking you tonight. We're gonna hand you around like a doll to be fucked and used. That pretty little virgin cunt is going to see more action than it will for the rest of your life, 'cause once we're finished, you'll want it, again and again and again."

I spread my legs wider, wider. Whimpering as he removed his fingers and snarled. "Get on your knees."

My legs trembled, unable to hold my weight I sank to the floor.

"Take it out."

I reached for his belt and yanked the tongue free. The gold clasp shuddered under my hands, still Kyle never moved. I could feel him take it all in. Every shudder, every whimper as the buckle came free. My hands trembled, unable to grip the button. Still, he watched with silent satisfaction. The button slid through the opening and I yanked his zipper down.

Kyle wove his fingers through my hair to press my head against his cotton boxers. "So timid." His grip on my head hardened, forcing my mouth to slide along the outline of his cock, all the way to the end. "Such a nice virgin slut. Open your mouth, virgin slut. Open wide."

Kyle pushed down the waistband, releasing his cock. I swallowed, staring at the thick veins that ran along the shaft. The throbbing muscle seared my lips with heat. I opened wide as he shifted the head toward me. The sight was overwhelming, softening my will to fight.

The smooth skin probed my mouth. Kyle moaned and the sound echoed through his body. The vibration tickled my tongue. His hold on my head forced me to open as he entered. His thick shaft stretched my lips, stinging the corners of my mouth and cutting off my air.

"Breathe, little slut. Just breathe."

I bucked under his grip. Still, he pushed deeper, shoving his cock over my tongue to probe my throat. My stomach tightened. I gagged, wrenching my fist backwards to slam against his thigh. My feeble blows were useless, my words nothing more than a gurgle in my throat. His grip in my hair tightened as I retched. My throat worked, trying to swallow, while fire tore through my chest.

My vision blurred. Hot, salty tears stung my face as the world greyed. My slaps barely grazing his thighs. *I can't breathe. I can't breathe.*

His hold on my head eased. Kyle pulled away and sweet air rushed in. I coughed and spluttered, dislodging the monster from my mouth. Spit drooled from the glistening head to my lips, a leash I wanted to break, but didn't dare. I forced my hand to swipe my mouth and gasped. "You fucking bastard. You almost killed me."

The devil wasn't done. Kyle growled. "Again."

Fear gripped me. My vision blurred, tears stung my eyes as his hold on my hair tightened until my view was warped and my head burned. I cowered from his touch, hitting the carved wooden legs of the billiard table. Kyle's angry cock bobbed against my face. The vicious pull on my hair made me whimper. "Please, no more."

"Again."

His other hand gripped my jaw. His fingers dug between my teeth, forcing my mouth open. His brutal grip on my hair a promise of how merciless he could be.

"Wider.

I trembled as my lips parted, unable to tear my gaze away from the slick cock, still dripping with my saliva. The moisture was cool, but his body was warm as he forced his way in. I tried to slow my panic, taking slower breaths as he slid over my tongue. The urge to gag tore through my stomach. I inhaled as my mouth was filled with spit.

"That's a girl, see? You can take more of me now."

Inch by inch, he stuffed my mouth until my jaw screamed from the violation. My pulse thundered. The rush of blood made my face burn and my vision blur. Each small inhale staved away the darkness a second longer.

Kyle slid out, only to push in. The pump of his hips and subsequent rocking motion of my head was slower now, letting me take air when I could. My tongue felt the friction. Each shove made my throat constrict, triggering a moan from Kyle. "That's the way. That's a good girl."

I focused on the air and on the rhythm of his hand on my head. My breaths turned into pants, matching the quickening strokes, until with a roar, he exploded in my mouth. I tried to swallow as the salty liquid hit my throat and gagged. Some dripped from my mouth to splatter my skirt.

His grip released and I sat there panting, trying to swallow. White cum coated the end of his prick as he slid free. The angry shaft still pulsed, trying to pump the last drop of semen over my lips.

The sharp tone of the doorbell ripped through the house, making me jump. Kyle stepped backward, his grin dark, as he stuffed his member into his pants. "You think Jared's going to give you what you need? He'll take, take, take. You won't ever be enough."

He reached for me and I couldn't stop myself from cowering. "You don't have to be afraid of me. I like a little force, but I'd never really hurt you. Maybe after Jared's had his fun, we can hook up sometime?"

He trailed his fingers down my cheek. The touch made my stomach lurch. A loud rap on the door drew his gaze. "You better wipe your mouth, sweetheart. Then be a nice hostess and see to the door."

I tried to make sense of his warning while I pulled myself from the floor. My knees were shaky as I stumbled to the front of the house. My clothes were a mess. I tried my best to straighten my skirt and wiped my mouth before I gripped the handle and opened the door.

Jared stood on the doorstep, his scowl like thunder, matching his snarl. "What took you so damn long?"

# Chapter Seven

MY JAW ACHED AND THE WORDS WOULDN'T COME. JARED just stood there until the silence became too much. The furrow in his brow deepened. "April, what's wrong?"

The sound of footsteps echoed from inside the house. Jared snapped his attention toward the sound. "Who's there?"

I could feel the tears coming. I parted my trembling lips, ready to spill everything. I hated the way Jared made me feel weak and I hated myself more.

Kyle stepped from the foyer, his smile ruthless. "It's me. Who else did you expect?"

My stepbrother's smooth complexion paled. He turned to look at me, then shoved the door form my grip as he barged in. "What the fuck are you doing here, Kyle? You've got no business... no, you've got no *right* to be anywhere near her."

Kyle's smug look wavered as Jared lunged. The small foyer table smashed against the wall. The vase on top tipped forward, and seemed to fall in slow motion until it shattered, sending bits of porcelain skidding across the floor. Jared grappled with Kyle, throwing him to the floor. But Kyle responded, moving quickly to step out of his way. "Why're you so upset? I mean, it's not as though you love her, right Jared?"

"That's none of your damn business, Kyle. You don't get to control her. You don't get to touch her, or I swear...."

Jesus. There was something wrong here, something really wrong. I could feel the tension swirling like a storm as Kyle took a step forward. Danger throbbed in his tone. "You swear? You *swear?* You break the oath, you even utter one fucking word to anyone, and *I* swear, I'll make good on my promise."

Kyle directed a look at me. I felt my stomach weaken as Jared's warning sounded like a siren. *Tell me to fuck off. Tell me you'll call the police. Tell me tonight in front of everyone. I... I can't say anymore, but there are things in play that I can't get out of. They'll hurt me, April. They'll hurt you, too, if they find out I told you anything.*

Kyle was threatening Jared and he needed me to play a pawn in this game, whatever it was. I couldn't deny my stepbrother now. "It's okay, Jared. Whatever you need from me, you'll have."

My stepbrother spun at the sound of my voice and his shoulders dropped. "April. You don't understand."

Shards of pain ripped through my heart at the tormented look on his face. He opened his mouth to speak, but there was nothing that needed to be said. Whatever he needed, whatever he wanted, I would freely give. This was what I'd wanted all along. The muscles of his throat worked, then he nodded.

"Good, now that's over, we can get on with things," Kyle snapped. But my stepbrother held my gaze. The world disappeared and my heart swelled.

"Well, I don't know about you, but I'm thirsty." Kyle walked toward the bar and disappeared.

The uneasiness grew. I took a step before Jared seized my hand and took a tentative step toward me. He kept his sight fixed on the doorway and his voice low. "Do you have those tablets Harmony gave you?"

My mind raced. How could he know about them, unless....

"Do you have them?" he growled. His hold on my arm tightened.

I nodded. "Yes."

"Good. Take one." I thought about the command for a second, and then nodded. "Whatever happens tonight, just go along with it. No one is going to hurt you. I wish there was something I could do to stop this from happening. But it's too late."

"We could go to the police. I could call Dad. He'll know what to do."

Jared shook his head. "These people will crush us if they knew we betrayed them. The only way out is to do exactly what I say. Go, take one of the pills. They'll relax you."

There was something in his voice and in his eyes. I couldn't help but nod then made for the kitchen. I pulled open the drawer and slipped my hand underneath the cloths to snag the bag. Five tiny white pills sat at the bottom. I glanced at the doorway, listening for footsteps while I broke the zipper seal and fished one out.

"April, where are you?" Kyle called.

I jumped at the sound of my name. My hands trembled as I shoved the tablet into my mouth then slipped the bag underneath the cloths. The colors outside were changing, darkening with a purple hue. The front doorbell sounded. The sound of male voices drew me. I swallowed the pill and headed for the foyer.

Jared turned from smiling at Maurie and Jed. "There you are. Our guests are waiting to be served."

I forced a smile, reaching to take their jackets. "Sorry."

A car door slammed in the driveway. I shifted to the side, allowing Maurie and Jed to pass as a sharp bark of laughter echoed. Heath and two women made their way from the driveway. I searched their faces for Harmony, but she hadn't come. I couldn't help but feel a sense of loss.

"Heath." Jared nodded as they passed.

I took their coats and smiled at their dates. Sparkling diamonds and designer labels covered their thin bodies. Only the brunette returned my smile. The blonde snarled, her distaste evident as she looked me up and down. "So this is the little sister."

Jared nodded. "Yes."

I felt naked under her scrutiny. She took a step toward me and lifted a finger to slide down my face. "How well behaved is she?"

Jared never flinched as I snapped. "I'm not well behaved at all."

"Good to hear it. I hate the meek and mild type." Without a second glance she strode into the house, followed by the others.

I could feel the weight of Jared's gaze as everyone left. "Remember, you hate me, okay? Go along with everything and don't cause a scene."

I shuddered as his words flipped a switch inside. Jared dropped his hand to slowly rub the inside of my thigh. His thumb caressed my sex.

"You love pain and pleasure. I can feel your heat against my hand. Hate me, April. Hate me."

I wanted to seize his hand and wrench it away in one second, then ached to spread my legs for him in the next. The conflict was driving me crazy. His hand dug against my mound. I arched my back, forcing his touch deeper and he complied. Jared slid his hand under my skirt and ran his hand along my crease.

"More." I growled as he pressed his body against my thigh.

The tiny white pill had me floating in desire. My brother's touch was all I felt. I could follow each imprint he left by the lick of fire that followed. He eased backwards and gripped my hand, dragging me after him. "Come on. Let's get this party started."

My feet moved, but my body felt numb. Where he led, I followed. I could already hear the others laughing and joking in the games room. They turned to watch me as we entered, all smiles, except for Kyle.

Jared let my hand fall and grabbed two glasses from the bar. Kyle searched my eyes, his mouth parted slightly as though he had something to say. He must've decided otherwise because he turned away.

"To money." Jared lifted his glass. "May it never stop buying happiness." Jared crooned and downed the contents. This Jared was different from the one who touched me minutes before. It was as though a switch had been tripped and he needed me to do the same. I reached for the glass on the counter, spying the red blinking light of the camera. *A camera? Are they going to tape me?* An icy chill ran across my arms, making me shudder.

Jared shot me a look, full of pleading and remorse. "It's just a drink, April." Jared shoved the glass into my hand, and lifted my elbow, urging me to swallow.

The room sparkled through the crystal tumblers as the rim touched my lips.

"Drink," Jared urged, while others in the room waited.

The scotch burned my throat all the way into my stomach, spreading out to warm the icy feeling inside. Still the heat wasn't enough.

Heath left his date and headed for me. I gripped the counter, watching him shrug out of his jacket and drop it to the floor. His body rippled underneath his clothes as he moved. I was spellbound. He held me trapped, dropping his hands to the buttons of his shirt.

Was this what Jared wanted all along? To watch me have sex with his best friend? Something in my chest fluttered at the thought. Smooth, tanned skin peeked from between the edges of his crisp white shirt. Jesus. I swallowed hard as he stopped an arm's reach away.

"Does this excite you, little sister?" Jared asked and I knew this was what he needed me to do.

Play the game. I nodded into Heath's brown eyes, stopping mid-movement as he turned toward my brother. My breath caught, staring as Heath leaned in and kissed my brother on the lips.

A small sound escaped, watching their lips caress. Through the movement of their mouth I glimpsed Jared's tongue dart into Heath's mouth. Their lips weren't hard, or cruel, like I thought they'd be when two men kissed. Jared lifted his hand sweeping Heath's shirt aside, exposing his shoulder. I expected cruelty. I expected pain. But what I got was something very different. My brother moved to stand behind Heath, reaching around to slide his hands along his chest.

My heart pounded. My mouth dried while I followed the movement of his hand, slipping lower. Heath sighed and dropped his head against Jared's shoulder. I caught every ripple of his skin, every tender touch, and I yearned for that caress to be mine.

Jared held my gaze, kissing Heath on the shoulder while his hand skirted the waistband of his trousers, then dropped lower. My brother cupped his friend's groin, sliding his hand between the valley of his thighs to slide back up again. Heath's body responded, swelling from the touch as Jared rubbed his big hands over the mound. Heath turned his face toward my brother, tongues encircled, dipping in to lap each others mouths. My nipples tightened at the sight, drawing a beat from my clit in response. Heath opened his eyes to mine, then held out his hand. "Come, April. Come and join us."

My feet refused to move. I stumbled, reaching for Heath's hand. Fire licked the inside of my core, threatening to ignite every nerve inside me. Heath dropped his head to kiss my bottom lip, then nipped the top one, working all the way to the edges of my mouth, then back again.

Heat wafted off his chest, penetrating the thin material of my blouse. Every rise and fall caused by his breathing rubbed my breasts. I was carried away by the work of his lips, by the feel of his hands—so carried away, I missed the sound of heels. I broke Heath's kiss at the touch of a hand on my stomach and turned to see sparkle of diamonds. I blinked and the rainbows resolved into the attractive face of Heath's date. Her blond hair fell across my shoulder as she kissed the nape of my neck.

My body responded to the gentle feeling of her hands on my nipples and the stronger touch of Heath's hand when he tugged my blouse from my skirt.

"Mine." Jared growled, rounding Heath in two steps to take his place. He grabbed my hand, guiding it to the front of his pants. A rigid shaft throbbed underneath the fabric. My skirt slid against my hips, the clasp undone by expert hands.

"We don't need this, do we?" She whispered against my ear.

I shook my head, watching her hands reach for the hem of my blouse. Two tugs and I was lifting my arms, the lace gone, leaving me in my panties and bra.

"You next." I breathed, staring at Jared, feeling vulnerable.

My fingers snagged his blue shirt, tugging the bottom free from his trousers as he dropped his fingers from one button to the next. His skin wasn't as tanned as Heath, yet his body was lean and muscled. Powerful. I'd seen him without a shirt before, but this time, his nakedness was for me.

He unclasped the buttons at his wrists and slipped the shirt free. Clasps snapped. I jumped as the cups of my bra slipped free. I slapped my hands over my breasts, covering what I could.

"No need to be shy here, baby." The blonde muttered behind me, sliding her hands along mine.

Jared snapped his belt, working the clasp open and fumbled for his zipper. Across the room, the brunette was shedding her dress like she was a professional, as was Jed. The only one who remained clothed was Kyle. He stared at me, his eyes dropped to skim my body before finding my eyes once more.

Electricity thrummed through my veins. I wanted Jared, but I wanted Kyle just as much. He rolled up his sleeves, keeping my gaze and moved toward me. I wanted to run my hands through his glistening midnight hair, but to do that would leave me exposed.

I could see he wasn't like the others. He moved with purpose, as though he was the dependable one. He was the one who got the job done. He reached for my hand, releasing my breast and slipped the bra free. His grip never left my wrist. The blonde's lips on the base of my neck kept me from focusing on what he was doing. The other strap slid free. My bra fell to the floor.

"Come, you're gonna enjoy this." Kyle growled, his voice husky and filled with need.

The drug mingled with the heat of the scotch, making me pliable. Kyle handled me with the touch of an expert, tugging me toward the games room. The aquamarine blue felt on the billiard table glimmered like the sea under the overhead lighting. Kyle led me to the table's edge. Steps behind had me glancing over his shoulder to see Jared follow. His pants gaped open, his erection strained the sliding zipper and I shuddered.

The sight of his body made mine react as though he'd touched me, and the resulting wave of heat snatched my thoughts. All I felt were his hands and the hard column of his cock at my back. He knocked me forward and I braced myself on the carved wood.

"You want to watch this, April. You want to see my cock slid into my own sister?"

His words tried to penetrate the void inside my head, but all I could do was nod. Jared's grip replaced Kyle's, spinning me around to face him. Jared gripped my hips, forcing his body between my legs. He'd seen me naked. He'd seen me vulnerable, but I'd never seen him. I dropped my gaze, my hand followed, shoving aside the waistband of his trousers and boxers.

*This is really happening.*

The thought filtered through my mind and then it was gone, replaced by the sight of my stepbrother's cock. The others followed us into the room. Someone slipped behind Jared's back to stand at the trophy case. My focus was wrenched to my stepbrother as he tugged on the edge of my panties, sliding them down my hips, exposing the thin line of dark hair that ran down my slit.

There was no waiting, no breathing. Jared trailed his hands down my stomach to hover at the edge of my pussy. One finger slipped in, paving the way for the other to follow.

His fingers were gentler this time, finding the nub that sent shocks through my body. I exhaled and leaned backwards, letting his fingers go where I needed them.

The tearing of Velcro made me jerk my head up. The hard plastic slid off my hand to secure my wrist. My stomach hardened. The excitement of Jared's expert fingers now gone. "What's going on?"

My brother smiled, his fingers still moving, circling my clit to dip lower and slip inside. "I told you, April. You're serving all of us tonight. Every, single one."

Kyle moved to grab my other wrist. I jerked my hand away and shook my head. "No, I don't...."

"It's fine. We're gonna give you the best sex of your life." Jared's fingers never stopped moving as he reached for my hand with his other. He gripped my wrist, extending my arm. Something hard encircled my wrist.

"Are you ready for this?"

The question took me by surprise. Jared's hand dropped to my breast, the pressure forcing me against the table. I lifted my head, staring at my stepbrother's cock inching toward the juncture of my thighs. The smooth contact of the head against the lips of my pussy froze me. The pressure at my entrance was unrelenting. A hiss escaped from my lips. I clawed the soft surface of the billiard table, trying to find something to hold as my stepbrother pushed in. He was too big, too hard. I opened my legs wider, clawing for a handhold against the table as he forced his way in.

"Jesus, you're so tight. Relax and breathe, little sister."

I couldn't breathe. I couldn't think. I felt like he was cleaving my body in two. I could feel him pushing against my insides, slipping out, only to try again.

"Fuck, your cunt feels so good. I'm going to fill you, then when I'm done, Monica here is gonna lick you clean. How does that sound, little sister?"

I whimpered as he thrust. He never slowed, never cared. He gave me only one violent stab after another until a delicious heat spread throughout my body.

The Velcro straps tightened as Jared gripped my hips. Each thrust moved me further onto the table. The smack of his hip against my inner thighs forced his cock deeper. I was lost on the rhythm, and the urgency building inside. I gripped the straps and lifted my hips to meet his, as the long, smooth thrusts turned frenzied. Pain mingled with pleasure. I couldn't catch my breath. I couldn't stem the tide.

The blonde leaned in to kiss me. Her lips were soft, supple, different from a man's. She tasted sweet, like cherries and champagne. Her tongue probed my mouth, the gentle thrusts twining with the hard pounding between my thighs. She pushed her tongue deeper inside me, as though spurred by Jared's hard bucking.

Her hands slid over my stomach to skirt my ribs. I arched my back, ready for her fingers on my breast. My breath caught with each blow. I was unable to hold on to the wave inside. Jared grunted, slamming home one last time before his warmth spread inside me.

The woman's expert fingers teased my clit. I shuddered and moaned as her teeth pulled my nipple. Her fingers replaced his cock. The brunette joined the blonde, climbing onto the table to suckle my breast.

This was wrong. I opened my mouth to say, "stop" as her fingers slid between my gaping slit, dancing around his cock inside me. Her mouth on my breast drew a shudder as Jared slipped from my pussy.

The blonde's mouth left my breast to rise and kiss me on the lips and whisper. "You want to feel one of Monica's special kisses?"

I was too breathless to answer. She didn't care, answering herself. "I hear she gives great tongue."

# Chapter Eight

Monica kissed my thigh, moving her lips down to my knee and traveling up the inside as she moved between my legs. My skin shuddered, and leaned back on the table as I followed the heat of her breath.

Her mouth traced the soft lips of my slit, her finger slid inside the spot where my stepbrother had been moments before, wrenching a whimper from me. Her finger worked in and out while she kissed the crest of my pussy. I opened my legs wider, allowing her tongue to dart around the hood of my clit.

My body quaked as her mouth stoked the fire between my legs. Tension climbed, twisting my guts with nothing more than the friction of her fingers and the gentle sucking of her mouth.

More. I wanted more. I needed more. Her warm tongue slid down to lap and my slit. She flattened the warm, wet muscle, licking me all the way up to the top. I lifted my hips to greet her mouth, grinding my pussy on her face as she probed me with her tongue. All thought fled from my mind as my body's needs took over.

I wanted to be used. To be fucked. I wanted more of her mouth. I wanted more cock and I wanted it deeper, harder. Heath climbed onto the table and jerked on my binds, setting me free. My gaze was seized by the smooth tanned chest and the thick cock that protruded from his pants. His gaze went from my open legs to my eyes as he growled. "My turn."

There was movement behind me, but I was transfixed by this gorgeous man between my legs. He leaned forward, gripping me with one hand around my waist, the other around my back. He lifted me as though I weighed nothing, pulling me onto his thighs as he moved backward.

Hands touched me everywhere. I turned to catch Jed's wicked smile and realized it was his fingers probing my anus. The sensation of his inquisitive fingers and Heath's thick cock pushing against my opening sent me over the edge. I gripped tight and whispered. "Do it."

His finger slipped in as Heath plunged inside. Pain flared for a second before Jed leaned forward to spit on his finger. The cool saliva was soothing against my pucker. Heath held me against his hips, bouncing nice and slow, spreading me wider as he inched his way deeper inside.

I felt myself widen as Jed's finger became two. I moaned at the sound of a zipper and the slick feel of a cock at my entrance.

"Smile for the camera, baby." Jed growled as he pushed against my walls.

I gripped Heath, my pucker burned, stretching. Pain mixed with pleasure as Heath never slowed. Thrust. Thrust.

"Relax, honey. Let me in." Jed's breath was hot against my ear.

He let go of my hips. The squirting sound, snagged my attention from Heath between my legs. I looked over my shoulder as Jed fisted his cock and gave it two hard pumps. The glistening lube covered the pulsing muscle, then he disappeared behind me. My body trembled with the shock of cold lube against my anus. Heath slowed, filling me wider with each thrust. Each time he withdrew Jed pushed against the tight ring of muscle around my anus.

Each sensation was overwhelming on their own, together with one thrusting my pussy, and the other a slow drive into my ass they stole my breath.

"Breathe baby. Breathe." Jed growled.

I swallowed a mouthful of air as my pucker stretched. My body worked to expel the intrusion, forcing his thick cock back out as Heath plunged in. Over and over, each one took turns stroking channels. Each time Jed made ground, driving his rod deeper, harder. The pain mixed with pleasure, each thrust became more forceful. I dug my nails into Heath's shoulder. He hissed with the pain and thrust harder. The look in his eyes was feral, need, hunger rode our bodies. I climaxed with a roar, my body quaking against these men as a scream tore through the room.

"You fucking piece of shit!"

Neither man stopped until the crack of breaking glass fractured the void.

Heath turned to the doorway. His face turned from tanned to a ghastly grey as he slid from my body and whispered. "Nathan."

"What is this, Heath? Another one of your games?"

Heath dropped my legs to the table. Jed slid from my ass to leave me trembling. I held onto the frame of the billiard table, trying to catch my breath while my mind caught up. The stranger held another crystal tumbler over his head. "You motherfucker. No, wait. Which one is she, Heath? She's got to be someone's sister, right? Whose sister is she?"

No one moved. I gripped the table, my throat was so dry I couldn't think, or speak. Heath moved toward him, one hand fumbling for his pants, the other held out, pleading. "Nathan, lower the glass. Let me explain."

Nathan shot me a look filled with pity and sorrow. His voice was husky. "They fucked me, too. Literally fucked me. My fiancée left me today. She found the recording while I was at work. I came home to find her stuff gone. Just like that, no note, nothing." He turned from me to Heath. "You've ruined me. Utterly ruined me. I thought you cared. Cared enough to get into my pants, I suppose. We're supposed to be family. That's what a stepbrother is, right? Family?"

I turned to Jared as the sound of his phone cut through the room. "Jared, what's happening?"

He never answered, just stared at the screen, and muttered. "Heath, you have to get him out of here. I've got to take this call."

The red blinking light of the camera caught my eye. The lens faced me and Nathan's words hit me like a sledgehammer. *She found the recording.*

Nathan stared as Heath advanced. His stepbrother kept his voice low and calm. The two women slowly retreated to the wall, stealing glances at Heath and Jared. One bent to fumble with something on the table. I didn't get a good look until she straightened, her bag in her hand. The blonde muttered as they made for the door. "We'll see ourselves out, gentlemen."

Heath and Jed made for Nathan, surrounding him. Heath's comforting voice drifted to my ears. I searched for my clothes, glimpsing Kyle standing next to the bar. While everyone else's attention was somewhere else, his was on me. Glass shattered as the fight broke out. I could hear the brutal thud of punches thrown, the agony in Nathan's scream as he lunged at his brother.

Blackmail. This is what this was all about. This was what Kyle had over my stepbrother. As I turned to the camera, I knew why his focus was no longer on Jared. Someone else took center stage now—me.

I huddled under the billiard table as Heath gripped his brother and wrestled him outside. Jared knew what they had planned. Had he betrayed me all along?

Tears sprang to my eyes as my brother walked into the room and headed for me, stopping to scoop my clothes from the floor. He held out his hand, helping me to stand and shoved my clothes into my hands. "We need to hurry. Get dressed."

I fumbled with the skirt. Nothing seemed to work. He held out the waistband for me to step through. "I want to tell you everything, but I can't. Not yet. But you're going to be okay. You believe me, right?"

Jared knew about the camera. He knew about everything. My trust, like my heart was breaking, shattering into a million pieces. I didn't know if I'd ever be able to put the fragments back together.

"It's doesn't matter anyway. By the end of this, you'll see," my brother muttered. "The phone call was Mom. It seems there was a problem with the honeymoon and they're coming home."

My hands stilled as I tugged the hem of my top down. My breaths were sharp, tearing through my chest. "What do you mean, coming home?"

"They'll be here in a few hours."

I stared at the ruined felt on the table, the shattered glass, just like my ravaged innocence. I could almost see the shattered look on my father's face when he saw me for what I was—a dirty slut who'd slept with her stepbrother. I'd be disowned. My life would be over. College gone and all because of... . "You. You did this to me? You are a sadistic piece of fucking shit."

Jared jerked as though slapped. "No. I promise. I'll fix this, April. I'll get the recording. I'll erase it. No one will ever know." He turned to the bar, then scanned the room. The sound of agony ripped from his mouth. "The camera, where's the fucking camera?"

## Chapter Nine

"Where's the fucking camera?" Jared's bellow ripped through the room. I jumped at the sound. My heart clenched tight, the fist unrelenting as I stumbled toward the bar. Outside, the shouts grew louder, shrill screams that curdled my blood.

I tried to make sense of what'd happened. Sex with Heath and Jed had drawn me into a dangerous current I couldn't get out of, until Nathan's screams wrenched me free. Now I tried to catch my breath in the wake of whatever the hell this was.

When had I turned into this person? One minute, I was making plans for college. The next, I was naked, writhing from each thrust from Heath and Jed, until Heath's stepbrother barged into the room.

Shattered crystal sparkled like diamonds on the floor. His words cut just as deep. *They fucked me, too. Literally fucked me. My fiancée left me today. She found the recording while I was at work. I came home to find her stuff gone. Just like that, no note, nothing. You've ruined me, Heath. Utterly ruined me. I thought you cared. Cared enough to get into my pants, I suppose. We're supposed to be family. That's what a stepbrother is, right? Family?*

Wasn't I Jared's family, too?

My stepbrother had begged me to do things I'd never even fantasized about. Degrading things that would destroy me if Dad ever found out. And he would find out. Everyone would find out. Because they recorded every single dirty deed.

*God, what have I done?*

Now the camera was gone. The device vanished while Heath and Jed wrestled Nathan outside. I glanced over to Jared. His skin looked ashen under the harsh overhead lights. Was this all just pretend? Could Jared lead me down the same destructive path?

My hands shook as I searched the glasses and half-filled bottles behind the bar. "It's not here, Jared. I don't know where the camera's gone, but it's not here."

"Kyle's taken it. That cheating, fucking bastard."

"You have to find it. That's me on that tape, Jared."

He rounded the counter and gripped my shoulders. I wanted to look into his eyes, but my world blurred. His strong arms pulled me against his chest. "It's going to be all right. I got you into this mess, so it's my responsibility to get you out, okay?" He slid his finger under my jaw, tilting my face up to his. You believe me, right, April?"

This was the Jared who was cruel, who'd taunted and ridiculed me in front of everyone. This was the same Jared who had refused to give me a ride home from school, leaving me to take the bus with the bullies and the freaks. His lips brushed mine, their touch sweet and gentle.

This was the Jared I'd longed for.

This was the Jared I wanted.

But, was this the Jared I could trust?

I opened my mouth, tasting his lips. My senses honed in on two things, the soft stroke of Jared's tongue and the tremor shuddering through his body. I wrapped my arms around him, melding into his warmth and the strength of his arms. In this moment, there was only him and me. His lips on mine. His breath in me, until a boom tore through the room, so loud it rattled the glasses.

Someone outside screamed. "Gun!"

Jared shoved me. I hit the floor hard, knocking the wind from my lungs. Each breath was a struggle against the force of his hand. Muffled shouts filtered to my ears, but all I could see was the gleam from the tiles and the shattered glass.

Jared pinned me. "Stay here, don't move."

The pressure eased as he climbed to his feet. "No." I grabbed his jacket. "Don't leave me."

"It's okay. I'm just going outside. I'll be right back. I promise." He whispered and edged toward the door of the games room.

I followed the sound of his steps out of the room and into the foyer. Each second felt like forever, while I waited for him to return. I shuddered against the cold floor. Was someone hurt? Were they dead?

I flinched at each tiny sound, waiting for the boom of a gun to shatter the silence once more. The faint wail of sirens drifted to my ears. *Thank God, that was quick.* Would Jared tell them what happened? Would they search the house and find the recording?

An ache settled in the back of my throat. If the police took custody of the video, my face would be splashed across the papers, all because the tape could be indirectly linked to Jared's father, Harmon Barnett. A few random kids making a sex tape wasn't news. But when one of those kids was the son of the man favored to become the next United States Senator from Massachusetts, the media outlets would foam at the mouth to get their hands on a copy.

*No, it'd just be taken into evidence.* And how long before word of who was on the tape leaked out and Barnett's opponent paid some cop more money than he could earn in three years to get a copy of the recording? A knot the size of a cannonball formed in my gut. Jared would be expelled from Harvard. His trust fund frozen. Any hopes of a future for him would be lost. His father could kiss goodbye any chance of running for office, no matter how good his chances were of winning. I shoved the thought aside. I didn't care about that.

If Jared was just a pawn in their game, could I let that happen?

If he wasn't, then how would I know for sure?

My damp palms slipped on the tiles as I climbed to my feet. The sirens were closer now. I followed Jared's steps, making my way toward the front door, shielding my eyes from the glare. The remnants of the vase were still scattered across the entrance. I edged around the shards to the open door, shielding my eyes from the light that flooded the front of the house.

Muffled grunts and cries came from somewhere near the front garden. I stepped onto the porch, staring into the light until my vision blurred. "Jared?"

Red and blue lights invaded the blinding headlights. I stepped out of the glare and into the soothing darkness. The pulsing lights splashed across a gold BMW I didn't recognize. I followed the pathway to the garden as the emergency lights stopped flashing. Two uniformed officers climbed out of their marked car and rounded the bank of roses to vanish behind the hedge.

Nathan's screams stilled me and my blood ran cold. "I'll fucking murder you, you sonofabitch! You ruined my fucking life. You ruined my fucking life!"

My whole body shook. The police would investigate. They'd have no choice.

"Is this the weapon?" a man cried.

The sound of my pulse drowned out the response as I stepped around the hedge and into view. The ratcheting sound of handcuffs drew my gaze. Nathan was on the ground, held down by his brother. An officer wrenched Nathan's hands behind his back. I spied a glint of steel.

"Tell them!" Nathan screamed and kicked. "Tell them what you've done to me!"

Everyone remained silent. I swallowed, trying to dampen the arid desert in my mouth, and crept past Jared toward Jed. He hovered a few steps away, close enough to tackle Nathan to the ground, but far enough to be out of danger.

One look at Jed and I knew he'd been fighting. His bare chest gleamed with sweat under the harsh beams of the police cruiser's headlights. He jerked his head toward me as I stepped behind Jared to move closer.

Something dark dripped from Jed's lip and slid down his chin. I lifted my hand, touching the lips that kissed me only moments before. Jed winced as the dark drop slid over my thumb. Black turned to red when I rubbed my thumb and finger. My heart lurched when I realized the stain was blood.

He shifted his gaze from my hand to my eyes. I could feel the need that still sizzled under the surface. He licked the cut on his lip. His husky voice was filled with lust and danger as he muttered, "You shouldn't be out here, April."

"No, you shouldn't be out here," Jared snapped. "I told you to wait for me inside."

Jared's cruel tone reminded me just who he was. His love could set me on fire, then in the next minute, his words could turn me to ice. I loved him, but I was done playing his games. "I'm not a child. So, stop treating me like one."

His dark eyes blazed. "Then stop acting like one and go back inside the house."

Behind him, the officer dropped to his knee. I shifted, catching the gleam of something silver in the grass. The cop grabbed the weapon, lifting it into the air with the barrel of an ink pen. I'd never seen a gun up close before. It was smaller than I expected, but the black hole in the barrel transfixed me. One shot could kill me. It could've killed Jared. I trembled in the night air and wrapped my arms around my body. Bloody thoughts ran though my mind.

"Miss, you okay?"

I jerked my gaze from the gun to the officer who held it, trying my best to catch my scattered thoughts. The drug raged through my blood, making me feel off balance. Crossing my arms over my chest, I tried to rub some warmth into them and nodded. "It's just...."

The cop shifted toward me, his eyes boring into mine. "Go on. It's just... what?"

"Jared, leash your bitch," came a snarl from the shadows. Kyle stepped into the light to glare at me.

"Do you live here?" The cop continued drawing my focus away from Kyle.

I looked to Jared. His pupils were wide, holding me. I was desperate to stay afloat in the whirlpool that dragged me under. "Yes."

The slight shake of my stepbrother's head was subtle, but the meaning wasn't lost as he spoke. "April's my stepsister. She didn't see anything when the gun went off. She was inside."

"And you are?" The officer evelled Jared with a dangerous stare.

I caught the square of his shoulders as he answered. "Jared Barnett."

One brow shot high as he focused on Jared once more. "Hey, I know you. You father's running for the Senate, right?"

Jared nodded, while Nathan thrashed on the ground at his back. "Ask her! Ask her what this is. Tell them the truth. Don't wait for them to ruin you, too!"

"Hush up," snapped the officer, scanning each of our faces. His tongue snaked across his bottom lip, until he settled on me. Placing his notebook into his pocket, he took a step in my direction. "Is that so, April? You didn't see anything?"

My brother's pleading gaze was more than I could take. I felt the drug surge in my bloodstream and I was too weak to fight anymore.

"How about you walk over to the car with me?"

I gulped, trapped by the command. Reluctantly, I followed the heavy tread toward the car. I hobbled behind, the pebbles hard under my soft feet. Pointing the gun away and toward the ground, he pressed a button that made a cylinder pop from the middle and emptied the bullet. "Damn thing only had one round."

One round.

That's all there had been.

I glanced to Nathan, who was being dragged to his feet by the other officer. The sound of the shot still rang inside my head. Was that shot meant for Heath, or himself? I swallowed hard. A loud snap had me wrenching my gaze to the officer. The cop slid the gun and the spent shell inside a plastic bag. Pulling the backing free from the edge of the bag, he sealed the top. He kept his voice low, so only I could hear. "You live here?"

I nodded. He asked my name. I stammered the answer. Then, he asked my father's name and occupation. He moved closer— too close, really. I almost took a step back, but he grabbed my arm. "Now, ordinarily, I wouldn't need a warrant to search these premises. The gunshot would be what we call 'exigent circumstances'. But, these rich boys have rich, powerful daddies. Do you know who they are? Just so I know that you know exactly what you're getting yourself into."

I could do nothing but nod.

"Right. Just so I know we're clear, cause I'm gonna be keepin' a real close eye on you and these young men here. You don't wanna mess with the wrong side of me, you understand?"

Each heartbeat took forever as I weighed the officer's words. One small motion on my part would change everything. If I asked, would he search each person here? He would search the house for the camera? Would he demand to know why I let three men fuck me, while someone else pressed 'record'?

One nod, that's all it would take. I fought the blur of my thoughts, trying desperately to get my head together. The unanswered question still waited. If I gave the word, this would all be over, for me at least. My future would be uncertain, but I would still have a future. But what would that do to Jared's future? I wasn't sure.

It was subtle, but I already sensed the rift between Jared and his friends. Nothing I thought someone else might see, but the truth lay in the arrogant expression on Kyle's face and the way Jared's eyes were wide with fear. Kyle smiled and laughed like the much older cop at his side was here to cut the grass. Such a contrast to the tight expression on Jared's face. The plea in his eyes sealed my lips.

I shook my head. "No. I was inside. I only heard the sound."

"And there's nothing you want to add here? Because what I see are three nearly naked males and one young woman who looks terrified. If something happened that you want to talk to someone about, you can come with me to the station."

My face burned under the scrutiny. I dropped my gaze and shook my head. Rape, that was what he was thinking. No wonder Jared was pissed. "No, it's nothing like that. I'm fine, thank you."

"Suit yourself," The cop muttered, staring as though he was trying to make up his mind if I was telling the truth. He reached into the car and straightened, handing me a card. "If you change your mind, call this number."

I nodded and stared at the card. The address wasn't the same as the nearby station's. "Is this the right card?"

"Yeah, it's a station we use sometimes. Just call the number. You'll get one of us, day or night."

I nodded. "Thank you. I will."

He jerked his head up, staring over the top of the marked car and called, "Driscoll, you ready to roll?"

The muffled sobs from Nathan tore at my heart as the officer walked him closer. The cop jerked the back door of the cruiser open, urging him inside with a hand on top of Nathan's head, but Heath's stepbrother resisted, staring at me. "Why won't you tell them? They're gonna do this to you, too. They'll ruin your life."

I stumbled away from the Police car as he disappeared into the backseat. The hard stones dug into my feet, but I no longer felt the pain as the older cop slammed the door, shutting off Nathan's cries.

"Are you okay?" Jared called. The crunch of stones sounded, then his arms were around me. No matter how tight he gripped, I still shuddered. The chill of the night had somehow snaked inside, filling me with its icy breath.

"Jesus, you're shaking," my brother whispered.

The blinding headlights stung my eyes, then twin beams swept the rolling lawn, leaving only the small pool of light from the porch lamps as the patrol car backed down the drive. "What have we done, Jared? He needed us, and we failed him."

"We didn't fail him, April. Nathan pulled the gun himself. He was the one who acted out tonight, not any of us. It'll be all right. Come on, let's go inside."

"Jared. You know the deal, right?" I shivered at the menacing sound of Kyle's voice, too close behind us.

There was no answer, but I didn't need words to know what would come next. "April, honey. We have to finish it. We have to go back inside."

I turned on my brother, piercing him with my stare. "Why, Jared? Why do we have to do this?"

"Please, baby. They'll—"

"They'll what?" I turned on him, making sure Kyle heard every word." They'll what, Jared? I really want to know what it is you think they'll do. Then, I want you to guarantee me that protecting them is worth what you're asking me to do. I'm a I little brat, right? So you're gonna have to spell it out for me. What are they gonna do to you and is it worth my soul? Cause that's what you're taking. It's me on that camera, being fucked by your friends." I laughed, but the sound came out as a snort as I found Heath and Jed. "What kind of person fucks their best friend's stepsister, anyway?"

Jared rose to their defense, just like I knew he would. "It's not their fault, we all...."

"You all what? You take turns? Is that what you're telling me? That you fucked their brothers and sisters?" My chest heaved, each breath felt like a sob. I wanted to cry, but even my damn tears fled in the face of my pain. "It was you on that tape with Nathan and Heath, wasn't it? It was you his fiancée watched, while Kyle stood back and taped the whole damn thing?"

"April, please." My brother gripped my arm. I dropped my hands, unable to shift the weight from my chest. His next words were so low I barely caught them. "They're gonna hurt me."

The night turned silent. I tried to process what he said as the others slinked off into the darkness, towards the house. "Who's going to hurt you?"

One shake of his head and I knew he was in deep, but what this was I had no idea. "What have you got yourself into, Jared?"

He lifted his head to trap me with a stare. His eyes were so dark, but I saw the boy he once was. The young child, shunned by his mother for her new boyfriend. The boy who just wanted to be held reached for me now. How could he not understand what he was asking me to do? What kind of man made his sister into a whore?

Fresh pain bloomed. An ache that was bottomless and greedy swelled where my heart once was. I knew better, but the drug took over again, making his scent sharp in a world where everything else was blurred or hidden in shadow. I sucked the scent deep into my lungs, needing so much more than he could ever give. Maybe there was a part of Jared that loved me. But another part of him needed me. Needed me to lie on my back and spread my legs. Needed to watch his friends fuck me.

That was all I was to him. A body to use. A mind to corrupt. I closed my eyes and fought the tremor building inside my chest, angry at myself for not seeing this sooner. Because he had corrupted me. He'd corrupted me in the worst way. I clung to his arms and pressed my breasts against his chest, knowing I was helpless when it came to my brother. "Then, you'd better kiss me."

# Chapter Ten

JARED LED ME BACK INSIDE THE HOUSE, STOPPING ONCE more beside the billiard table I was coming to hate. He dropped his head to kiss the corners of my mouth. Taking more than he wanted to give, I captured his lips with my own. Anger flared and stoked the fuel to something far-reaching inside me, fanning the flames until my body trembled. There was no love here. Jared didn't love me. My brother had incurred a debt he could never pay and my body was the price.

Through my thin blouse, I felt his heartbeat. The vibration was so strong, pulsing in time with the thudding of my own heart. I released his mouth, leaving him to falter, and tried to regain the upper hand. This anger in me changed everything. My brother expected me to be the weeping little school girl I'd always been... *no, what did he call me? You know what happens to little mice who get fat and just sit in one spot all day? They become the meal.*

*That's right. Little mouse.* He retraced the path over my lips, taking his time. The heat of his breath tickled my face. I wanted to slap that mouth. I wanted to hurt him, just as he was hurting me.

I was no mouse and I was no one's meal. Not unless I wanted to be.

The thought bloomed. Hitting my brother was less than he deserved. I wanted him to feel the hurt I felt. To know this was all because of he was weak.

When the ripping of the Velcro sounded, I shoved my hands out to the side. The soft cuffs wound around my wrists, biting into my flesh as I strained against the bindings. I scanned the room to find Heath standing to the side. My anger was a torrent, sweeping any sense of modesty aside. I was here for a purpose. One I would devour with a ravenous hunger.

"Fuck me." The words tasted vile in my mouth.

I swallowed the bitterness, and enjoyed how Jared's eyes widened with my words. "April, you don't have to be like this."

"Be like what? Like one of them?" I jerked my head around the room. Every single person here was a spineless piece of shit—and my brother was the worst.

"I don't like to hear you talk like that."

*Good.* I turned my gaze on Heath, who shifted from one foot to the other, as though he didn't have a clue how to act. "Fuck me, Heath. Fuck me until I scream."

He looked from Jared to me. I kept my eyes steady on his pale face. "But, you're gonna have to take my clothes off to do it."

If he was waiting for my brother's approval, then he wasn't going to get it. I didn't have to look into Jared's eyes to see the pain. I could feel the emptiness radiate from him. It was the same look he had when he told me he was leaving for Harvard. The memory now resurrected. *"Mom, doesn't want me around anymore. It seems your Dad needs her more than I do."*

Heath moved, edging around my brother to stand in front of me. He fumbled with my blouse. I clenched my jaw, fighting the need to scream. *Hurry the fuck up!*

I helped him along, shrugging out of my blouse. He released the cuffs one at a time, jerking my sleeves over my clenched fists before refastening them. They thought I'd try to run? Who were the real cowards here?

The skirt was easier. Still, Heath's awkward movements—such a contrast to the seductive skills he'd shown before—took the heat right out of my anger.

Kyle moved, drawing my gaze. The sting of outrage fought the drugs in my blood. I tried to focus on his movements as he walked over to a rack on the wall and picked up a billiard cue, weighing the slender staff in his hands before moving close by my side. "How about this to get you warmed up a little?"

I tried to hide the flinch, but it was impossible. "Fuck you. You fucking piece of shit."

His sick grin widened as Heath picked me up and placed me on the table. The straps tightened around my wrists. I tilted my head, catching sight of Jed at the far end before he bent and disappeared from view.

I felt the hard, rounded end of the cue push against my slit. A whimper tore from my lips. My mind fought my body as the smooth end slid up and down, pressing against my clit, sending shivers racing across my skin. I shook my head, as Kyle worked the object inside, only to pull it out. Thick and hard. Part of me wanted it. Part of me opened my legs, wanting to feel used. My body took over. My throat burned as I grew wet. My hips moved against the cold intrusion. I wanted more.

"She likes that. Look at her riding this fucking stick like it was your cock." Kyle's jeering laughter rang in my ears.

My knuckles popped from my grip on the table edges.

"Take it out of her, or I'll break it over your head, and stab you with what's left." Jared snarled.

The thick shaft withdrew and Kyle was blocked from view as Heath climbed onto the table and crawled between my legs. I searched inside for the anger. I needed to feel the pain—and like it. I had to find my desire and let it take over, and melt everything away.

My body was on fire. My pussy was filled with an ache that needed only one thing. Heath stood in front of me. He wasn't even my type. Short, muscled—too muscled. A head full of curls that glistened under the games room lights. But he was here to fuck and so was I.

I licked my lips. Kyle held a stick, like he was some animal trainer and I was just another animal. All I had were words. "Fill me up, Heath. Slide that delicious cock of yours inside me."

Heath smiled, mashing his lips together to stifle a giggle. "You don't really pull off the dirty talk, April. You look too sweet and innocent."

I clenched my jaw. Another shove from Kyle and the anger I needed was back, but Heath's too-kind remark threatened to overwhelm me with the wrong emotion. I splayed my thighs wide and pushed my buttocks off the itchy felt surface. "Does this look innocent to you?"

Heath swept his gaze along my slit and the thin thatch of hair above it. I opened my legs wider, feeling the lips of my pussy gape just a little. "I'm hurting here. Can't you see I'm hurting? Please, Heath. I'm already wet. Just fuck me. Please fuck me. "

I shoved those filthy words from my mind. There was no going back now. I'd been reduced to a rutting whore—for Jared. Heath let out a shuddering breath at the last words. That was what men wanted, right? A tight fuck? I scanned the room, finding the camera perched in the spot where it'd been earlier, on a shelf behind the bar. That red, winking light was all I focused on. I smiled. The words came easier now that the nice April was someplace safe. I doubted I'd ever see her again. "I want to feel every inch of you stretch me."

I smiled as Heath lunged forward. My lips stretched wider when a tortured sound came from my brother. *This is for you, Jared. All for you, my darling brother.*

I arched as Heath's warm shaft eased into me. I didn't want soft and tender. I wanted hard. I wanted to burn from the inside. I clenched my ass, feeling the hard slap of skin against skin as our hips met. Each jolt spurred on by my harsh breaths and wordless sounds. "Uh. Uh. Uh."

I held onto the sensation of hard flesh gliding over slick flesh, urging him deeper with each thrust. I could feel the head of his cock work in and out of my entrance, drawing me toward the end—an ending I didn't want. I gripped the table and turned my head toward Jared, using the sight of him to shove away my climax.

He stared at Heath between my legs. Did a mixture of jealousy and rage dance in his eyes, or was I merely wishing it was so? There was no pain, not yet. The chemicals raced through my blood, stirring me. I was grateful I'd taken the pill, because I sensed the drug-induced arousal let me hold the pain I sensed Kyle craved inflicting on others at bay. I shifted my attention to the man between my legs, hating him inside me. Hating the way he made me feel. Each violent stab was slower now—taking a part of me that was not for sale. I strained to lift my body, as far as the cuffs would allow, and met his soft brown eyes. "Don't look at me. Fuck me. That's what we're here to do right?"

I wanted the guttural, craven need. The mindless fucking. Just like goddamned pool cue had been—a mindless tool, an unthinking thing. But these men... oh, they knew what they did, and they liked doing it.

Heath pumped like a madman. His face turned red, sweat broke out on his sculpted chest until his eyelids fluttered and he sighed. When he opened his eyes and stared at me, something had changed. Now there was a longing in his gaze I'd never seen before. "April."

"Get the fuck off me." I snarled, wrenching my gaze from his eyes.

"We haven't got all night, Heath." Kyle snapped, killing the moment. Heath slipped from the table, his once-swollen cock now soft and limp. My juices gleamed on his shrinking skin.

"I'm so sorry, April. I got myself ready. I won't take long," Jed whispered, taking Heath's place.

I shook my head, feeling sick with the sight of twisted, fucked-up longing in Heath's eyes, so I turned my head toward Jared. "I don't care how long you take, Jed. I like it. Make it last." *Flinch, go on, Jared, flinch. That's right.*

This was Jared's fault. Every little depraved thought I had was because of this moment and these men. "This is what I'm here for, right? To be fucked? I think I could get used to this. We could make this a weekend thing. Heath would like that, wouldn't you, Heath?"

From the corner of my eye, I caught Heath's flushed cheeks, but I jerked my gaze to the next fuck. Jed's cock stood ramrod straight, the tip flushed bright red. It was his hand on my knee, coaxing my thighs apart. I didn't fight him, allowing him to open my legs and work his body against the juncture of my thighs.

My body jolted up and down on the table. I was lost for a while in the trance, drawn back by the pain in my hips. Jed held onto whatever he could as he rammed his cock home. This was the frenzy I needed, but the moment was gone, lost somewhere between Heath's pathetic gaze and the pain that swelled inside my chest when I looked at my brother.

Jolt after jolt. My body grew numb. As though from far away, I heard Jared snarl. "Jed, you're hurting her." But I covered the sound with made-up moans of pleasure, because if I had to suffer, so did Jared.

Jed's hard thrusts became a languid slide, rocking my body back and forth. He reached for my breasts, rolling my puckered nipple between his fingers. The pain melted into a slow burn. One stroke after another fanned the flames between my thighs to life once more. His abdomen rippled with taut muscle. I followed the powerful flex of his muscular arms as he strained for his release. Jed held nothing back, rolling his hips so that his cock hit a spot inside me that made the fire burn.

"Harder." I panted.

Jed was losing constraint, thrusting harder, but no matter how hard he tried, I couldn't get there.

"Oh, Jesus." He whimpered, pushing his cock deeper and holding the position. Warmth spread through out my body, filling me with his seed. I wasn't on the Pill and no one had used protection. My needs shoved aside for my brother's. God, what if I got pregnant?

"This was the last one, April. I'm gonna take good care of you. I'll make everything all right." Jared leaned down to whisper against my ear, brushing my hair from my face.

I jerked away from his touch and glared. "Don't you dare touch me."

Kyle stepped up beside the table. "What do you mean, last one? This party's only getting started. You know the deal, Jared. She has to take us all."

I flinched. No. Not Kyle.

I tried to block the movement as Jared stood. "Fuck you, Kyle. You piece of shit."

"You want me to make the call? I can tell them you won't be playing our little game anymore? But you know what happens after that, don't you? So, just give the word and it's done."

I waited for Jared to say something. To stand up and be the man I needed him to be. I wanted him to launch across the table and beat Kyle to a bloody pulp. No one would stop him. Hell, his little sister would take the fall, just like I did now.

But Jared never moved, only stood there, allowing Kyle to finish the argument for him. "If you're not man enough, Jared, then shut your mouth and climb aboard. Or wait for last. Makes no difference to me."

Spittle flew from my mouth as my rage poured out. "Say something! Do something you spineless piece of shit!"

He flinched at the sound, but stood there, too much a man to leave, yet too much of a boy to meet my eyes. The silence stretched so thin I couldn't stand it. I shifted my gaze from his face and opened my legs. "Get it over with. Then, get out."

Kyle's sniggers came closer as the sound of a zipper tore through the silent room. "Your little sister's got more balls than you."

I felt the dull thud on the billiard table. There was nowhere else to look. My gaze fell to Kyle's cruel smile. I wanted to feel the rage I felt seconds ago, but the drug pumped pure emptiness into my bloodstream now, and the void swallowed me. I flinched from Jared's touch, instead staring down Kyle's body, settling on the thick cock in his grip.

This was what they wanted, wasn't it? To see me whimper and cower. To see my brother stand by as each of his so-called friend took turns fucking me. This was the game, in all its fucking glory and I'd fallen for it, hook, line, and virginity.

The pain in my chest felt like a leaking wound. There was nothing else to hold onto and I was lost. I focused on Kyle, hating how my voice trembled. "Fuck me. Make me scream, if you can manage that."

His eyes widened and he smiled.

I shifted my gaze away. "You fucking disgust me."

"I disgust you, huh?" Kyle leaned over me. He prodded my pussy with cruel fingers. So cruel, it seemed a relief when his cock pressed against my opening, but the relief soon fled. My body stretched wide, until I could take no more. I clawed the table, hearing the cloth rip as Kyle snarled. "How do you like me now?"

I opened my mouth to scream, but only a hiss escaped. The air cut off as pain speared my insides. I clenched, trying to force him out of me, and heard him hiss. "Fuck you're a tight bitch, aren't you? No wonder big brother here's all choked up."

Kyle lunged forward, using his hips like a wedge to force my legs wider. His sweat dripped onto my breast and the cool droplets felt like acid. The tendons between my thighs strained like overwound strings. Any moment they'd snap. Kyle worked his way inside, only to slide out and try again, fighting my body for one more inch. "How does your cunt like me now? Fuck, I knew you'd be good. Breathe, bitch. You haven't even taken half of me yet."

I held on to anything I could feel. The hollowness when he withdrew and the sting and swell of delicate tissues inside me as he worked his way into my channel once more. Pain cleaved through my body with each powerful stoke and a dark need to hurt my brother flared to life.

I timed the thrusts and forced a moan. The pathetic sound slid from my lips as a lie, but it found its mark.

"Oh Jesus. Fuck, I want this bitch. I want this every night, all fucking night." Kyle cried, pumping like a man possessed.

Instead of tensing, I opened myself wider, squeezing at the right moment to make him shudder. "Oh shit, I'm gonna come...."

Kyle gripped my hips as he shuddered. His cock pulsed, spilling deep inside me. My body felt numb as he slid free, but inside my head, I rejoiced because I'd survived the worst this night, this *game* had to offer. My entrance gaped, the air felt cold against my hot flesh.

"Now for the main attraction. Come on, Jared. I warmed her up nicely for you."

I turned my head and stared at the wall.

"April," Jared whispered. But his words meant nothing to me anymore. I swallowed hard.

"Please, look at me. I'm begging you."

I squeezed my eyes closed, trapping a tear. How could I have been so I?

"Just say the word and I won't do it. They can do whatever they want to me, I don't care. Just please, don't shut me out, April."

"It's a bit late for that, don't you think?" I said and opened my eyes to stare at the paint. Connie would be mad. Someone had scuffed the wall with the end of a cue.

"I don't know how to fix this, to fix us. Please don't give up on me. I...."

His touch was soft. I felt his lips on my knee, on my thigh and I flinched. His lips were warm, but I resented him taking the time to tantalize my skin. I'd finally found my inner nirvana. Even my heart felt numb, but my stupid stepbrother seemed determined to drag me back to painful life with each brush of his lips.

"I love you," he whispered, kissing my flesh between breathless sentences. "I love that awkward girl who was forced into my world, the one with sad eyes and perfect lips. I love the way you flick your hair from shoulder and the way you sing in the shower. I love your innocence and nothing will take that from you. Not this night or any other night. Do you hear me, April?"

I squeezed my eyes tight, trying to block him from my new, unfeeling world. But each kiss pierced the wall I tried to build. I sucked my breath in as something that wasn't a cock slid between my thighs. I looked down, catching sight of his expensive shirt, now stained with the spoils of his friends.

"Don't think about them. It's just me here. Just me." He tossed the shirt and leaned over me, then dropped to lie at my side. I wrenched my head away from his kiss. But something far more powerful than the chemical speeding through my body made me helpless when he traced my jaw with his fingers, gently turning my head so my eyes were on his face.

His mouth found mine, and as much as I hated my body for responding, I couldn't stop it, but this wasn't the drug. His lips were sweet and hungry. His tongue probed my mouth and the sensation was more erotic than anything else that had happened tonight. My nipples tightened. Blood pooled and heat flared between my legs, until he broke the kiss.

"Do you know how beautiful you are to me?" His breath tickled my mouth. His face blurred as he moved in to kiss the corners of my mouth as he fumbled with my wrists, tearing the Velcro cuffs free to fall onto the floor. The hard table was awkward, but my brother managed to lift my body and slide his arm underneath to my legs so he could cradle me against him. I tried to hate the way his chest felt against mine. I wanted to despise the scent of his cologne as I climbed on top, straddling him.

I held onto my anger, to the hurt, and the betrayal. His cock pressed against the crease of my ass. I focused on the pain in my knees from the slate top underneath the thin layer of blue felt. This was what I wanted. This was what I'd listened to outside his room and ached for it to be me with him and not... whoever the hell he'd brought home. My fantasies had been warped by him. He'd taken something sensual, something perfect, and traded it for fucking. My brother needed to fuck his sister. I'd already given him my heart, my soul, so why not this?

I rocked and my small breasts moved with the motion. Jared remained silent, his touch didn't demand more than I was prepared to give. This tenderness was by far the cruelest thing I'd been subjected to tonight, because the loving touches took me to places I didn't want to go. But I would go there tonight, and come tomorrow, I'd work on forgetting I ever had a brother.

I reached behind my body, raking my nails over the puckered flesh of his balls, and gripped his cock. He stilled. There was no moan, no hiss of breath, as though he was terrified I'd stop, or keep going. I could see the stark cold fear in his eyes. I slid my grip low, then back up the rigid column. Movement to my left snatched his focus. I spied the red blinking light move in slowly, just waiting for the climax to this all. With each stroke of my hand, the icy reserve in his gaze started to melt.

His body stiffened under my grip and his fingers on my thigh became feather light touches, moving in time with the motion of my hand. My body relaxed, as though sex with my brother was the most natural thing in the world. I eased back on my haunches and his cock slid into me as if... as if it belonged there.

*Shut up. Can't think like that.* But this was out of my control. Even my body betrayed me. The ache in my muscles from trying to accommodate Kyle melted away as Jared filled me, stretching my walls, until all I felt was him.

I reached for him, entwining my fingers with his and, we rocked together This moment was sacred. Each motion rubbed a part of me that sizzled, setting fire to my soul or my mind, I didn't know which. Slow and steady our bodies met as the heat built. Jared's grip tightened. I spied the strain in his face, but he let me set the tempo, no matter how desperate he might be. I took my time, relishing in the feel of his body inside mine until the flames licked deep, wrenching a moan from my lips.

Jared bore down on my hands, lifting his hips to meet my body, thrusting hard, and then slowed. His eyes bore into mine and he gasped. I felt his cock jerk and he leaned forward to press his forehead to mine. His eyes were deep pools and I let myself fall in.

"So touching, you two. For a second there I forgot this was all for the camera." Kyle snarled, snapping the viewfinder closed. "Well, I guess I'm done here."

Jared's gaze never left mine. "Get out, everyone. Heath—"

"I got it, buddy. You just take care of her."

I ignored the shuffling around us and the heavy tread of footsteps as the room emptied. The click of the front door echoed just as loud as the gunshot, and then, there was only us.

"I had no right to ask you to do this. I had no idea...." My brother's tortured expression said enough. "But I swear I'll make it up to you."

My voice was weak and pathetic, but I was past caring. I'd done what needed to be done for him. Someone had to think about me. "I'm not on the Pill and no one used protection."

He flinched as though I'd hit him. "Oh shit, April. I didn't even think. I mean, I thought you'd be on the Pill, at least."

I couldn't stop my bottom lip from trembling, no matter how hard I tried. "Why would I be, Jared? I was a virgin, remember?"

"Oh, Jesus. Shh, it's okay. I'll make a call and get you taken care of. Don't you worry."

I let Jared pull me into his arms before whispering. "Get me off this table, Jared. I never want to see it ever again."

# Chapter Eleven

Jared lifted me, cradling my head against his neck. I felt numb, lost in what I'd done and the words I'd said. Lost in everything. Higher and higher, my brother carried me, up the stairs, then left toward the bathroom.

My legs trembled. My knees locked and unlocked as Jared lowered me to the ground. I clenched my muscles, determined to stand on my own as he stepped back. I lashed out, my palm struck the side of his face. The blow tingled, barely registering.

The dam inside burst with the impact. I wrenched my arm back and struck again, this time with all the force I could muster. Skin stung against skin. The heat traveled into my arm and I stumbled backward, gripping the sink to keep from falling. Then the words came, tumbling out of some dark need to maim and hurt. I wanted blood. His blood.

"You sonofabitch! You sick sonofabitch! Why? Why did you have to come back here? Why couldn't you have stayed away in your rich, fucking life with your goddamn fancy cars and perverted friends? Why did my father have to love your mother? Why did I have to love you? I could've loved anyone. I could've loved someone who deserves me, instead of the gutless fucking cunt you are. Why did it have to be you Jared? Tell me, why?"

He glanced down at me then. His eyes were already red, glistening tears ran down his cheeks. Had he been crying this whole time?

When he spoke his voice was raw, carrying with it the pain I'd wanted to inflict. "I should've stayed away. I should've known family isn't for me. I've always been a slow learner. I should've known after the first time, right?"

The gnawing pain ravaged my chest at the sight of his pain. This was about me. This was my moment to hate him for what he'd done and turn my back on the kind of man he was. "What do you mean by that? What do you mean, you should've known after the first time, Jared?"

He shook his head, dropping his gaze and the ache in my chest flared. "This moment isn't about me, April. It's about you and the horror you've suffered because of me. Hit me. Hurt me, just please, don't shut me out."

I shook my head, wanting to lash out once more. But the fire was gone, doused by the tears sliding down his face.

"I know I don't deserve this. I don't deserve you, but please, let me make it up to you. Please, I'm begging you, let me try."

He waited for what felt like forever, then took a tiny step toward me. I gripped the basin, wanting to tell him to go to hell and run. But I was helpless to do either. He moved closer, slowly closing the distance. His hand trembled as he reached for me. I cowered from his touch but said nothing to stop him.

"Just one chance, that's all I'm asking. One chance to be different. One chance to be who you need me to be."

I said nothing as he brushed my cheek. The touch stayed with me as he turned and opened the shower door and pulled the lever, sending jets of water to the floor. The heat moved fast to fog the mirror. One chance, that's all he was asking for. But I didn't know if I had one chance left to give him.

Jared reached for my hand, his touch so gentle as he guided me into the spray. The hot water stung my skin and beat against my scalp until he hit the plunger, dividing the water between the overhead jet and the handheld showerhead.

Half the spray ran over my shoulders, plastering my hair to my face. The other shot fine needles between my legs. I opened my thighs wider, feeling the sting of sensitive flesh until the pain melted into the pulsing rhythm. I didn't speak and I didn't move, only laid my head against the tiles and tried to feel something other than the pain in my chest.

He soaped the sponge, running it over my shoulders and my arms, moving in to kiss me. I didn't want to think. I wanted only to feel his hands on me, the real me, not the monster he'd turned me into. I needed to find her and I didn't care who helped me do it.

Jared drew the sponge in circles around my breasts, following the trail of the soap down my stomach to disappear between my legs. My stepbrother dropped to his knees and gripped my leg behind my knee, washing me over and over, until I was lost in the feel of his fingers. There were no more demands. I had a feeling after tonight, he'd never ask me for anything again. The remnants of this night would linger for a long time to come. Whatever happened between us would be given freely, or not at all.

I lifted my leg, allowing Jared to place it on his shoulder. He moved the sponge over my other leg. I leaned against the tiles, relishing the heat of the water and his tender touch. The sponge slid over my stomach, then my hip, to fall into the crevice between my thighs. My foot slipped lower down his back as he moved against me, kissing the top of my mound.

His hands never stopped. The circular motion washed everything away but the pressure of his hand and the feel of his lips. His tongue slid into the top of my slit, probing tender flesh. I wanted to tell him to stop, but my body needed this. I needed this.

He dipped lower, angling his head upwards to suckle the outer edges of my entrance. I trembled as he gently pulled my soft lips into his mouth before dipping in to lick my channel. His tongue danced around my clit. A wet splat sounded, the sponge discarded. His fingers followed his tongue, trailing the crease to slip inside. I rocked my body against his mouth, urging his mouth deeper as my focus narrowed to the need inside. My eyes stung and my tears fell, but the shower swept them away. The pressure in my core climbed with each drag of his tongue. He worked his fingers in and out while I sobbed, shedding the filth of tonight in this moment.

I wound my fingers through his hair, pressing his face against me while I rocked. He sucked my nub, drawing the end close. My body pulsed, the beat sending me over the edge. Jared held me while I cried out and gripped the walls. My knees shook from the effort of standing. Jared rose from the floor and leaned over, trapping me with his body to kiss me. His mouth tasted warm and salty, taking my breath. I clung to him, sliding my hands around his back until he broke the kiss.

He stared down into my eyes. His broad shoulders divided the flow of water to splatter into my eyes. My eyelids fluttered, fighting the sting. The intensity returned to his eyes. Twin laser beams, directed at me, exposing my hopeless longing. My need for him, my stupid, little girl dreams that wouldn't let go, mixed with the pain inside me. He licked the water from his lips. I followed the trail of his tongue, remembering the sensation of where it'd been only moments before.

"You need to sleep. Your body needs to rest. Tomorrow I'll start making this right. I promise. Just say you'll give me one thing tonight. One thing is all I'm hoping for."

He took my silence as permission to continue. "Don't think tonight. Don't replay any of this until I have a chance to do right by you. If you start thinking and remembering you're never going to give me that chance and right now, that's all I've got holding me together. Just rest that beautiful mind of yours, and sleep. And when you wake, I'll have a plan. I'll have a way to try to fix what we have. I'm not giving up on this, April, so please don't give up on me. Tomorrow, our other life is going to come crashing down on us when our parents come home, and I need you to be prepared for that."

The phone call. Our parents. I closed my eyes. I'd forgotten all about them coming home early. Would my brother return to the cruel jerk he'd always been? How had these past two days changed us?

Jared hit the tap, ending the stream, and stepped out of the stall. I wanted to ask the questions that crowded my mind. I didn't want whatever this was between us to end. Deep down, I knew everything had changed—for me at least.

## Chapter Twelve

"April. Have you listened to a word I've been saying to you?"

I glanced up from my bowl of yogurt to catch the glint of annoyance in my stepmother's eyes. "Sorry. What were you saying?"

"I was telling you how the fire destroyed the entire wing where we were staying on the island. What's gotten into you today? You've been off with the fairies ever since we came home."

Connie stifled a yawn and picked at her fruit.

I fumbled for something to say. "Sorry, just thinking about my first semester classes. Getting excited, that kind of thing. You look tired. Jet lag's a bitch, isn't it?"

I'd do anything to get rid of her and my father for a while. Jared was gone when I woke this morning. Even though I'd promised my brother I wouldn't let my mind take over, I couldn't stop worrying. The memory of last night slapped me awake. All the hurt and the pain. All the things I'd said and the promises Jared made. Promises that sounded empty in the harsh light of reality.

There was still the tape to consider. The thought was enough to curdle the yogurt in my stomach.

I searched the house as Connie unpacked. The place was all but perfect. The vase in the foyer had been replaced by something just as ugly and the games room sparkled. The only reminder of what happened was the bare billiard table. The ruined felt was gone, leaving the slate exposed. The table wasn't mentioned, nor the vase. I guessed Jared had taken care of that as well.

The only questions were from Dad as he climbed from the cab and pulled me into his arms. Had Jared taken good care of me? Was I packed for college? Then, my feeble answers were brushed aside by Connie and her drama. I stepped backward and gave her the spotlight, just as I'd done for years. But this time, shrinking into a non-entity was a conscious choice I'd made, wanting to avoid them. I wasn't the same person. I was different somehow, as though I'd finally shed being a kid. Dad glanced over as Connie rambled on about how horrible that place had been. But Dad ignored her, staring at me instead with his brow raised. Had he sensed the change in me, too?

Now that they were home, I wanted to disappear into my room. I wanted Jared to call, and not call all at the same time. Part of me waited for the pain to start, so I could mourn, then move on with my life. Another part of me knew I couldn't give up on him, that the pain of losing him would be too much. The uncertainty made me feel like the kid that I'd been three days before all over again.

"Maybe I could do with a nap. I am feeling rather flat."

I jumped at the chance to steer her into her bedroom. "I'm sure you'll feel better after you've had a rest. It sounds like an exhausting trip."

Connie nodded and I rose from the bar, heading for the dishwasher. My thoughts were already on escaping as I placed my bowl and spoon inside.

I made for the stairs, mumbling something about packing as I passed, but I needn't have bothered. My father was already asleep and stepmother barely batted an eyelash. I hurried to my room and closed the door behind me. My phone on the dresser beeped. My heart sped as I snatched the handset, swiping the screen to stare at the display. *Missed Call: Jared.*

He answered on the third ring. His voice a whisper. "April. Something's happened. Heath's brother killed himself this morning, so the police are looking into what happened last night at the house. They're calling it a suicide, but Heath's saying different."

I sat on the bed. My mind numb. "Oh, no. Oh, God, Jared."

"He said Nathan was threatened, that someone was following him."

"Who? Was it Kyle?"

"I don't think it was any of us and I don't think it was suicide, either. I think someone killed Nathan to keep him quiet."

*And as a warning to us.* I thought the words, but couldn't say them. Jesus, Nathan was dead. I'd failed him. I left him feeling alone when he needed someone the most. If only I'd—

"Are you there?" Jared whispered.

I swallowed the lump in my throat. "Yes. It was my fault, Jared. I should've spoken up last night, then maybe he wouldn't have—"

"You don't know that. No one does. I spent half the damn night watching you sleep, asking myself if I could ever look at you in the eye again, after what you did for me. I realized that I couldn't, April. I couldn't allow myself to stand by, knowing there's a tape of you out there. Just waiting for someone to press a damn button and upload it for everyone to see. I can't stand the thought of your beautiful face on that screen. It's eating me alive, just thinking about it. I should've done the right thing at the start. I should've told them to go to hell."

"You need to tell me now, Jared. Why are they forcing you to do this?"

The heavy sound of his breath filled the silence. "I don't know. I never saw it coming. I thought Kyle was just a good friend, you know? Someone to listen while I moaned about my father and his damn campaign. We went out one night. I think it was Kyle's idea to hang out this local dive. When I woke, I was tied to a chair with a gun to my head. I had no idea where I was, April. I had no idea who had me. I didn't see who they were. Their damn masks covered their faces. But they knew everything about me, about you, about my mom and your dad. They told me they required a little insurance. I had no idea this is what they meant until... until I was told to have sex with Nathan. He was the first. Jesus, if I'd only been stronger and said no."

My chest tightened. The pain in his voice plunged a dagger through my heart. Jared was hurting and my feeble words were useless.

"So, that's why I'm calling you. I didn't want you to think I'd given up, that I wasn't strong enough to fight for you. I'm parked on the street outside Kyle's apartment. I'm going to break in and steal all the recordings back. I'll fucking torch the place if I have to. I may not've been the man you needed me to be last night, April. But I sure as hell will man up now."

Guns. Death.

"Jared don't. If they find you they'll—"

His haunted words cut me off. "It doesn't matter anymore. I should've told them to hurt me if they had to, but to stay away from my family. It's what I should've done the first time they took me and it's what I should've done last night to protect you."

"Let me come with you. Tell me where you are. I can be there in a few minutes. You don't have to do this alone."

"No, April. It's too dangerous."

"It will be safer if you have someone watching your back, don't you think? Let me do this with you." I had no other card to play. I was stumbling, ready to use anything I could to make him agree. So I put my final card on the table and prayed those two were enough. "You said you wanted to make it up to me. Then let me do this with you. Don't make me sit here and wait for the call, Jared. It's killing me being here when you're there. I hate not being with you."

I thought he was going to brush me off or make some excuse. I waited for his answer, praying he would see sense. "Okay. 'Cause, I've been thinking about you all morning anyway. I can't seem to get you out of my head, little sister. I'll text you the address. And, April?"

"Yes." I breathed into the phone.

"Be careful, okay?"

"I will."

I felt the heat in my cheeks as I ended the call. Jared wanted to be with me just as much as I wanted to be with him. My hands shook as I pulled on my shoes and grabbed my bag. I wouldn't let him deal with this alone, no matter what happened.

I grabbed my keys and slipped from my room, keeping one eye on Dad's bedroom as I hit the first stair. There were so many things I wanted to say before I left. The harsh words we spoke on the day they departed still seemed to linger between us. *I love you Dad. I never meant to be in your way, only in your life.*

I clenched my jaw, steeling my nerve, and ran down the stairs.

Jared was out there somewhere, waiting for me. I opened the front door and pressed the lock, hearing it snap as I closed it behind me. I slid into the seat of my little car and turned the key. I punched in the address Jared gave me and stared at the GPS screen. The building overlooked the Charles River. How hard would it be to get into without a key? Maybe Jared had one?

I backed out of the drive and wove through the streets of Back Bay, headed for Cambridge, following the directions until I eased into a parking space two doors down. Jared's Maserati sat up ahead, drawing longing gazes as people drove by. "Good way to be inconspicuous, Jared."

For someone so smart, he sure wasn't with the program on going unseen. My body buzzed with the thought of seeing my brother again. Each step felt like I was walking on air. The driver's side sat empty. I turned, scanning the trees and found my brother leaning against the broad trunk of a majestic oak, watching me. Heat raced to my face. I kept my head down, watching my steps until I rounded the thick trunk of the tree and stopped.

"I hate that you're here, but I'm really glad to see you."

It wasn't the welcome I'd envisioned. "Good to see you too," I muttered.

He reached for me, pulling me around the trunk and into his arms. "Come here. I just hate the thought of you in danger, that's all."

"And I hate being away from you."

His lips brushed my cheek as Jared bent to kiss my neck. I couldn't help but stiffen. "Jared, stop. What if someone sees us?" How many friends did Connie have who lived in this part of town?

His words made my heart soar. "Let them. I don't care anymore."

I wanted to stand there and listen to him but we had a plan that right now was more important. "Jared, the recordings."

He straightened and my skin cooled away from his warm breath. "You're to stay here and keep a lookout. You can see both sides of the street and you're far enough away not to be in any danger. Ring me if you see Kyle or any of the others. But stay here. You got me April? Stay right here. Do not move, no matter what. I got you this. Take it as soon as you get home. The doctor says to expect some cramping and discharge. But you'll be okay."

I stared at the small white box. "Thanks."

"It's the least I could do." For a second I wanted to tell him to forget the recordings, forget everything. I wanted to ask him to run away with me and I'd spend my days counting the sparkle of stars in his eyes. Then, I remembered Nathan and the words were lost.

"Remember, call me if someone comes, but stay here."

Jared dipped his head for one last kiss, then he was gone.

I watched my stepbrother cross the street and move among the traffic, terrified I was going to lose him.

# Chapter Thirteen

The apartment complex towered over fifteen stories. I glanced up at the top floor silently trying to figure out how long this should take. Minutes crawled by while I scanned the street for Kyle's vehicle and waited for my brother to exit.

The park filled with joggers and yoga classes. People came and went and still there was no sign of Jared or Kyle. I paced the sidewalk, following each crack in the concrete to the end. What was taking him so long? I checked my phone and chewed my nails while the minutes ticked by. I should've taken note of the time he went in. It had to be at least an hour. The tiny windows of the penthouse gave me nothing to go on.

My stomach felt heavy, weighed down with the dark seed of fear. Standing out here was killing me. I focused on the front doors of the building and found myself stepping off the pavement. My feet hit the asphalt without my permission, but I kept moving forward.

Horns blared from the oncoming traffic. I jumped backward as a yellow cab shot past. The driver shouted, waiving his fist from behind the windshield. I held my breath and surged forward, finding the pavement on the other side. My whole body shook. I gripped the bench outside the building, scanning those headed toward me until I could catch my breath.

The lobby was a hive of activity, flower deliveries, package deliveries, and a bunch of kids mobbed the front desk. No one stopped me as I headed for the elevators. I took a glance at the stairwell, searching for any sign of Jared. The heavy weight in my stomach was slowly burning a hole through my insides. I stared at the red directional arrows above the elevators. *Please be in there, Jared. Just, please be in there.*

The bell pinged and the doors slid open. I stepped inside the elegant carriage and punched the top floor button, waiting for the door to slide shut. My chest ached with each sluggish beat of my heart, drowning out the clunk as the door slid closed. Images crowded my head. Jared hurt. Jared changing his mind. Jared running, leaving me here alone and staring at the elevator numbers as they slipped by. Jared bleeding.

Five.

The weak girl inside me had whispered about our future all morning. No matter how much I tried, I couldn't shut her up.

Ten.

Jared was here, he was doing the right thing, and his change of heart wasn't just for me. It was for Nathan and all the Nathans and the Aprils to come. Someone had to stop Kyle. My chest swelled with pride.

Fourteen.

I held onto that feeling as I watched the floors tick by. Jared was going to be standing there when the doors opened. His smiling face would be the first thing I'd see.

Fifteen.

The elevator shuddered to a halt. My breath was weightless, trapped in my chest as the door slid open. I exhaled at the sight of dirty blonde hair, until he turned around. Cold eyes narrowed on me. One corner of his mouth turned up into a sneer. "Hello, April."

I scanned the rest of the empty hallway and returned my gaze to the man in front of me. He stepped forward, placing his boot in front of the closing door. The panel slid backward.

"I did warn you, didn't I? I told you to be careful. Don't you remember?"

The white lights of the elevator grew brighter, drowning out the blue uniform shirt in front of me. I tried to lift my hands to shield my eyes, but my arms were so heavy. Jared's warning echoed inside my head. *I don't think this was suicide, April. I think someone killed Nathan to keep him quiet.*

My trapped breath sounded like a hiss as the officer took another step, moving into the elevator. I shuffled backwards until I hit the wall. The police had arrived at the house too quickly last night. At the time, I thought their rapid response was strange, but with Nathan's threats and screams, I hadn't been able to think about anything else.

My legs felt weak and dark spots clouded my vision as this all started to make terrible sense. First Nathan, now Jared and me. I had to find him. I had to find my stepbrother.

"Where is he?"

The doors closed behind him, locking me and the policeman who'd asked to search our home in the tiny space together. He was so casual, reaching out to hit the basement button, while my heart thrashed in my ears. "Where is he? Where's my brother?"

## Chapter Fourteen



"Where's Jared? Where's my brother?"

The officer's cold gaze filled me with fear, standing the hairs on my arm on end. He took a step inside the elevator, blocking me in. I shifted my gaze. One quick look to search the corridor to Kyle's apartment behind him, but the carpeted hallway was empty.

We'd come for the recordings, hoping to find every dirty sex tape Kyle ever made, and burn the place down if we didn't. I'd waited for ages, standing across the road like Jared wanted me to, until I couldn't stand the waiting any longer.

The shine of gold on the officer's uniform drew my focus. The words ablaze on his chest read, *Boston Police.* I prayed there was a way we could get out of this mess. "Please tell me where he is. I promise not to cause trouble. Just tell me, where is my brother?"

His smile chilled me to the bone. "Now, you're going to behave, aren't you? I had to get a little rough with your boyfriend before. You don't want to make the same mistake. Not that I wouldn't mind getting rough with a young thing like you."

He took another step. The lift doors shuddered and slid closed, leaving me trapped. I could feel his eyes move over me, slick like a slug. I shuddered and moved backwards until I hit the far wall. "My brother has rights. I demand to know where you've taken him."

My voice shook, sounding weak, but I didn't care. This was the police. They had a duty of care. They had to abide by the law, didn't they?

Dark eyes glinted. "Rights, huh? Tell me, April. What rights do you think you have?"

I swallowed as the elevator dropped. "He has the right to call his lawyer. His father, do you know who he is? You can't just take him without letting him call someone and tell them he's been arrested."

The cop just leered at me with the devil in his eyes, until it hit me. I shook my head. "You can't arrest me. I haven't done anything wrong."

"Can't I? Arrest, seems such a formal word. How about detained for questioning? That seems a little more appropriate."

"Detained." I whispered feeling the steel walls closing in around me. "What for? I don't know anything. I didn't do anything."

The sneer on his face bought back the terror in Jared's words from this morning. *Heath's brother killed himself, so the police are looking into what happened last night at the house. They're calling it a suicide, but Heath's saying different.*

The elevator jerked to a stop and the doors slid open. I spied the open garage behind him. Cars parked in neat lines on either side. The black and white marked vehicle sat in the middle, with no one else in sight.

"So, I'll ask again. You gonna come quietly, or do I have to restrain you?"

He reached for his waist and snapped open a pouch. I glanced to the steel handcuffs nestled inside. I could already feel the metal biting my wrists. My head ached from the thumping of my damn heart. I couldn't think over the noise. They had Jared. I glanced up into his eyes and whispered, "I'll be good. I'll come quietly."

He nodded. The smile widened, as though he was pleased with himself, and reached into his pocket for his keys. "That's what I thought."

As soon as he turned, I dropped my head and shot forward. I hit the cop side on. The impact stopped me cold. He was bigger, stronger. Still, I had momentum on my side. I barged out of the lift and into the garage as he spun. I raced past the black and white toward the entrance to the lower level.

Heavy footsteps pounded the concrete behind me. His steps were faster, outmatching mine. I pumped my arms, my chest burning with the force of my breath as I surged ahead. The soles of my shoes slapped loud against the ground, echoing until I didn't know which were his steps and which were mine. I timed my steps to scramble over the metal barrier to the lower level and reached out.

My palms was slick with sweat, my fingers numb as I gripped the metal pole. His heavy breaths were all I could hear, drowning out the sound of my own. I shoved one leg through and bent low as my head was wrenched backwards, slamming me into the railing. "Where the fuck you think you're going?"

The pain scattered my thoughts. Momentum took me over the barrier as I toppled to the level below and out of reach. The cop reached for me again. "Get back here, you fucking bitch."

I scurried out of reach, staring up at the menace in his face. My legs wouldn't work. Fear rooted me to the spot as the cop slid through the same opening. *I gotta get out of here. I gotta find a way out.*

I spun, searching the cars for someone to help me and realized no one would. I was a young woman, running away from the police. No one would dare get involved. The row of four-wheel drives hid the end of the garage from view. I stumbled forward, glancing back one last time as the cop squeezed through to fall to the ground. If I could just make it across the street, I could lose him in the park.

I slipped behind a dark blue truck, keeping my steps as light as I could and worked my way around the rusted brown SUV, watching behind and in front.

"There's no way out of this, April. I'm gonna catch you, and when I do, you're gonna wish you'd played nice."

I tried to focus on slowing my breaths and the heavy pounding of my heart. I was sure he could hear the deafening sound. The yellow boom gate glared like a neon sign at the end of the parking bay. I dipped low, tracked his heavy steps, and glanced across to the other side. If I made it over there without him hearing, I could slip behind the parked cars and I'd be out. Even if he chased me, I'd make it in time.

My dry lips stuck to my teeth. I slid my tongue across the ridges, wetting the inside of my mouth and knelt to search for his boots.

"There you are, you little cunt."

I swiveled at the sound as the cop pounced. He gripped my hair and wrenched me backwards, dragging my feet along the ground. My head was on fire. The pain, scalding, tearing through my scalp. "Stop. Let me go. Let me go!"

My steps slipped and caught, each time the pain burned. My nails found his hand as I tried to slip his hold. I clawed and twisted. His hold on my hair went slack, then his cruel fingers gripped my neck. One hard jerk and I slammed into the front of the SUV. My head hit the chrome plated grill. Stars danced in my eyes. The dull thud ripped through my head and pain flared, my chest crushed by the bumper bar.

Dried bugs crushed against my cheek under the impact and fell to the ground as the cop shoved me to the ground. My head hit the concrete so hard, it bounced. I couldn't move. I couldn't think, only watch the navy blue cover my vision as the cop dropped to his knees on top of me.

The air left my body under the force of his weight. Heavy. He was so heavy and I couldn't breathe. His breaths blew against my face. I could feel his hands on my body, clawing my clothes. All I thought about was one tiny breath as my lungs burned. I felt weighed down by all the mistakes I made.

I dug deep, shoving my chest out as far as I could go, and inhaled. The air was cold, and there wasn't nearly enough of it going into my lungs. *Once more.* This time I shoved harder, taking in what air I could get, and ignoring the hard bulge grind against my sex.

The sound of an engine drew my gaze as I took another breath, clearing the fog from my mind. The motor came closer. I focused on the crunch of the tires, praying they would see what was happening. If I could only shift my head I'd see the car. I closed my eyes. My skin rubbed against the rough concrete, riding the slow thrust of his body. I prayed those in the car saw what was happening before he yanked my jeans down and finished what he started.

The car slowed, bits of gravel grated under the tires. I shifted my head, one quick glance as the car turned into the bay on the other side, directly behind the SUV. As soon as they got out of the car they'd see us and if they didn't I'd make damn sure they heard me.

"No you don't, you fucking bitch." The cop dropped his head to whisper against my ear. His breath blew hot against my face.

I realized I could die here, amongst the cars in this dirty garage, far away from the glitz and the glamor of my home. Far away from the college I was to attend next week. They would find me raped, of that I was sure. My throat felt thick. I tried to swallow the hard lump in my throat. They wouldn't kill Jared, no. My brother, like the others of his group, were untouchable. But ones like Nathan and like me, we were disposable. We were here to be used as bait and discarded just as quick.

I stared into the cop's eyes. Hate and fear flickered amongst the stars floating over my vision as a car door slammed. The sonofabitch slapped his hand over my mouth, muffling my cries for help. I kicked my feet against the ground and wrenched my head back and forwards.

My screams were nothing but stifled grunts that warmed his hand against my mouth. My feet slapped against the floor, until he shifted, pinning my legs with his own.

"Make one more sound and I'm gonna fuck you so hard, I'm gonna split that pretty little cunt of yours."

I stilled as his words sunk in.

"Me and the boys are looking forward to getting to know you, April. There's plenty of us to go around, although you may not look so pretty afterwards."

My stomach filled with ice. Cold and hard, it sank inside me, along with my resolve. Footsteps echoed. I hung onto each beat as the heavy tread lingered in the carpark. Then they died away, disappearing amongst the dull roar of the busy street.

His weight shifted, releasing my chest as he climbed off. "Now then, I'm glad we're both on the same page. It will be much easier when I take you back to the station."

My voice was nothing more than a lifeless whisper. "Why are you doing this?"

He stilled. I followed the slow blink of his eyes, then he answered, "Because it's my job."

Something sour crawled into my mouth. I swallowed the acid and it burned all the way down my throat. The cop reached for his belt and the snap of handcuffs sounded seconds later. The steel bit into my wrists. He shook the chains, grinding the metal edges on my jutting bones, and smiled as I whimpered.

It was his job. Nothing more, nothing less.

Yet this was my life. This was Jared's life, and if ours were so easily discarded, what hope did we have? The officer jerked on the chain, pulling me to stand. If we were to survive this, we'd never be free, not while we remained here. My feet moved on their own as he led me from behind the four-wheel drive. I felt my heartbeat in the deep crescents the shackles cut into my wrists as I trudged up the steep embankment to the upper level.

The black and white waited and my steps slowed. There'd always been stories about corruption among the Boston police. Officers taking bribes, some getting away with speeding or other crimes while off duty. But I never imagined anything like this. He hit the button, unlocking the doors and gripped the handle for the backseat.

The sour smell of vomit assaulted me as he opened the door. "Get in."

I shook my head, trying one last time. "Please, you don't have to do this. I don't know what you want, but I don't have anything. My father isn't rich. I have no connections, I have nothing you can use. Just let me go. I promise not to say a word to anyone what happened. I promise not to say a word."

My words failed to connect. There was no remorse in his gaze. No hint of anything but cold cruelty. There was no amount of pleading, no amount of crying, that would change this. I sank into the back seat as he placed a hand on my head and pushed me down.

He moved in, bending to lean over me and reached for the belt. The leather seats refused to give as I shoved my heels against the floor and away from his touch. It didn't matter. He took what he wanted anyway, wrenching on the belt until it snapped tight and grabbed my breast. "Nice, very nice. I always had a thing for perky little tits like yours."

I wrenched my head to the right and away from the smirk on his face. The car door slammed shut. A second later, his door followed suit. The engine started, filling the interior with a growl. There had to be someone at the station who could help me. Surely not every officer in the Boston PD was involved. I'd demand to speak to a captain. Tears blurred the bank of parked cars as my captor turned the wheel and eased away from the elevator.

The rubber squealed as the car raced down the garage ramp. I glimpsed the rust colored SUV, my chance at escape had been pathetic. I'd gained nothing but an enemy, of that I was sure.

The boom gate lifted out of view. The park outside seemed like a mirage now. Just a painting of people who walked their dogs and pushed strollers. What felt so vibrant and happy a mere hour ago was now nothing more than a hopeless beginning, only to end with me in handcuffs.

I rested my cuffed hands on my thighs, watching as the outside world rushed by. Street after street we passed, until an unsettled feeling filled my stomach forced me to turn and scan the buildings rushing by. "Where are we going? The police station's back there."

There was no answer from the front seat. The only noise was a crackle of the radio. No station meant no captain. No one I could speak to. No one to help me. "Please, tell me where I'm going. Where are you taking me?"

Please. Please. Please. "Why won't you answer me? Why won't you tell me where you're taking me? "I clenched my hands, the hard cuffs cut into the thin skin of my wrists. "I have a right to know where you're taking me. I have a right to know where I'm going!"

The officer leaned forward and switched on the radio, blasting a heavy beat through the interior of the car. I blinked back my tears, refusing to succumb to my fear.

The car slowed outside an ugly brown brick building that backed onto another, equally ugly, building. There were no signs posted outside, nothing that told me where I was. I spied one other marked car as it drove past and caught the nod of my captor's head in greeting. I should've known something was wrong last night when this bastard handed me his card. It was all too late now as the cop's words echoed back to me. *It's a station we use sometimes. Just call the number. You'll get one of us, day or night.*

This plain building didn't look like any station. It looked like a quiet place to do whatever they wanted, away from prying eyes and demanding questions. The car turned into a back lane and slowed at a single door at the rear of the building.

I fought to swallow the retch as my belly rolled. I breathed the putrid air deep into my lungs. Feeling the burn deep inside. The gears shifted. The engine died.

*I'm alone and in serious trouble.*

# Chapter Fifteen

The officer climbed out of the driver's side and strode around to open my door. "Scream in here, and I won't be the worst one you'll have to deal with. You understand me?"

One slow nod felt like it sealed my fate. He bent over my lap, hitting the clasp and the belt slid free. I had to try once more. I had to find my brother. "Tell me that Jared's in here. Is this where you're taken him, too?"

The cop wrenched my cuffs and I sprawled forward. My hands slapped the door in time to stop myself from hitting the pavement and I crawled from the car. I stared up at the building, scanning the windows, trying to find Jared among the movement as the door slammed shut behind me.

He had to be somewhere inside.

"Move."

The cop's tightening grip on my arm made me wince as he dragged me toward the door. We stopped long enough for him to punch a set of numbers into a lock. The door clicked open and he strode through, dragging me behind him. Paint hung from the walls in thin strips. The long corridor behind a set of stairs was half hidden in the shadows and stank of mold. I lifted my arms, burying my face into the soft sleeve of my shirt as the cop mounted the stairs.

"What am I doing here?" My words sounded muffled. I slowed my steps, using each second to think. "I don't understand what I'm doing here."

He stopped climbing, turning to glare down at me. "I'm sick of hearing your whiny fucking voice. Shut your fucking mouth, or I'll stick something in it so you can't talk."

I swallowed hard, knowing he would, and he'd enjoy every damn minute. Chill bumps raced along my skin and I shivered. The cop climbed, yanking me from the standstill to stumble forward. We passed one stairwell and kept climbing, until he stopped at the second. The door was old, the swollen wood shrieked in the frame as the officer gripped the handle and yanked it open. The low hum of voices drifted to me as I stepped through the doorway.

Doors lined the first half of the corridor, the rumble of voices came from somewhere in the back. I tried to focus, singling one voice out from the rest, searching for a name, anything I could use. A sharp bark of laughter drew my focus as the officer dragged me toward a door. IO 1 stood out in brass letters. IO, what could that mean? Interrogation Office? I couldn't come up with a better—more comforting—guess. My steps slowed as we neared the room. I tugged against his grip on the cuffs and dug my heels into the floor. "Please, stop. I want to call my Dad. I just want to call my Dad."

The door unlocked and swung open. A detective—at least, I thought he was a detective, since he wore plain clothes—moved to stand in front of a table. He folded his arms across his chest and looked me up and down. Gravity pulled me into the room. I resisted, wrenching on the metal bindings. Agony flared along my arm and into my elbows. I didn't care. The harder he pulled, the more I resisted. I threw my leg around the doorframe as we passed, straddling the flaking wood with my thighs.

I had to try again. I had no other choice but to keep fighting. " Please don't do this. Let me call someone. Let me call my Dad. I just want to call my Dad."

The detective lunged forward. He gripped my hair and wrenched my head back as his other hand wound around my throat. "Let go. I said let go."

I gripped as hard as I could. The muscles of my thighs strained. I clasped my elbows around the wood, holding on for my life. My head yanked back and I stared into the detective's blue eyes. They seemed to pierce right through me. His perfect lips slid back, uncovering his teeth in a sneer. "I'm gonna like breaking a little cunt like you."

"Murphy, get her legs." The uniformed bastard growled.

The detective snapped his head toward my abductor. "No names, you dumb fuck."

"Fuck. Just get the bitch's legs."

*No. No.* My arms strained as I dug my elbows into the frame. Their fingers dug into my muscles and the grip around my throat squeezed. I could feel my pulse ponding inside my ears and my face burned. Spittle flew from my mouth as I choked, using the last ounce of energy I had left to scream. "Stop. Stop. I want my Dad. Dad!"

Their forceful fingers wormed under my elbows and between my thighs. A hard pinch to the soft flesh between my legs had me whimpering. The lights on the ceiling dimmed. I clung to the last traces of consciousness as my face burned and my head pounded. Their hands were cruel, someone gripped between my legs. My feet left the floor as they carried me into the room and threw me against the table.

Sparks danced in my eyes as the back of my head impacted with the wood. I tried to inhale as the air left my lungs. Fresh agony bloomed inside my head and clawed at the muscles along my neck.

Their heavy breathing filled the room. "Now, you're gonna pay for that, fucking bitch."

These men were bigger, stronger. I felt dwarfed in size. Each pulse of my head was like a knife inside my skull. I tried to focus on my breaths, forcing them through my arid mouth. A whisper was all I had left, so I made it count.

"Fuck you."

The movement on a screen drew my focus. I tried to gather my thoughts as the grainy image flickered. A man paced back and forward in front of a camera. I couldn't make him out from the back. My stomach tightened as he turned his face toward me and the air left my lungs.

Jared.

My stepbrother paced the room behind the camera, moving to slam his fists against the wall. I could see the agony on his face, distorting his beautiful mouth. The shine on his cheeks made me think he was crying. The pain dropped from my head into my chest. I held my breath and rolled to my side, using what little strength I had left to pull myself up and stare at my captors. "What are you doing to him?"

These two animals only stepped back and smiled. Their badges sparkled under the overhead lights. They weren't cops. They were nothing but scum. No amount of begging and pleading would help us in here. There was no law here and no rights. This place never existed. Inside these walls, we never existed.

I only hoped we'd get out alive.

I tried to keep the tremor from my voice as I wrenched my gaze from the monitor. "What do you want from us?"

The uniformed bastard turned to Murphy. "See, I told you she's no dumb slut."

"She still has to pay, and I been itchin' to get inside that tight cunt since I saw the recording."

I held my breath, unable to stop the tremors in my arms as his words sank in. *The recording.* I closed my eyes, feeling the room sway. The repercussions battered the walls inside me as the tears finally slipped free. This was why I was here. This was no arrest. There was no investigation. These weren't police officers. These were animals, intent only on rape.

I caught the sound of a footstep and forced open my eyes. The uniformed cop moved closer and fumbled with the buckle on his belt. "I warned you. Still, you made me chase you down the damn carpark. You almost ruined the entire fucking thing, kickin' and screamin' like a damn lunatic." His twisted mouth broke into a grin as he pulled his nightstick from his waist and slammed the thick baton against his palm. "I liked the feel of you squirmin' underneath me. I'm thinking we might reenact that bit."

The movement on the screen drew my focus. Jared's mouth stretched wide. His soundless screams tore my heart. Through my tears, I turned to my abductors. "Do whatever you want, just let Jared go."

"Oh, look here. The little girlfriend wants to save this gutless pissant from listening to us fuck his sister," Murphy muttered, then chuckled.

I focused on the uniformed bastard. "Let my brother go."

The screen was a blur as Jared threw himself against the wall. The camera shook with the impact and my world trembled.

"Let Jared go. I'll do anything. You want to fuck me, fine. Just don't hurt him."

The officer swung his arm, bring his nightstick down on the desk beside me. "I'll fuck you, all right. There'll be plenty of others after me as well. Cruel bastards that will take those tears as though they were diamonds and use that pretty cunt of yours until you're raw."

"Enough talking. Hold her down." The detective snarled.

The unformed cop yanked the cuffs over my head. He gripped my ankles, wrenching along the table, my legs spread wide as Murphy bore between my thighs. My arms strained. I stretched until my back bowed. "Stop. You're hurting me. You're hurting me."

I inhaled the sickly-sweet scent of fabric softener from the cop's shirt as he smothered my face with his chest. Something hard rubbed between my thighs. The pressure increased, even when the bastard moved to hold my arms over my head.

Murphy grinned, probing the crease of my jeans with the nightstick. "I saw how you enjoyed the billiard cue. I wonder if you'd enjoy something with a bit more girth?"

"Fuck you, you sick piece of shit." I spat and my arms jerked taut, jutting my breasts high.

"Oh, you're gonna fuck me all right. You're gonna taste my cock. Look at those titties. So nice." He reached up with one hand, keeping the stick hard against the crease of my jeans and gripped my breast.

The pinch made me whimper and the detective hissed. His eyes were bright, focused on my pain. He squeezed harder, kneading the flesh until pain flared in my breast and I cried louder.

The image through the monitor shook above me. The monitor blurred, bouncing around in my field of vision as the cop rubbed the stick again and again. I stared at the black and white mess as a dull thud echoed through the walls, followed by another. Hot tears slid down my face. *Jared.* The blur stopped. The camera focused on my brother. He slid down the wall to sit on the floor. I watched through the monitor as he dropped his head into his hands.

*Don't give up. Fight for me.*

"You know your brother in there could stop this. All he has to do is say yes." The cop above me spoke. "One little word for the sake of his sister. I mean, don't get me wrong. I'm almost coming in my fucking pants with the thought of being balls deep in your little cunt. But one word from little Jared in there is all it takes for this to stop."

I shifted under the grip on my breast. The hard end of the nightstick ground into the crease of my jeans. Why did Jared fight them?

"It's not a bad deal." The officer above yanked on my cuffs, wrenching me from my thoughts. "All he has to do is whip out that little cock and fuck the next guy. He's done it before, and I've gotta say, he makes dude-on-dude hot as fucking hell. But this time, little brother in there isn't playin' the game. Says he's in love. Says he'll take whatever punishment we give him. But see, the punishment was never for him, was it?"

The pressure against my sex eased. The detective's hand was heavy against my stomach. No. I yanked my arms and swung my legs. My heart thundering as I kicked him away. "Stop. No. Stop!"

He took every blow, gripping my hips so my feet hit nothing but air. The button of my jeans popped open. The zipper slid down underneath his insistent fingers as he wormed his way underneath the elastic of my panties.

"All he has to say is yes. One little word."

"Fuck you! Fuck you! Don't do it! Don't do it Jared!" I screamed until my throat burned and his fingers slid down the hair of my sex and slipped into my crease.

"So warm." The bastard slid deeper. I could feel his probing fingers, pushing in deep.

I felt the walls of my pussy stretched wider with two fingers inside. He worked his hand up and down, rubbing against my clit. I whimpered as the harsh stokes turned slow, creating heat where there had been none before. I turned my head from the monitor to stare at the empty room.

"Get those jeans down. I wanna see her tight pussy." The voice growled above me.

I closed my eyes, feeling the waistband of my jeans slide from underneath my ass, exposing my body. A hiss of breath was followed by a deep moan as my right shoe slid from my foot to hit the ground. He squashed my face underneath his chest. His greedy fingers spread me wide. "Fuck, she's wet. This one likes it rough."

The pressure increased, then stopped.

"That's the signal. We broke him, he's gonna do it."

The vibration of his voice tickled my cheek. His words rebounded through my head as a muffled growl. The pressure against my head eased. The invasion retreated. The click of the handcuffs above my head made me jump and my hands were set free.

"Five more fucking minutes and you would've been mine. It's lucky your boyfriend in there gave in. Once I start, I don't normally stop, especially not with something like this."

I felt his thumb slide down my crease, parting my folds. My thighs clamped around his hand and I turned over. The desk was hard under my body, but I didn't care. I lifted my foot and grabbed the other half of my jeans.

"Shit. The message from Kyle was he gave in when we dragged her in here. Huh, we must've missed that message, Murphy. Lucky the microphone caught everything though. I bet the little boyfriend in there loved hearing his bitch scream."

The detective pinned me with his hard gaze. "Just wanted to make sure we got the point across." He leaned in, making sure his words never carried. "The new senator will learn who's in charge here. When Mr. Brontie says jump, we wanna feel the earth shake, understand? Tell that to your little fuckbuddy in there. His daddy needs to know who is really calling the shots around here. You try to come after the recording again, and you'll end up like your friend's poor little stepbrother. You feel me?"

I nodded and slid my foot through my panties and into the leg of my jeans. His words sank in as I lifted my ass and jerked the waist underneath me. These corrupt cops could do anything they wanted to us. *Dance, little puppet.* My strings felt like they'd been stretched too tight.

My fingers shook and I worked the button closed and snagged the zipper, sliding it up. The detective gave me one last glance before sauntering to the door. It was over, they'd won. We had no recording, it was in the possession of these animals. Worse, with the tape, they could force us to do this all over again, anytime they liked. Jed and his stepbrother were next. We were all pawns in this sick little game and there was nothing we could do to stop them.

The uniformed cop patted my leg as he walked past. "I hope we see each other again, April. For now, I'll keep your recording close. After all, it's my favorite."

I tracked his heavy steps when he strode out of the doorway, leaving me curled up on the desk, alone.

## Chapter Sixteen

"April! April! Where is she? Where is she!"

Tears filled my eyes at the sound of his voice. I scrambled from the desk and raced from the room. Jared was a blur as he stumbled down the corridor toward me.

The impact jarred the thoughts in my head. Jared's arms were there to grab me. He lifted me, cradling me against him, as close as our bodies would allow.

"I'm here. It's okay. I'm here now." I clung to his voice and to his arms as he carried me from that corridor. I must've been heavy, too heavy for him to cart down the stairs. I could feel his muscles strain and his chest swell. His grip tightened around my body, as though he could hold onto me forever. And that's exactly what I wanted him to do. Hold onto me forever and never let me go.

He made it to the base of the stairs before his body shuddered under the strain. I leaned in close, kissing his shoulder and whispered. "Put me down, Jared. It's okay. We'll get out of here faster if I walk."

He dropped my feet to the ground and grabbed my hand. "Let's get the fuck out of this place."

His voice was husky. He must've screamed so much he was almost hoarse. I blinked away the tears and tugged his hand, pulling him along as we shoved the door open to escape. The world outside hadn't changed. The sun felt just as warm on my skin, but there was something different. Something had changed inside me and when Jared clenched my hand, I knew he felt it, too.

There was darkness now. Something cold lurked in the background of my world, waiting for the moment to snatch everything from me. I followed Jared out of the building and onto the street. He stared at the cars, running his hand through his hair, while he held onto me with the other.

I wanted to save him from the torment in his eyes. He was drowning, and there was nothing I could do to save him. I couldn't even save myself. I reached for him, running my hand down his arm, waiting for him to turn to me. "We need somewhere where we can think. A motel, or something." It hurt me to say the words, because I knew they would hurt him more. "I need someplace I can shower. I can still smell them on me. I have to get it off me, Jared. I have to...."

"It's okay. I'll find us a place and we can try to work this out." He whispered, turning to hail a cab.

I nodded, but inside, I knew there was nothing to workout. They mapped everything out for us. In this moment, I realized it wasn't Jared who was drowning—it was me.

The yellow cab pulled up hard against the curb. I could smell the rubber burning as I climbed into the backseat. Jared let me go and I slid across the ruptured leather and fastened the seatbelt. I massaged the raw scrapes over my wrist bones, knowing that tomorrow, they'd turn angry and purple. But those were hardly the worst of my injuries, not by far.

My knees started shaking. By the time the cab pulled out into the street, the tremors overtook my limbs. I hugged my stomach and tried to keep myself from falling apart as Jared gave the driver the address to Kyle's apartment. It took me a second before I understood. Our cars were still there, parked outside for all to see.

I wanted to speak my mind. Instead, I sat back against the rough seat and focused on his arm against mine. In this moment, the slight connection was enough. Just to touch him, to know whatever happened, what we had right now was real. We were holding tight to this slippery slope with everything we had, not wanting to take others down along with us. But sooner or later, we had to let go.

Familiar buildings raced by as the cab slowed. I forced myself to look past Jared to Kyle's building. It seemed like forever since we were here last. We'd both been naïve, thinking we could waltz in there and get the recording back. We'd had no idea of the people we were dealing with. Now, we knew who we were up against, and the knowledge scared the hell out of me.

Jared's black sports car stood out. I shifted in the seat and glanced back at my blue little hatchback. There was no way we could go anywhere in the Maserati. Everyone knew who drove the sleek vehicle. Jared pulled his wallet from his jeans and slipped the driver a twenty as I opened my door and climbed out. I tried not to look at the carpark and the yellow boom gate. The agony in my head was reminder enough. I reached up, probing the tender flesh. My scalp was swollen. I sucked in a sharp breath at the sting.

"Are you okay?" Jared reached out, touching my arm.

I shook my head. There was no denying the obvious. "We can't take your car, those cops are probably watching us. We'll be spotted in that for sure."

He glanced toward the black beast and stood there for a long time before he turned and smiled. "Yeah, I know. Hand me your keys and let's get you out of here."

I dug into my left pocket and snagged my keys. "No one will notice us in this. We can come back for your car later."

He held out his hands for my keys. "Let me take care of you. We can work everything out later."

He took the keys from my hand and slid his arm around my waist, holding me close. My legs were shaking so, I could barely stand, let alone walk. I focused on my car, making my knees lock with each step. I trailed my fingers over the hood. The metal was warm from the sun. Jared moved around me, opening the door for me to climb inside. I breathed deep, watching, Jared walk around to the other side and slide in behind the wheel.

"We'll find somewhere close so you can shower. I'm sorry we don't have any spare clothes for you."

I shook my head. "It's okay. I just need someplace to think."

He leaned forward and started the car. I had a feeling we both needed to make some serious decisions.

## Chapter Seventeen

Jared winced at the broken sign that flashed, Vacancy.

I reached over to squeeze his hand. "It's not forever, only for a few hours."

"You're right. I'm too damn picky. Wait here while I pay and get us a room key."

This was the first time we'd been together like this. It felt strange, as though we were a couple, until I scratched the surface and realized why we were here. He cut the engine and climbed out, leaving me in silence. I had things to say, things Jared wouldn't want to hear. But he would listen, even if they were painful to hear.

I watched him walk out of the reception with a thick key tag in hand. To me he was so out of place in the parking lot of a cheap motel. He was used to butler service and the best money could buy. But here, he was no different than those on the street, or me. We were worlds apart, and yet here he was, trying his best.

My chest panged. The ache I felt for him was dangerous and yet this was the choice I made. Love, loss, or never love at all. It'd never been about any of the others. I only ever wanted Jared. But Nathan's death had shaken me to the core, even more now that I'd been threatened.

The end was so clear to me now. This dark ride would end in bloodshed, of that I was sure. My birthday loomed so close and eighteen seemed too young to die.

The door yanked open and Jared slid inside. He started the engine and slowly backed my car between two other vehicles before shutting the engine off once more. One quick scan of the parking lot and he pointed toward the back of the motel block. "Our room is over there. Parking here should buy us a little time before anyone sees us."

"Okay." My voice no longer sounded like my own. There was no life, no spark. I held onto whatever I could as Jared climbed out of the driver's side. I followed his lead, walking to the front of the car and crossing the parking lot.

A car door slammed out on the street and I flinched. Each step seemed to drive me further from my life. Instead of planning one last dinner before I went away to college I was planning how I would die. Would it be a crack of gunfire, or a hand around my throat? This game I'd been forced to play was no longer for love, it was for life.

Jared stopped outside the room. The number thirteen hung limply to one side. He caught my gaze. "It was the only one they had away from the road."

"It's okay. Really, it's fine." I whispered as he twisted the lock and pushed the door in.

I scanned the faded carpet and the dirt-stained chair, pushed hard underneath the small desk. The bed was sunken in the middle, framed by two small desks with matching orange lamps. The room smelled of cigarettes and pine. I forced myself not to look too close.

Jared locked the door behind me and noted the comforting jungle of the chain sliding across the frame—not that such a small thing could protect us. I slumped to the bed and stared at my hands in my lap. I wanted to cry, to scream. I wanted to fall apart. The empty hole inside swallowed everything.

"Let me get the shower going for you. The hot water will make you feel better."

He was so careful, so tender. I stared at him as he walked into the bathroom. This wasn't the same man who made fun of me at our parent's wedding. The one who touched my body in just the right places to make a naive girl whimper in delight.

I could see he was trying, and in a way, his efforts made being here harder. I stood from the bed and pulled my shirt over my head watching his gaze slide over my body.

Even through the horror, I felt my pulse quicken. I kicked off my shoes and reached to undo my jeans. My zipper was already half open. I needed a mental escape from that horrible place more than I cared for my dignity. It didn't take much effort for the rest of my clothing to fall. I shed my jeans, along with my panties, and reached behind my back, snagging the straps of my bra.

My brother gripped the bottom of his dirty T-shirt and pulled it over his head. A shuffled step and his shoes were discarded. His jeans fell soon after. Everything about this felt natural as Jared took my hand and led me into the shower stall and under the spray.

I twisted the tap, adjusting the temperature. No matter how far I turned the fixture, the water wasn't hot enough. Jared winced and stepped to the side. "You're scalding yourself, April."

I trembled under the water. My teeth chatted together. The sound was all I could hear. "I can't get warm. I'm so cold."

"Let me hold you." He reached past me, adjusting the spray until it cooled, then pulled me against his body.

I stiffened as his hands went to my hips. I held my breath, waiting for the pain to come.

"It's okay. You're here with me now. Relax, baby. Let me take care of you."

No matter how hard I tried, I couldn't relax. The sensation of his hands on my body was too much. The walls of the bathroom closed in. I had to get out of here. I had to run. My chest rose and fell in sharp bursts. I shoved open the stall door and stumbled out. My footing slipped on the wet tiles and I fell.

I could hear Jared's voice echoing in the tiny bathroom, trying to break through the screaming inside my head. But the shrill sound was all I could hear. I landed on my knee on the tile floor. Jared grabbed me and I lashed out. My foot hit him in the thigh and he went down on the floor. I scrambled out of the bathroom. The front door was all I saw. Freedom, just a few steps away.

"April, stop. April listen to me."

I lunged for the door and fumbled with the lock. The afternoon sun streamed through the opening as I yanked the door open. The chain snapped tight. The door barely opened. Not even enough for my hand to pass through. Spittle flew from my mouth landing on my arm as I cried out. "I gotta get out of here. I gotta get out of here."

My mind was stuck, unable to think about anything but those warm rays of light. I closed the door, to wrench it open once more. The chain wouldn't give. Nothing would give.

"It's okay. I'm not going to touch you, April. It's okay to cry. You can stand there and look at the sun if you want, or you can close the door and we can sit here. See, we can sit here and I'll try not to touch you. But you're naked and dripping wet and you'll probably give the old guy next door a damn heart attack."

His smile looked more like a grimace. The fact that he was trying tugged at my heart. I glanced at the sun, taking in all the warmth I could before I closed the door and sank to the filthy carpet. Jared lowered himself to the floor with his back against the bed, keeping his hand out in front. "I'm not going to touch you, not ever again, if that's what you need. We're just going to sit here and when you're ready, we can talk about anything you want."

I drew my knees up to my chest, not caring that I was naked any longer. My chest burned from the force of my breaths. I forced myself to concentrate on the rise and the fall, slowing each inhalation until the fire subsided. There was no silence, even though neither of us spoke. My head filled with voices. Each one demanded I listen, but it was the whisper in the back that held my attention. I didn't know I spoke until Jared's voice pulled me from the noise.

"Say that again."

I glanced up, finding his piercing focus on me. I swallowed and repeated the words. "Who is Mr. Brontie?"

A scowl crossed his face. He opened his mouth to speak, but nothing came out for a few seconds. "I don't know. Why?"

"That's who's behind all this. Mr. Brontie. The detective threatened me back there. He told me if I came after the recording again, I'd end up like Nathan."

"Jesus." Jared stared at a spot on the carpet, then seized my gaze. "I didn't hear them say that. Tell me exactly what he said, word for word."

"He said, when Mr. Brontie says jump we wanna feel the earth shake, and that if I go after the recording again that I'll end up like my friend's poor little stepbrother. He's talking about Nathan, Jared. He's talking about killing me like they did Nathan."

"Don't say that. You're not going to die."

My brother tried to sound sincere, but his voice trembled. Both of us knew what was coming and we were powerless to stop it. I nodded. "I can't go through this again, Jared. I'm not going to drag someone else along with me."

"So, what are we going to do?" The tremor in his voice disappeared.

I just sat there, feeling the distance between us widen, although neither of us moved. "I don't know. But while I think, would you just hold me?"

He opened his arms as I crawled across the floor toward him. "I'd hold you every night for the rest of my life, if I could."

His body felt warm as I slid underneath the crook of his shoulder. I turned my head, feeling the water still on his skin and inhaled the sweet scent of my stepbrother. One slow trickle of water ran from the base of his neck and down his chest. I licked my lips and followed the trail, dipping in at the last minute to lick the trickle from his skin.

Jared never moved, letting me slide my lips across his perfect skin. He was so warm, so smooth. I didn't want sex. I didn't want love. I needed comfort, in whatever way his body could give me.

I rolled on top of him, straddling his hips with my knees. His hands went to my hips and never moved, allowing me to lean in and kiss his lips. He opened his mouth for me, taking nothing. The water turned his blonde hair brown. I combed my fingers through the strands, then dragged them down his neck to his chest.

The warmth of his body seemed to melt the ice inside my chest. I wound my arms around his neck, rising up for him to take my nipple in his mouth. His slow draw on my breast was all I cared about. I tracked the movement of his hands sliding up to cup my ass. I pressed against him, forcing his mouth wider. His fingers kneaded my flesh, opening my thighs wider. I dropped my weight. My nipple slipped from his mouth. The warmth of his saliva still lingered as I slid his cock against the rising heat of my channel.

His hands felt so good sliding up my back, holding me as I rocked back and forth. His cock grew harder with the motion, teasing my opening. I glanced up to the ugly pastel comforter and whispered. "The bed."

"You sure?" Jared whispered, but his eyes never shifted from my face.

I nodded climbed to my feet, giving him room to move. I couldn't tear myself away from staring at his nakedness, his body hard and lean as he stood and yanked back the covers. His jutting cock held my gaze. Every inch of this man filled me with a ferocious need. He turned, catching my stare, allowing himself to be vulnerable—for me.

I stepped closer and wound my arms around his neck, letting his hands slide down to my hips. I wanted this moment to last forever, just him and me. I didn't care that we were in some cheap motel because I'd have this moment with him forever—

however long my forever might be. He lifted me against his chest and we fell against the white cotton sheets.

His mouth was on mine, biting my lips, searching for my tongue, and I opened myself up to him. His cock was hard against my mound. I splayed my legs wider, welcoming the pressure as Jared moved his cock at my entrance. These seconds I'd relive forever. His eyes blazed with need. His mouth opened. Warm breaths danced across my cheek as his cock slid inside.

Our hips rocked with the same motion, each rise filling me that little bit more until I gasped. I held onto my stepbrother's arms, mesmerized by sensation as his body met mine. Delicious, warm energy flowed through me. I focused on heat and the friction, bearing down as each thrust turned more urgent.

"Look at me." He whispered and I shifted my gaze to his. His face grew flushed. His chest glowed as he pumped harder. My nails dug into his arms as the primal need washed over me.

We raced toward that ending with each hard slap. My body clenched deep, tiny spasms gripped his cock, and he met my channel with one more thrust, then filled my body with his seed.

"I love you," he murmured, then collapsed onto the bed beside me. I rolled with the motion, feeling the loss as he slid from my body. Yet, I was content here with my head in the crook of his shoulder, my body buzzing with his lovemaking.

"I love you, too." I wanted those words to fill me with something other than fear. I was afraid for him and for me. I was afraid of what would come next. I pressed my ear against his chest and listened to his racing heart.

Seconds turned into minutes, then minutes into hours. The sun lost its bite through the cheap blinds. The inevitable waited in the corner of the dimming room. I took a breath, trying to steel my nerve.

"They know everything about me. My name, my address, probably where I plan to go to college. They'd know everything about you too."

"Our only option is to call my father. We have a name, so that's a start. He can help us." He implored me with his eyes. "He can try."

I took a breath and the ache in my chest turned harsh. "And if he can't?"

Hope seemed to fade in his eyes. "Don't think like that, he'll know what to do. Just give him a chance, April."

"Once we tell him, then we're putting his life in danger as well. I'm just not sure if I can do that."

Jared shook his head. "Don't you see? His life is already in danger. These bastards are after my father, by doing this to you and me. Jed's father is just as powerful, you don't get to own an oil company without playing dirty. They have no idea who they're messing with. Dad hasn't got to where he is by bowing under pressure and I won't put Jed into this same mess. Trust me, can you do that?"

I tried to be the voice of reason, searching the doors for another way out of this mess, but everywhere I turned the way was closed.

"Okay, do it. Call your dad and tell him what's happened. Tell him everything, get him to call your mom and tell them something. Dad will be freaking out right about now."

He sat up and swung his legs from the bed. "I won't use the phone here, they might be able to trace it. There's a payphone just down the street. I'll make the call and hope to God my father has enough pull in this damn city to set this right."

"Tell him everything, Jared. The tape, tell him what they tried to do to us today. Tell him about Nathan."

My stepbrother nodded and walked into the bathroom. There was a heavy silence in the room now. Jared returned, dressed in his jeans, tugging his T-shirt into place, then bent to kiss me. "I'll be back as quick as I can."

"Okay, just hurry."

He moved toward the door, sliding the chain free before yanking the door open. He was gone in the blink of an eye. Jared became only a shadow that moved across the window, and when the dark shape disappeared, I finally cried. My tears came hot and fast. I sat up with the sheets around my waist and wept like a child.

I held my head. The tortured sounds echoed back to me and my tears fell to splatter on the sheets in my lap. I cried until my tears ran dry, then I crawled from the bed and made my way into the bathroom. The shower spray warmed me. Every part of me ached, but my head was the worst. I rubbed my scalp gently with soap, feeling the sting of torn skin, then rinsed and shut off the water.

My old clothes would have to do, I had nothing else. I tugged on my jeans, feeling my underwear stick to my damp skin, then stared at my bleak gaze in the mirror. The eyes staring back at me made me wince and look away.

I gathered the room key and locked the door, feeling the flutter of hope in my belly. Maybe Jared's father would set everything right. That feeling grew as I walked along the building to the reception office, turning into butterflies in my stomach. I glanced right and left, spying the phone booth. My steps felt lighter as I walked along the footpath, until I drew alongside the plastic wall. The stall was empty. I scanned the cars, then the footpath.

Jared was nowhere in sight.

I clenched my hands into fists and whipped my head in each direction. He had to be here. He wouldn't just leave. I stilled and closed my eyes. My head shook, seemingly of its own accord, as the thought settled in. *No. No. No.* My eyes burned. There were no tears left, only a sinking of my stomach as I understood what had happened.

Jared had left. He couldn't leave his father, or his life. So, he'd returned to his cushy life, leaving me alone. The concrete path seemed to swallow me. I dragged my feet, turning back toward the motel as my thoughts raced. There was no way I could stay in Boston, not if I wanted to survive.

I trudged back to the reception door and slipped the room key in through the after-hours slot. Had he known all along? Had he played me for one last fuck before he slipped away? The pain in my chest was savage, puncturing my heart with the memory of each thrust between my legs.

The games my stepbrother played had finally broken me. I felt numb as I made my way over to my car and unlocked the door. Those cruel games were designed to destroy. The engine started quickly. I shifted into gear and turned the wheel. I crept out of the parking space, heading for the driveway. I couldn't even scan the traffic. Instead, I waited, unable to think, unable to feel and let my foot slip from the brake.

A bang on the hood made me wrench my gaze up. I slammed on the brake and stared through the windshield. Jared stood there, wide-eyed, gripping the car. "Jesus, April. You almost hit me."

I couldn't move as he stumbled around to the passenger side. I'd never even seen him. He'd come from the opposite direction. His harsh breaths filled the car as he opened the door and collapsed inside. The passenger door slammed shut. Jared closed his eyes, panting before he opened them and stared at me. "You were going to leave?"

I shook my head. "I thought you'd left me. I thought—"

"The phone wasn't working. I had to run about two blocks in the other direction to find one that did."

"I thought you decided to go back. I thought I was all alone."

"Never. I told you I wouldn't leave. But we have bigger problems now."

I saw the worry in his eyes. His hand shook as he reached for mine. "We've got to leave. This guy, this Mr. Brontie, he's bad news April. Real fucking bad. Dad's gonna do his best, but I dunno, even he sounded rattled. He said the best thing is for us to leave town, lay low."

I couldn't feel his touch anymore as I thought about my future. "For how long?"

"A few weeks. A few months, maybe longer."

Leave, just like that? I turned to stare through the windscreen as his words sank in.

"Dad will give us money, even get new IDs if we have to. We can't stay here April, they already got to us once, and they can do it again—anytime they want."

The tank on the car was near full. It would get us out of the city limits. What other choice did we have?

I nodded, feeling the weightlessness swallow me. "Just you and me."

He reached over and gripped my hand. "Forever."

The End

# Volume Two

## Chapter One

FOREVER. THE WORD RANG IN MY HEAD AS I DRAGGED MY knees higher and pressed my back against the headboard of the bed in the dingy motel room we stayed in. It was the twelfth one, or was it the thirteenth? I'd lost track. Lost count of the cockroaches I'd seen and the scummy guys who hit me up for a blow-job for crack.

I lost count of the number of times Jared swore things would get better, and the number of times I believed him. But I didn't need to count these things. Not anymore. His rhythmic snores rang out in the darkness. Sleep came so easily to him, like it always did. But not me...*never me*.

Sleep was a savage beast. One that swiped at me when I came too close. One with jagged claws that tore me open, and flickers of the past spilled out. The attack at the so-called police station. The corrupt cop's hand down my pants. *"Fuck you feel tight."*

I flinched, drawing my knees closer as Jared's snores deepened. But the attack by those disgusting *animals* wasn't the real reason sleep wouldn't come. No, the truth was far more disturbing, far more cruel. I glanced at him, tracking the line of his bare back as he lay on his stomach, his arm curled under the pillow. No...the truth was something I didn't want to deal with.

I wasn't ready.

I carefully slid from the bed and made my way toward the table, bending to slip on my sneakers before grabbing the room key, my hoodie and left. Sirens were the background track for this disgusting place. Just another city. Just another place to hide. I stopped in the yellow light that splashed against the motel door and tugged on my sweater, pulling my hood low.

Out here I could be anyone, and no one all at the same time. Out here, I was alone. I glanced over my shoulder, finding a glimpse of him through the tiny gap in the curtain and turned away, making my way from the block of rooms and across the car park.

The old white Toyota sat lonely against the wooden fence. We bought it with the stack of cash given to us by a friend of Jared's dad. A man who met us in some empty playground in the dead of night.

There were no names exchanged, especially on his side. But one glance toward me and the slow rake of his gaze down my body told me he knew plenty about us. I stood back, arms crossed, keeping a lookout while Jared headed for the swing set and took the money. They exchanged words after the fat envelope was handed over. Then it all changed.

The man pulled out even more money, this time from a leather billfold in his jacket pocket. One glance my way and he opened it, pulling out a thick wad. Jared stared at the money, then jerked his gaze to the man. A heartbeat was all it took before he lunged, swinging his fist and punched him in the nose.

"*Fuck you!*" He screamed as the guy reached for his nose and stumbled away.

Screams came from the guy as he clutched his nose. I caught the splash of blood that looked black, seeping it through his fingers as Jared strode toward me, grabbed my hand and dragged me away.

I wanted to know what it was all about. But he refused to tell me. Not who the man was or what the fight was about. But as we walked through the dark empty streets and back to the dive we stayed in, I slowly pieced it all together.

He wanted to give Jared money...in exchange for me.

The thought first made me sick. There was only one reason he would think that'd be okay.

*That's if he saw the recording.*

The recording of me being fucked by Jared's friends.

I stilled at the corner of the street, and glanced back to the motel, my breaths coming hard and fast as I glanced at the car. A wince twitched at the corner of my cheek before I turned away.

If the Senator's friends thought it was okay to buy me for an hour or a night, then what must his dad think? Had he seen the recording? Did he know how deep this corruption went?

Who the fuck was Mr. Brontie, and what did he want with Jared's dad?

I walked along the dark street, heading to the flashing neon lights, and yet all I saw was that fat billfold filled with cash, and as the thud of the seedy nightclub grew louder, luring me closer the memory of Monica's tongue sliding deep rushed back to me.

I stopped at the corner, braced my hand against the wall and closed my eyes. He fucking did this...he did this to me. My stepbrother. *The man I fucked every morning and night.* The heavy thud of the music reverberated the walls.

This was the sickness I didn't want to acknowledge.

The one that made me feel sick and depraved. The one that drew me back to places like this, places where dark deeds were done in dark corners. Anger rippled through me. The kind that cut like a knife.

*April, I love you...*

Jared's words invaded.

He told me the words over and over and yet since we'd fled the city with nothing more than the clothes on our back and Jared's unmistakable Maserati, I couldn't say the words back.

Days became weeks.

My brother felt the divide growing.

He'd done all he could to bring me back from the empty pit he pushed me into. But the truth was...*I was enjoying the dark.*

I opened my eyes at the squeal of hinges, watching as a guy stumbled from the seedy dive. I steeped closer, that endless chasm inside me calling. I could go in there, pull my hood low, let them see me.

I'd have men offering to buy me drinks in an instant...women too, if I looked their way. I imagined that as I stared at the door slowly closing. *You want to feel one of Monica's special kisses?* The memory came rushing back to me. *I hear she gives great tongue.*

I reached the door before it slammed closed, grabbing it and holding it open. I wasn't into girls, not really. But I couldn't escape it, not the depravity or the need. My brother made me like this.

He took my innocence and fucked me with the kind of depravity that left a mark.

That mark that I felt now as I opened the door to that seedy bar.

My pussy clenched, warming with the memory of lips and tongues and the brutal invasion of another's cock. I hadn't been able to come since we'd run. Not from Jared's lack of trying. My body refused, growing colder the harder he tried. So he just stopped trying.

Instead, he used me, grunting and grinding on top of me. Using his cock as a weapon to punish me. Every time I didn't climax was just one more slap in his face. One more reason to hate himself...and one more reason for me to feel that desperate need to just disappear.

I ached to disappear, to get away from him, and this entire fucked up situation. But I couldn't, because they tied me to this entire mess. My body hungered with a sick, ravenous need. One triggered by that night. The night I couldn't get out of my head.

I licked my lips, listening to the music and looked across the tables and the packed bar. But as I took a step inside, that twisted hunger shifted under my skin, sinking its claws deeper. It wasn't here I wanted to be...wasn't these strangers I wanted to be with.

*I'm sorry, April.* Jed's voice invaded. *I'll be as quick as I can.*

*Get on your knees.* Kyle's savage snarl broke in. *I want to feel you suck my cock.*

My breaths turned hard and insistent. I stood in that dark emptiness, staring at the pit where my brother left me and realized this wasn't where I wanted to be.

I stepped backwards, leaving the heavy steel door close with a *thud.* I can't...no I...

*I can't.*

Everything collided inside me. The threats, the terror, the fact we'd lived in these same fucking motels for months now and still there was no word from Jared's father or anyone on what was happening.

I turned, leaving the thud of the music behind and stepped out of the alley, glancing down the street.

"Hey, don't I know you from somewhere?" The deep snarl came from behind me.

I kept walking as fire lashed my cheeks.

"Hey." The guy was insistent.

Footsteps thudded, ringing louder in my ears as I hurried toward the murky glow of a streetlight.

"I know you."

He was right behind me. "No, you don't." I snapped. "You don't me at all."

Cruel hands grabbed my arm, fingers dug in as I was whipped around...and stared into familiar eyes. Eyes I never thought I'd see again. Eyes I didn't want to see...not in my nightmares or my fantasies.

"You not going to say hello, April?" The familiar tone hit me as he moved closer, leaning out of the shadow and into the light. "Cause I remember a time where you did a lot more than that."

My body clenched. Heart hammered. I bucked in his hold, tried to wrench my arms away. But his grip was unmerciful, like a vise around my arm. *Fight!* That voice inside me screamed. Fight him...*FIGHT HIM!*

But the beast in my nightmares wasn't letting me go. A coldness swept through me, plunging me down into that terror once more. It was all I could do not to scream as I whispered the name of the devil in my dreams. "Get your fucking hands off me, Kyle, before I scream."

There was a twitch in the corner of his mouth. "You forget, April. I liked it when you bucked and howled…" sinister eyes lowered, taking in my disheveled appearance, but it didn't matter to him what clothes I'd worn, because he already knew what was underneath. "Maybe it's about time I give you a reminder?"

# Chapter Two

"Get the Hell off me, Kyle!" I screamed as he pulled me against him.

His hand clamped over my breast, pawing me through the thick hoodie. "You think I haven't watched you for fucking weeks come to this goddamn bar looking for what you crave?"

I struggled, turning to shove him away as terror punched through me. "You don't understand a goddamn thing!"

His hold slipped, leaving me to shove backwards and drive my elbow into his stomach. He gave a hard grunt as I spun, stumbling away from him. "You...goddamn bastard."

But that cruel glint in his eyes still shone, mirroring the sick smirk as he stepped closer, driving me against the wall. "I might be a bastard, April. But at least I'm not the one lying to myself. I know what I am and what I want. Can you say the same, or are you just lying to yourself?"

My breaths were hard, tearing through my chest as I tried to get away. "Leave me alone."

"You think about that night, don't you? You think about all of us, the way we used you, the way Monica licked you. The way you didn't exist outside of *our* pleasure. Your brother handed you around like some filthy fucking rag for us to use however we wanted. Only he forgot to mention one thing." He pressed against me. "That little, dirty rag becomes stained."

I jerked my gaze to his. Cold, black pools drew me in deeper as he stared into mine.

"Of all the ones we recorded, you've been my favorite." He lifted his hand, fingers reaching for my hoodie.

I flinched at his touch, revolted.

"You've been a favorite to many of us, including Mr. Brontie. You know he'll use it against Jared's if he has to. He'll break the truce."

I stilled. "Truce?" I whispered. "What truce?"

He searched my gaze, searching for something. "The truce the Senator demanded. They didn't tell you, did they? No one told you. There's been no reason for you to be in hiding, April, and there hasn't been for months now."

"What the fuck are you saying?" My mind spun as I tried to understand. "We've been fucking hiding because of you."

Kyle's smile grew wider. "No, you've been hiding because that's what Jared and your step-father wanted. No other reason, April. You want the truth? Then there it is. Don't believe me? Ask Mr. Brontie yourself."

He dropped his hand from against the wall and stepped away, motioning to the black Lamborghini parked in the distance. "Let me take you back home. You can ask him yourself."

I shook my head, staring at the car. My skin itched from the hard water in the motel. I hadn't seen a proper meal for weeks, surviving on week old, pre-packaged sandwiches from graffitied vending machines. "You're lying." I tore my gaze from the sleek sports car.

"Am I?" He stepped away, crossing his arms. "How much do you want to bet on that? A month in that filthy fucking dive? A week...*a day?* I'm offering to take you home." He raked his gaze down my disgusting clothes, by way of a damn shower and some fucking clothes. Your brothers been lying to you, April. He's been lying this entire time."

"Why?"

That smile returned. "I think maybe that's a question you want to ask him and his damn father. But might I suggest you do that when you hold the power and not give it all to him?"

*Power...*

That's what this was all about, wasn't it?

Sickening, corrupt power and the games people played to get it...*and keep it.*

Kyle took a step backwards. Kyle with his perfect open collared black shirt and Armani trousers. The heady scent of something sultry and masculine carried on the wind to hit me. God, he smelled good. Even if the thought of him touching me made me want to retch.

"The power can be yours, April." He hit the button of his car and the doors unlocked. "All you need to do is take it."

*Take it. Take...it.*

He turned his back on me, giving me a chance to run. I glanced back down the road, at the direction of the motel. The motel where Jared would be sleeping, his body spent at the sacrifice of my soul. He used me. I still couldn't get that out of my head. I still couldn't work through the lies, not on all the sleepless fucking nights.

Kyle was right, I was stained.

I was their ruined, filthy rag, and I was stained.

*Why else was I out here ready to walk into some strange bar...just to feel that stain once more?*

I turned back to Kyle, watching as he glanced over his shoulder. I took a step toward him, my heart clenched so tight I could barely breathe.

"That's my good little whore." He murmured and yanked open the passenger's door for me as I slipped in.

My fingers brushed cool leather. The rich scent invading my nose to fill my lungs. I hated that I sucked down the air, hated even more that I pushed back into the seat and fought back the need to sigh. Kyle closed the door behind me and the rounded to climb in behind the wheel. In an instant, the sports car came to life with a throbbing snarl. Piercing white headlights carved through the night.

We were pulling away from the curb before I knew, leaving me to fumble for the seatbelt. My mind was racing with everything Kyle told me. As much as I despised him, I couldn't deny that whisper inside my head. The one that asked the same questions over and over.

*Why me?*

What could they hope to gain from having a recording of me? Kyle punched the accelerator, spearing us through the night, weaving through street after street of this derelict part of the city to come out to where the bright lights sparkled and the shops weren't permanently guarded with bars.

"I've booked us into a room for the night."

Panic surged through me as I jerked my gaze to him.

"Don't worry, we're not staying. But I thought you might appreciate a long, hot shower, some clean clothes and some food. No offence, April, but you smell worse than a goddamn dumpster and you've lost far too much weight. All I see is bones."

His words hit me like a slap as he drove toward the Marriot Hotel and pulled up outside the expansive glass doors. He didn't even kill the engine, just shoved the car into park and climbed out round the front in long, sleek strides to open my door.

In the bright glare of the luxury hotel, he was even more beautiful. Harsh edges made his face look cruel. Dark pools of his eyes made me feel like I was drowning as he opened the door for me.

He never said a word. Just let me sit for a second, like I was watching for sharks before stepping into the water. But how did I know which cold-blooded predator was after me...*when they all looked the same?*

I unbuckled my belt and stepped out, leaving him to shove the door closed as the valet rounded the car, heading for the driver's side.

"Keep it close." Kyle demanded. "I'll let you know when I'm ready."

"Yes, Sir." The attendant nodded, climbing in.

I followed Kyle through the doors, glancing at the receptionist as she stared. I knew what this must look like to her. Someone like Kyle returning with some street rat.

Someone who'd do anything for money or drugs. I tore my gaze away, following Kyle as he stepped into the elevator. He watched me like how a viper watches a mouse. He leaned back against the wall and crossed his arms as we rose.

"Did you never ask yourself why all the running? Why all the hiding? Did you ever ask him?" He never waited for an answer as we came to a stop. "I guess you didn't. After all, it was easier to lie to yourself than face the truth."

He stepped out when the doors opened. No longer waiting to make sure I followed. It was almost like he knew I would. I was desperate enough...and sick enough. Shame swallowed me as the doors closed, but then I was moving, slipping between them before they closed with a thud.

The click of a lock sounded before the door opened. Just one door though...

*One door to one room.*

I followed, my heart thundering as I followed him inside, lingering in the darkened entrance.

"Clean clothes are through there, food is on its way up. I ordered seared steak and charred green vegetables with fresh strawberries and fruit. Take as long as you need, April...I'm not going anywhere."

I stepped closer, moving in to peer at the bedroom with an array of clothes spread across the foot. "You knew I'd come, you bastard."

He helped himself to the bar, pouring two glasses of scotch before tuning. One glass had more in it than the other. That glass he offered to me as he headed my way. "This city, the next. I knew it was only a matter of time...before you broke."

I stared at the glass, then reached out with a trembling hand and took it.

"The shower is waiting." He offered, glancing at my sweater. "Leave those behind when you're done."

I took the glass with me and hurried for the bedroom, closing the door behind me. Fire burned my lips as I took a swallow and it carried to the pit of my stomach. I placed the glass down, looking at the black slacks, and high-necked sheer lace bodysuit with matching jacket.

It was a power suit, one designed to seduce.

I made for the bathroom, desperate to rid myself of these clothes. In the harsh lights of the bathroom, I saw the truth. I was thin...too thin. I peeled the sweater free, then the stained t-shirt and jeans I'd been wearing for months before lifting my gaze to the mirror.

Gone were the thick thighs I once carried. Gone was that innocent spark.

I was supposed to start college at once stage, but standing here I couldn't for the life of me remember why. I tugged off my filthy bra and stepped out of my hand washed panties before moving to the shower.

Steam filled the room in an instant. I let out a guttural moan as I stepped backwards and into the heat. Heaven, this is what it felt like. Fine needles massaging my scalp, working away months of oil and dirt. I used the hotel's expensive wash and shampoo, scrubbing my hair twice before working the conditioner through the lengths.

I closed my eyes, lulled by the scent of cleanliness and the feel of the water on my skin. When the brush of fingers came against my breasts, it took me a moment to understand what was happening.

I jerked open my eyes to find Kyle standing naked in front of me, his lean body bare, his cock hard and demanding.

"Now you didn't think I'd come all this way to play saviour now, did you?" He asked, reaching up to grasp a handful of my wet hair. "You know how I like you on your knees, April...so how about we start there?"

# Chapter Three

## KYLE

I STEPPED INTO THE SPRAY, LOOKING OVER HER SMALL breasts and bony body. My gaze trailed down dusty pink nipples, her stomach, and the trail of dark hair on her perfect, little cunt. Fuck, she still looked good. Too good to be fucking a loser like her goddamn stepbrother.

"What the fuck are you doing, Kyle?"

I braced one hand on the wall and fisted her hair with the other. "I think you know exactly what's going on here." Her nipples hardened, the sight of that wasn't lost on me. "But if you need a step by step, I can do that as well, or maybe we call it a *blow... by...blow?*"

I clenched my grip on her hair. Not enough to hurt her...but enough to let her know who was in control. And she fucking knew it, looking up at me with those big doe eyes. "No." She fought, trying to shove me away.

But her blows were weak...and pathetic.

Because she wanted them like that.

Just enough to keep up the pretence...still acting like a goddamn virgin...

We both know she wasn't.

Not after that night.

The video of her replayed in my head in damn stereo. I knew each scene off by heart now. Every one of her whimpers, every one of her sighs seared into my fucking mind. Just like she was. It was the only thing that drove me. The only thing that kept me going after all these months, tracking her from city to city, finding those cheap, filthy fucking motels...and the crumbs of her life she left behind.

Months I'd been searching.

Until last week...

When I finally found her.

I licked my lips, gripped her hair and snarled. "On your fucking knees."

She bucked, spine bowing backwards. Her breasts jiggling until resignation moved into those perfect brown eyes. She gave in, sinking to the tiles with barely more than a fuss. "Perfect little kitten, aren't you?" I whispered, her gaze running down my stomach to my cock.

Her gaze made me flinch. Christ. Electricity shot from my balls and along my shaft, making me throb. One fucking look and this is what she did to me. Little fucking April Harkness.

"Open your mouth, Princess." My voice choked. "I want to feel you..."

Her breath caught. A look of pain and hunger moved through her eyes, carving deep enough to make me still. Her hair fisted in my hand. What the fuck was that? That look...*that need.* What the fuck was that?

The spray of the water ran down her body, droplets beading on her lips. She pulled her head forward, mouth widening as her tongue peeked out, flattening as it grazed the head of my cock.

I hissed with the sensation. My fucking hold weakening. Still, I couldn't look away, not when she bent her head to the task. Lips stretched wide as she took me into her mouth. I fucked her warmth, sliding along that delicious tongue until the sensation unleashed a savage sound in the back of my throat.

*Fucking months.*

*Months of searching.*

*Months of craving...this.*

"More." I croaked, driving her head forward, sliding deeper until I felt the graze of her teeth, and then pulled out. She didn't buck this time. Didn't fight. Didn't give so much as a whimper. A stark contrast to the first time I took her.

Instead, her body trembled. Tiny shudders I felt along her tongue as I drove back inside. Rhythmic motions bucked my hips. I drove her head forward, setting the pace. *My pace.* The only pace I wanted, using her mouth, taking more and more from her with every thrust.

Her throat worked with the invasion, clamping around me until that fight took over and I let her release. She gasped for air when I withdrew, her tits jiggling with the effort. *Fuck, it wasn't enough. This...whatever this was, wasn't enough.* I just wanted this to be over. I wanted to relive that fantasy and be done with her.

I'd take her to Brontie...and leave her behind, exactly like I was instructed.

I'd use her. Because that's what I was good that...

*It's all I knew.*

"Get up." I demanded. "Get the fuck up."

I eased her head backwards. Saliva strung from stretched lips as she pulled away and lifted her head. Our gaze collided. There was that look again. Haunted. *Desperate.* The same one I'd seen as she stood in that alley. The same glimpse I caught tonight.

Something deep in me trembled as she rose. I leaned forward, hit the spray. "Bedroom...*now.*"

I hated that coldness in my tone. But she didn't seem to notice, stepping out of the shower, grabbing a towel from the rack as she passed. I grabbed the other towel, running it across my chest and lower. Hunger roared with the brush against my cock.

I strode out, cast the towel to the floor as she climbed onto the bed and lay down.

"I don't think so, Princess." I demanded. "I don't fuck like your goddamn brother. Get on your knees."

She did meekly, climbing to all fours, legs splayed, pussy parted. Pink was all I saw. I shoved the clothes from the bed and moved behind her. I didn't care about the others I fucked. Didn't touch them, didn't tease them. I didn't care if they enjoyed it, and I sure as hell didn't care if they came.

But as I moved behind her, my gaze taking in her bowed head. Her brown hair dripping onto the sheets. I sank to the floor. This felt different.

My knees hit the plush rug as I ran my hands along her thighs, my gaze fixed on her crease, from the puckered tight hole to her perfect slit. Something dangerous rumbled in the back of my throat as I dipped my head, my tongue seeking. She jerked with the contact. I stilled, curling my tongue, drawing away.

I met the touch with my finger, sliding along her slit until I found that tiny nub. My touch danced around, drawing a shudder from her body.

"No." she whispered, her voice detached and strange. "You don't get that from me."

"Don't I?" I found her again, that hunger burning in me.

I knew what it was now. What this conquest was.

It sure as hell wasn't her mouth.

I had that.

Tasted her fight.

Revelled in her meekness.

But this...this thing I drove toward now was so much more. More addictive. More dangerous. *Deeper than I'd ever felt before.* I rounded her clit with my finger and slipped inside. Her eyes closed, shutting me out. But it wasn't that easy...*I'd make her see.*

I shoved upwards, grabbed her around the waist and hauled her from the bed. Her eyes flew open as I dragged her back against my chest. "You want to shut me out?" I growled, anger burning inside me. "I don't fucking think so, April."

The floor-length mirror sat at the end of the walk in robe. I strode to the end and reached around her body, grasped the inside of her thigh and forced her legs to part. My cock nestled between her thighs as I stopped in front of the mirror.

Fear widened her eyes as she met my gaze in the reflection. "No." She hissed, shaking her head.

"You will watch, April." I forced through clenched teeth. "You'll watch or I'll never let you out of this goddamn room. I'll fuck you, day and night, if I have to."

She flinched as though I slapped her. Her hands grasping my wrists, shoving down, trying her best to break the hold. But it didn't matter. I yanked her thigh, stretching that cunt wide and angled my hips. She shoved out a hand, falling forward and braced against the mirror.

In the reflection, I breached her. Her tiny little slit clamping down as I slipped the thick head of my cock inside. My heart was thundering, the thrashing sound filling my ears as I drove upwards. Her body bucked against me as she took me to the hilt.

"Fuck, I missed this." The words escaped before I knew. "I missed you."

"Fuck you." She spat, her gaze riveted on the mirror, fixed on the point of our bodies where I sank into her.

"No." I gripped her hips, lifting her before I slammed her back down. "I'm the one fucking you."

She let out a moan, her little pussy clenching. I moved my hand around, finding her clit.

"I won't do it." She whimpered, thrashing her head from side to side as that warmth in her body grew. "I won't do it."

She fought.

She raged.

Hate burning in her eyes as they met mine in the mirror. Jesus, she was cold. Cold to her soul. Cold and empty even as I filled her. I rounded that tiny nub, circled and teased, lifting my hand to her lower abdomen and pressed down.

She unleashed a trapped moan, letting her head roll backwards. Her wet hair lashing my chest. Blush pink nipples hardened, but she moved, rocking her hips forward as the pressure mingled with the thrust, finding that spot that made her slam her eyes closed once more.

But it didn't matter.

I was already claiming what I wanted.

She grew slick around me, her hands stopped trying to push me away. Instead, they clamped down, riding me as I rode her.

"Fuck I missed you." I whispered, as that heady feeling rushed toward me. "So much I can;t let you go."

Over and over I thrust, drawing her closer and closer, until a tortured look creased her brow. I pressed down harder, feeling that invasion inside. I claimed her...wanted her.

So fucking...*much*.

She let out a cry and bucked, her cunt clamping around me, milking me until that vein throbbed along my cock and I kicked inside her body, releasing. I dropped my head forward, resting on her back. Christ, I never wanted to leave. Not her body...not her presence.

Never.

I rocked slowly, letting the aftershocks claim me, until I grew soft inside.

"Get...get the fuck out of me, Kyle." She whispered.

I lifted my head, expecting to see that vibrant woman I knew before.

But I didn't. She was even colder. Even more consumed by hate. Tears slipped from the corner of her eyes. I could tell myself it was just water, just the remnant of the shower.

But then I'd be lying.

Maybe that was all I was good at...

*Maybe that's all I knew?*

I slipped out of her, that ache booming in the center of my chest. Telling me that everything was changed now. Lying was the old me. The me who wouldn't waste a goddamn second thinking about someone other than myself. But I'd travelled across the country to find her.

*Now I had...I didn't want to let her go.*

# Chapter Four

I turned and shoved, driving my fist against his chest to push away from me. "Get the fuck off me."

He just stared at me, those dark eyes fixed on my every move. I didn't like him staring...didn't like him seeing. Didn't like him searching for a way to crawl under my skin. There wasn't enough room...not enough for them, or me.

That was the truth.

It was them or me.

*Them or me...or I wouldn't survive.*

He lowered his gaze, searching my body, his cock falling against his thigh. I sucked in hard breaths, finding the glistening remnant of my body along his length. My body quaked, pussy throbbed with a pulse of its own.

He took that from me.

My power...

Claiming it like they always did for their own selfish needs. "You bastard." I stumbled past him and out into the bedroom.

Tears sprang to my eyes as the sight of those clothes now shoved to the floor.

They didn't care. Not about me, or my needs.

"I ordered food." Kyle started.

I spun, my body shaking and screamed. *"FUCK YOU!"*

He stood there, stunned. His brow narrowing. But if I thought I was going to get a hint of kindness from Kyle, then I'd be delusional. A sharp knock came at the door, tearing my gaze. Kyle strode forward, snagging his towel from the floor as he passed, winding it around his waist before he strode from the room.

The bedroom.

In the motel where I came, following Kyle and his lies out of that dingy fucking place. *Jared.* I left him behind, left him sleeping. *Oh, Jesus...*I doubled over, unable to breathe.

What the fuck was I thinking coming here.

Voices carried. Kyle's deep bass voice came a second before the thud of the door. I bent, grabbed soft lace panties, a size too big. A size I once was, and slipped them on. The bra was next. I clasped it closed around me as Kyle carried in the large tray.

The scent of food hit me, making my mouth water instantly.

Food. Proper food. He placed it down on the bed and took a step backwards. "I'll give you a little privacy."

I glared at him, hating him with all I had.

Some of what I had, anyway.

Hate was endless for me.

A black void that seemed to go on forever.

I licked my lips, my gaze drifting to the food. Still, he cared enough to feed me. The idea of that didn't sit right. My belly clenched as I took a step closer, drawing in the heady scent of steak. I lifted the silver lid and groaned and the perfect, thick round morsel, lightly charred with scalloped potatoes and seared green vegetables.

My knees trembled, I almost buckled at the sight.

But there were more, two more plates sat covered. I lifted the lid on the next one, fresh fruit and cream. The next one held the most delicious sticky chocolate fudge cake. I unleashed a moan at the sight.

"Take as long as you want. If you're still hungry, I can order more. Whatever you want, April."

I lifted my head, finding Kyle as he stepped through the door, now dressed once more. He carried a bottle of water. My pulse raced, knowing what we'd just done.

Kyle was supposed to be my enemy, one of them at least.

He glanced toward the food. "Eat, enjoy it. I only ever want to give you something you enjoy."

My core softened as I swallowed.

"Then give me something more than food. Give me answers. Who is behind all this, and what does it have to do with me?"

He stilled, his gaze searching mine. I didn't like the warmth I saw, didn't like the way he licked his lips, his chest rising with a deeper breath when he looked at me. I didn't like the way he licked me, the way he touched me...the way he way he bought something in me crashing to the surface, until I gave in.

"I wish I could, but the truth is, I don't have the information you want. The best I can do is deliver you to the one who has."

"And then?" I took a step closer, moving through the doorway to stand in front of him. "What will you do then?"

"I'll do what I always do," he answered coldly. "I'll leave."

I swallowed hard, forcing the truth down. "At least you're fucking honest."

I turned then, strode into the bedroom and slammed the door shut with a *boom!*

My breaths were savage, sawing through my chest as I dropped to the side of the bed, wrapped my arms around my body and rocked under the pain. He wasn't going to help me. No one would. It'd spent months living in some filthy fucking hovel at Jared's whim, and now I was about to be handed over to this manipulative, calculated animal.

I stilled, my body trembling as I lifted my head.

But I refused to be a victim.

I glanced at the plate of food. Food, Kyle ordered or me. Ordered with care. I glanced at the closed door, the boom of my force still lingering in the air. He lied to me just now. He lied, and he tried to hide it.

The way he touched me was the truth.

This wasn't just a job to Kyle. This was more.

I reached over, grabbed the plate of steak and the cutlery before rising and in my underwear I strode to the door and yanked it open. He flinched, his eyes widening for a second with surprise as I walked out.

"Do you want to share it?" I offered.

"Share you food?" He scowled. "No."

I placed the plate down, grabbed the knife and fork, slicing off the browned edge and stepped closer. "Open."

My pulse raced, my mouth went dry. This was a test...a test to find my boundaries. A test to see the truth. Perfect dark lips parted as I stepped closer and lifted the fork to his lips. He held my gaze, riveted on what I held inside, leaving me to slide the steak inside before he chewed.

Juices dribbled down his lips, making them glisten.

Lips that seconds ago glistened because of me.

I reached up to slide my thumb across them. He moved fast, lashing out to grasp my wrist, his hold painful. "Careful." He murmured. "You don't know what you're playing at."

But that was the point...I did.

I knew exactly the games we played here...better than anyone.

He released me, stepping around me. "I'll make sure the car is ready."

Then he left, heading to the front door as fast as he could.

I scared him.

No, *I fucking terrified him.*

Adrenaline surged through me at the thought. My stomach howled, unable to be silent anymore. I walked to the table and sank to the floor, before picking up the cutlery and attacked.

Each bite was heaven. Even if it lost some of the heat, it was still delicious. I devoured it, slicing morsels of steak before chewing and swallowing, chasing it down with potatoes and vegetables until the plate was empty.

I rose, made my way back into the bedroom. Kyle didn't come back as I scraped cream on the chocolate cake and consumed that too, leaving the fruit for last. By the time I was done, my belly was heavy and my mind blissfully happy, buzzing with sugar and happiness.

I picked up the clothes from the floor, pulling on the bodysuit before the slacks and jacket. A pair of black, scrappy Armani heels sat beside the bedside drawer.

Clothes like this weren't cheap.

Nor were off the rack.

Kyle chose them carefully, just like the food.

*Careful.* His warning rang in my head as I threaded the last strap through. I stood, wobbled for a second before I found my strength and made my way back into that walk in robe.

The scent of sex still lingered. Kyle might've fucked me, but he also fucked himself.

He showed me a glimpse of something.

Something that was far more powerful than fear.

*Hope.*

I strode out of the wardrobe, then the bedroom and the room, finding him standing in the hall. He turned as I opened the door and stepped out, his gaze taking me in from head to toe. "It's a start." He murmured. "Until the next stop."

"Next stop?"

His smile was sinister. "I drove across the country to find you, April. I'll have to drive back. Don't tell be you're scared of spending the next three days and nights with me?"

He expected me to whimper.

Expected me to cower.

But I didn't. Instead, I smiled. That tiny spark of desire grew stronger as I whispered. "Not half as much as you're scared of spending it with me."

His smile faltered.

Growing stony.

I'd let Kyle fuck me as many times as he wanted. I'd make him buy me clothes and food and everything else. I'd feed him kindness. I'd draw him into me...and when it came time for me to face my monsters, I'd see if he ran.

I was betting he wouldn't.

Because I now knew the game I was playing...and I was determined to win.

# Chapter Five

JARED

THE FAINT SOUND OF A SIREN INVADED. I CRACKED OPEN my eyes, finding darkness before closing them once more. Then stilled. The air felt different, *lonely different.*

*Beep.*

I opened my eyes, the screen on my phone illuminating. Panic punched through my chest. The only person who had that number was my father. I shoved up from the bed, my gaze sweeping the dark, finding the room empty. "April?"

Sleep slipped away as I came awake. I looked to the bathroom, finding it dark and quiet. My gaze drifting to the open door. A chill raced through me as I shoved from the bed and grabbed the phone.

I pressed the button, illuminating the screen as I made for the door. "April?" I called, turning the lock on the door and stepped outside.

But she wasn't out there. My gaze went to the car, relief flooding me when I found the white Toyota where I left it. I glanced along the outside of the rooms, searching. She must've gone for a walk…

She did that sometimes.

Everything else I could handle. I glanced down to the screen, finding a message from an unknown number. "What the fuck?"

I stepped back inside and closed the door, hitting the message. It was a video, one that played out on the screen as it opened. The bright lights of a bathroom were blinding, the hiss of water the rush filled the air. April stood under a shower, her head tilted back, eyes closed with a look of ecstasy. Her breasts and body on full display.

"She's thinner than the last time I saw her."

I froze with the voice, that chill plunging all the way into the pit of my stomach as I watched the camera tilt, catching Kyle's face in the bathroom mirror. He was naked, his cock hard and ready. "But it's okay, old friend." He said, staring into the mirror. "I'm here to take care of her now."

"What the fuck?" I jerked my gaze around the room, then strode out into the night. "April!"

Panic rose inside me as I strode out naked into the parking lot. *"APRIL!"*

*"Hey! Shut the fuck up!"* someone screamed from the room next to ours.

I strode back inside, grabbed my jeans from the chair and yanked them on. My mind was racing, running that scene over and over in my head. It was a trick. It had to be. Just a goddamn trick.

I shoved my feet into my boots and yanked my shirt over my head, grabbing my keys before lifting the phone and playing the message again. I tried to look at his cock, shoving aside the fucking fantasy of what they'd been doing. Instead, I rewound the video to play it over and over again.

*It might not be her.*

The panic words a rush.

*It...might not be her.*

I blinked, lifted the phone to my face and pressed play once more.

I searched her body, small tits, nipples dusty pink and tight. Her waist was thin, bony. Fuck, it sure looked like her. But it could be a goddamn lie. After all, this was Kyle we were talking about. I strode toward the Toyota, shoved the key into the lock and climbed in, starting the old thing with a whine.

Lights came on from the room next to ours. The door flew open, and some fat fuck strode out as I shoved the car into gear and backed out. I didn't give a fuck about him, my mind screaming with thoughts about where my stepsister was.

She wasn't with him...

*No fucking way would she be with him.*

I glanced at the phone in my hand, my fingers fumbling as I pressed play once more.

"She's thinner than the last time I saw her. But it's okay, old friend. I'm here to take care of her now."

"No." I forced the words through clenched teeth and turned toward the bar two blocks away. *"No fucking way."*

But if it was her...if it was her, then it was over.

A wounded sound tore from the back of my throat as that fantasy I tried so hard to ignore came rushing back to the surface. He'd fuck her. Christ he'd fuck her. He ride her body, taking her over and over again. He'd take her hard.

Without mercy.

He'd punish her, turn her...he'd fuck her until there was no part of me left inside her. I knew that...because that's what I'd. I'd mark her like he would mark her. I'd stain her if I was him, then I'd turn her against me.

*"FUCK!"* I screamed and drove past the bar, the lights now dark. What time was it? I glanced at my phone, almost five a.m. When did she leave? I tried to think, but the truth was, I didn't know.

"This can't be happening. Can't be..."

If she was with Kyle then there was only one place he'd take her.

*To Brontie.*

My foot slipped from the accelerator. I pushed the brake, coming to a stop in the middle of the street. The repercussions of that resounded like a boom in my head. If she went to him... they we'd lost her.

I picked up my cell and pressed the button on the only number in the burner cell. The car rolled forward as I released the brake. I pressed the accelerator listening to the phone ring on the other side of the country.

"Jared?" Dad's slur came through. "What's wrong?"

I accelerated harder. "She's gone..."

"Gone?" His tone sharpened. "What do you mean, gone?"

I fumbled with the phone, hitting the message and forwarding it to his number. Through the speaker I heard it hit, then the scene played out, my stepsister naked in front of me father...and Kyle's smug fucking voice.

"Jesus." Dad whispered. "Jared..."

"I know."

"If Brontie gets his hands on her..."

I winced. "I...know."

"We should've told her the truth."

"And have her turn against us?" I headed toward the city. "She'd hate me more than she already does."

"You tried to protect her."

"She won't understand that. Brontie will take her, he'll turn her. He'll induct her into his sick fucking Order."

"I'll destroy them...*all of them*."

"And you'll destroy yourself too."

"This video was just sent, right?" The thud of dad's footsteps sounded, muffled by the rush of his breaths.

"Yes."

"So she's still there, you can still find her."

I'd been just driving, heading to where I didn't know. But now... now purpose roared through me. "Yeah, yeah I can."

"She's still in the city. The hotel looks expensive. Let me search for the one's he'd stay at and send you the addresses."

I shoved my foot against the accelerator, purpose driving me now as my phone gave a *beep*.

"That's the first one." Dad spoke. "I'll hang up and send you the rest. Find her, Jared. Find her and bring her home, it's about time she knew everything."

I jerked my gaze to the phone as the call went dead. Tell her the truth? How would that work...

*Hey, April...you might not know about this...but your blood father is really fucking powerful and there's assholes who will use you and hurt you to get to him. You know, assholes like me.*

I gripped the steering wheel and drove the piece of shit harder, weaving my way through the early traffic to the most expensive hotels in the city.

Hotels we should've been staying. No, instead I kept her kept her in fucking squalor. What kind of asshole does that? I glanced at the address, then hit the link to the map, finding the first one in the heart of the city.

I followed the directions, pulling up outside the Four Seasons and killed the engine. Desperation fueled me as I shoved open the door and raced out. It was still early...too fucking early. I stopped at the window, spied the asshole behind the counter and thumped my fist against the glass.

He looked at me, then scowled and shook his head. "Motherfucker." I snarled.

I knew what I looked like. Just a bum, right? A nobody, some broke asshole off the street with a Maserati still parked in the garage at home and about ten million sitting in my bank untouched. I curled my lip and punched the glass once more, only this time...*hard.*

His head snapped upwards with an annoyed look. But he shoved upwards and rounded the desk, striding toward me.

"No beggars." He snarled when he shoved open the door.

"Not a beggar, asshole. I was fucking robbed. I need to get into my room."

His eyes widened with words. Only the rich talked down to people, and he heard the dollars signs in my tone. "Oh, I'm so sorry. I didn't realise."

He opened the door for me, striding to the computer to punch in the name I gave him. But there was no record of Kyle's name in the register. He looked at me like I was stupid before I turned and left. He wasn't there... nor was he in the next hotel I forced my way into.

An hour it took me. An hour I didn't have.

By the time I forced myself into the last hotel on the list, the fucking Marriott, they bought up his details.

"Yes, Sir." The desk manager murmured, lifting his gaze from the screen. "I have your room details here. But Mr. Blackburn." He said, lifting his head with a look of confusion. "It says you've already checked out."

"When." I leaned across the desk, grabbing his shirt and hauled him closer, desperation roaring in my head. *"When?"*

"T-twenty minutes ago." He stuttered. "It's says you're already gone."

I shoved away from the counter, scanning the empty foyer and screamed. "Fuck!"

# Chapter Six

"So what kind of music do you like?" Kyle hit the button on his steering wheel, skipping the heavy beat and screaming in my ear.

"Anything that doesn't sound like torture." I watched the song titles flash across the display.

"Life is torture, April. At least you can listen to this and enjoy the ride."

I glanced at him. His focus divided between the road and the stereo. A scowl grew as he skipped song after song. And all of this hit me. We're really doing this? Really pretending we were...*friendly*. My breaths sped, racing along with my pulse.

He glanced my way. "Pink. Do you like Pink? I think I have some of hers somewhere."

My stomach rolled violently. I was going to be sick all over his expensive car.

"April?" He glanced my way.

"Pull over."

His scowl deepened.

*"I said pull the fuck over!"* I roared, clawing the doorhandle.

The car swerved hard, pulling us over to the dirt shoulder of the road somewhere an hour out of the city. Rocks kicked up, peppering the underbelly of the car as I yanked the handle and shoved. My belly rolled violently as I stumbled toward the bank of darkened trees. Acid spilled, splashing the grass, leaving me to fall to my knees.

"Jesus, April."

I closed my eyes, unable to get the feel of his body out of my mind. This couldn't be happening. Kyle. Jared. My world was one big battleground. I opened my eyes at the sound of his steps behind me.

I flinched at the touch on my shoulder, shrugging him off. *"Get the fuck off me!"*

"Jesus, April. Take it easy." He sounded hurt.

Hurt while revulsion churned in my stomach, sending me spiraling inside. He stepped away as I swiped the back of my mouth. All I could hear was the crunch of his boots, then the sound of the car door as it opened, then closed. I sucked in a hard breath and shoved to stand, staring into the murky gloom as he returned.

"Here." He handed me a bottle of water.

I turned, meeting his gaze. I expected to find revulsion in his otherwise icy stare. But there wasn't anything like that shining back at me. God, if that was genuine concern in his eyes, I think I'd be sick all over again. This can't be happening. Not with him...anyone else but Kyle.

But he neared, cracking open a bottle of water and handed it to me. He said nothing as I took it and filled my mouth, swishing the liquid around before I spat.

"Better?"

I nodded, handing him back the bottle.

"Keep it, April." He started toward the car and then stopped, staring at the car. "You know, I'm hoping on this drive you can see as someone other than the bad guy."

He left me then, heading back to the driver's side and climbed in. I stared at him, did I just hear right? He wanted me to...*like him?* I sucked in hard breaths as the memory of him came roaring back at me.

But it wasn't disgust I felt.

No...it was worse.

I swallowed a shiver and headed back to the car as the engine started. I climbed in, my belly aching, my nerves fried. Kyle glanced into the side mirror and pulled back out onto the highway. I felt raw and empty, watching him from the corner of my eye as we drove in silence.

"London Grammar." I murmured twenty minutes later.

"What?" He glanced my way.

"You asked what music I like. It's London Grammar."

He frowned. "That's a little serious."

I gave a shrug and turned to the wash of headlights out my window. "You asked."

He moved, holding the wheel with one hand and punched in the detail on his stereo. The smooth, soulful feminine tone filled the car. Seconds was all it took for me to ease into the seat and relax. I twisted, curling my body toward him.

He drove without a word. The dashboard lights and the muffled sound of the car on the road lulled me. I found my eyes closing. Still I fought, forcing them open.

"Sleep, April." Kyle murmured. "You're safe here."

Safe.

Safe with him...

My body still trembled at the feel of him inside me. The feeling carried me down, into the darkness.

I WOKE with the blast of a horn, jerked my eyes open...and found myself in a car. *What the fuck?* The events of last night trickled in slowly. The motel, the bar...then someone grabbing me. The automatic doors of the gas station opened and Kyle strode out, carrying two large coffees. It was morning, still early and barely light outside.

He lifted his head and his gaze collided with mine as he stopped at the door, shifting the cup in his hand to his arm, pressed against his side, and opened the door. The cold rush of air made me shudder as he climbed in and closed the door. "Figured you'd be desperate for a coffee."

"Thanks." I took the cup when he offered, curling my hands around the warmth. "Where are we?"

"About three hours from Allenstown."

"Oh." My mind raced, trying to place where we were. But everything was foggy.

I lifted the cup to my lips, blew gently and then sipped. The brew was bitter and hot, still it was bliss. I licked the plastic rim, catching the drop left behind, drawing Kyle's gaze as he just sat there.

I didn't like this new version of Kyle, nor did I like how he was making me feel. Gratitude felt far too comfortable. I knew Kyle well enough to know that was he dangerous. I focused on his gaze. "Aren't you going to drink?"

"I'd much rather watch you chase the drop of coffee with your tongue."

I stilled, my pulse racing as I met his gaze. He searched my eyes, then slowly reached up, brushing the hair from against my face. I flinched, jerking from his touch. He stilled, a twitch coming at the corner of his mouth before he dropped his hand.

Then in an instant he turned away, dropping his hand to start the engine and put the car into reverse. We didn't speak, not when he pulled out of the service station and kept driving. Not even he stopped a little while later pulling up at a discreet block of amenities. He watched me as I climbed out and headed for the ladies.

It felt strange in this skin, strange wearing these clothes. Clothes Kyle picked out. I tried not to think of that, feeling the weight of his stare as I rounded the building and hurried for the ladies' restroom. Someone else was in the other stall. I used the toilet, sighing at the relief as the woman next to me flushed and stepped out. I followed, opening the door, forcing a smile as our gaze met awkwardly in the mirror and washed my hands.

I looked haunted and strange. These clothes a little too big. I ran my hands down my bodysuit to my waist before washing and walking out. But the moment I stepped out, I spied the pay phone.

"Excuse me." I called to the woman.

The woman stopped and turned. "Yes?"

I winced, hating how desperate I felt. "Do you have any change for the phone?"

She took one look at my expensive clothes as she stood in baggy sweats that looked like the ones I'd left behind in the hotel. "You've got to be shitting me?" With a sigh, she dug into her pocket, pulling out a few coins and stepped closer. "Here."

I took her change. "Thank you."

"Sure." she muttered, then strode away.

I felt like an asshole clutching her money in my hand. Still, my gaze went to the payphone. Jared would be awake by now. Would he be pissed, hurt...*relieved?* I stepped closer to the phone and picked up the receiver. But the moment my fingers touched the button, I froze.

All I could see was the filthy motel room.

All I could feel were his hands on my body.

And hear his lies in my head.

A shudder tore through me. "Why Jared? Why lie to me all this time?"

Pain tore through me with the words. Did I believe Kyle? Not really...but then again, it never felt right. We hid for so long with no word of when we could come home. The haunting questions kept me awake.

I dropped my hand and placed the receiver back down. Maybe it was good for him to find me gone, or maybe he'd never even care...

Maybe it was good for us...*to be done.*

Pain carved through my chest at the sight. I closed my eyes and curled my shoulders. But I refused to cry...I refused to shed one more tear over my stepbrother. I opened my eyes, placed the phone back into the cradle, then made for the car.

Kyle lifted his gaze, watching me as I strode to the passenger's side and climbed in.

"Everything okay?" He asked.

I just stabbed the armrest, waiting for the console to pop open and tossed the coins inside, earning a confused glance from him. "Fine." I muttered. "Let's just drive."

Questions raged in stare. Still, he never voiced them. Just shoved the car into reverse and backed out of the space before driving away.

I left a piece of my heart at that payphone. By the time I realised it, there was no going back. Not for me...or my stepbrother. Instead, I glanced at the man who had once been as much an enemy as anyone could be...and felt a flicker of gratitude.

We drove, heading through the city and it wasn't until we were out the other side he spoke. "Did you call him?"

I froze, swallowing the last sip of warm coffee I had left. "What?"

He glanced my way, the side of his face bathed in the morning sun. Those careful eyes were a little colder, a little more cutting.

"Do you think I'm stupid?" He glanced at the console between us, the one where I threw in the spare change. "Back at the rest stop, you left with nothing and came back with change. So, either you miraculously found a pile of coins in the ladies' bathroom, the moment before some strange woman strode out muttering and shaking her head, or you asked for it." He punched the accelerator harder, driving my body back against the seat. My question is not how you got the money, that's pretty fucking obvious. But I want to know if you used the money and called him...*did you call your stepbrother?"*

My breath caught. Panic rose as I shook my head. "There were no—"

"Liar." He murmured quietly, grabbing his phone and unlocking the screen.

*Payphones in my area*

The question was in the search...and underneath it was a section of a map. One that showed a satellite view of the rest stop we'd been at...and the highlighted pointer showing the phone behind the block of amenities.

"Did you call him...tell me now or so help me God, I'll pull this car over. Did you call your fucking brother to come save you?"

I shook my head, meeting his dangerous stare. The words were right there. The truth mingled with my desperation. I opened my mouth to say exactly what happened...but there was a small part of me that whispered, *what if he's driving me to my death... what then? I needed someone to know where I was.*

Then I answered. "Yes. Yes, I called him."

Kyle froze. There was a twitch in the corner of his eye. A strangled nerve that kicked and bucked, right before he slammed on the brakes...and pulled us over to the side of the road. "Get the fuck out..." He demanded, staring straight ahead. "April, get the fuck out of the car now."

I swallowed hard. My pulse booming...*oh shit.*

# Chapter Seven

KYLE

I SHOVED OPEN THE DOOR, LEAVING THE ENGINE IDLING. The smell of the warm engine pungent in the air as I rounded the front of the car and headed for her.

"No." She stumbled back on the gravelled shoulder of the road, her eyes wide. "Kyle, *stop!*"

But fuck me. There was a spark of defiance in her eyes, lingering under the fear. I lunged, closing the distance between us. She cried out, yanked her hand in front defensively and stumbled backwards. But the shoulder of the road wasn't big enough. She slipped, windmilling her hand instead.

"Fuck!" I grabbed her, pulling her forward hard enough to slam into me.

She clutched hold of my shirt, fisting it as she stared up at me, terrified. I gripped her too hard, I knew that. But she bought out the animal in me. I held her against me, even as she struggled.

"You think Jared is going to come and save you from the goodness of his heart?" I snarled.

She winced, pulling her arms from my hold. "Get *off me, Kyle!*"

I sucked in hard breaths as the memory of that gritstone time with her came back to me. How she looked up at me with those big doe eyes while I gripped her head, making her swallow my cock. *Christ*. I grew hard with the memory. Her mouth stretched wide, that look of utter shame.

I wanted to shame her...

Right here.

*Right now.*

I licked my lips; the words roaring in my mind...*get on your knees, April. Get on your goddamn knees and unzip my pants.* I wanted to make her do it all, unbutton, unzip, slid my cock from my boxers and take it between those lips. I wanted her mouth more than I'd ever wanted anything else in my entire goddamn life.

But I didn't...instead, I released my hold, leaving her to stumble away. "Get back in the goddamn car." I demanded, shifting my gaze to the trees in the distance. "Before you force me to do something, I'll regret."

I caught the movement in the corner of my eye as she opened her mouth to speak. But no words came. She took a slow step backwards before she turned and hurried for the car. I let her go, fighting that primal urge to take her to the ground. I'd have her pants shoved over her ass be inside her in a goddamn second. But that wasn't what I wanted...

Not anymore.

I closed my eyes and sucked in a hard breath. When that bestial side of my nature drew back into the darker corners of my mind, I turned and made for the car, climbing inside and slammed the door closed.

We didn't speak, not for the next few hours and when I pulled over, making the first stop, she climbed out, slamming the door behind and made for the ladies restroom.

"April." I growled out her name.

She stopped, facing away from me. But she never turned, just stared at the restroom door at the gas station and muttered. "Don't worry, Kyle. I'm not running."

I had to take her at her word, but when she walked away like that, it hurt. I forced myself to move, use the restroom and head to the service center, grabbing food while I watched for her through the window.

Heat coursed through my chest as she stepped through the doors, not bothering to look my way. She made her way to the counter, grabbing a sandwich, a water and a packet of gum on the way, like she was seventeen all over again.

She waited at the counter while I grabbed the last of my things.

"You two together?" The attendant grabbed her things, scanning them before he glanced my way.

"Yes." She answered, stony. "We are."

He just gave a shrug and reached for my things, flinching when I handed him my black Amex. I grabbed my things, waiting for her before we headed for the car and climbed in, taking off once more.

The soulful sounds of London Grammar turned into something just as depressing as she took over searching for music. But slowly, that heavy silence between us grew lighter.

"Can we stop at a diner or a park?" She asked. "I need to stretch my legs."

I glance toward her, finding her watching me. "Sure."

The first rest area I found, I pulled in. She moaned, grabbing the small of her back as she climbed out. I narrowed in, finding her pale, her skin shiny with sweat. "April, are you okay?"

She nodded, wavering me away. "I'm fine, I just—"

Her knees buckled in that moment. There was no ending in the sentence as she crashed to the ground.

"*April!*" I roared, driving my body forward and grabbed her from the grass. "What the fuck?"

She shook and shuddered, a bead of sweat beading on her brow before slipping down. I grabbed her, turned and raced for the car, piling her into the seat before I yanked the seatbelt across.

"Wait." She slurred, cracking open her eyes.

"I'm not waiting." I barked, closing the door and around to the front.

But the moment I slid in behind the wheel, I realised I couldn't take her to the damn hospital. Not with her damn name, for every motherfucker to track. "Shit." I glanced her way as she shook and shivered.

I hadn't noticed her unwell before...*why the fuck hadn't I noticed?*

I grabbed my phone and called Brontie's right-hand man, Alex. He answered on the second ring. "Kyle."

"April is sick." I snapped. "She's fucking sick and I can't take her to a damn hospital."

"*Whoa.* Slow, down...what's happening?"

"*Don't tell me to slow down!*" I roared as she winced and shuddered beside me.

She was sick this morning. Christ, she was sick this morning, and I didn't nothing. I shouldn't have pushed her...*fuck, what a damn idiot!*

"Talk to me," Alex brought me back to the moment. "What's happened?"

I told him how she was ill this morning, then she just collapsed.

"She's conscious?" He asked.

I glanced her way, finding her brow furrowed tight. "Yeah."

"And you're what, on the outskirts of Desolation?"

I lifted my gaze to the city skyline. "Yeah."

"Give me five minutes and I'll get back to you with directions. Head for the city, Kyle. We'll get this figured out."

I started the car, shoved it into gear and peeled out of the rest area, punching the accelerator and headed for the city. April moaned, rolling against the seat. "I feel like I'd been kicked in the back."

I reached across the seat and pressed my hand against her forehead. "Christ, you're burning up."

She opened her eyes and looked at me with the kind of desperation that made me catch my breath, my heart hammering before I looked away.

No.

This wasn't good. Not the tightness in my chest at the sight of her like this...or the savage need to rip something apart. Starting with her damn stepbrother.

My phone ran ten minutes later. By then I was strangling the steering wheel, my nerves frayed.

"I'm sending you directions to a private doctor. He's expecting you and don't worry, he's vetted."

Vetted...

More like paid off. I didn't care in this moment. I would've taken her to the Devil himself if he was qualified and kept his mouth shut.

*Beep...*

A message popped up on the screen of my car. I pressed it, watching a map appear with directions. I drove harder, hugging the speed limit and made my way to a towering medical building on the outskirts of the city. By the time I pulled into their car park, my pulse was racing.

I'd never felt this out of control. I climbed out, rounded the front of the car and opened her door.

"Come on." I bent, sliding my arms under her and lifted. "We're going to get you fixed up."

I carried her, locking the car before striding through the automatic doors and headed for the reception. "Dominic Wilde." I snapped.

The woman behind the counter glanced at April in my arms. "And you are?"

"It's fine, Jessica." Came a careful murmur behind me.

I turned, finding a grey-haired older male striding toward me. One look at me and he knew. He lowered his gaze to April in my arms and motioned me forward. "This way."

I carried her after him, through a door and into some kind of secure treatment room.

"Place her on the bed." He gave a wave of his hand. "Then step outside. I'll come and get you when we're done."

I laid her carefully down, watching her grimace with the movement. "I'm staying."

"No, you're not." He turned, grabbed his stethoscope from around his neck and gave a jerk of his head. "Out, or she doesn't get treated, not by me or anyone else here."

I flinched, finding nothing but determination in his eyes.

"Go, Kyle." April moaned, looking at the doctor. "I'll be fine."

But I didn't want to go. *I couldn't go*...not without tearing myself apart.

"I'm going to take good care of her. But I need her to...I need her to talk to me." He mumbled. "Nothing will be recorded. I've made my peace with that. But I refuse to treat someone who isn't honest with me, and that will not happen with you in the room. So, either wait outside, or take her and leave."

I flinched. My breath caught as I looked at her. She was trying to be strong, but her body gave it all away. Her fists were clenched. Her entire body trembled.

"Fine." I lifted my hand and stabbed a finger at the doctor's chest. "But anything happens to her. I'm holding *you* personally responsible."

"I understand." He said calmly.

While I felt out of fucking control. I dragged my fingers through my hair, then turned and stepped out of the treatment room. But I'd be fucked if I was waiting in the goddamn waiting room with all the pathetic husbands.

I froze...*Christ did I just think that?*

I strode out of the door and headed for the rear of the surgery, to a small outdoor area complete with towering palms and a pond.

There I grabbed my phone, called Alex and filled him in on the details, then paced.

Thirty minutes...

Thirty minutes and I thought I was going to lose control. I didn't drive across the country to finally find her and have her taken from me in the blink of an eye. Fuck, I sounded like a man possessed.

More like obsessed.

I shook my head, then turned at the sound of the door.

"I figured I'd find you here, Mr. Blackburn."

I scowled, taking a step closer. "Is she okay?"

He stopped walking, meeting my gaze. "It depends what you consider 'okay'"

Panic rose inside me. "If you don't come straight with me, doc, I'll go fucking insane."

"I figured that was the case..." he looked away, seeming to fight with his own conscience. "What I'm about to tell you is sensitive, and it's only because of your current circumstance, I'm willing to stay anything out of patient confidentiality at all."

Mt stomach dropped as I stepped closer. "Then tell me...tell me. Now."

# Chapter Eight

JARED

I STEPPED OUT OF THE STORE AND ADJUSTED THE COLLAR OF my black shirt, then dropped my hand to my designer jeans. My pulse was still thundering from the moment I swiped my credit card, knowing full well it'd come up on their systems.

If I thought they weren't waiting for me to surface, then I'd be wrong. The growl of a Hemi engine drew my gaze as the black Chrysler pulled up against the curb in front of me and a driver climbed out.

"Mr. Barnett." He strode around the rear of the vehicle.

"Yes." I lifted my bag, filled with brand new clothes and opened my hand, taking the keys from him.

"It's all fueled and ready for you, sir." He tried to hold my gaze as I pressed the button for the boot and stowed my bag inside before closing the boot.

"Thank you." I muttered, yanking open the driver's door and slid behind the wheel.

I knew exactly where they were. Kyle was taking my stepsister. The one place I didn't want to go—right into the Devil's lair.

I pressed the button, started the V8 engine and shoved the car into gear. They had a head start on me, at least five hours. But I'd drive day and night if I had to...I wouldn't let her face Brontie alone.

I pulled out, tires squealing as I pulled into the traffic and hit the button on my cell, calling my father. It took him five rings to answer. That only meant one thing. He was dealing with Connie.

"I'm here." He murmured into the phone.

The heavy thud of his steps echoing through the speaker before the soft click of a lock.

"Any information?"

"None as yet." He answered. "But its early days. Are you on the road?"

"Yes." I pushed the car harder, making my way to the on-ramp to the freeway that'd take me out of the city. "My cover is blown. They'll track me."

"Then I'll be expecting a visit." He muttered. "But if Brontie thinks he's going to make me bend like I did before, then he's in for a nasty fucking surprise. I won't crumble this time...won't break."

"You do, father and this time we won't have to worry about them sending a hitman to our door...because I'll kill you myself."

"April..." He started. "You need to get her back. If they tell her the truth."

"She won't believe them, anyway." I answered as pressed the button activating the cruise control. "I made sure of that."

"Are you that convinced? Do you have her...handled?"

"I have her handled." I murmured, remembering the way she looked at me. "Have Leon call me if they come."

"I will...and Jared."

Silence filled the air.

"Thank you."

I winced and reached out, hitting the button and ending the call. I was serious about what I said. Father or no father, what he made me do was sickening...even for me. I gripped the steering wheel and focused on the road, stopping in some small town about an hour out of the city.

There, I grabbed a toothbrush and toothpaste, some soap and a towel. I'd sleep in truck stops, shower in service stations. I'd eat as I drove. Every second was precious. More precious than anything else at this moment.

Brontie's men would track me, pinning markers along the map the further I drove. I focused on the freeway as it blurred. White lines faded into one until it was all I could see, until she came. The one I never wanted, the one I shouldn't have wanted...and still I did. God help me, I did.

I licked my lips and deepened my breaths, still seeing her as I did that first night. Her fingers were deep inside her pussy as she sat on the toilet of our bathroom. The sound of my name, a guttural groan from her lips.

Fuck, I'd never seen something so desperate, so raw and humiliated. She made me as hard as she did now. My little stepsister. I winced at the thought. It shouldn't have happened... none of this should've happened. Not to her and not like this.

I dragged my fingers through my hair and glanced into the rear-view mirror. New clothes were one thing, but nothing could hide the dark circles and haunted look in my eyes. Nothing could hide the truth...that I was a fucking monster.

The end result of something that was used to manipulate and destroy.

But it didn't start with me...and it wouldn't end there either.

Not unless I blew the entire thing sky high.

Only then would she be truly safe.

But could I do it? Could I expose one of the most corrupt and sadistic manipulation rings to ever exist? One, my own father was part of? That thought filled me as I drove, pushing the Chrysler to the speed limit as I inched my way closer to her.

I stopped three hours later, refueled and grabbed some food before climbing back into the car. By the afternoon, my mind felt heavy. No matter how hard I tried, I couldn't shift the thought of exposing them all...including my own father.

It was the only way she'd truly be safe. I'd keep her name out of the media, pay to have it suppressed. Kyle would go down with the others like the piece of shit he was. I clenched my grip around the steering wheel, strangling the damn thing like I wanted to strangle them.

By the afternoon my calves were cramping, even with the cruise control. I pulled into the gas station, refuelled and parked, walking around the building to the restrooms. The place was filthy, but no different to the damn hovels we'd been living in.

I used the stall, unzipping my fly and pulled my out my cock as a snarling came from the cubicle beside me. Mutters followed as that hot stream shot out, splashing against the stained enamel. The door flew in the cubicle beside me flew open with a *bang!* I ground my jaw, listening to footsteps before the door was yanked open, then slowly closed Hinges squealing with the force.

Filthy animal hadn't even bothered to wash his damn hands. I winced, tucked myself back in and hit the button. The roar of the water filled the space as I unlocked the door and stepped out...coming face to face with a guy just standing there.

I flinched, glanced behind him. I hadn't heard anyone come in... that's when it dawned. No one had.

"Fucking stink." He muttered, looking at me with blood-shot eyes. "Stink like them...like the—" he wrenched his hand up and bashed the side of his head with a clenched fist. "Like those rich assholes."

I licked my lips, then spoke carefully. "I just want to get past." I moved to the side, drawing his focus.

His head snapped upwards, hate blinding in his eyes, driving home as he curled thick lips over yellowed teeth. "You think you can tell me what to do?"

I swallowed and shook my head. "No."

"'Cause you motherfuckers are all the same." He lifted his other hand...

That's when I saw it, the long, honed shank that's been once a screwdriver and now was a fucking weapon. My heart clenched tight, igniting the booming sound of my pulse.

"I don't know you." I said carefully. "I don't know you at all."

"Rich fuckers." He spat and stabbed the weapon at me. "Give me your money."

"No."

"What?" He spat.

"I said no. I'm not going to do that."

He stepped closer, gripping the screwdriver. "Give...me...your...*fucking...money.*"

I swallowed, holding myself still before he stumbled forward, driving the end of that fucking shank toward me. But there was nowhere to move, wedged between the stalls and the wall. I grabbed his wrist, wrestling with him as he charged, pushing me backwards.

Grunts echoed in my ears. His. Mine. He was strong, incensed by fucking madness. I lifted my hand, watching the honed steel edge come closer, aiming at my stomach.

*April...*

Her face filled me as a man twice my sized and hyped up on some fucking drug unleashed a roar and slammed me backwards until I hit the wall at the end of the toilet stalls. My head slammed backwards, hitting with a *crack!*

Stars tore through my head. Bursting behind my eyes with neon white. Still, I never lost my grip, twisting my body as agony cleaved through my mind and yanked him toward me with all I hard, then moved.

Stepping to the side as the drugged-up asshole drove headfirst into the tiles. His footing slipped, sending him crashing to the floor. I acted before I knew. The rage I'd suppressed since getting that message from Kyle broke free.

Cold.

Hard.

*Rage.*

I unleashed, slamming my fist into the side of his face. He hit the tiles with a sickening *crunch.* Blood spurted from his nose.

But I didn't stop...*I couldn't stop.* Blow after blow, they became a blur of red, until my knuckles throbbed and he let out a sickening moan. His arms, a cage over his head, protecting him from my fists.

Hard breaths consumed me as I stumbled from the exertion and hit the wall, sucking in hard breaths. He moaned, bloody and ruined, curled into a ball against the stained, broken tiled wall.

Until I shoved upwards and stumbled out of the bathroom... making sure to wash my hands before I left. But I didn't lift my gaze at the mirror. Didn't see the monster I'd become.

I left the bathroom, stumbling out and headed for the Chrysler parked at the end of the gas station. I unlocked and climbed back in...my head roaring with rage.

*Beep.*

My phone buzzed with an incoming call. I glanced at the Chrysler's display. *Caller Unknown.*

Unknown.

But they knew me.

I hit the button and answered the call. "Yeah?"

"Jared?" April's voice cut through the speaker. "It's me..."

# Chapter Nine

KYLE

I STARED AT THE DOCTOR AND CLENCHED MY FIST. HIS words resounded in my head, along with that wince of sympathy. "I'm sorry, but it's just too risky."

I swallowed hard, then shifted my gaze. "I understand."

"Hospital—"

"No goddamn hospital, doctor. I'll take care of it."

I left him behind, striding to the door to the surgery and pushed through. My mind was a blur of words and medical terminology. None of which I gave a damn about. But what it boiled down to, I did...very much so. I turned, striding back to his offices and yanked open the door.

Rage seethed inside me, blistering the edges of my soul. If Jared was here, I would've beaten the spineless fucking prick to an inch of his goddamn life.

I wanted to...

*Christ, I wanted to.*

I strode through the door and headed to the doctor's office, hearing April's faint voice as I stepped inside. She lifted her gaze, her hand placing the handset on the phone back into the cradle. *What the fuck?* I wanted to tear my focus from her hand, but I couldn't. Her fingers shook, the tremors racing along her arm into her body.

"Stop staring at me like that." She gripped the edge of the desk and tried to stand.

But her knees buckled, sending her crashing to the floor.

*"Jesus!"* I lunged, grabbing her arm at the last minute, then picked her up, easing her back against the hard bed.

"I'm okay." She whispered.

But she was anything *but* okay. Her skin was pale...so goddamn pale and her eyes were dark and sunken, like she hadn't slept in a goddamn month. She probably hadn't.

Footsteps came from behind me before the doctor gently cleared his throat. "I'm stressing how important it is for you to get expert care here. You need to be monitored and be on an intravenous drip with antibiotics. A severe kindness infection like this is no joke."

"No one's laughing." I answered, staring at her.

"No hospital." April shook her head.

"Then I *implore* you to stay in the city for a few nights at least." The doctor headed for his desk and pulled out his chair. "I'll write you a prescription for the most powerful antibiotics you can get over the counter. It will take longer to get into your system than what can give you in an IV. But if you insist on no admittance, then this is the best I can do.

He scribbled on his notepad, then tore off the script and handed it to me. I just stared at the sheet in his outstretched hand and winced.

"It's fine." April tried to push up on trembling arms and slid her feet from the bed. "I can take care—"

The moment her feet hit the ground, she fell once more. "Jesus Christ, April!" I grabbed her, yanking her against me. She was so fucking thin...*too thin.* Which was the entire fucking reason for her collapse. I braced her against me with one hand, reached out and snatched the damn prescription with the other.

"Come on. We're getting the fuck out of here."

She cried out when I lifted her. Her spine arched, fingers dug into my arm as her face twisted with pain. I looked at the phone on his desk once more, then hauled her into my arms. "It's fine, doc." I turned, shoved the script into my pocket and strode for the door.

I yanked the handle, making my way out into the reception with April in my arms. The receptionists watched me as I left, heading out the door and made for the Maserati once more.

April whimpered with each step, gripping my arm, agony tearing across her face. I slowed my steps, rolling my feet as I walked. That tortured look on her face eased to some sickened look as I eased to the side of the car and opened the passenger's door. I was as gentle as I could, easing her inside and lowered her to the seat. "You okay?"

A sheen of sweat glistened on her bow and beaded across her top lip. Her breaths were fast, panting, making her pupils wide until they swallowed the brown.

"Y-yeah."

I winced, gripped her arm, bending low to stare into her eyes. "Don't lie to me...don't *ever* lie to me."

"You mean like you lie to me?" She murmured, then lifted her gaze to mine.

I pulled away from her, closed the door and strode around the front of the car, my hands clenched in fists before I yanked open the driver's door and slipped behind the wheel.

"Seatbelt." I muttered, stabbed the button and started the engine.

Watching her from the corner of my eye before I swore under my breath as she lifted her arm and caught her breath. I leaned across, making sure not to press against her and yanked the belt across, snapping it in place.

"I'm getting you the Hell out of here." I muttered, slid backwards in the seat and shoved the car into gear.

I drove as careful as I could, used one hand to press the button calling Alex.

"How is she?"

"Infected." I muttered and cast her a look as I drove out of the car park and into the street. "The meeting needs to be delayed."

"Impossible."

She stiffened, grabbed the armrest as I hit the street and turned. I winced, muttered under my breath and tapped the brakes, slowing the sports car. My pulse was racing, mind spinning out of control. "Then make it possible."

"You know that can't happen, Kyle."

I snatched the phone from the cradle, pressed the button, switching it from hands free to direct as I snarled. "I'm not asking...I'm telling. We're holing up here for a couple of days.

She's too sick...to sick to keep driving. So it's that or she's in the goddamn hospital."

"That happens and she's dead."

"Exactly. Which is why we're staying in a goddamn motel until it's safe for her to move."

"*Shit...* " He muttered. "Okay, how long?"

I glanced her way. "As long as it takes."

"Where?"

"Where ever you find us a place, text me the address. I'll punch it into the GPS. And Alex...make it nice." I pressed the button and ended the call, making my way to the city centre and pulled up outside a row of boutique shops. "Wait here."

I climbed out, closed the door behind me, making my way to the drugstore and handed over the prescription to be filled. I grabbed a handful of other items, toiletries I hadn't had a chance to get for her before, then placed them on the counter. "Ring those up when it's ready. I'll come back."

The assistant just nodded and stared. I ignored her, leaving the drugstore behind. I glanced at her, fighting that flare of panic as I prepared myself to find the car empty and her gone.

But she wasn't. She had her head tilted back, eyes closed. Relief washed over me as I strode into the small sports clothing store, grabbing a few items before walking out.

*Beep.*

I glanced at my cell, finding an address to the hotel. So I clicked the link, letting it load before finding my way back to the drugstore. By the time I climbed back into the car, Anna's teeth were chattering so hard, the gnashing sound made me wince.

"Here." I yanked open the brown bag, grabbed out the pain killers first and a bottle of electrolytes before cracking the lid.

I pressed out the tablets, and handed her the drink, watching as she took them with shaking hands. The longer I watched, the more enraged I became. Sonofagoddamnbitch.

He did this...

Letting her live in squalor.

Living on fucking scraps for food and tainted, rusted water from the taps.

He fucking did this to her.

She deserved better...

*You mean, you?* The thought surfaced as she swallowed the painkillers. Then I cracked open the bottle for the antibiotics and handed them over. But my mind didn't give me an answer. Did I want April for my own?

I didn't know. Did I want her? *Sure.*

But was it out of jealousy and spite? Or was it something else? She took a last swallow and handed the bottle back to me. "T-thank you." She closed her eyes and tilted her head back once more.

I started the engine and pulled out, making sure I took care, braking softer, turning gentler and when I pulled into the car park of the hotel I slipped out, rounding the car to the passenger's seat.

Her breaths were slower and steady, eyelids barely flickering open when I opened her door, unbuckled her bet and gently lifted her from the car. I carried her inside, checking in with a mutter and a glare, before their concierge scurried after me all the way to the penthouse suite.

The room came with a butler and its own concierge. I tossed him the keys with instructions to bring our things to the room while I strode into the expansive bedroom overlooking the city with walls made of glass and gently lowered her to the bed.

Any other time I'd take my time with the view, taking comfort with a glass of scotch as I watched day turn to night and the true face of the city to be revealed. But I cared about none of that now, instead as I laid her gently on the bed, I pressed the button, turning the now afternoon into night time in the blink of an eye.

Our things were carried up and unpacked. I ordered food, drink, a few things she might need and waited for the staff to leave with a nod. The door clicked as it closed and we were alone.

She shuddered and shook, her teeth chattering, arms wrapped herself around her body as though she was freezing. I rolled up my sleeves, bending over to press the back of my hand against the furnace of her forehead.

*Malnourishment, kidney infection that's been left untreated. Dehydration and a fragile state of mind.* The doctor's words rang in my ears. *I don't know what you're doing with this girl, but if you continue to treat her like this, then her body will shut down and she could die.*

Could die.

I winced with the words, touching her forehead, then brushed the strands of her hair from her face. Her eyes were closed, breaths a shudder as I leaned down and gently kissed her.

I didn't kiss...

Not like this.

I took and demanded. I didn't care.

So why the fuck was this now changing?

# Chapter Ten

I was so cold...so very cold, shifting, moving. Searching and finding warmth at my back, then scooted backwards. There was a grunt, but I didn't care. I was frozen on the inside, unable to feel alive. A dull ache spread along my back as I rolled, reaching out, finding a broad chest.

Jared...

Jared was here.

"I missed you." I whispered, sliding my leg over his, craving every pulse of his radiating heat. I'd climb inside him if I could.

He wrapped his arms around me, drawing me close, pulling up the comforter until I sank into it like a cocoon. My breath blew back against him, and I was filled with his scent. Deep, masculine. My breaths slowed, that darkness came for me once more.

I slept, dreaming of bright lights and dirty motel rooms.

Until the fantasy took hold.

"Little sister." He called.

"Stepsister." I reminded him as he strode toward me wearing the most stunning black tuxedo I'd ever seen.

He still made my heart flutter.

"Even if he hurt you." Came the faintly familiar voice at my right.

I turned, watching Kyle stride toward me wearing an open white collared shirt against fitted black trousers. Those dark eyes glinted with cruelty. He stopped in front of me. I lifted my gaze to his as he lifted his hand, his thumb smoothing the bottom of my lip with a possessive stroke. "You're just a game to him."

My pulse stammered, then raced to catch up. "I'm just a game to both of you."

Movement came at the corner of my eye. I glanced toward Jared as he came closer, moving to stand at my back.

"He can't be trusted, April." Jared murmured in my ear.

"No." Kyle's glare was icy at my stepbrother. "He can't..."

Jared lifted his hands and gripped my shoulders, his lips finding my shoulder. Hands landed on my hips. I knew who's hands they were. Big hands circled my waist as Jared's lips moved higher, moving to the long line of my neck.

I dropped my head to the side, letting him go where he wanted as Kyle knelt in front of me. I was so powerful in this moment, so in control of these two powerful men. Men who were all mine and as I lifted my head, that pool room from my old home beckoned.

The blue felt top of the pool table.

Memories hovered in the back of my mind.

Cruel twisted memories.

And in the middle of that games room stood a tripod, the cameras angled at us. I reached over my shoulder, sliding my fingers through Jared's hair and stared into the camera.

*Just a game...*

*That's all this was.*

*Just a game.*

And they were playing to win.

"April." Kyle called, sliding his hands along my thigh, sliding my dress higher. "April, you're dreaming." He slowly rose, drawing my dress up and over my head. "You're just dreaming."

"I know." I whispered, raising my arms over my head. "I'd never let this happen otherwise."

Jared reached round, his hands moving to cover my bare breasts as he kissed my neck. I let them touch me, let them undress me. Let them take me down to the floor.

"It's just a dream." Jared whispered as he lowered his mouth to my breasts.

Warmth moved over my breasts as Kyle sank lower, gently driving my knees apart. "A beautiful, dangerous dream." He murmured, lowering his head to kiss the inside of my thighs. Then he moved higher.

His mouth found my slit, his tongue pushing deep as he worked his way to my clit. I was all about me in this moment. Their touch, their desire...was all focused on my desire.

Until pain stabbed along my back, making me cry out.

"April."

I wrenched open my eyes to darkness and cried out.

"Easy." Something cold and wet pressed against my forehead. "I got you." Kyle pressed a cool cloth to my forehead. "Jesus, you're burning up."

He moved in the bed, sending a wave of agony tearing through my body. I unleashed a cry as he picked me up, lifting me from the bed. My body stiffened as I grabbed my back. The agony was consuming, stabbing, cleaving, until it was all there was.

Every step was agony, every rock and roll and twist made me whimper until the hiss of the water sounded. Cold rushed over me, like ice against my skin. I screamed, the sound muffled and blubbered under the freezing spray.

"I got you." The words resounded through his chest. I turned my head, burying my face against his body.

I needed his heat...his warmth. I needed. "Please."

"Hold on to me."

I did, my fingers driving against the muscles of his arm. Somewhere in the back of my mind, I knew it must've hurt. But I was helpless to stop it, swallowed by the agonising throbbing that coursed across my lower back and lunged inside.

So, I gripped him, holding on while the freezing water splashed against my face and soaked through to my skin.

"Easy, now...*easy.*"

My teeth gnashed. Body jerked and spasmed until that bitter sting of the icy water eased. The seizures slowed, leaving me flinching instead.

"There you go." That deep tone resonated.

I eased my grip around his arm, sliding my hands around his waist and lowered my body, pressing the side of my face against his stomach. His hands were gentle and sure, smoothing sodden strands of my hair from my face as the cold water rushed over us sitting on the shower floor...and slowly the shudders eased.

I closed my eyes, giving into the feel of his hands and the sound of his voice as he soothed me. The water turned warm against my face until it slowly ended. Weightless. That's how I felt.

Weightless and boneless.

Something slid against my skin before a *plop* came next to me. Then softness...softness and warmth and the feel of his hands.

"Kyle..." I whispered.

The movement stilled. "Yeah?"

"T-thank you."

He never continued, not in words at least, dragging the towel across my hair, then my face before wrapping it around me. Strong arms lifted me. He was sure and powerful, carrying me from the bathroom. His wet feet slopping against the tiles, until the dull came from soft carpet.

My body sank into the bed, my head against the soft pillow before the towel was tugged from me. I shivered for a second before the covers were pulled high. Kyle left me then, his steps growing fainter as he walked back into the bathroom.

The *click* of the light snagged my focus. I cracked open my eyes, watching as he strode naked from the bathroom, running the towel through his hair. My body ached and throbbed. The pain dull and gnawing. Still, I watched him as he stared at me in the faint wash of the lights.

There were no words between us.

There rarely was.

Just action.

Just touch.

That raw brutality that burned between us from the moment we met.

"Why?" The word was a croak. "Why are you being nice to me?"

He stepped closer, standing above me. His cock was soft and swaying as he ruffled the towel through his hair. Then he stopped and leaned down, bracing his hands on the side of the bed.

The answer was right there, sparking in the depths of his stare. One that seemed to plunge deeper than the tremors that coursed through me. Deeper than anything else I'd ever felt before. His lips parted, his breath a rush.

He looked like a God in this moment, bare, beautiful and commanding. "I don't know." He finally murmured. "I just don't know."

I waited for more, but there was nothing else to say. He was just as conflicted as I was. Just as awkward and as tense. Just as scared...

He rose, dragged the towel from around his shoulders and wrapped it around his body. I didn't want him, not like that. Not in this moment. Still, I couldn't help myself staring, taking in the hard ridges of his toned stomach and the V at his hips. But it was his chest that drew my gaze. That warm, expansive chest I laid my head against, taking comfort where I could.

He seemed to understand. Walking around the foot of the bed and climbed in between the sheets, moving against me.

I slowly turned, sliding my arm around him, my head instantly finding the crook of his shoulder. His arm went around me, pulling me in close. I'd fucked Kyle, and I'd let him fuck me. But in this moment, with my head pressed against his chest and his arms wrapped around me, this felt more like a betrayal than anything I'd ever done.

Before was a matter of survival.

But this...this was because I wanted to.

I closed my eyes, seeing Jared's face. Tears slipped from the corners of my eyes. I lay there, crying...and finally slept.

# Chapter Eleven

DARKNESS HELD ME UNDER, COMMANDING DARKNESS, until it slowly brightened. I crackled open my eyes, finding nothing but gloom. I waited for the howl of sirens, for the screams that always came with living in seedy motels, but there was none of that. There was just the soft muffled drove of cars somewhere in the distance.

The cool air was clean and crisp, drawing me closer to the surface. I blinked, coming away and shifted my foot, finding clean, cold sheets, then slowly lifted my head. Kyle was asleep in the chair next to the bed, his head dropped low, still wearing his clothes from yesterday...or I think it was yesterday.

An ache moved through my body as I pushed upwards. I winced and bit down. But the moment I rose, he cracked open his eyes and lifted his head. I froze, finding his stare.

"Morning." He said carefully.

"Morning."

He lowered his gaze, searching my body, but for some reason I knew this time it wasn't sexual.

"Are you in pain?"

I shook my head. "Maybe a little."

"Thirsty?" He pushed upwards, dislodging a damn cloth that dropped from the armrest of the seat to fall to the ground with a *splat.*

I licked arid lips and nodded. "Yes."

He moved soundlessly, bare feet padding against the carpet. But I couldn't look away from his crumpled white shirt, which looked like he slept in it. Had he been awake all night? The heavy ache in my bones whispered the truth, *yes.*

Memories came back to me. The icy shower, his hands running that cold cloth against my across my forehead and around my neck. *Easy, April. His* soothing, deep voice resounded in my head, making me catch my breath.

The sound of a refrigerator opening came from outside the bedroom.

He'd taken care of me. Not just watched me from the armchair next to the bed either, but wiped my face, given me pain killers, carried me to the shower to break my fever. Which is why I felt so goddamn achy.

Footsteps resounded as he came back carrying a large glass filled with what looked like Apple juice. He held my gaze, handing it over. The first sip was icy, tearing through my teeth. I winced, then sipped slowly until my mouth became used to the sensation.

He moved away, grabbing a bottle of pills and shook out two large white tablets, then a smaller pill before handing them over. "Pain killers and antibiotic."

I took them, vaguely remembering me doing the same thing before. "How long have we been here?"

"Two days."

I met his gaze. He gave a shrug. "Fridge is stocked. Room service is fast and enjoyable. Made sense."

"Sure." I swallowed the tablets and turned, holding the glass in my hand.

Exhaustion hit me, and that dull ache across my back returned. "What happened to me?"

"What do you remember?"

I tried to think. The car ride, the park. Then I collapsed and found myself at some random doctor's surgery. "The doctor. He was nice."

"And insistent. You had an infection, a serious one. You're just lucky I could talk him out of admitting you to hospital."

"Talk him out of, or the threaten?" I glanced his way.

He said nothing. That gave me the answer I needed. I took a sip, then glanced around the expansive room. "So what now?"

"Now we leave." He took a step toward the bedroom, then stopped, turning to me once more. "When you're ready. Are you up for this, April? Tell me if you're not and we can stay."

"I thought we had to go."

He scowled, thinking, then answered. "Yes. We do."

The low, dull pain in my back was insistent, but not like the agony it was before. "Then we'll go."

He waited, then slowly gave a nod. "I'll take a shower." He murmured. "Then when you're ready, we'll go."

He walked into the bedroom. I lifted the glass of apple juice, sipping it as the hiss of the water came floating through the door.

I took a step, drawn by the sound and stepped back into the bedroom.

The hiss was so loud, steam billowed from the doorway, enticing me to step in.

But once I did...

Once I did, everything would change.

I glanced at the rumpled sheets on the bed and that damn cloth in a pile on the floor where it fell. He took care of me. He was savage with the doctor, demanding, furious. Then when he carried me from the car, he was so gentle, so unbelievably gentle.

My clothes stuck to my body, damn with sweat and smelling foul. I stepped into the bathroom doorway, then into the steam that wafted from the shower and placed my glass on the bathroom counter.

He turned as I gripped my shirt and dragged it over my head, then reached around and unhooked my bra. Kyle never once moved, just stood there under the spray. Rivulets ran down over his hard chest and plunged down his stomach.

I couldn't help but look. Strong legs and powerful thighs. A small thatch of dark hair around his long, soft cock. A cock I'd had inside me. I shivered and shoved down my pants before stepping into the spray. He moved to the side, letting the warm rain over my arms and then over my shoulder.

There was nothing sexual in this moment, and yet everything was sexual with Kyle. He reached for the bar of soap as I tilted my head back.

"It'll take us another two days to get there." He started talking, running the soap over my shoulder and along my arm. "When we get there, you're going to need to be careful. There'll be people you'll meet with. Brontie for one, but there are others. You're going to need to keep your wits about you. Do you understand what I'm saying?"

I closed my eyes at the sound of his voice. "Yes."

"No matter what they say, you need to keep your cool. It's all a game to them, everything. The game for you is to not let your emotions run away. You trust them with your heart and you'll get hurt."

"Don't trust them." I murmured as he stopped rubbing my body.

The squeeze of a bottle came. Sure fingers rubbed my hair and massaged my scalp. I let him touch where he wanted to, melting into the feel of his care. A feeling that was starting to become a little too familiar.

"They might not let me in there with you." His voice deepened, as though he didn't like that at all.

As though he was scared...And I was guessing for Kyle that was something he wasn't accustomed to.

I opened my eyes as he smoothed conditioner down the strands of my hair, then found the worry in his stare. "I'm stronger than I look."

He scowled, but there was more than fear in his eyes. Stars ignited as his fingers stilled, combing through my hair, then he bent and kissed me. Only this wasn't the cruel, savage way he'd been before. This kiss was soft and passionate, giving away far more than he wanted.

My pulse raced, body softened, making me turn and lift my arms, wrapping them around his neck. I didn't want to feel like this about Kyle, didn't want to feel this way about anyone. My heart only made me vulnerable and right now, more than ever, that wasn't a good thing.

He broke the kiss, pulling away enough to look into my eyes. My body shivered with his touch as he dragged his fingers along the underside of my arm, skirting the outside of my breast. This was getting far too real between us...far too...everything.

"Are you ready for this?"

My breath caught. Ready for what? Him...them...wasn't it all the same?

"No." I answered. "But I'll do it, anyway."

He gave a small smile, then reached up, angling the water down my hair as he washed the conditioner from my hair and then switched off the shower. We dried, then dressed before he grabbed our luggage and carried it all from the room, leading the way to the elevator. He carried our things to the car, stoking them away before opening the passenger's door for me to slip inside.

Everything was different with us now. He reached across, grabbing my hand and placed it on his thigh before he started the engine and pulled out of the parking garage. By the time we hit the city streets, the morning sun was only just rising, giving way to a brand new day.

...and a new beginning for us.

That terrified me, more than ever before.

# Chapter Twelve

## JARED

I stared at my cell as the screen went dead. For a second I couldn't think...I couldn't speak.

She called me...

April sounded weak, desperate. Her hushed words were nothing more than a whisper that spilled through the phone. Still, she called. She called me. My pulse raced at the thought as I strode back to the Chrysler and climbed inside. I tried to get information from her, find out where she was and what happened. But she was vague, not giving me anything other than the fact that she was safe...and with Kyle.

*Fucking Kyle.*

I wanted to strangle the bastard. I clenched my fists around the steering wheel, drawing in the rich scent of the leather and froze. *"Fuck!"*

Dark thoughts burned in my mind. I'd kill him...I stared at my hands around the wheel. I could almost feel them around his neck. I'd kill him, nice and slow. Take a knife to his pretty face. I'd cut him...

*I'd fucking cut him.*

I glanced at my cell before I grabbed it, unlocked the screen and brought up the call log. The number was right there. *Incoming...*

I pressed the number, listening to the phone ring before it diverted.

"Doctor Wilde's office." A woman answered.

I scowled, stared at the dashboard...*Doctor Wild?*

"I had a call from there, a woman...April—."

"Is she a patient, Sir?"

*A patient?* Panicked thoughts moved through my mind. "N—I don't know. *Maybe.*"

"I'm sorry, Sir. There's nothing coming up by that name."

"There has to be...it was fifteen minutes ago. Check again."

I listened to her typing, scanning the patient logs. "Nope. Nothing."

"Look again." I demanded.

The cheeriness slipped from her tone. There was no typing this time. "I'm *sorry*, Sir. But there's nothing by that name."

"She was just there."

"I'm sorry—"

*"I don't want you to be fucking sorry."* I spat.

The call went silent, then she responded in a bitter tone. "I'm hanging up now. Like I said...I'm really sorry."

"Wai—"

But the call was dead. Wild...*Wild*...I bought up my phone and punched in the number, tracing it to a doctor in Desolation.

*Desolation...*that's not too far from here. I stabbed the button, starting the car and pulled out of the parking lot and back onto the freeway.

I drove hard, punching the accelerator and forced the speedometer to climb. I hit the GPS, bringing up the map. Two hours. Two hours until hit the city limits. I checked the rear-view mirror and pushed the car harder, risking the attention of the cops.

By the time I hit the city limits I was cold, savage, glancing at the GPS and followed the directions to a sleek, towering building and pulled up outside. My hands were shaking, fear filled me, but desperation was there, snuffing out any voice inside my head that whispered, *maybe I shouldn't do this?*

All I heard was April's small voice on the other end of the call...and all I saw was Kyle's fucking cock in the video footage he sent me. Jealousy burned inside me. I wanted this rage to burn because she was in danger. At least she was on her own. But when I opened myself to that anger, it was selfish and cruel.

I wanted her because *he* wanted her.

I wanted her because she belonged to *me.*

I reached over, yanked open the glove box and reached inside. The car had been hired, and damn well expensive, but that wasn't the only request when I called. I gripped the cold steel and pulled the gun free, leaning forward to tuck it against the small of my back before I turned my gaze to the front door.

It was late, almost closing...but not quite. I still had time.

I shoved open my door and climbed out, scanning the car park as I headed to the front door and strode in. The reception was busy, the phone still ringing non-stop. And voice that answered was chirpy and familiar. The same woman who answered my call smiled her fake smile, wearing her headset and typed frantically on the keyboard in front of her.

"Can I help?"

I glanced toward a brunette who stepped around the end of the counter and the brass plague engraved with the doctor's names. "Dominic Wilde."

"Do you have an appointment?" She stepped back around the counter and headed for the computer.

"No."

She stopped, forced a smile. "Oh, did you need to make one?"

"No. I glanced at the others. The woman with headset glanced my way.

She scowled for a second, glanced at the other receptionist, then back to me as I reached around my back and grabbed my gun. "I want to talk to him...*now.*" She didn't understand at first, not until I lifted the gun and sat it carefully on the counter. "Dominic Wilde."

The phone rang and rang and *rang.*

"No..." The brunette glanced at the gun, and then me. Before she did the one fucking thing I didn't want her to do...*she ran.*

I snatched the gun from the counter and lunged, slamming into her before she reached the end of the cupboards. She let out a shriek, one that turned savage and loud as I grasped a handful of her hair and yanked hard.

Her spine bowed, tears were in her eyes as I snapped. "Why the fuck would you do that?"

Panicked cries echoed through the waiting room. I lifted my head, scanning the elderly and a woman with a toddler perched on her hip. "Stupid fucking bitch!" I snarled and shoved her forward.

She stumbled, throwing up her hands to brace against the cupboard before she hit.

"Wilde..." I demanded. *"Now."*

And under the sound came a deep, throaty murmur. Heads turned as a silver-haired man wearing an open-collared white shirt and black trousers headed our way, walking with an older woman.

"So I'll see you next week, Mary." He smiled as he glanced my way...and then smile faltered.

He glanced at the receptionist, then the gun in my hand. It didn't take a genius to know it was him. Dominic Wilde.

"Office...*now.*" I demanded.

Cries tore through the reception as I strode forward. But I didn't lift the gun, didn't shove it in his damn face, although I wanted to.

"I'm calling the police." The blonde in front of the computer muttered, her fingers moving before I knew.

Anger lashed, and that panic I'd tried so hard to keep check punched its way to the surface. But I didn't need to answer...

"No." Dominic Wild shook his head. "No need for that, Stacey. I'll take care of this." She slowly stood as Dominic turned, then glanced my way over his shoulder. "This way."

He walked carefully, as though he were somehow expecting me. I took one look toward the receptionist and followed, stepping through glass double doors to the large, expansive office inside.

"I knew this wasn't over." He turned, glanced at the gun in his hand. "Are you here to kill me?"

"Kill you?"

He swallowed hard and met my gaze. "You're a hitman, right? Kyle...sent you?"

"Kyle sent me?" I snarled. I took a step closer. "No. But the woman...I want to know about the woman."

He stilled, scowled. "Why?'

"Why?" I stepped closer, bent down to brace my hand against the side of the desk and glared at him. "Because he's my goddamn stepsister."

He flinched, his eyes widening.

"He fucking *took* her from me. *He took what wasn't his to take.*" I glanced at the splayed files on top of his desk. "She was here...*why?*"

He shook his head, but then he moved, leaning forward. His arm sliding across the desk...as though he tried to keep something from me. My pulse stuttered, then grew louder until the booming sound filled my head. "She was here...*wasn't she?*"

He shook his head.

"She was *fucking* here."

He swallowed hard before he lunged, grabbed the shack of files, but I was already moving, shoving him aside. My anger igniting like fuel. I shoved him aside. He fought a little, grasping the edges of the coloured folders and wrenched them from his grasp.

I stared at the names, throwing aside one, and then another... and another.

Until I came to a file unmarked.

I opened the yellow folder, my gaze scanning the details *Jane Doe, age 18, presenting with lower back pain consistent with Urinary Tract Infection.*

I scanned across the details, then stopped. UTI...she had a UTI. "She was in pain?" I met his focus.

"Considerable."

"You saw her?"

"I did." He answered. "And her boyfriend, too."

"He's not her goddamn *boyfriend.*"

He flinched. Still, I held onto every part of her, my gaze moving to the rest of the information in neat scrawl...until I froze.

The black ink blurred.

Pregnancy: Positive.

I read the words...again...*and again*...and whispered. "Jesus...*no.*"

# Chapter Thirteen

APRIL

We drove all day, pulling up that night in a motel on the side of the road. But even without the penthouse views and room service on hand, Kyle made it feel almost...*nice*. We slept that night, him beside me with his head braced under his arms and me curled against the side, as far away from him as possible. At the start, at least.

When I woke, I was against his side, his arm wrapped securely around me. Protecting me...warming me. My pulse pounded when I surfaced and cracked open my eyes. He was awake, staring down at me with that dangerous glint in his eyes...

One flinch and I pulled away...

He let me go, never once saying a word as I mumbled some excuse about needing the bathroom and as I scurried away.

Whatever we once had between us now was forever changed. I didn't hate him. *I couldn't hate him.* Not after all he'd done. Emotions collided inside me. I used the toilet, flushing before I stepped into the shower, watching the unlocked bathroom door in the corner of my eye. But he never came in, never forced himself on me, not like he'd done before and as I washed and scrubbed, easing my head back into the warm spray, I found myself wanting him.

It was wrong...*very wrong.*

Still, the memory of his hands and his savagery made me feel things no one else had. He threatened that doctor for me; I knew that. And he'd deliver too...

My hand dropped, fingers trembling as I skirted my belly.

*Pregnant.*

A chill coursed along my spine in response. *God, this shouldn't have happened.* I pulled my hand away, twisted the taps and stepped out. But by the time I dried, dressed and stepped out, Kyle was already up, and mostly packed. His dark eyes boring into mine as he stepped past and into the bathroom, closing the door behind him.

I had all the time in the universe as I sat on the end of the bed. Seconds past, achingly slow, the background was a hiss of the shower spray. Leaving me to contemplate how in the Hell I was going to say the words out loud. "I..." I tried, and closed my eyes. "I'm..."

"You're what?" I jerked open my eyes to find Kyle staring down at me. His slicked black hair was still wet as he buttoned his shirt. "You're what, April?"

My pulse spiked...

*Tell him...*

*Tell him now.*

But the words wouldn't come.

"Nothing." I answered, my belly unleashing a snarl. "Just hungry is all."

"Good. We'll grab food on the road." He moved past, grabbing the last of my belongings and strode to the door, before looking back over his shoulder at me. "Coming?"

I swallowed hard, pushing my desperation down and rose from the bed, following him out to the care once more. We climbed in and pulled out of the parking lot.

All through the drive, it was quiet and awkward. I caught Kyle sneaking glances my way, checking on my pain. I just meekly nodded, giving him as much conversation as I could. But the floodgates were open now...

And I couldn't stop hearing the doctor's words in my head. *"This is very serious. I need to know if you're safe...or if you're being held against your will."*

Held against my will?

This entire thing was against my will, starting from the moment I had feelings for my stepbrother. I stared out of the window. God, what a goddamn mess.

We pulled up at lunch, refuelled and grabbed food before we started off again.

"We'll be there tonight."

My breath stilled. I swallowed and turned my gaze toward him.

He divided his attention from the road to me. "I have a place booked for us for tonight, then tomorrow I'll take you to meet him."

*Him...Brontie. The man who was behind this.*

I didn't know how to feel numb from the inside out.

Do I attack him? Kill him with my bare hands? I glanced to Kyle as he watched to road. He'd have a gun somewhere, I knew that.

In the car maybe? I hadn't seen it in his things...but then again... I hadn't really checked.

I swallowed hard. I wanted to ask him about Brontie, wanted to get all the information I could. But would he tell me? He glanced my way, forcing me to break the stare and look away. "I'm nervous."

"About tomorrow?"

I gave a slow nod. "Will you let him hurt me?" The question hung in the air.

He jerked his head toward me, his expression a mixture of shock and anger. "I told you before I wouldn't."

"How can I believe you?"

"You really going to ask me that, after everything I've done?"

"Yes." I answered. "Because a few good deeds doesn't cancel out all the other shitty ones you've done to me. You know more than anyone, I have to protect myself." *And my baby.*

The last words lingered in my head.

He went quiet. Too quiet...then carefully. "I guess whatever I say is meaningless. I'm going to have to prove it to you instead."

My heart skipped a beat. There was danger in that tone, a quiet edge that sent a shiver along my spine as he glanced my way. "Aren't you?"

That thunder in my chest reverberated. "Yes."

He turned back to the road, leaving me terrified of what those words meant. Every mile that went past, I felt the tension grow inside me, and when the faint sparkle of city lights grew bolder against the darkening sky, I wanted to tell him to pull over.

My pulse raced, my breaths panted. I leaned forward, sliding my hands down my legs and unleashed a moan.

"Breathe, April." Kyle urged. "Just breathe."

But I couldn't...couldn't seem to catch my breath or slow my racing thoughts. All could think of was that fucking camera with the footage of me on it. The footage that right now was being used to blackmail. Heat raced to my face as I opened my eyes.

I was being pushed into a corner here...one dark and dangerous corner. The end rushed toward me, just like those glittering city lights. Too fast...*too fast*.

Oncoming headlights seemed to blur as we drove into the city. Kyle pulled up outside the Grand Hyatt. "I figured you'd be tired and desperate for a hot shower." He muttered, sounding pissed.

I unbuckled my belt and stifled a moan as I climbed out of the car. He waved the porter close, opening the back of the car and hauled our luggage out. I followed him inside, glancing at the stacked cases on the trolley as he busied himself with checking us in. My mind went to the thought of a gun once more.

The sound of his voice drifted into the background as the valet climbed into Kyle's car in the corner of my eye. If there was a weapon, then it'd be in the car, or in the suitcases. I needed someway to check.

"I'll be back in a second, forgot something in the car." I muttered.

He glanced my way as I headed for the glass double doors of the expensive hotel and waved my hand to the valet as he started the engine.

"Ma'am?" He glanced across from the driver's seat as I opened the passenger's side door.

"Sorry." I forced a smile. "Forgot something."

I lowered my head, sneaking a glance under my arm at the hotel's foyer. But Kyle wasn't looking at me anymore. So I yanked the latch from the glove compartment and scanned the contents.

My heart was hammering. Sweat rose along the back of my neck.

But there was nothing inside. Nothing more than the service log for the car and a few naps. Frustrated, I closed the compartment and straightened. "You're good now."

I closed the door and stepped backwards, watching as the Lamborghini slowly drove past. Then i turned, meeting Kyle's confused stare as he waited just inside the doors.

"Everything okay?"

I didn't his stare, just nodded and started walking, heading to the elevator, my gaze drifted to the stacked suitcases on the trolley. I followed Kyle into the elevator, staring at the floor as he pressed the button and waited for the doors to close.

"You're not thinking of running now, are you?" His voice was dark and dangerous. "Because that would be very bad indeed."

The threat stayed with me as we rose upwards, and as I followed him into the suite. *Run...that's* what he thought I was planning? I made for the bedroom, kicking off my shoes as I stepped inside and headed for the bathroom.

*Run?*

Desperation hummed as I flicked on the light and closed the bathroom door. I switched on the tap at the handbasin and stared into the reflection of my gaze. Run...

I wanted to...but that wasn't an option. I knew that. So running wasn't what I thought of, not anymore. I used the toilet, then washed my hands before making my way out.

But when I stepped into the bedroom, Kyle was waiting for me.

"Last night, April." He came closer, reaching out to tuck a wayward strand of hair behind my ear. "Good or bad, tomorrow everything changes." My heart hammered as he leaned down, his lips brushed mine. "So how about we lose ourselves a little?"

His fingers were already tugging my shirt from my pants, then moved to the buttons of my blouse. Pinpricks of heat crept into my face. I should be slapping his hands away.

I should be screaming at him to stop.

I should be planning at how to unleash my rage on all of them.

But I didn't do any of that. Not in this moment.

Instead, I tried to slow my panicked thoughts and opened my mouth, deepening Kyle's kiss. My mind fixed on one thing...

*Finding a weapon.*

# Chapter Fourteen

## KYLE

SHE WAS HIDING SOMETHING FROM ME. I STARED AT HER AS she walked into the room. Her steps were slow, like her mind was elsewhere. Maybe it was elsewhere. Maybe it was on one thing entirely. Maybe her thoughts were on Brontie.

*Give her a break. She's panicking...you know, like you're panicking.* I walked in behind her, closed the door and headed for the kitchen. "Do you want a shower first or food?"

There was no response, just a slow stride through the living room to the windows that overlooked the city.

"April?"

"Yeah?"

"Do you want food first, or a shower?"

"Whatever."

The knock came at the door. I walked to the damn thing, yanked it open, ready to snap and then saw it was the porter.

"Your bags, Sir."

"The bedroom." I stepped aside and jerked my head, leaving the guy to wheel the carrier inside without a word.

*Thud.* The door closed behind me. I followed the guy inside, watching April as she turned from the window, her gaze following the bags as they were wheeled into the bedroom.

"Fine." I muttered, moving to the phone and dialled reception.

"Reception, Mr.Blackburn."

"A shower." She muttered and strode into the bedroom.

"Room service." I murmured. "Steak, medium rare, steamed vegetables, some kind of fruit, something for desert times two." I glanced as the porter left, and the bedroom door was closed behind him. That nagging concern rose once more. I stared at the closed bedroom door. "On second thoughts, add something chocolate, decadent, with whipped cream."

"Of course, Mr. Blackburn. Is there anything else I can assist you with?"

My stomach tightened as I stared at that door. "No. Have it ready in half an hour."

"Of course, Sir."

I hung up the phone and stepped toward the bedroom door, listening to the rushed slide of a zipper.

*A zipper?*

The only thing that was zipped was my suitcases. What was she doing, going through my stuff? A chill tore through me when I remembered my gun secured against the side. I shoved down the door handle and pushed in, finding her jerking her gaze upward.

I glanced at my open case. "Help you with something, April?"

She just lifted one of my t-shirts and gave a weak smile. "Just needed something comfortable to wear."

I stared at the shirt in her hand as she closed the suitcase and straightened, her hands moving to the buttons of her blouse. "That's okay, isn't it?" She asked.

I was captured by the sight of those buttons as they widened and exposed the dusty pink bra I bought her. The bra I chose carefully...for her.

I swallowed hard. "Of course."

She slid her blouse free and dropped it to the floor before she hooked her fingers into the waistband of her slacks and slid them over her hips. "Then I'll take that shower."

I flinched, jerking back to reality with her words and nodded.

She turned then, leaving her clothes in a mess. I was riveted by her, by the sweet curve of her ass as she walked away, disappearing into the bathroom and closed the door. *Will you let them hurt me?*

Her words haunted me as the hiss of the shower spray started.

My unzipped suitcase called me. I stepped closer and bent, sliding my hand along the inside until I touched cold steel. Would I let them? I lifted my head to the bathroom door.

*No...*

I busied myself unpacking our luggage and took our worn clothes out into the suite, then called the concierge to have them washed, pressed and ready for us by morning. By the time she stepped out wearing nothing more than my t-shirt that was about four sizes too big on her, then knock came for our food.

I tore my focus from the way the fabric moulded against her body and headed for the door, opening it as our food was wheeled inside.

"There was some laundry, Sir?" The waiter murmured.

I grabbed our clothes, handing them to him before he left.

"Smells good. I'm starving." She stepped closer, lifting the dome cover from the plates.

"Sit." I strode to the kitchen, grabbed two glasses and a bottle of wine, opening it as I went. "It'll help you relax a little." I poured her a glass and handed it to her. "And you need to relax, April."

My tone was husky...*too husky*.

But Christ, seeing her there, dressing in my shirt made something primal rise inside me. Something I'd held at bad for the last two goddamn days...but not anymore.

I placed the glasses down, and then the bottle, moving closer until she jerked that gaze to me. There was a hint of panic...one that only incited that beast inside me.

"Kyle..." She started as I slid my hand around the back of her neck and pulled her close.

"No more talking, April." I murmured before I kissed her.

She stiffened under me, then bucked, pulling away. But I knew her...knew her better than she thought I did. I'd replayed our moments over and over in my head until it was all I thought of. All I *wanted* to think of.

The fight.

The fear.

Then the giving in...

Fuck me, she gave in. I kissed her harder, my hand a vise around the back of her neck before I broke away. Her breaths were hard and heavy, driving those tight peaks against my damn shirt, leaving me to cup them gently. Her breath caught with the slid of my thumb across the peak.

"Kyle...*no*." She moaned right before I slowly knelt.

I dropped my hands to her thighs, sliding the hemline of my shirt higher, until her black lace panties were exposed.

"No?" I murmured and leaned close, breathing in clean scent of her. I kissed her pussy, moving my fingers to the edge of the elastic.

"No." She moaned as my finger slipped under the edge.

"Just tell me when to stop, then." I whispered, my finger finding the edge of her slit and sank in to her warmth.

"Oh." She moaned, her hand falling to the back of my head.

I circled that tiny nub, smiling when she parted her legs wider.

"Here?" I asked, sliding my finger deep. "Is this where you want me to stop?"

I lowered my head, tugging her panties to the side, and widened her pussy for my tongue. "How about here?" I murmured, my lips brushing her clit, before I slit my finger all the way inside. "You want me to stop here?"

"Oh, God." She moaned, low and throaty.

Fuck, Jared must've been a pathetic lover. She was so horny, so ready...*so fucking wet.*

"You wear my shirt." I slid my hand down the back of her thigh, grasped her knee and lifted it over my shoulder as I licked and fingered her pussy. "The least you can do is wear my cum."

She didn't hear me. Caught up in the wave of desire, I stroked her body, pushing her closer and closer to the edge before I eased her leg from my shoulder and rose. One hand went to my trousers, unbuckling my belt, then worked the button and the zipper.

I had her panties yanked to the side in an instant. One hand went around the small of her back as she gripped me, staring up into my eyes. I kissed her with the taste of her desire o my lips. I plunged my tongue into her mouth as I rammed myself inside, shuddering with the feel of her.

So he clawed for a hold, desperate to hold on. My desperation was in the driver's seat now, forcing me to grab her around the waist and lift her.

Her legs wrapped around me as I carried her back into that bedroom and laid her on the bed. I saw her, the *real* her, as she stared up into my eyes. I fucked her, bucking my hips upward. Driving myself all the way inside.

She moaned around panting breaths.

"You want me to stop here?" I growled, bracing one hand above her in the bed as I buried myself in her heat.

I never wanted to stop.

Never wanted it to be anyone else.

I was on the edge of a precipice...one gaping black hole that held nothing but danger for me...*nothing but despair.*

But at the end was her...*April.*

The woman I was falling for.

I lowered my head, listening to her pants as her pussy clenched around my cock and she tumbled into ecstasy...at the same time, I fell headfirst into that darkness.

*I love you...*

The words were nothing more than a groan as I gave one hard thrust and stilled, emptying deep inside her. *I love you, April. I fucking love you.*

I pulled away. My breaths savage as I stared into her eyes. I didn't know if she heard me. Christ, I hoped she heard me...*I hope she realised what she'd done.*

She'd turned a monster.

Into a man.

One who was ready to burn down the world to save her.

Maybe not the world...*just Brontie.*

# Chapter Fifteen

My body ached when I cracked open my eyes. Like always reality took a second to rush in, leaving me floating in that space between my dreams and the feel of crisp, clean sheets. In that space, I felt free and hopeful. I closed my eyes once more...*floating*.

Until the bed shifted. A soft, deep snore followed a hand as it slid over my stomach and curled around my waist. But the hand didn't feel right. It was heavier than Jared's, not that Jared ever comforted me like this. I breathed deep, unable to shift my focus from the touch. Fingers splayed, like he just couldn't touch enough of me.

"No," he whispered. The word heavy with sleep. "No, you need to run...*April...you need to run.*"

I wrenched open my eyes. My pulse thundered, leaving a gash in the fantasy where the real world rushed in, leaving me to turn my head.

Kyle lay beside me.

*Kyle.*

I swallowed a moan and tried to shift away from his touch, but the moment I shifted, that dull, aching heaviness moved inside me. That softness between my legs, a feeling I didn't understand...until I did.

Satisfaction.

That's what it was. My body was warm and sated, limbs soft, sleep deep and restful. The kind you have in the wake of sex. No, not just sex. *Good sex.* The kind that blew your mind. And that's what Kyle gave me last night.

I licked my lips, remembering the feel of his mouth, his fingers, then his cock inside me. I climaxed hard...the first time, right before he made me sit and eat until my belly was full and my mind was swimming with the glass of alcohol. Then he took me to bed and made slow, comforting love to me.

I turned my head, finding those intense eyes still closed. Midnight hair against pale skin. His fingers curled against my stomach, gripping, touching me. He always touched me now, with a deep rush of a breath he cracked open his eyes.

There was nothing slow and tentative about Kyle. No, once he switched on, he was all the way on. That intense stare cut all the way through me. Like sleep didn't award him the same dreamy transition to real life. No, he was just...*there* the moment he came awake.

"You okay?" He murmured.

I nodded. "Just didn't want to wake you."

"I'm awake now. You hungry?"

*Hungry?* I searched my body, but the moment I did, my throat tightened and my stomach rolled. *Oh, God...I was going to be sick.* I shoved upright, tearing out from under his touch as I raced for the bathroom.

"April?"

I shoved the door closed with a *boom!* Hunched over, I sprinted for the toilet, making it just in time as acid flew from my mouth to splash against the back of the toilet. My knees trembled, leaving me to crouch against the cold enamel. My body took over, clenching, heaving.

"April...you okay?"

*Go away!* The roar resounding in my head. But I just held onto the toilet, unable to answer him as my body tried to expel whatever was inside me. Only it couldn't...because it was what was inside me that caused this.

*The baby.*

*Oh, no...the baby. The baby because I was pregnant. I was pregnant and having sex with Kyle.* My body eased with the thought, stomach settled...leaving fear to push in. I was meeting with Brontie today. The man who not only had the video footage of me having sex with a group of strangers as well as my step-brother, but who was using it to blackmail my father.

A father I left behind...

"April?" Kyle called from behind the door.

I shoved up on trembling legs and looked at the yellow acid swirling around the water and hit the button, flushing it all down before I forced myself to straighten and made for the door. I opened it, then stepped back, moving to the shower.

I didn't hide my body from him anymore. What was the damn point? It seemed my needs knew what it wanted, never mind what my head screamed.

"You okay?" He stepped in as the hot water slipped into the spray.

"Yeah." I adjusted the temperature and stepped. "Just…"

"Nerves."

I nodded. *Yeah, nerves.* I stepped in, watching as he strode to the toilet, cupped his cock and unleashed a spray. I shifted my attention from him peeing, hating how we'd arrived at this state of being this comfortable around each other.

He flushed as I washed my hair, then scrubbed my body, my touch careful across my belly. My breath caught as he stepped into the shower, moving under the large overhead spray that rained down from the ceiling. God…the way he looked at me.

He grabbed the soap, squeezed some into the cloth and ran it over his powerful chest, then down his rippled abs. I looked away as he washed, his gaze fixed on me. Water cascaded around his neck, running down his chest as he lowered his head. God, he was beautiful. Strong. Demanding…

*And my enemy, remember?*

I flinched with the words and stepped around him, moving out to grab a towel and hurry from the bathroom. I didn't give myself time to worry about the nausea that burned in the pit of my stomach. After sliding on clean underwear, I looked at the clothes hanging in the wardrobe.

Kyle had unpacked the suitcases last night, stowing my things away before removing the suitcases…and the gun from my reach. I glanced over my shoulder, to the open bathroom door, listening to the rush of the water before I hurried around the bed and made for his wardrobe.

But I barely reached into the hanging area before the shower spray ended, leaving silence in its wake. "Shit."

I glanced at the edge of the suitcase peeking out, then tore myself away, making it back around the end of the bed before

Kyle strode out, towelling dry his hair. He glanced my way as I pulled on a pair of navy blur slacks, and a white blouse with puffy sleeves and a tie high around my neck, leaving an opening that showed the tops of my breasts.

"I like that on you," he murmured, pulling his own clothes from the wardrobe, slipping on trunks, then black trousers and a navy blue shirt that almost matched the color of my pants. Was it a choice by accident, or a simple statement?

I didn't know, and I sure as Hell wasn't game to ask.

"Do you want to eat before we go?"

My stomach clenched at the thought. I shook my head. "No. Thank you."

I sat at the edge of the bed, slipped my feet into strappy heels, buckled them at the side of my ankles before I rose.

My thoughts were racing as I made my way back into the bathroom and used the dryer on my hair, taking my time to get my makeup just right, what little I had to work with. Kyle had called ahead, had some things delivered to the room before we arrived, still it wasn't mine.

Not my colors, or my cheap knock-off brands. This stuff was...*expensive.*

"Ready?" He asked from the doorway.

I lifted my gaze to the reflection, to the strange woman staring back at me. The one who looked haunted and older, aged by every secret she held. But did any of it matter when I was about to face the devil himself?

No.

That was the truth...

It didn't.

Mr. Brontie sent his henchman across the country to track me down and drag me back here. Just like the fairytale Snow White the henchman was falling for me, I knew that. But was it too little too late? Would this be the day they served my heart up on a platter for the villain? Or would Kyle be the man he said he was…and set me free…

Free to run back to Jared?

Pain carved through my chest at the thought. I winced and jerked my gaze from my reflection. There was no way I wanted to see the truth in that. That was a lot to unpack, more than I dared, as I turned and nodded to Kyle. "Ready."

I followed him out of the suite and into the elevator. As usual, Kyle was quiet, wrapped up in his thoughts, leaving me to a thorny briar of my own. The more I fought, the more trapped I became. So I closed my eyes and thought about one thing…and one thing alone.

*Making it out of this alive.*

The elevator shuddered as it came to a stop. I opened my eyes and followed Kyle out of the reception. But instead of the familiar Lamborghini waiting for us, there was a black, sleek Bentley. The driver stepped forward and opened the rear door, nodding to Kyle. "Mr. Blackburn."

Kyle just waited, motioning me inside, his gaze cold and steely. Gone was the man who lay next to me an hour ago…gone was the man who wiped the sweat from my body and fed me when I was too weak to feed myself.

This was the Kyle I met the first time. The cold, controlled, savage bastard. Hate seethed in his eyes as the door closed behind him and the driver climbed in behind the steering wheel.

*Thud.*

The locks engaged, sending panic surging through me. I jerked my gaze to Kyle, but he said nothing, just stared ahead as the car rolled forward, out of the pickup point of the hotel, then out into the steady stream of morning traffic.

"Just keep your cool," he urged. "Remember what I told you."

He glanced my way, and that savage gaze softened before he turned away. It wasn't much, just a flicker of the man he was behind closed doors. But out here he was the bastard once more. There was no room for softness here, or anything that might be considered weak. He shifted carefully as we drove through the city and out the other side. His hand moved to his jacket, pulling it tighter...until I caught the hard bulge.

The gun...

My pulse thundered.

He bought the gun from his suitcase. The one I tried to steal for myself.

And as he glanced my way, I understood...everything he told me was real.

He was ready to protect me, however he had to.

"We're here." He glanced out of the tinted windows at the towering, gated entrance.

My pulse kicked hard as the car turned and suddenly this became all too real...

Gravel crunched under the tires. The car made its way slowly along the drive until it pulled up outside a towering mansion hidden from the street. For a second, I thought I knew this place. It seemed...*familiar*. Too familiar.

The driver climbed out, leaving the door open behind him.

"Just stay with me." Kyle said a second before his door opened.

He climbed out, leaving me behind, then looked over his shoulder. Only I couldn't move. I was frozen with fear, with my heart racing.

"April." Kyle carefully called my name.

I tore my gaze from the house to him, swallowed hard and then shoved forward. My heels sank into the ground as I climbed out.

"This way." The driver motioned us forward. My knees trembled, my steps fragile. I wanted to reach out to Kyle, to hold on to his arm, but I didn't. Instead, I forced my head upwards, ground my jaw and drove myself forward.

With each step I grew bolder...angrier...more determined they wouldn't see me weak. I climbed the stairs behind Kyle, making my way to the large double doors which opened when we neared.

Boots thudded.

Heels clacked.

The place made grand seem...*pathetic*. Polished marble and gold crowded the expansive foyer. I followed the driver as he headed deeper into the house and stopped at a set of wooden double doors.

"Through there, Sir. They're waiting for you." The driver stepped to the side, watching as Kyle neared, bore down on the door handle and swung open the doors.

"Kyle wait," I whispered.

But I was too late. He disappeared inside, leaving me panicked and...alone. "Shit." I followed him in, my pulse erratic and my knees weak.

The room wasn't just a room, but an entire wing. My heels sank into the soft, cream coloured pile of expensive carpet. A receptionist rose from behind a desk. Her eyes were wide, stunned, as she turned from Kyle to me. I guessed she wasn't expecting me. But Kyle never slowed, just headed toward another set of double doors at the end of the large room.

But before he reached for the handle, the doors swung open and a man stepped out. I froze. Stunned. My mind unable to catch up with my heart as it stuttered and I whispered. "Dad?"

## Chapter Sixteen

"April." Dad strode through the door and grabbed me in a hug. A hug that was tight, crushing me against his chest, before he pulled me away. There was a panicked look that found Kyle before he settled that frantic gaze on me. "You shouldn't have come here...you shouldn't have—"

"Nonsense." A deep booming voice came from behind him. "Of course she should. Why else would April know the truth? After all, don't you think she deserves it?"

That voice triggered something inside me.

Something cold.

Something cruel.

Like the point of a knife dragged down my spine.

From behind the sagging shoulders of my dad, he stepped out of the doorway and for the first time in my life, I came to face with a monster. The one called Mr. Brontie. He smiled at me. I both wanted to scream and vomit and hurl myself at him, tearing open his face with my nails—all at the same time. I would. I knew I would. Give me that gun that was under Kyle's jacket and I'd do worse.

I stiffened as he came closer. He was younger than I expected, not fat or blading that I'd hoped for. In fact, he was gorgeous. Too gorgeous. He glanced at my father. "How about a proper introduction?"

Dad's arm tightened around me.

"I don't need to be introduced to you." I answered. "This is neither pleasurable for me, nor wanted. But then again, I guess you're good at that. Forcing people to do things they don't want."

There was a flicker of amusement in those blue-green eyes. His lips pursed for a second. But if I was waiting for any kind of apology, then I'd be disappointed.

"April." Dad started.

"No, it's fine. She has a right to be angry." Brontie answered.

Dad spun so fast he knocked me backwards. I stumbled as he lunged, cocked his fist like he was about to lay Brontie flat. But he didn't. He just bare his teeth while the sick sonofabitch met his stare.

"You quite finished?" Brontie murmured. "Or did you want to tell her yourself?"

My heart was pounding as I glanced from dad to Brontie. "Tell me what?"

Dad glared at him, lips curled, teeth bared. I'd never seen him so fucking furious.

"No."

I stiffened at the voice behind me. A voice I didn't want to hear...a voice I didn't expect to hear, not here...not now. *Jared.*

I turned, watching him stride through the door, looking like he hadn't slept in days. Dark circles, sunken eyes. His clothes were dirty and wrinkled, still he made my heart race. I could stop from glancing at Kyle as he turned around and took a step sideways, right in Jared's path to me.

"What the fuck are you doing here?" Kyle barked.

There was no answer, other than a battle cry that ripped from Jared's lips as he lunged through the air and punched Kyle in the mouth. Kyle's head cracked backwards. Blood was a trickle at the corner of his mouth, one that he licked away.

"Guys..." Brontie started.

But there was no stopping them. You couldn't even if you wanted to. It was like holding back to cyclones that were destined to collide. Fists and grunts filled the space. Kyle grabbed Jared by his shirt and rammed him backwards, slamming him against the wall.

Expensive paintings jumped, then thudded with the blow. Security rushed toward us from the doorway at the end of the hall. Men dressed in black, who moved fast, grabbing Kyle and Jared and pulled them apart.

"I'll fucking *kill you!*" Jared roared. "You hear me? *You're fucking dead!*"

"Stop it!" I screamed. "Both of you, *just stop it!*"

"You are *pathetic!*" Kyle roared. "You fucking come here thinking what? She's going to go back to you? Why? So you can lie to her, keep her filthy fucking motels and starve her?" Kyle yanked his arm from the bouncer and stabbed the air. "You're the fucking dead man, Jared. I ought to beat the shit out of you for what you've done."

*"ENOUGH!"*

I flinched with the boom. Kyle and Jared sucked in hard breaths. Their gazes savage and chilling as they stared each other down. Agony tore through my chest with the panicked thrumming of my heart. My fists shook, clenched at my side. I couldn't seem to catch my breath...and there was only one man responsible for all of this.

I spun with a scream trapped in the back of my throat. Tears welled in my eyes. But they weren't tears of pain. They were tears of anger...rage that had nowhere else to go but down my cheek. I took a step around my father to stare this cruel, vindictive bastard in the eyes. "You wanted me here, well, here I am. Get this over with...and let me go."

He met my stare, then gave a simple nod and motioned with his hand. "By all means."

I glanced to where he pointed, to another hallway and another wooden door. Then I stepped forward, leaving everyone behind and followed him to that room.

"April." Kyle called my name.

His voice was wounded and strained, stopping me cold. "It's okay." I answered, not turning to meet his gaze.

I knew if I did, I'd never go into that room, never hear what this manipulative bastard had to say, and I'd never leave this place and him behind.

*But with who?*

That voice inside me whispered. But the answer was too much to unpack. I shoved it aside and headed for that room. My steps were muffled against the plush carpet.

"Let me through." Jared growled. "I said...*let me the fuck through.*"

I didn't need to look behind me to know Jared was trying to muscle his way in. He was desperate, unhinged. To catch up to us, he must've driven all day and most of the night. But was he worried about me, or what I was about to find out?

Brontie opened the door and stood outside, glancing behind me to the others as I strode through the door. Then we were alone, the door closing with a soft thud behind me. I looked around the room. Every inch reeked of money from the large wooden desk that sat in the middle of the room, and chesterfield sofa that sat facing a bank of monitors fixed to the wall.

I was aware of him, of his movements and his presence. Of his slow, calm breaths and the way he turned and leaned against the desk, watching me.

"You're prettier than I expected." He said.

"And you're uglier." I met his gaze. "And crueler, and a lot more pathetic."

He smiled, but it wasn't one that reached his eyes. "I guess I deserved that."

I glanced to the monitors on screen and suppressed a shudder. I didn't need an explanation to know what he had watched. "How many times?"

"Excuse me?"

I met his gaze. "How many times have you watched it?"

*You're prettier than I expected...*

I swallowed hard.

That smile turned into a smirk, one that gave me the answer I didn't want...*a lot...he watched it a lot.* "You liked it?" I stepped closer. "You enjoyed watching me being...*forced to do that.*"

"You could've left." He answered. "Could've screamed, could've run away, you had a car, if I'm correct. You could've done many things, but you chose not to." He shoved off the desk and took a step closer until he towered over me. "You stayed to do what Jared wanted you to do. You and your step-brother alone are solely accountable for what you did. Do not assume to place the blame squarely on me."

The words were a slap in my face. But they weren't new, were they? They were the same words I'd been telling myself over and over again. "That might be the case." I crossed my arms over my chest. "But the recording is all on you. I might've been fucking naïve, but you...you used it to your advantage. That's why I'm here, right? For you to hold it over me once more. What do you want, Brontie? What more could you possibly want? You've already destroyed my soul...do you want my blood too? Or is it my body?"

The idea sickened me, still I knew this was what it had to be. Why else was I here? I dropped my hands and unbuttoned my jacket, pulling it free to expose the black lace bodysuit. "Is this what you want now?"

He shoved off the desk and strode across the room to stand in front of me. Those blue-green eyes reminded me of fresh spring grass, but there was nothing fresh or sweet about this man. He licked his lips and lowered his gaze. "If I told you I hadn't watched the recording, then I'd be lying."

I flinched with the words.

"The truth is, I've watched it many times." He reached up, slid his finger under the thin strap of my bra and slowly dragged it over my shoulder. "More times than I should."

Inch by inch, the top of my breast was exposed. I caught my breath, my pulse a trapped, thrashing animal in my head. He lowered his gaze, the movement stopping at the edge of my nipple.

I didn't need a blow by blow account to know what he wanted.

My body tensed...

*Me.*

That's what he wanted. His sick, demented hunger raged in his eyes. I knew what he was imagining...me on that pool table, only it wasn't Jared or Kyle or any of the others between my legs. It was him. Fucking me...*owning me.*

Until he did the one thing I wasn't expecting.

He tugged my strap back into place and dropped his hand, stepping away. "I want you...want you in ways that's...*immoral.* But that's not why you're here."

I swallowed hard, my throat dry. My voice scratchy and trembling. "Then tell me...tell me what you want..."

"What I want, April...is for your father to fall to his fucking knees. And I'm not talking about that schmuck out there." He gave a jerk of his head. "I'm talking about your real father. The one you were taken from...the one you've been kept from your entire life. I want him to yield to me. Only then will he have you back. Until then, consider this place your home...for the foreseeable future."

"My home?" My blood left my face. My pulse stuttered. *This couldn't be happening...this couldn't be...*

Darkness reached for me, swimming up like a commanding tide, making the world darkness and my future grey. Still, I held on... biting the inside of my cheek...and did the only thing I could.

*I lunged for him...*

# Chapter Seventeen

I stared at that open door and gripped my cell phone, knowing that once I stepped inside that room, everything would change. The bouncer moved closer, drawing my gaze.

"In or out, April." Brontie murmured. "It's your choice."

My choice? How was any of this my choice? I should never have stepped into the car. I should've kept on walking. I should've run and kept on running. I should've never been born.

Those words stopped me cold.

*Boom!*

I flinched at the sound and stumbled. Brontie started forward, grabbing me by the shoulders and shoved me aside. *"Stay here!"* He roared to the bouncer. *"Make sure she's protected!"*

He left, charging through the hallway, leaving me and the bouncer who was prepared to put me in the hospital behind. I jerked my gaze to him and then to the open door of that room.

*Boom!* The explosion came again.

I pressed my spine against the wall and jerked my gaze to the bouncer. "What the fuck are you waiting for? *Go!*"

Panic tore through his gaze as he glanced toward the sound.

I stumbled forward, giving him a shove. *"He could die out there!"*

There was a second where I thought he wasn't going, but then he gave a snarl and charged forward. *Go...GO!* He left in a deafening thunder of footsteps. I didn't waste a second. Glancing over my shoulder at that open door, I grabbed my dress and charged ahead.

Screams filled the restaurant, people shoved and lunged, driving from the front of the restaurant and into the back. I moved with the rush, pushing past the swinging doors that led to the kitchen. A man pushed behind me, blood trickled down his cheek.

"Get out of the way!" He barged me to the side, pushing his way past the stoves crammed with pots and pans.

I stumbled forward, shoving out my hand as I hit the bench. Agony tore through my side. A cry ripped fire. I shoved backwards and kept on moving, driving myself toward the rear door. I pushed through, scanning the back alley and kept on running.

*Get out...get out of here.*

Terror spilled around me. I risked a glance over my shoulder and kept on moving, running with the rest of the crowd and caught sight of the guard as he stumbled out of the restaurant and scanned the others. I had to get away from him...like...*now*.

I glanced down at my dress. Of course I'd have to wear something like this. The wail of sirens cut through the air up ahead. I stumbled to the side, hugging the other buildings and spied the opening of an alley up ahead. I just had to get there. I kicked off my heels, bent and snatched them from the asphalt and raced ahead, my bare feet slapping on the road. A cop car tore along the street, screeching to a halt at the rear of the restaurant. I didn't know what happened, but I sure as hell knew they wouldn't protect me. Not from someone like Brontie.

So I kept running, tearing down the alley as most of those running from the restaurant carried on ahead. Footsteps thundered, rebounding against the side of the building as we ran...until I slowed. The fence of a house was on one side. The corrugated iron damaged and buckled in one section, covered by thick green plastic...the corner flapping in the wind. Clothes were draped over the line that ran from what looked like a lean-to at the rear. I glanced at the others who kept running, heading back to the main road and away from the blast of the restaurant.

I still didn't know what happened, if it was the explosion came from restaurant itself or more. All I knew, there was no way I was going back there, not with Brontie, or his fucking bodyguard. I turned to that flapping plastic, hiked my dress up and lunged forward.

"Please don't have a dog. *Please don't have a dog.*" I yanked my dress up with one hand and gripped the fence with the other and lunged.

My dress snagged on the wire, tearing with a rip. But then I was over, stumbling through someone's backyard and raced for the clothes draped over the line.

They were a woman's. About the same size as me, jeans, t-shirts, and a man's sweater. I snatched them free and hurried for shelter, reaching around for the zipper on my dress and yanked it down.

I dressed, watching the alley, desperation screaming inside me. They'd come...and soon. I tossed the dress over the line and hurried forward, yanking on the sweater as I went. The heels I couldn't do anything about not yet. I slipped them on and stumbled forward. Dogs barked at me from the neighbouring yard. I watched them, hurrying forward along the side of the house and out to the street.

There was no one home. The house was quiet, no cars were parked out front. Red and blue lights of emergency services crammed the street out in front of the restaurant. The flickering bright the lights glaring against the night. The pathway was blocked off, police held back the growing crowd. But through the gaps of those gathering, I saw the remains of Brontie's Maserati...now blown apart in ruins.

That was the explosion. I stopped, stared, unable to recognise the ruins. The doors were thrown open. The windows were shattered. It hardly looked like a car, not one I recognised. Someone was out for him. It didn't take a genius to know Brontie had enemies, ones who were now making their presence known.

I stumbled backwards, away from the restaurant and everyone else. My heels clattered, too damn loud, but I couldn't do anything about that. I just lowered my head, hunched my shoulders and started walking, leaving the restaurant and the few houses far behind.

Sirens howled as they raced past. With every piercing sound, my pulse jacked that little bit higher. I walked until my feet burned, then took off my heels, casting them aside into a dumpster. I was in a strange city with no money and no friends, no one who wasn't Jared or Kyle.

And they weren't friends.

For all I knew, they could be in on this.

My cell vibrated in my pocket. I pulled it free and caught the No Caller ID before quickly stabbing the button and killing the screen. Panic made me look over my shoulder as I stepped up onto the sidewalk, heading past more shops.

My bare feet slapped against the pavement. I tucked my hair into the collar of my sweater and glanced over my shoulder. *Smack!* I hit something hard and stumbled sideways.

"Hey!" He barked.

"Sorry...*I'm so sorry.*" I mumbled, righting myself and kept on walking.

I hurried, until my feet burned and I was breathless, and when the crowd grew dangerous. Catcalls rang out from guys across the street. Shouts of men on the fringes of a fistfight. I slid my hands into my pockets, lowered my gaze and kept on walking until I realised I had nowhere else to turn.

It was getting too dangerous to be out here.

A small neon sight beckoned *Warm Meals. Soup Kitchen.* I made for that sign, stepping around men and women chatting and lingering outside. They looked at me, then down to my bare feet as I stepped inside, shivering. It was getting cold, and there was no way I could survive a night on the streets. No way I *would* survive. Not now...not when I had more than myself to think about.

"Hey." A soft male voice came from behind me. "Are you okay?"

I turned to find a man with the kindest brown eyes I'd ever seen. He took one look at me, smiled and said, "Let me get you some place quiet to sit."

I just nodded, desperation roaring through me. He nursed me, guiding me through the crowd with a hand on my arm, until we found a quiet corner away from the crowd. "Here." He motioned to a seat.

I dropped, pulling my bare feet up to massage the burn. He took one look at me, his expression softening. "Let me get you a blanket and some food."

I shook my head, shivering. "I'm not hungry, thank you. But I will take the blanket."

He gave a nod and left, returning a minute later with a heavy, grey wooden blanket. "Do you have someone I can call? Someone who can come and get you?"

Someone he can call? My cell rang. I jerked my gaze to the screen and pressed the button, sending it to voice mail. I swallowed hard. "I don't know."

He looked at my bare feet, then at my shaking hands. "Are you in trouble?"

A soft chuckle slipped free. *Am I in trouble?* I lifted my gaze to his. He wouldn't believe me, even if I told him.

And I couldn't tell him.

I couldn't tell anyone.

Brontie was a man who not just track anyone down I spoke to but would also destroy them. I glanced around at the many people in needed. There was no way I'd bring that man's wrath to this place of kindness. So I shook my head. "No, thank you. The blanket is perfect."

"How about a coffee?"

I smiled, giving him a nod. "How about tea?"

He beamed. "Tea we have."

He left, making his way through those in need. Those who had life harder than me. Those who struggled to find a purpose. I lowered my hand, my fingers finding my stomach. My cell vibrated once more and even though I knew who it was, still I looked.

*Jared.*

His name glared on the screen. Fear punched through my chest, following with a wave of desperation. One so powerful it hit me like a blow. I was lifting my cell and pressing the button before I knew.

"April?" He cried. *"April?"*

"It's me." I said quietly as tears blurred the room around me.

"Jesus Christ, we heard about the explosion. Are you okay?"

I licked my lips, the words a hard knot in the back of my throat. "I'm okay. But I'm not coming back, Jared. I'm not coming back to you or Kyle...and not to Brontie."

"What?" He murmured.

Silence filled the air.

"April?"

I lowered my hand...the sound of his voice was so small.

*"April?"*

I lifted my finger, hovering over the button to end the call... when he said.

"I know about the baby." His words drifted, so faint. "April, I know."

# Chapter Eighteen

## KYLE

I *HATED* KNOWING SHE WAS IN THERE. HATED KNOWING SHE was in that room with Brontie. I hated not knowing what he was telling her even more.

"How..." the word came from behind me. "How is she?"

I winced, my gaze fixed on the door in front of me. *How is she? How the fuck is she?*

"You going to answer me?"

I spun, hate bubbling up to the surface. "You've got to be *shitting me.*" He stood there, that smug fucking look on his face. A look I wanted to wipe off on the end of my goddamn fist. "How is she? How the fuck is she? Weak. Malnutritioned. Dangerously close to death. Is that what you want to hear?"

He paled, flinched. At least the sonovabitch had the decency to do that. I took a step closer, getting into his space.

"Kyle." April's father warned.

I whirled on the bastard, unable to fathom how the bastard could stand there and hear this. "She's your fucking daughter!

*Your fucking blood! How are you not fucking murderous? Answer me that? How are you not calling for blood?"*

He said nothing, just stared at me with that same stony stare. "You don't understand."

"Oh, don't I? Seems you've both made it *abundantly* clear where your loyalties lie...and it sure as Hell, isn't with April. She doesn't want you here." I stared Jared down. "She doesn't care about you, nor does she want to see you. So why don't you do her a favor and fuck off?"

But he didn't fuck off. He just my gaze and kept prodding. "Did she tell you that? That she doesn't want me? Because if she did—"

I grabbed his shirt and shoved him toward the door. "She doesn't have to."

He stumbled backwards, then punched my hand away. "Because you make all her decisions for her, right? You decide what she wears, where she sleeps. No doubt in your goddamn bed. Are you fucking her?"

I stilled, then let a slow, bitter smile creep across my lips. My heart thundered watching the bastard squirm. I wanted nothing more than to tell him in intimate detail how I fucked her and how much she liked it, how that after one fucking night she stopped calling out Jared's name and now, when she looked at me, she didn't wince.

Christ, I didn't think something that small could make me feel so goddamn powerful—but it did. She didn't flinch, didn't look away...didn't stiffen when I touched her now. No. She met my gaze, watching when I went down on her. Those eyes were still so fucking innocent when I licked her cunt and brought her to the heights of euphoria.

She was warming to me. A few more days without this motherfucker and she would've dismissed him entirely. All I needed was time to turn her against him—he couldn't even give me that.

Here he was. I lowered my gaze to his filthy, wrinkled shirt and the unkempt shadow on his face. "Let yourself go, haven't you?" I sneered. "No fucking wonder she comes so goddamn hard around my cock. It's been a while since she had a real man."

The bastard lunged then, and I fucking welcomed it.

He swung, but the blow was wide and fucking pathetic. I dodged it easy enough. All I wanted was a fucking opportunity, and he gave it to me. I lunged, grabbed the bastard around his throat. He drove back, short, sharp blows around my middle.

I tensed, wincing with the pain and then drove my fist into the bastard's cheek. His head snapped to the side before he turned that savage gaze to me. A ripple of fear tore through me as Jared roared, sounding like a man unhinged as he punched me in the mouth, snapping my head sideways.

I swung, driving him into the wall and hit him, unleashing a barrage of blows. Blood splattered, flecks flew through the air as I split the bastard's lip.

"For fuck's sake!" April's dad roared and the heavy thud of boots echoed.

I was grabbed from behind. But not before I got one more blow in, cracking the bastard in the nose. "Stay the fuck away from her! *You hear me? Stay the fuck away!*"

"*Try to make me!*" He roared as April's dad grabbed his arm and hauled him backwards.

"You need to come with us, Mr. Blackburn." The asshole behind me growled. "*Now, Sir.*"

I yanked my arm from his hold. "Fine! *Get the fuck off me!*" Savage rage burned inside me as I turned and strode away, leaving the bleeding piece of shit behind.

The tang of blood bloomed in the back of my throat. I licked my lips, wincing at the sing as I headed for the door.

*"You think you fucking know her, don't you?"* Jared roared behind me. "You don't know fucking anything! You're gonna lose her, *Blackburn! You're gonna fucking lose her, because you never had her in the first place!"*

I clenched my fists and ground my jaw. It took every inch of my willpower not to turn around, take out the gun under my jacket and take the bastard out once and for all. But doing that here and now, I knew without a doubt, I'd lose her for sure.

That I couldn't risk.

I followed the guard through the door and reached up, touching the sting in my mouth as Jared's words hit harder than I wanted them to. I winced and strode along the hallway, leaving the security to close the door behind me and block the bastard's voice out. Still, his words lingered. *You're gonna lose her, Blackburn!*

"We'll see about that." I snarled and headed to the far end of the mansion.

Red cedar railing, Italian carpets and paintings that would be considered an art exhibition itself, and that was just the goddamn foyer. The place was made from money...old money. The kind that just gives those who wielded the power an open playground to do whatever they wanted.

And what Brontie wanted was to own the players of the world.

The real players. Senators, Justices. Hell, even the White House. He'd do it too. After all...he had power and money on his side. I shoved open the door and stepped into the east wing of the house and watched Alexi uncross his legs and lift his gaze from the iPad in his hand.

One glance was all it took. He winced, placed the iPad down beside him and rose. "I see you've had fun."

I ignored the comment and headed straight for the bar, pouring myself a scotch, then downed it in one swallow and refilled.

"Show me." Alexi grabbed my jaw and forced my gaze on his. I let him manhandle me like I was one of his 'boys' for a second at least, before I bared my teeth and jerked my head away.

"Christ, you're feisty." Alexi snapped. But there was a bite of his lip. He liked it. Liked me savage and cruel.

"I don't like the fact she's in there without me."

Alexi's brow rose. "Territorial, are we?"

I glanced at Brontie's right-hand man and then looked away. *Keep it together…keep it fucking leashed.* The last thing I needed was them knowing how fucking invested I was. For all they knew, I was just the hunter, nothing more than a dog, right? "No, I just want to know what's said, that's all."

"Sure…" Alexi said, like he didn't believe me one fucking bit.

The truth screamed in the silence. "Say anything about this and I'll come for you."

"Please." Alexi rolled his eyes. "You think I'm that bitchy?"

"No." I muttered. "I fucking *know you are.*"

Another eye roll. "Maybe if this was about something else, but you know I hate this as much as you do. I have a sister April's age. You think I'd let them…you think I'd let them be used like that?"

My pulse kicked. I took a step forward, scenting not blood in the water, but an opportunity. "Then help me, Alexi. Help me get into that room before it's too late."

"You know I can't." He whispered. "Mr. Brontie—"

"Pull the fucking fire alarm, detonate a goddamn bomb. Hell, shoot me in the fucking shoulder if that's what it takes. Just get me in there. Get me in there...*now*."

There was a tiny shake of his head.

His eyes widened.

I'd use him any way I could.

Hell, I'd use them all if it meant I could get her away from Brontie. I just needed to take her out of the equation, to make her less useful. I narrowed in on Alexi. The guy knew Brontie better than anyone. He knew what he was planning...he also knew the other players.

"There are others, aren't there?" I took a step closer, almost urging him to touch me once more. I'd have his hands on me. If it meant I'd get the information I needed, I'd let hi do almost anything. "Other women...other...*targets*."

Alexi stiffened, then swallowed hard.

It was a tell.

One I needed.

One I'd *exploit*.

"Tell me who they are, the other...*women*."

"Kyle, no." Alexi shook my head. "I can't."

I moved closer, hunting like a shark hunts. "You can, Alexi...and you will."

# Chapter Nineteen



*My home for the foreseeable future?*

*Fuck you!*

My nails raked down his cheek before he grabbed my wrists. "Get the fuck off me! *Let me go!*" I screamed, yanking and thrashing in his hold. *"You fucking bastard!"*

"Stop it!" He commanded, but there wasn't a bark of rage, or a spark of violence in his eyes, even as a bead of blood bloomed and then dripped from his cheek. There was nothing but that cold, sickening hunger. "You'll hurt yourself."

*"Hurt myself?"* I let out a bark of laughter, staring at him.

He licked his lips, taking in my pain and rage and then lowered his gaze to the hanging strap of my bra. "What you're feeling now is shock and rage, but neither of those things are useful to you right now. You need to keep your head, April. Control. It's the only thing that matters." He dragged his gaze along the exposed top of my breast. "Control can change your future in the blink of an eye and those around you."

My pulse was thundering. The sound was a roar in my head.

He was so calm, so...*cold.*

"Breathe." He commanded, his hold softening around my wrists.

I did, sucking in hard breaths while rage seethed in my veins.

"That's the way." He stared into my eyes, and there was almost a flicker of approval. "Now, you have questions. Important questions."

*Questions?*

His words settled in my head, and when they did, they hit me hard. "You're a liar."

"I'm many things, April, and I lie when the conversation calls for it, but not here and not now. You wanted to know why you, then I'm explaining why."

"My father..." I started.

"Isn't the man standing out there?"

I flinched with the words and shook my head. "No, he..."

"Want to take a paternity test? I can have one ready in the hour, but think about it...think about your entire relationship. Has he ever been a real father to you?"

I swallowed hard, the answer a roar in my head. He let my wrists go, leaving them to drop to my side. Then he pushed from the desk and strode to a bar at the end of his study, grabbing a crystal decanter and pouring a splash of amber into two glasses before he grabbed them and turned to me. "They call it power roulette, where oligarchs and magnates from the most powerful and wealthiest families have children, daughters specifically."

He handed me the glass and for some stupid reason I took it, like his spell already ensnared me as that howling anger roared. Still, I took it and when he lifted the rim to his lips; I did the same.

Heat burned all the way down the back of my throat.

"And they trade them, use them like a get out of jail card." Every movement and every flinch captured Brontie. "It was a failsafe. Come after one family and you risk the blood of your enemy. A safety trigger."

"A safety trigger?" I whispered.

None of this made sense.

"So the family of your enemy would take your daughter, and they'd raise them, all the while knowing that if it all went south, they could use the daughter as a bargaining chip, a get out of jail free card, so to speak."

Acid burned in my belly.

I was going to be sick...

Throw up on this expensive carpet. My knees shook, making me reach out and steady myself against the desk. I closed my eyes, hating how his words resounded inside me. All these years I never had love from my father, not like I should've from him.

"But your father refused."

I flinched, opened my eyes and found him. "What?"

"He refused, so he did the only thing he could. He paid someone to raise you. Paid him to hide you. Paid him to pretend he was your family."

That resounding booming in my head grew louder. "He paid him?"

"Handsomely and he did his job, for a time a least." Brontie lifted his glass and swallowed.

I didn't think about anything else in this moment, not the life I carried inside me, or the ache in my heart. "That man..."

"Is not your father." Brontie stepped closer.

"And Jared…"

"Isn't your brother."

I rocked with the guilt. I'd spent the last few months hating myself. Guilt driving my every reaction. "Then who the Hell is my real father?"

But Brontie just shook his head. "That will come. But know this, there are others out there who'd love to do nothing more than to hurt you." He came closer. "Even worse than I'm doing right now."

Worse?

What could be worse?

"This was never about Jared, was it?"

Brontie shook his head. "No."

"You used him to get to me."

"Yes." He answered so coldly. "And would again."

"The tape?"

"Used as a threat, but nothing more. If your real father is smart, then he'd see this as an opportunity to do the right thing."

"And what?"

Brontie smiled. "Give me what I want."

I flinched and lowered the glass. He was a monster. A fucking vile monster with no heart and no soul. I wanted to sink to the carpet in front of him. I wanted to scream and howl and scream. *Why me?* But I didn't. I stayed upright, even when my knees felt weak.

"I want to know everything." Trying to keep the revulsion from my tone, I met that sickening gaze. "I want to know it all now."

He moved closer, and I had to fight the urge to whimper and flinch from his touch. "All in good time. Right now, you need to focus on staying in control. He reached into his pocket and pulled his cell free, typing out a message before pocketing it once more.

In an instant, the rear door at the other end of the massive study opened, and a guard stepped in. "Harley will escort you to your private wing. I've had your things sent over from the hotel, along with Mr. Blackburns." He stepped around the desk. "Please let Harley know if there's anything you require, making your stay here a little more comfortable."

"Stay?" I muttered as it dawned. He was serious. "I'm not staying here. Not with you, not *anywhere* near you."

"You will if you want answers, or if you ever want to see those you care about ever again."

I sucked in a hard breath and shook my head. This entire time, I'd been pushed and prodded. I'd had my decisions made for me every step of the damn way. I tried to think as the guard stepped closer. The lingering taste of Scotch tasted bitter in my mouth, making my stomach clench. I had to snap out of this. I had more than myself to think about.

"You're holding me hostage?" I asked.

"Not at all." He gave a shrug. "If there's anywhere you wish to go, day or night, my drivers are at your disposal. Think of this as...ensure your safety."

Ensuring my safety, my ass. He wanted to keep control over me, watch me...protect me? Protect me from what I didn't know. But what was the difference between staying here or staying at the damn hotel with Kyle? The response was simple...

*Answers.*

And with answers came control. The same control he spoke so highly of. Brontie pulled out the high-backed leather seat at his desk. "Now if you'll excuse me, April." He said curtly. "I have some other business to attend to. But I very much look forward to more of our conversations. I only hope you'll come to not see me as the enemy, more as the...*catalyst of change.*"

Catalyst of change? What the Hell did that mean?

I swallowed hard, realising I had little a choice at all. Not if I wanted to find out the truth. I glanced at the guard and then took a step forward. "Don't delude yourself, Brontie. You will always be my enemy in all of this. By the time this is over, I hope you're dead."

He never flinched with the words. Instead, a tiny smile tugged at the corners of his mouth, almost like he was expecting them. Like anything less than venom would be considered...*weak.* "Please enjoy your stay, April."

I wanted to scream, *fuck you!* I wanted to spit in his face. His eyes were ugly, and I wanted to scratch and claw them out. But I didn't. I turned and followed the guard as he motioned toward the door, and I left Brontie and his study behind.

There was no control when it came to the truth and there were no alliances either. Not from those I called family, or the ones I gave my heart to. I stepped out, waiting for the guard to close the door, then followed him deeper into the house.

I wasn't about to take Brontie's words as the truth. I wanted to talk to dad, to ask him to his face. Then I'd see what I needed to decide. I'd know the reason he'd been distant my entire life. As I walked, I couldn't help but see the way he'd treated me, and I hated how Brontie's words resounded a little too well.

My heels sank into the plush carpet, drawing me back to where I was heading. We were moving deeper into the house, then turned to the rear, taking the right-hand hallway to another wing of the house. I slowed and glanced over my shoulder at the opposite wing. The white double doors firmly closed.

A shudder coursed through me at the sight. I didn't need to ask if that was Brontie's personal wing. I just knew.

"There's a fully equipped gym at the rear of the house." The guard spoke, drawing my focus back to him. "As well as a heated pool. The maids come every day, so please let them know if you require anything personal and we are on call twenty-four seven if you should require an escort into the city."

He turned once more as the hallway split once more. "There's a private living room and bathroom in your suite. Meals are at your request, feel free to order anything you want. We have a range of staff on hand."

"I bet you do." I answered, as he stopped at a set of double doors at the end of the hallway. He opened the doors and stepped in after I looked left at another set of double doors.

"We have all your belongings set aside and a full range of personal items you might wish to take advantage of."

"Kyle..." I started, hating how my mind went immediately to him.

The guard motioned at the other set of double doors. "Has been placed in the other suite. If you don't wish to be near him."

"No." My pulse sped as I shook my head. "It's fine."

"Then I'll leave you to get settled. The phone on the desk will connect you with anyone you might need, Ma'am." He nodded carefully and then turned.

He left me standing at the entrance to my room. I glanced to Kyle's room and fought the need to knock on his door. The thought of being here alone was daunting and as much as I hated him, I'd come to need him all at the same time.

Kyle was a drug, one I couldn't fight. But I didn't allow myself to sink to that low, not yet at least. I stepped into the room and closed the doors behind me before I turned and took in the suite's grandeur. White and gold, plush carpet and white sheer ceiling to floor curtains. The place was mind-blowing.

I walked deeper into the place, making my way to the double sliding doors and opened them to a stunning bedroom with a king-sized bed. They indeed hung my clothes neatly in the wardrobe and, well as placed other items in the spaces next to them, bathing suits, lingerie in my size, with the tags still attached plush bathrobes.

The Devil spared no expense. Was this his way of an apology, or something else?

Something sinister?

I swallowed a shudder as my skin crawled, hating how my thoughts turned to Kyle once more. I wanted to talk to him, wanted to look into his eyes as I demanded to know how much of this he knew.

*Just stay close to me.* His words resounded.

The sound of a door opening came from outside the bedroom. Heavy footsteps thudded as they came my way. I turned as the shadow fell against the doorframe and held my breath, ready to face whoever it was...in complete control.

# Chapter Twenty

## KYLE

I stepped into the doorway, watching her eyes widen and her breath catch. Relief flooded through me...for a second at least until I saw the hate and the rage and the desperation in her eyes. Then I stopped. Frozen. Aching. Desperate to go to her.

But what if she hated me?

What if she blamed me for what Brontie did to her...*what did Brontie do to her?* I searched her face, then her body, finding red marks around her wrists. Sonovabitch.

"Did you know?"

I flinched, jerked my gaze to hers. That panicked flicker died like an ember growing darker and colder, just like she grew colder.

"Did. You. Know?"

"Some." The word slipped free before I knew.

"You knew Jared wasn't my brother?"

I nodded.

"You knew my father wasn't my father?"

I nodded again.

"You knew they wanted to use me, that this was never about Jared but about me?"

"Not in the beginning, no."

"But at the end, at the end, you knew." She searched my eyes. "Before or after you fucked me."

Panic filled me as I tried to find the words. But I didn't too. She just nodded, slow and careful. That cold, detached look returned in her eyes. The same look she had when I took her from *him*. The same look *I saved her from.*

Now it was back, and it was back with a vengeance.

"You want to hate me?" I murmured. "Go ahead, I hate myself. I'd give anything to know then what I knew now. If I did...then I'd hurt you worse." She flinched, and I took that flinch to my soul. I stepped closer, watching her breath catch and her lips press together. "I'd hurt you so much you'd run and you'd never look back. You'd hate me. You'd hate me and you'd be safe."

"And pathetically naïve." She answered.

"Yes." I stopped in front of her. "Pathetically naïve. Would you prefer that over this?"

Her gaze danced as it searched mine. I'd never wanted to invade another's thoughts as badly as I did right now. I needed to know...*I was desperate to know.*

"You never gave me the option." She said coldly. "And for that, you can get the fuck away from me."

I stiffened. My pulse booming, driving that panic like a knife through my chest. "No."

The curl of her lips was instant. Teeth bared. Feral and cold. She closed the distance in a heartbeat, rearing her hand backwards before it flew through the air. *Slap.*

Fire lashed my cheek with the sting. I stood there, stunned. Panicked. That desperation howling inside my head like a desperate beast, until I lunged. She whimpered as I grabbed her arms, driving her backwards and onto the bed. I couldn't stop, couldn't slow. I yanked her pants, tearing them down her hips even as I caught the blur of her hand.

*Slap.*

My head snapped sideways before I slowly tuned back. Heat seared my face in the outline of her hand as I fisted her hair, forced her head back to the bed and kissed her hard. The metallic tang of blood bloomed in my mouth. I didn't know if it was her blood or mine.

She lifted her hand again, only this time she didn't lash out. Instead she grabbed me, pulling me hard against her until my lips mashed against my teeth and her hand grab my hair. Her heels fell to the floor with a thud. I frantically tore her pants free before she reached for my zipper.

Anger turned to desperation. I needed to be inside her. "Fuck." I snarled, tearing at her body suit until the snaps ripped free. One yank of my zipper and my cock sprang free. I braced myself, lifted her leg and then rammed inside.

She stiffened, arched her back and released a guttural groan. "Harder."

I pulled free, then bucked my hips, ramming all the way inside her. "You fucking tell me to leave again." I thrust. "I'll take you down to the floor right there and—" thrust. "Fuck the shit out of you." She moaned, bucking and arching, clawing my back with her nails until l hissed with the sting. I lowered my head, my words nothing more than a growl against her ear. "I'm never leaving. Not now...*not ever.*"

My thrusts eased into a rhythm, no longer brutal, more desperate.

She consumed me. The sting of her blows.

The heat of her breath.

The way her body moved under mine.

"Fuck me." She moaned. "Fuck me and make me yours."

*Mine.* That word was a growl in my head. *Mine...mine...MINE.*

She moaned and panted, lifting her head to watch the moment where my body met hers. I pulled free and slowed, driving in hard, slow, stroking that urgency as her pussy clenched around my cock. "That's it." I moaned. "Come for me, April...*come.*"

She rocked her hips, watching as I invaded her body over and over. Slick sounds filled my ears. That slap of our bodies colliding until she dropped her head backwards.

"Look at me." I demanded. "Look at me when you come."

She did, staring into my soul. That detached look driven away, for the moment at last. Here and now she was mine. I gripped her hair, holding her in place as her lips parted with panting breaths. Tight. So fucking tight. She climaxed, letting out a moan as I bucked one last time and came hard.

My balls tightened. Warmth spilled as I filled her.

"Mine." I groaned as I stared into her eyes. "Mine."

We lay like that for a second. I grew soft inside her, slick and warm. Her hands slid over my shoulder, fingers finding the ridge of corded muscles. She hated me. I knew that, but there was a bigger part that needed me as well.

"We'll figure this out." I murmured. "We'll figure this out."

I pulled free and rose, leaving her laying on the bed, the black lace bodysuit unsnapped around her waist and her cunt glistening with cum. She moved, closing her legs.

"No." I demanded, leaning over and moved her leg aside before I looked down.

I wanted to see the remnant of our desire. Wanted to see her my seed spill from her body. I wanted to mark her as my own. "Marry me."

Her eyes widened. "What?"

"Marry me." I knelt over her body. "We can do it tonight. Find a celebrant, say our vows. I can submit the paperwork to the courthouse in the morning. No one needs to know but us."

"Why?" She searched my eyes. "We barely like each other."

I winced with the words. My hammering heart pained with her words. *Barely like each other. We barely like each other.* I pulled away, rising from her. This time when she closed her legs, I made no move to stop her. I adjusted myself, zipped up my pants, watching as she slowly rose. "What?"

I didn't meet her gaze. "Nothing."

There was an awkward silence. I masked the pang in my chest and glanced around her room. It was the same as mine, only this one looked...*prettier.* "He wants you, you know." I turned back to her, watching her reach underneath and grasp the clasps. "Brontie...he wants you."

"So you figured you'd get in first, right?" She snapped the suit closed and lifted her head. "Fuck me, mark me...own me. That's why the desperate attempt to marry me, right?" She rose. "Is that all I am to you, to all of you? A well you can dip your cock into anytime you want. You, Jared...Brontie. When will it be enough?"

She stepped closer, lifting her head to meet my gaze. "When will it be enough?"

The answer echoed in that ache in my chest, and this time the words reached my lips. "When it comes to you...*never*."

# Chapter Twenty-One

I didn't want to feel that rush when Kyle looked at me. Didn't want my body to want him. Even now, as he adjusted his belt and looked down at me, I wanted him. I wanted his body and his love. The thought of that terrified me. "Get out." I forced the words. "Get the fuck out."

He nodded, smothering that flicker of pain. "I'll leave, if that's what you want. But don't think for a second I'll be gone for long. Wherever you go, I go." He stepped closer, looking down at me. "Got that?"

Rage and desperation tore through me. I reached up, grasped the pillow above my head and hurled it through the air at him. "Get the fuck out *now!*"

He slapped the pillow away, leaving it to fall to the floor. One glare and he turned and left, yanking the door closed with a *bang!* I didn't flinch at the sound. Just ground my teeth together and seethed.

"Fuck you!" I roared, then threw myself back on the bed.

I covered my eyes with my hands. I wanted nothing more than to sink into this comforter and disappear. But no matter how much I wanted to, my mind wouldn't switch off.

My father wasn't my father.

Jared wasn't my stepbrother.

And my life...was nothing more than a lie.

I let out a moan and rose from the bed, adjusting the snaps on my bodysuit, tugged on my pants and strode for the bathroom. The heady scent of sex filled the air. I used the toilet and wiped, then touched my belly. I didn't think about the pregnancy. I couldn't afford to. Not yet.

My fingers trembled. My breath caught. It was still early, too early. No one knew about the baby and I had no intention of telling anyone. Including Kyle. The *thud* of a door came from outside. I turned and strode from the bedroom. "If you think for one minute I'm going to sleep with you again—"

I stopped, watching as a maid stepped in, smiled and nodded. "I'm sorry."

She smiled once more and nodded again, pushing a cart into the room, one laden with fresh fruit, wine and chocolate covered strawberries. I stared at it all, then at her, before stepping closer and lowering my voice. "I want to get out of here. Is there anyway you can help me?"

She just looked at me, that detached look in her eyes as she nodded.

"Can you help me?" I repeated. That same smile was there, making me still. "Do you understand what I'm asking?"

Smile. Nod.

"Do you speak English?"

She stilled, then gave a shake of her head.

"You don't speak English."

Another shake.

"And you can't help me, can you?"

Another shake.

I turned away. Of course, Brontie made sure the maids couldn't help me. I let out a groan and turned away. He was probably watching me at this very moment. I froze. My heart hammered as I lifted my gaze, searching the ceiling and the walls.

Cameras...

I swallowed hard and took a step forward as the maid stoked the refrigerator and then hurried from the room. There was no getting out of this for me. No escaping whatever Brontie had in store. Hate rippled through me, burning like fire in my belly.

The maid was no more out the door than a soft knock came. It was the guard, the same one from before. Only this time, he carried a clothes bag over his arm. "Your dress, Ms. Barnett."

He walked in, glanced around the kitchen and stopped. "Would you like it on the sofa, or the bed?"

"What dress? I don't have a dress."

"The one you're to wear to dinner, of course."

"Dinner?"

"With Mr. Brontie."

I froze, then shook my head. "Oh, hell no."

But there was no anger, not even a flicker of displeasure. "Sofa or bed." He asked once more.

I swallowed, my mind racing, trying to weigh up my options.

"Mr. Brontie has specifically instructed you're to attend...*with or without the dress.*"

With or without the dress. The words stopped me cold. I glanced at the carrier over his arm, knowing full well this man would take me kicking and screaming and naked if he had to. He was loyal to one man and one man alone. Whoever wasn't, I suspected, was beaten into submission or taken care of. Either way, Brontie got what he wanted.

"The bed." I answered meekly.

One nod and he strode into the room, placed the dress down and stepped out. "I'll be ready to pick you up at five. Please be ready."

I watched him leave, my heart heavy and aching. I strode to the counter and picked up my phone, glancing. It was only two in the afternoon and yet it felt like today had lasted forever. My belly burned, and I didn't know if it was because I was physically fucking sick from being here, or the fact I had hardly eaten all day. So I made my way to the refrigerator, grabbed out a bottle of water and some grapes.

I drank and ate, hating the way the food tasted so damn good and fought the need to glance at the bedroom door. I wanted to look at the dress. Wanted to see just what Brontie thought he could use to bribe me, or force me to wear.

My hand trembled as I placed the water down on the counter and slowly made my way into the room. I didn't know if it was the covering that made me want to look...or the need to hate it and I would *hate it.* I'd hate everything about the damn dress and him. I'd fucking despise it.

Still, that didn't stop me from dragging down the zipper, revealing inch by inch the elegant, sparkling, figure-hugging gown. "Jesus." I whispered, touching the fabric.

No...

Just no.

I pulled it out of the covering, leaving the bottom of the dress to fall. *My God, it was stunning.* I let out a wounded sound. Why couldn't it be hideous? Why did it have to something that looked stunning? I searched for a tag but of course there was none. It didn't matter. I knew this was expensive.

Probably the most expensive thing I'd ever seen, and defiantly the most I'd ever worn. Now I just felt guilty for wanting to put it on. But of course, that was Brontie's plan all along, wasn't it? Guilt. Threats. Intimation. It was all in his arsenal.

His damn MO.

*Knock. Knock.* "April?" Dad's voice carried.

I dropped the dress to the bed and turned. Fear coursed through my body as I stepped out of the bedroom, finding my dad inside the door. But he wasn't my dad...was he? *He was nothing more than a stranger...*

He looked like a stranger now. Standing there, wringing his hands as he looked at me.

"A dad for hire." The words were free before I realised I spoke them. "I always wondered why you never spoke of my mom much. I just figured the breakup was messy, and I wasn't what she wanted. But now, now this has opened up a massive wound, hasn't it?"

Pain coursed through his face. He took a step forward. "I never meant to hurt you."

"No?" I crossed my arms. "Exactly how did you think something like this would play out? Hey, April. Just FYI. I'm not your dad. I'm just a damn stand in...a paid performer."

"It was never a performance. I care for you."

*"YOU DON'T KNOW ME!"* I screamed. "You don't know a goddamn thing about me!"

He stilled, my torment lingering in the air. Then quietly. "That's where you're wrong."

I sucked in a hard breath, staring at him. Agony coursed through my chest as he came closer, stopping in front of me.

"You're the girl who refused to cry when she fell and scraped her knee when she was three. The girl who came tearing through my study when I was in a meeting to scream at the top of your lungs how Miss Martha was getting married. You're the girl who ate only chicken and noddle soup for an entire month because all the kids had the flu at school and you were sure that you were getting it and the young woman who refused to give up on her dreams when she was knocked back from Dartmouth. You think being blood makes me any less proud of you? Or stops me from loving you? I couldn't love you more even if I tried."

I didn't know what to say.

"You want to blame me for lying? Go ahead, I deserve it. But what I don't deserve is to have my love discounted just because you don't carry my DNA. I love you, April. I've always loved you."

"Even so, instead of telling me the truth and protecting me from any of this, you let it all play out." I answered coldly. He might think that recounting my childhood was enough to hide the truth. "Like a real father would."

He stilled. HIs breaths making his chest rise.

"Because you knew, right? You knew what kind of man Brontie was, and you knew you were backed into a corner. What does he want from my father? *My real father.*"

This stranger shook his head.

I stepped closer, hiding the sting. "Money, power."

"Everything. You father is a very rich man, April. Turn on the TV and you'll find his name mentioned at least twice in the hour. Brontie wants to force him into the deals that could take it from him."

I winced at the words, my heart hurting as my mind raced. "I'd give it all...if it was me."

But that was it, wasn't it? They wouldn't. Not these men with their money and their power. They wouldn't sacrifice for me.

"But you didn't answer the question. Did you know? The day you and Connie left for your honeymoon, did you know?"

"Yes." The answer was a fist to my chest. "I knew he'd come after me, but I had no idea—"

"Get out." The words were a hiss.

"April."

I stepped backwards. "Get the fuck out now. I never want to see you again."

There was a tiny shake of his head.

*"GET THE FUCK OUT!"* I screamed. *"LEAVE!"*

He stumbled backwards, that agony cutting deep. Then, with a slow nod, he turned and left, quietly closing the door behind him. I waited for that *thud* before I fell apart. The agony I'd held at bay from the past few days hit me. Tears came in a torrent, sliding down my face.

I raced for the bedroom, slamming the door behind me as heavy sobs came. I couldn't get away fast enough. Couldn't hide myself away further enough. I closed myself in the bathroom and stumbled to the far wall before I sank to the cold tiled floor.

I cried. Cried for me...cried for everything. For Jared and Kyle.

For the positions we found ourselves in.

There was no getting out of this. Not from a man like Brontie.

What he wanted...he got.

I pulled my knees to my chest, knowing I'd have no choice but to get ready in the next few hours. I'd have to put on the dress and play this game. The game that started and ended with him... I only hoped I'd survive tonight...

*With my body and soul intact.*

## Chapter Twenty-Two

I DIDN'T LIKE THIS DRESS, DIDN'T LIKE THIS MAKEUP. I didn't like the expensive body wash I squeezed onto the loofah and scrubbed along my arm. The scent hit me, soft, seductive and carnal. I closed my eyes, hating how something inside me sighed with relief.

No...just no.

I scrubbed and washed, digging my fingers into my scalp as I massaged. I didn't want this. Not from Brontie, or any of his asshole guards he had worked for him. I slid the conditioner along the strands, working the ends until they slipped through my fingers.

A tremble of fear moved through me as I rinsed and switched off the water. The room was quiet, too quiet. I wrapped a towel around my body and one around my hair before I stepped out into the bedroom and attempted to avoid looking at the dress splayed out on the end of the bed.

Kyle...

I licked my lips and stepped out of the bedroom and glanced around the empty sitting area, and then through the sheer curtains that led to a private balcony. The place was stunning, truly stunning. Pity it was owned by a soulless, black-hearted, pathetic excuse for a man.

My stomach gave a tremble, drawing my focus to the life growing inside me. A life I needed to think about. A life, "I am thinking about."

Kinda…

I unwrapped the towel from my hair and glanced toward the door. Time was ticking. I massaged the back of my neck and glanced toward the bedroom. The gold dress drawing my gaze. "Goddamnit."

I made my way back inside, unwrapped the towel from my body and picked up the sheer black panties and matching bra. "A dinner with Lucifer. Why the fuck not?"

I slipped the underwear on, hooked the bra and slid the straps in place. With every second, I felt my life slipping away. I wasn't in control of this shit show. My future was about to change dramatically, baby, or no baby.

Jared, Kyle and now Brontie saw to that.

I made my way to the bathroom, hit the overhead mirror lights and glanced along the brand new selection of makeup that was in my perfect shade. "Fuck you, asshole."

I applied my makeup carefully, keeping it light. Christ, I gave a shit about my makeup now? I applied powder and stepped away, hating that I looked…*nice.*

The dress slid on perfectly. The damn heels even better. I tugged up the zipper and turned to the full-length mirror as a sharp *knock* came from outside the bedroom. I ground my jaw as met my gaze. Outside, the door opened. A wince came from the corner of my eye.

"April?"

I jerked my gaze upwards at the familiar voice and to the bedroom door. *No...God, no.* The one voice I didn't want to hear...the one man I didn't want to see...my stepbrother—*Jared.*

For a second, I was frozen, my knees locked. Fear rooting me in the same spot as a shadow spilled across the doorframe. But there was no way I was letting him in this bedroom. I straightened my spine, hating how that flutter in my belly came at the sound of his voice.

I straightened my spine and forced myself to move, stepping into the doorway and then headed for the kitchenette. "What do you want, Jared?"

He froze when I walked out, his gaze moving from my face, then along my body as he took in the dress. "Wow, okay. You look..."

I jerked my gaze his way. "Clean? Nourished? Healthy? Are those the words you're going for?"

He winced at the bite in my tone. My hands were shaking when I grabbed a fresh bottle of water from the refrigerator and cracked open the cap. I gripped the bottle tighter, trying to still the shake in my hand...but I couldn't. Water sloshed against the sides, hitting my chest. The blast of cold was instant, soaking through the dress. "Shit." I snapped.

Jared moved fast. "Here." He snatched the clean towel from the counter and strode forward.

But the last thing I wanted was him touching me. "I've got it." I snatched the towel from his hand and gave him my back.

"Oh...okay." He murmured, sounding hurt. Like he had a goddamn nerve to feel anything when it came to me.

I spun, desperation and anger a dangerous combination. "What the fuck do you want, Jared?"

His brows narrowed. His mouth opened. But I didn't give him a chance to speak. The cold, hard truth was I didn't want to know. I didn't want to hear his voice…it haunted me enough as it was. I dabbed the water that darkened the top of the dress.

"April…can we at least talk?"

My hand stilled, pressing the cloth to the dress as another knock came at the door. From the corner of my eye, Brontie's bodyguard strode through the door and into the room, casting my stepbrother a glare. "Jared." He muttered.

I turned around, catching a bemused smirk on his face as the guard glanced my way. "Am I interrupting?"

"No." I answered instantly.

"*Yes.*" Jared tried to stare him down.

But he wasn't the one calling the shots here—not anymore. I never looked my stepbrother's way. Just faced the bodyguard, Harley. "Are we doing this, or what?"

One brow rose on the bodyguard. "Sure." He gave a slow jerk of his head. "If you'd like to follow me."

I wouldn't…

I'd rather walk barefoot across broken glass…

But I'd take that over being in the same room as Jared any day. I couldn't face him. Not yet. I wasn't ready. Maybe I'd never be ready. I swallowed at the thought and stepped around my stepbrother, making my way to the door.

My heels clacked against the expensive Italian tiles as I headed along the hallway, not even stopping for the guard to open the door. Just yanked it and was out in an instant. A pent up breath released in a *whoosh* and the corridor greyed at the edges, leaving me wobbly.

"Easy." Harley grabbed my arm. "You okay?"

I nodded...but it was a lie.

I wasn't okay. I wasn't anywhere near okay. But there was no way out of this for me. I was backed into a corner...or a series of corners. One side Jared, the other side Kyle and the beast who came for me was Brontie taking swipes anyway he could.

All wanted their pound of flesh.

But I had nothing left to give.

"Fine." I focused on slowing my breaths and slowly the grey at the edges of my vision brightened. I ground my jaw and forced myself to walk, slowing enough for Harley to surge ahead, opening doors as he went. He led me to the side of the sprawling mansion, then to a small door that led outside to a path of cobblestone steps and lush gardens.

The place was an oasis and any other time I might have enjoyed staying here. Might even allow myself to fall in love with it a little. But this place wasn't an oasis...it was a trap. The path led down to the towering concrete wall and small black gate.

Harley punched in a code. But he wasn't fast enough...9...9...3... 3. The lock gave a *click*, and the gate released. I glanced away, making a mental note of the code and stepped out. A sleek Maserati waited parked at the curb. Brontie climbed out of the open driver's door and rounded the back of the sports car. "Thanks, Harley, I can take it from here."

*No.* I froze watching him. Dressed in neat black pants, a white, open-collared shirt with sleeves rolled against powerful forearms. He looked *stunning*. The kind of stunning that turned heads everywhere he went. *Oh, hell no...*

I swallowed and glanced at the bodyguard, silently pleading for him not to leave.

But he didn't see my pleas, just nodded. "Of course, Mr. Brontie."

I shook my head when he turned. "Wait."

Harley stopped, his gaze moving to mine.

"April!" Kyle roared from behind the towering wall. *"April! Where the fuck are you?"*

"APRIL!" Jared roared from the left behind the wall. *"I'm not leaving until we damn well talk!"*

My heart boomed. Thundering. The sound swallowing everything else and in an instant my world seemed to sway once more.

"When you're ready." Brontie urged, his voice a deep, resounding murmur.

I jerked my gaze to his. He knew. God, he knew. He gave a smirk and motioned to the open car door.

"April, for fuck's sake!" Jared pleaded. "Let's talk about this."

Jared...

Kyle...

*Brontie.*

"I'm done." The words slipped out before I knew. "I'm just fucking done."

I stepped forward, and for a second Brontie's grin grew wider, until I stepped past the open door of his sports car and rounded the front, heading for the street.

Fuck them all.

I was done playing their games...

*I was done with them all.*

I wanted out of this. They can use the footage. They can trash my name.

I pressed my hand to my stomach. I was putting me first.

For once...and for all.

# Chapter Twenty-Three



"April!" Kyle screamed from behind me.

A grunt came from somewhere closer as a hand was thrown over the top of the fence. "April." Jared grunted as he crawled and heaved himself over the top of the fence. "Wait. Come on..."

*Fuck no.*

I kept on walking, leaving Kyle, Jared and Brontie behind, until a hand clamped around my wrist and I was jerked around.

"I don't think so, sweetheart." Brontie growled and with a step forward, he bent, picked me up around the waist and hauled me over his shoulder.

"Let me down!" I roared, catching the blur as Jared hit the ground with a *thud.* Kyle followed, lunging over the top of the fence with barely a grunt.

"In." Brontie turned his head to meet my gaze as he lowered me to the ground. "Unless you prefer, I leave you with these two?"

Jared and Kyle rose, brushed their pants and both stared at me with needy glances. I looked at the open door and then Brontie as he jerked his head to the open car door. I didn't have a choice, not really. As much as I wanted to walk away from all of them and never look back, I wouldn't get far. Not in these heels.

I glanced at my stepbrother and the moody glare from Kyle as they looked at me longingly before I met Brontie's stare. "Touch me like that again and I'll kick you in the balls."

I didn't give him an opportunity to speak, just stepped into the car and yanked the seatbelt across. Brontie climbed in behind the wheel, hit the button for the doors to close and started the engine. He pulled the car out and accelerated hard. I didn't want to see them, didn't want to feel the pang in my chest. But I did. I lowered my gaze to the side mirror, watching them as we drove away.

———

Kyle

"WAIT! *APRIL!*" I roared and stumbled forward, watching the Maserati drive away. The gate behind me gave a beep. But I didn't care who it was. I didn't even turn around, just stood there, next to that fucking asshole, Jared, as he pathetically watched them drive away.

"You know he's going to take her."

I winced at Alexi's voice.

"If you don't do some—"

I spun. "What? What do you suggest I do?"

Alexi just stood there, arms crossed, gaze tortured. "Maybe pull your head out of your ass."

Jared smirked and shook his head, drawing Alexi's gaze. "Same goes for you!"

The smile faltered on the sonofabitch's face I fought the surge of enjoyment at the sight.

"You want her away from him?" Alexi watched the Maserati drive away. "I want her away from him. But how much are you willing to pay for that to happen?"

"As much as it takes." I said.

"Everything." Jared answered at the same time.

Alexi turned his head to meet my gaze. "I told you before, Jared. You need to give him someone else. Someone he wants more than he wants April."

"Who?" I stepped closer.

Alexi scowled, conflicted. "I shouldn't." He murmured and turned away, heading for the locked gaze.

"Wait." Jared lunged forward, baring the way. "I don't fucking think so. What the Hell do you mean, *'give him someone else'*?"

"Nothing." Alexi side-stepped him and reached for the keypad on the gate. "Forget I said a word."

The code entry made a beep before the gate clicked open. Alexi was striding through, leaving Jared to stride after him. *He was going after him...to find a way to save April.* "Like fucking Hell he is."

I made for the gate, lengthening my stride. "There are others." I repeated the words from before. "Other women. Other targets."

Alexi's stride quickened, leaving Jared to shoot me a glare over his shoulder. "What women?"

"What the fuck do you think?" I shoved forward, barging him out of the way. He stumbled off the slate stone path and into the garden. I smirked at the sight as Alexi headed for the side door and stepped into the house.

He tried to slam the door on me...asshole. I grabbed it, wincing as it was crushed in the doorjamb and shoved it open. "There *are* others."

"No." Alexi barked. "No...*no*...*no*...*no*. Not going to happen."

I barged in. "You *think* I want this? You think I'd trade her life for another?"

"That's exactly what you're asking." He hissed at me. "I can't give *you* the names. He'll kill *me*."

"He won't." I stepped closer.

"Get the fuck out of the way." Jared growled behind me.

I caught sight of the gun before the *bang!* The gunshot tore through the room as Alexi stumbled backwards, his eyes widening in shock.

"What the fuck?" I roared and spun.

Alexi buckled, blood blooming through the white shirt on his shoulder. He looked down. "You...y-you *shot me?*"

"And I'll shoot you again." Jared stepped forward, taking aim at Alexi's head.

I looked around, panicked that one of the guards was going to step around the corner and open fire. "Jared, what the fuck are you trying to do? Get us killed?"

"You? Maybe." He muttered. "Whatever it takes to get April back."

"Fuck you, asshole." I snapped, then turned my attention to Alexi shivering and whimpering on the ground. "The files, Alexi."

"No." He shook his head. "I won't do it."

I glanced at the gun and then Jared. "Doesn't look like you have a choice."

"*We* don't have a choice." Jared answered. "Not anymore."

There was something in words, or in his voice. A tremor of fear coursed through me. Still I jerked my gaze to Alexi. "The files."

"Please." He muttered, his skin turning a pasty grey. "You don't want to do this."

"Oh, I'm pretty sure we do." I answered.

"Files." Jared commanded. "Now."

My breaths were racing as I stepped forward, bent and grabbed Alexi's arm, hauling him to his feet. "Don't make us hurt you."

He glared at me, the spark of hate and fear colliding. "You know he'll kill you for this?"

I just nodded as I pushed Alexi toward the hallway and the back of the house. I did know that, but right now, I didn't care. I wasn't going to lose her, not to a destructive bastard like Brontie —I glanced over my shoulder to find Jared following—not to anyone.

"You'd do the same thing," I murmured. "For the person you loved."

Guilt swallowed me, taking down into the seven levels of Hell as I pushed Alexi to the double doors of his wing, then topped him, opening the door, and shoved him inside. Jared followed us in, closing and locking the door behind us.

"I'm bleeding." Alexi whimpered as he looked down at the wound.

I led him to the sofa and eased him down. "Let me look." I stared into his eyes and bent down, working the buttons of his shirt.

"You know, I fantasised about this." He muttered, holding my gaze. "I just didn't think I'd take me getting shot for it to happen."

"While you two lovebirds are getting your flirt on, I want the files." Jared neared the large desk in the middle of the room. Where, and don't make me shoot you again."

Alexi jerked his gaze upwards as a hard knock at the door came.

"*Alexi.*" Came the deep snarl from one of the guards. "We heard a gunshot. Is everything okay?"

Panic surged inside me. Jared stopped rifling through the contents on Alexi's desk and straightened, glancing from me to Alexi.

"Get me up." Alexi forced the words through clenched teeth.

There was nothing I could do, only watch as Alexi snarled, baring his teeth and muttering under his breath as he grabbed my arm and hauled himself to his feet instead. He snapped his focus to Jared. "Your jacket...*now.*"

"Alexi?" Came the insistent guard through the door.

"I'm coming!" He snapped. "Just hold the fuck on."

He held out his hand to Jared, motioning him to hurry. The trigger-happy asshole had the gall to glance my way, as if I would be the one to save his pathetic ass. I'd rather throw him under the fucking bus. But the problem with feeding Jared to the wolves was, the bastard would take me with him.

I gave a nod, leaving him to place his gun down on the desk and shrug out of his jacket before handing it over. Alexi slipped it on, then turned his attention to the door as the guard gave a *boom!*

The guy stumbled, then braced his hand against the door, before jutting his chin high and straightening his spine. He twisted the lock and jerked open the door, wide enough for the guard to see me sitting on the sofa and Jared now standing in the middle of the room.

"This better be fucking important." Alexi snarled at the guard.

I knew what it looked like from where the security stood. Alexi with his shirt half undone, me sitting on the sofa looking guilty as fuck, and Jared glaring as the guard scanned the room.

"There was a gunshot." The guard murmured.

"Well, as you can see, there's no problem. Interrupt me again without good fucking reason and I'll have your balls, understand that?"

The guard glanced my way once more, his cheeks rushing. "Sure." He muttered and stepped away.

I wanted for Alexi to close and lock the door, and the fading thud of the guard's footsteps before I released a pent up breath.

"Now." Alexi turned to Jared and me. "I give you this name, and you get me to a goddamn hospital."

"Agreed." Jared said to the both of us.

I rose from the sofa. We were really doing this, giving Brontie someone he wanted more than he wanted April...

*Jesus, we truly were monsters.*

*God save us all.*

# Chapter Twenty-Four

I EXPECTED US TO DRIVE TO THE RESTAURANT STRAIGHT away. I hoped for that really, desperate to spend as little time with my abductor as possible. But we didn't. Instead, Brontie took his time heading out of the city, working the horsepower of the sleek sports car as we climbed.

I spent my time staring out of the window, pressed against the door. It felt too awkward. Too much like I gave in, like I didn't fight him hard enough, or scream loud enough. Or do a million other things that raced through my mind?

"You're quiet."

I flinched at the sound of his voice, but kept my gaze focused on the darkening skyline as we climbed higher and higher until we levelled out and stopped along the edge of the lookout. My breath caught at the sight, my words escaping me. Below was a blanket of stars. Stars that crawled, glinting red and blue and white, and behind the city dark, towering mountains stood protectively.

"It's beautiful, isn't it?"

I'd almost forgotten he was there, wished for it hard enough and it still didn't come true. But he was, and the more I grew aware of him, the more I wanted out. The car throbbed as it idled. It wasn't lost on me that a few weeks ago I was scrounging stale food out of motel vending machines and wearing clothes that's been washed in a handbasin.

Now here I was, sitting in a half a million dollar car, wearing a dress that was far more expensive than anything else I'd ever hoped to wear and I hated it. I hated it all. I hated the fact that both Jared and Kyle were in my life, hated the fact that a part of me wanted them there. That I *ached* to have them there. Even if both of them were after blood.

"You can spend all night in silence, if that's what you wish. Maybe you'd be more comfortable if I did all the talking?"

I clenched my jaw, staring at the tiny trail of cars until they were a blur.

"I didn't start with money." He started. "I fact I started in similar circumstances like you did, destitute, homeless, a thief, until one day I was abducted, just like you."

I lifted my hand to the door handle. I wanted out of here, out without hearing another word out of his mou—

"I was taken by a man, a cruel man. A man who called himself family. We might've shared blood, but we were nothing alike."

*No...no, don't listen.* My fingers were curled around the handle, pulling it until I felt the lock grab.

"I was forced into a position I didn't want, so I know how much you might hate me right now."

"I doubt that." I forced the words through clenched teeth. My gaze fixed on my fingers around the handle.

"Which is why I bought you up here to offer you a way out. I'm prepared to let you leave."

I froze. "Leave?" I glanced his way.

He just nodded. "Tonight, if you want to. Let me take you to dinner, after all you're wearing the dress. Then after that, if you chose to, you can pack up your things and walk out. I'll even have my driver take you to the airport."

My heart was booming. "Just like that?"

"Just like that."

"No strings?"

"Not after tonight, where you're concerned."

That elation died away in an instant. "What does that mean?"

"Your father stays." Brontie held my gaze. "To fulfil his obligations, as well as Mr. Blackburn and your stepbrother, Jared."

A pang tore across my chest. I swallowed hard, finding that sparkle in his eyes.

"Take the night to think about it." He leaned forward, shoved the car into gear. "Then when we're done, you can let me know what you decide."

*You bastard...*

I wanted to say the words out loud. I wanted to tell him exactly what I thought of him nd his goddamn offer. But I couldn't, because Brontie knew exactly what he was doing. He was pushing me into a corner, making me choose between my own well-being and those who I love.

Love...

That ache in my chest grew colder, sending a chill through me as Jared and Kyle filled my mind. My father, who wasn't really my father, was much to blame for this as anybody. But Jared and Kyle were forced into this just as much as I was. They didn't want this whole filthy game Brontie forced us to play.

That ache grew inside me as Brontie drove us down the mountain and headed into the city, pulling up outside a very expensive restaurant and parked the car.

He climbed out, rounded the rear and opened my door. I didn't want to take his hand, didn't want to touch him at all. But his words and his proposition stayed with me. I'd be lying if I didn't say part of me wanted away from him and his entire disgusting mess.

That was the only reason I took his hand. The only reason I swallowed the acid that rose in the back of my throat and the only reason I followed Brontie into the restaurant. We didn't have to stop inside the entry, didn't have to give our name. The maître d smiled as Brontie neared, then ushered us to a table toward the rear of the restaurant.

Smoked salmon crepes came first, then braised duck and vegetables. We ate in silence and as the servers fussed around Brontie, I through of his offer. Leave, just like that. Could I do that?

"Would you care for the deserts menu?" The waiter asked.

Brontie glanced at my plate, still half full and shook his head. "No, thank you." His dark eyes sparkled when he glanced at my untouched wine. "You don't like it?"

"I'm not in the mood."

"Something stronger, perhaps?"

I just shook my head and picked up the glass of water instead. Brontie's brow rose, which made my pulse jump and race. "Are you ready to leave, then?"

I gave a nod, pushed my chair out as I rose. Brontie strode to the front, signed the bill and then waited for me. *Leave.* That word haunted me, just like he knew it would. I walked out and slipped inside the car when Brontie opened the door.

He climbed in behind the wheel and started the engine. I didn't know what I expected when it came to tonight. But it certainly wasn't an opportunity for a way out. My belly was full, too full, making me feel drowsy as Brontie started the engine and pulled out.

He drove, and I was lost in the smooth movement of the car as he took the long way through the city. But we didn't go back to his house. Instead, we pulled up outside some kind of club. Brontie killed the engine and was out before I realised.

He opened my door. "One last surprise." He offered his hand, giving me a sly smile. "Humour me."

I glanced to the dark, brick painted building with its dark tinted windows. "What place is this?"

"Only the most decadent desert you've ever had in your life." He answered. "After this, I'll take you back...to your brother."

I glanced at the building, then took his hand and rose. Jared and Kyle's screams still rang in my head. I wasn't in any rush to go back to that. So I took his hand and climbed out. My body felt slow from the floor as Brontie closed the door behind me and led me not to the front door, but to a gated entrance where he punched in a code, then opened the door. "After you."

"A desert that has this kind of security has to be good." I muttered, glancing around.

A flutter of nerves filled my chest. I glanced around as we walked, heading to a door where Brontie knocked twice hard. It was opened by a bouncer and the moment it did, the heavy throb of music spilled through.

"April." Brontie lingered in the door.

I didn't want to go in there. I wanted to go back...*where?* Home? I had no home, not the one where I grew up, or the filthy motels I shared with Jared, or the hotel rooms I had with Kyle, and home sure as hell wasn't the luxury suite I was staying in now.

That desperation filled me and Brontie saw it all. "You can leave after tonight." He urged carefully. "I give you my word."

That flutter of panic in my chest turned to hope. I forced myself to move and took a step, following him inside what some kind of club. The bouncer locked the door behind us.

"Wage we met earlier today, I told you about my plans, and how they involve your father." Brontie started. "Your real father."

I jerked my gaze to his as he led me past a dark and empty bar. There were no people sitting at the tables, no dancers on the softly lit stage, even though the soft, seductive music filled the air.

"What I didn't tell you was, I wasn't the only one with an image of the future. A certain kind of future. One, a select few of us control."

I was so caught up in that growing confusion and the deep baritone of his voice; I found myself in a hallway, standing outside a door. One turn of the handle and he pushed the door wide.

Darkness waited inside.

"We will control the narrative of society, April, with money, power, and fear if we have to." He stepped aside, motioning me inside that room. "You can now be part of that narrative. You want out, then I'll grant you that. It will come with consequences of course."

Movement came from behind me, making me jerk my gaze over my shoulder. The bouncer from the door stepped up behind me, his hard gaze fixed on me.

"Consequence like that life inside you." Brontie murmured. "I said you could leave after tonight...and we still have a quite a few hours left. Hours that could be spent inside that room...or in the hospital's emergency ward."

I flinched and jerked my gaze to his. Brontie stepped closer, lifting his hand to graze my cheek. "We wouldn't want anything to happen to that life, would we?"

My senses screamed. Cold danced across my skin.

"So make the choice, April. Step inside the room and join me... or I'll have Peter here escort you home."

I stared at that open door, knowing exactly what waited for me if I didn't step inside. Pain. Loss...*terror*. I lifted my gaze to Brontie and found that cruel sparkle in his eyes.

"I told you before, I'd have you either way." He murmured. "You just didn't listen."

# Chapter Twenty-Five

I STARED AT THAT OPEN DOOR AND GRIPPED MY CELL phone, knowing that once I stepped inside that room, everything would change. The bouncer moved closer, drawing my gaze.

"In or out, April." Brontie murmured. "It's your choice."

My choice? How was any of this my choice? I should never have stepped into the car. I should've kept on walking. I should've run and kept on running. I should've never been born.

Those words stopped me cold.

*Boom!*

I flinched at the sound and stumbled. Brontie started forward, grabbing me by the shoulders and shoved me aside. *"Stay here!"* He roared to the bouncer. *"Make sure she's protected!"*

He left, charging through the hallway, leaving me and the bouncer who was prepared to put me in the hospital behind. I jerked my gaze to him and then to the open door of that room.

*Boom!* The explosion came again.

I pressed my spine against the wall and jerked my gaze to the bouncer. "What the fuck are you waiting for? *Go!*"

Panic tore through his gaze as he glanced toward the sound.

I stumbled forward, giving him a shove. *"He could die out there!"*

There was a second where I thought he wasn't going, but then he gave a snarl and charged forward. *Go...GO!* He left in a deafening thunder of footsteps. I didn't waste a second. Glancing over my shoulder at that open door, I grabbed my dress and charged ahead.

Screams filled the restaurant, people shoved and lunged, driving from the front of the restaurant and into the back. I moved with the rush, pushing past the swinging doors that led to the kitchen. A man pushed behind me, blood trickled down his cheek.

"Get out of the way!" He barged me to the side, pushing his way past the stoves crammed with pots and pans.

I stumbled forward, shoving out my hand as I hit the bench. Agony tore through my side. A cry ripped fire. I shoved backwards and kept on moving, driving myself toward the rear door. I pushed through, scanning the back alley and kept on running.

*Get out...get out of here.*

Terror spilled around me. I risked a glance over my shoulder and kept on moving, running with the rest of the crowd and caught sight of the guard as he stumbled out of the restaurant and scanned the others. I had to get away from him...like...*now.*

I glanced down at my dress. Of course I'd have to wear something like this. The wail of sirens cut through the air up ahead. I stumbled to the side, hugging the other buildings and spied the opening of an alley up ahead. I just had to get there. I kicked off my heels, bent and snatched them from the asphalt and raced ahead, my bare feet slapping on the road. A cop car tore along the street, screeching to a halt at the rear of the restaurant. I didn't know what happened, but I sure as hell knew they wouldn't protect me. Not from someone like Brontie.

So I kept running, tearing down the alley as most of those running from the restaurant carried on ahead. Footsteps thundered, rebounding against the side of the building as we ran...until I slowed. The fence of a house was on one side. The corrugated iron damaged and buckled in one section, covered by thick green plastic...the corner flapping in the wind. Clothes were draped over the line that ran from what looked like a lean-to at the rear. I glanced at the others who kept running, heading back to the main road and away from the blast of the restaurant.

I still didn't know what happened, if it was the explosion came from restaurant itself or more. All I knew, there was no way I was going back there, not with Brontie, or his fucking bodyguard. I turned to that flapping plastic, hiked my dress up and lunged forward.

"Please don't have a dog. *Please don't have a dog.*" I yanked my dress up with one hand and gripped the fence with the other and lunged.

My dress snagged on the wire, tearing with a rip. But then I was over, stumbling through someone's backyard and raced for the clothes draped over the line.

They were a woman's. About the same size as me, jeans, t-shirts, and a man's sweater. I snatched them free and hurried for shelter, reaching around for the zipper on my dress and yanked it down.

I dressed, watching the alley, desperation screaming inside me. They'd come...and soon. I tossed the dress over the line and hurried forward, yanking on the sweater as I went. The heels I couldn't do anything about not yet. I slipped them on and stumbled forward. Dogs barked at me from the neighbouring yard. I watched them, hurrying forward along the side of the house and out to the street.

There was no one home. The house was quiet, no cars were parked out front. Red and blue lights of emergency services crammed the street out in front of the restaurant. The flickering bright the lights glaring against the night. The pathway was blocked off, police held back the growing crowd. But through the gaps of those gathering, I saw the remains of Brontie's Maserati...now blown apart in ruins.

That was the explosion. I stopped, stared, unable to recognise the ruins. The doors were thrown open. The windows were shattered. It hardly looked like a car, not one I recognised. Someone was out for him. It didn't take a genius to know Brontie had enemies, ones who were now making their presence known.

I stumbled backwards, away from the restaurant and everyone else. My heels clattered, too damn loud, but I couldn't do anything about that. I just lowered my head, hunched my shoulders and started walking, leaving the restaurant and the few houses far behind.

Sirens howled as they raced past. With every piercing sound, my pulse jacked that little bit higher. I walked until my feet burned, then took off my heels, casting them aside into a dumpster. I was in a strange city with no money and no friends, no one who wasn't Jared or Kyle.

And they weren't friends.

For all I knew, they could be in on this.

My cell vibrated in my pocket. I pulled it free and caught the No Caller ID before quickly stabbing the button and killing the screen. Panic made me look over my shoulder as I stepped up onto the sidewalk, heading past more shops.

My bare feet slapped against the pavement. I tucked my hair into the collar of my sweater and glanced over my shoulder. *Smack!* I hit something hard and stumbled sideways.

"Hey!" He barked.

"Sorry...*I'm so sorry.*" I mumbled, righting myself and kept on walking.

I hurried, until my feet burned and I was breathless, and when the crowd grew dangerous. Catcalls rang out from guys across the street. Shouts of men on the fringes of a fistfight. I slid my hands into my pockets, lowered my gaze and kept on walking until I realised I had nowhere else to turn.

It was getting too dangerous to be out here.

A small neon sight beckoned *Warm Meals. Soup Kitchen.* I made for that sign, stepping around men and women chatting and lingering outside. They looked at me, then down to my bare feet as I stepped inside, shivering. It was getting cold, and there was no way I could survive a night on the streets. No way I *would* survive. Not now...not when I had more than myself to think about.

"Hey." A soft male voice came from behind me. "Are you okay?"

I turned to find a man with the kindest brown eyes I'd ever seen. He took one look at me, smiled and said, "Let me get you some place quiet to sit."

I just nodded, desperation roaring through me. He nursed me, guiding me through the crowd with a hand on my arm, until we found a quiet corner away from the crowd. "Here." He motioned to a seat.

I dropped, pulling my bare feet up to massage the burn. He took one look at me, his expression softening. "Let me get you a blanket and some food."

I shook my head, shivering. "I'm not hungry, thank you. But I will take the blanket."

He gave a nod and left, returning a minute later with a heavy, grey wooden blanket. "Do you have someone I can call? Someone who can come and get you?"

Someone he can call? My cell rang. I jerked my gaze to the screen and pressed the button, sending it to voice mail. I swallowed hard. "I don't know."

He looked at my bare feet, then at my shaking hands. "Are you in trouble?"

A soft chuckle slipped free. *Am I in trouble?* I lifted my gaze to his. He wouldn't believe me, even if I told him.

And I couldn't tell him.

I couldn't tell anyone.

Brontie was a man who not just track anyone down I spoke to but would also destroy them. I glanced around at the many people in needed. There was no way I'd bring that man's wrath to this place of kindness. So I shook my head. "No, thank you. The blanket is perfect."

"How about a coffee?"

I smiled, giving him a nod. "How about tea?"

He beamed. "Tea we have."

He left, making his way through those in need. Those who had life harder than me. Those who struggled to find a purpose. I lowered my hand, my fingers finding my stomach. My cell vibrated once more and even though I knew who it was, still I looked.

*Jared.*

His name glared on the screen. Fear punched through my chest, following with a wave of desperation. One so powerful it hit me like a blow. I was lifting my cell and pressing the button before I knew.

"April?" He cried. *"April?"*

"It's me." I said quietly as tears blurred the room around me.

"Jesus Christ, we heard about the explosion. Are you okay?"

I licked my lips, the words a hard knot in the back of my throat. "I'm okay. But I'm not coming back, Jared. I'm not coming back to you or Kyle...and not to Brontie."

"What?" He murmured.

Silence filled the air.

"April?"

I lowered my hand...the sound of his voice was so small.

*"April?"*

I lifted my finger, hovering over the button to end the call... when he said.

"I know about the baby." His words drifted, so faint. "April, I know."

# Chapter Twenty-Six

JARED

"You okay here?" Kyle muttered, staring at the hive of doctors and nurses that rushed around us.

Alexi winced. "Sure, great." He muttered, glaring at me. "I mean sitting here with a bullet wound the size of the Grand Canyon in my damn shoulder."

"It's a flesh wound." I stared at the dressing taped across his arm.

"It's a *very large* flesh wound." He snapped, glanced at the nearby doctors, and then hissed at me. "You could've *killed me.*"

I stepped closer and bent down. "If I wanted to do that, I'd aim a little higher than your damn shoulder."

Kyle cut me a glare. Fuck him. Fuck this asshole, too. I straightened, feeling that hum of desperation inside me. They didn't understand a goddamn thing. But I did. I understood perfectly what was happening.

My fucking woman was in the car with a goddamn viper.

"Mr. Roth?" I glanced toward the young male doctor as he stepped closer. There was a scowl on his face as he looked at me and then Kyle. "I was wondering if we could have a word in private?"

Alex flinched. "Okay."

"We'll be out in the waiting room." Kyle turned, jerked his head at me, motioning for me to follow.

I clenched my jaw. Every time the bastard looked my way, I wanted to empty my fucking gun at him. Put him in my line of fire and see if I aimed at his shoulder. I'd move the muzzle to his heart if I knew the piece of shit had one.

Still, I followed, making my way out into the waiting area. It was a fucking flesh wound. How damaging could it be? I ignored the scowling looks from Kyle. I looked at that bastard one more time and I'd do something I'd regret.

"We need to find these files." Kyle pushed through the doors and stepped out into the waiting room. He cast a snarl my way, before meeting my gaze. "We find these files and we find someone else who can take April's place. Don't give me any fucking shit about throwing someone—"

"I agree."

He stopped, turned and finally met my stare. "You do?"

He had no fucking idea, did he? I stepped closer, staring into his eyes. "Whatever it takes to get my...to get April away from Brontie."

There was a second where he almost got it, almost saw how desperate I was to have her back. "How far are you willing to go?" He asked. "This could get messy."

He expected me to flinch. He expected me to back out and give up on her. He didn't know how dark my world became the moment she left me. No, not left—*taken*. My lips curled. "I'll let you know when I reach the end."

A nerve twitched in the corner of his eye. He didn't like that, didn't like that. I refused to just...*go away*. He didn't know me very well...and he sure as hell didn't know my goddamn stepsister. Not as well as he thought, anyway.

He finally broke the stare, turning instead to pace the waiting room in front of a young mother and her screaming baby. I watched him from the corner of my eye, just as I'd been watching him since the moment I turned up. He didn't like me being here...and he didn't know about the baby.

I smiled.

*He didn't know about the baby.*

I thought about that as we waited...and waited. I glanced toward the door when the woman and her screaming kid went with one of nurses. By the time Alex slowly walked out, looking even worse than he was when he walked in, Kyle was ready to snap.

"What the fuck took so damn long?" He barked.

"Nothing." Alex muttered and walked past.

I turned my head after him and followed out of the emergency department. I was halfway out the door, watching Kyle as he strode ahead to grab Alex's arm. Their voices drifting to me as Alex's cell rang.

He reached down, grabbed his phone, scowling at the caller ID and answered it instantly. "Yes?" He muttered, before he stiffened and a look of horror crossed his face. "What? *Oh my God.*"

"What?" Kyle stepped closer, moving out of the way as others rushed toward the automatic doors of the emergency department. "What is it?"

But Alex didn't answer. He just walked numbly as he murmured. "I can't believe it. I can't...is Mr. Brontie. Is he *dead?*"

I jerked my gaze to Blackburn. "What the fuck is going on?"

"Hell if I know." He stared at Alex.

He didn't seem to care, didn't seem to realise. I lunged, grabbed his shirt and yanked him closer. "April is with him, for Christ's sake!"

His eyes widened as he jerked his gaze to Alex.

"An explosion." Alex muttered.

*What the fuck?* Those words made my blood run cold. I grabbed my cell and pressed her number. The phone rang...and rang. While Kyle left me, striding toward Alex and out of earshot. I could hear them talking. While my pulse thundered, I moved away, listening as she answered. "Jared?"

"April?" I cried. "*April?*"

"It's me." Her voice was cold, careful. Totally unlike the woman I knew...or I thought I knew.

"Jesus Christ, we heard about the explosion. Are you okay?"

There was silence, then carefully. "I'm okay. But I'm not coming back, Jared. I'm not coming back to you or Kyle...and not to Brontie."

All I heard was: *Me. She's not coming back to me.* "What?"

Silence filled the air.

"April?"

My heart was screaming as agony plunged through my chest.

"*April?*"

*Say SOMETHING!*

"I know about the baby." The words tore free without thinking. "April, I know."

There was silence. Silence while my world fell apart. She let out a whimper, then a moan. "Jared, you don't know a goddamn thing. Stay the fuck away from me."

Kyle swung his gaze my way as though he now heard me speaking. "Is that...is that April?"

Hate burned through me as he strode forward. But the need quickly smothered that anger for her to be safe. I lifted my gaze, then held out my phone, desperation fuelling me. "Talk to her. Talk to her and tell her we need her to stay."

He stilled, his eyes widening as he looked at the phone in my hand and then took it. "April?"

I had to look away when he said her name like that. Had to close my heart off to the tender way he spoke. A way I never thought a man like Kyle Blackburn was capable of. But here he was, not caring, not even remembering anyone else was around him when he said. "Talk to me, baby. Talk to me."

I didn't want her to speak to him for a second. My heart too fucking weak. Then I was turning toward them, seeing the way his brows pinched and his body tensed. I had to wonder, when would she tell him about the baby?

I could hear her voice, her words too faint for me to pick up. Still, Blackburn turned, speaking slowly and carefully. "Are you safe, where you are? Now? No, no, it doesn't matter about that now. I don't care. I don't care about any of that. I only care that you're safe."

That pang in my chest grew claws.

"Gotta think about you now. I know you don't want me near you. But let me wire you some money. Let me give you what you need to take care of yourself." He sucked in a breath and I hated myself more than I'd ever done before. Why didn't I say that? Why the fuck didn't I give her that?

*Why didn't I care about that more than I cared about myself?*

I didn't deserve her.

Not like this.

I winced, listening to him as his voice softened and his words hit me harder than any words could.

But she's still mine. *She's still mine.*

My stepsister. My woman. The mother of my child.

"Okay, text me your bank account information. I'll send you enough money to find a place to stay and food and anything else you need, and April...don't give up on me, don't give up on us. We have a plan." He glanced at Alex. "No, I can't say anything else. But just know that I'll do whatever it takes to keep you safe. Yes, good. Stay safe. I'll contact you as soon as I can."

He hung up the call. Not once asking me if there was anything left to say. What could I say he hadn't already? *I love you*, that's all I could say. But in the wake of Kyle's words, they'd no doubt fall flat.

Love.

I didn't know if this sick feeling in my gut was love. Didn't know if that dark, yawning pit inside me was love. What I knew was that desperation I felt in the hours and the days he took her from me was an anguish I never wanted to feel again.

So I took my cell, slipped it into my pocket as Kyle turned to Alex. "The files, my friend."

Alex looked sickened. His hands shook as he met Kyle's gaze.

"What is it?" Kyle stepped forward, jerking his gaze to the emergency department behind us. "What did they tell you?"

"I'm..." He started. "I'm sick."

"Sick?" Kyle looked down at him. "How sick?"

"My blood pressure is through the roof and there's some kind of problem with the rhythm. They need to run more tests, but it's not good. If Brontie finds out."

"If he finds out, he'll..."

"He won't find out." Kyle gripped his face in his hands. "Do you hear me? He won't find out. Now, tell us what we need to know. Give us the name of the woman who can take April's place."

## Chapter Twenty-Seven

CONTENT WARNING: THIS CHAPTER CONTAINS sensitive subjects, including potential/pregnancy loss. Please take care of yourself and if this is a trigger for you, skip this chapter.

"WAIT." I called and lifted my head, finding the kind man's gaze once more. "I do need some help. I mean, if you're still offering?"

The soup kitchen stranger smiled, and I felt that warmness, just like I felt Kyle's words when he said he'd take care of me. My cell gave a *beep, and* I looked down to find an automated message. *Incoming funds, click here to view your account.* I clicked the link and logged into my bank to find a deposit of 25,000 *dollars.* "Shit. You weren't kidding."

"Sorry?"

I jerked my head up and forced a smile. "Nothing. But I do need your help...I need somewhere to stay. Somewhere quiet. Somewhere I can—"

"Hide." His smile softened as he stepped closer. "It's okay, you can say the words out loud. Somewhere you can hide."

I nodded. "Yes, somewhere I can hide."

Even if my bare feet stung and my mind was in turmoil, there were things I could do to keep us safe. I touched my stomach, drawing this man's gaze. My pulse thundered as he looked at my hand against my stomach. A knowing passed between us. My pulse sped as he met my gaze. He was the first person...the first real person standing in front of me who knew. *Who I allowed to know.*

"Keep the blanket." He motioned. "Come with me. Let's get you someplace safe."

The burn in my feet grew claws as I rose. A hot shower and a soft bed were exactly what I needed. Some place away from all this, where I could sit and think and be still. I followed this man to the rear of the kitchen and then out the door to where an old grey Toyota waited, the rear doors open. Care bags filled with hot meals, and some personal items were stacked inside.

"Wait just two seconds." He motioned with his hand. "I'll be back."

He took off to the rear door of the building once more and disappeared inside. My nerves were wound tight like a string. I scanned the other cars in the carpark, then to a car as it rolled slowly along the back alley and drove away. What the hell was he doing in there?

*Calling Brontie to come and get me...*

Panic hit me for a second before he strode out carrying a large bag.

"What were you doing?" I asked.

The smile on his face fell and a look of concern made his brows furrow. "I was..."

"Did you call him?" I took a step, then another and before I knew it, I grabbed his arm. "Did you call Brontie?"

Pain carved deep as he grabbed my hand. "No. Look. I got these from the back room. I had to hunt through a heap of clothes to find ones I think are your size."

I looked down to the bag stuffed with clothes in his hand. Clothes that's been washed and folded.

"It's okay." He said softly. "I get that you're scared, but I promise you're safe with me."

I glanced back at the soup kitchen. The murmur of voices drifted out. No one who did this night in, and night out was dangerous. They couldn't be, could they? I stepped closer and yanked open the passenger's side door before sliding in.

He closed the rear doors and slid behind the wheel. "I have a couple of deliveries to make, but then I'll drop you off. It's a small hotel, but it's clean and cheap. We take a lot of the DV cases there."

"DV?"

He glanced my way and started the engine. "Domestic violence."

"Oh." I just nodded, unable to understand how I got here, not here at this kitchen...but here, in this position. Alone, frightened, barefoot and pregnant. "Thanks."

He was true to his word, stopping off at two places before he pulled into a quiet motel that had a no vacancy light out front.

"Wait here." He said before climbing out.

I clutched the surrounding blanket, watching as he disappeared into the reception office and winced as a stab of pain tore through my belly. I caught my breath, gritted my teeth and rocked forward, unleashing alone moan. My fingers danced across my stomach is that pain grew intensity.

Oh God…

My heart raced, and my mouth went dry as panic rose, until in a heartbeat the pain eased. Movement came in the side-mirror of the car. The reception door opened, and he strode out, heading toward the car once more. I sucked in a hard breath, pressing my hand against my stomach. Everything was okay, everything was fine. It was just the stress of the explosion and tonight. Those words resounded in my head is the drivers-side door opened and he leaned down. "I've got you a room for as long as you need it. Come on, let's get you settled."

I reached for the door handle, my hand shaking as I pushed. But that pain never came again as I stepped out of the car and close the door behind me. He opened the rear door, grabbed out one of the care packages from the seat and the bag of clothes before closing the door and heading to the room at the far end of the motel.

There was just a numbness inside me, that sinking feeling in the wake of terror. He shoved the key into the lock and pushed open the door to room number thirteen.

I didn't want to take it as an omen. Jared and I had stayed in many room thirteen's before, and there was nothing different about this one. He pushed the door open and switched on the light before stepping to the side. "It's not the Ritz by any stretch of the imagination. But it's clean and safe and no one will find you here."

He moved to the small table in the single room and placed the care package down. "I have you listed under her cousin's name Harlow Otter. Anyone asks, and that's the information she'll give. Marion knows exactly what you're going through. We helped her escape an abusive partner quite a few years ago. Now she makes it her mission to help anyone else in need." He stepped closer. "So you're safe here."

Safe...

I hadn't the heart to tell him nowhere was safe when it came to men like Brontie.

A tiny twitch came in my belly, forcing me to step closer. "Thank you."

"Here." He said, turning to scan the rooms and strode toward a small desk. He yanked out a notepad and scribbled something down. "This is me, and my number. If you need anything... anything at all, please reach out, day or night. I have a feeling about you. I hope I'm wrong, but I think you're in a lot more trouble than you're letting on. You might need a friend, someone you can trust. I can be that person for you."

My cheeks burned. Still, I took the slip of paper.

Just nod, that small voice inside whispered. Nod and say *thank you*. Then we never call him. We never drag him into our mess. Because we know what happens. I stared at that piece of paper with his name printed on it. "Thank you, Liam." I murmured and lowered my hand. "I appreciate it."

He just nodded, gave me a smile. "Sure. Like I said, anytime, day or night."

He walked to the door, and I took a step to follow. That gripping pain tore through me, not as bad as it was before, leaving me to clench my jaw, force a smile.

"Take care." He murmured as I closed the door behind him.

I just nodded, and slid the chain in place, before I closed my eyes and leaned on the door.

Footsteps sounded as I moaned and rocked.

That agony stabbed deeper.

I shoved away from the door as the faint sound of a car started and scanned the motel room, finding the bathroom on the other side of the queen-sized bed. A cry tore free as I stumbled for the bathroom. The pain made my knee buckled halfway along, sending me crashing against the end of the bed.

I whimpered and pushed against the mattress. My arms shook as I shoved upright and stumbled into the bathroom. The overhead light was glaring as it blinked on. I stumbled to the toilet and shoved my pants down.

There was nothing on my panties.

No spotting. Nothing of any kind.

But there was no relief waiting for me. I shoved upwards, yanking up my pants as I went and made for the bed. That stabbing pain grew worse, making my insides tightened.

"Please, no." I whimpered as I fell to the bed. "No...*no...no...*"

I didn't want this baby, not before, not when all I saw was this was one more battle. Not when this was just another thing happening *to me.* But in the days that passed. When the numbness of what was really happening wore off, I thought about this baby more.

And I wasn't scared.

Not anymore.

I closed my eyes and rocked forward. Something wet spilled between my legs. I didn't want to look. Didn't want to know. If I prayed and pleaded, then this would stop. This would all stop. *All of it.*

But that wetness between my legs grew, making me reach under my pants.

Slick warmth coated my fingers. My heart grew heavy.

"No. Please, God, no."

# Chapter Twenty-Eight

KYLE

"Get in and out." Headlights of the Maserati splashed against the compound as I pulled up outside the gates. "We need those files, Alex. We'll be waiting."

Alex gave a nod before he yanked the handle of the rear door and pushed it open. He was gone in a hurry. One shoulder hung lower than the other as he stabbed his code into the lock and moved through the gate. I gritted my teeth and forced my gaze straight ahead. I didn't want to look across to the passenger's seat. I didn't want to see anyone other than April sitting beside me. I sure as *Hell* didn't want to see her goddamn stepbrother.

So I sat in silence, staring at the towering wall. And every second is a goddamn eternity.

"Are we really doing this?"

I winced at the question. "If you have a better plan, I'm all ears."

He didn't and I'm not, not for him at least.

"So we find them and we exploit them." He stared straight ahead.

"When you want out, Jared, just fucking say." I muttered as the gate re-opened and Alex came back out.

Only he didn't climb back into the car. He made his way to my window, waiting as I punched the button and lowered the glass.

"Here." He shoved the files at me, then stepped away, his eyes wide and haunted. "I want no part in this. Not anymore."

I gripped the correspondence. Anger moved through me as I do something I loathed to do and handed it across the seat. "You are involved, my friend. Whether you like it or not. Betray me, Alex, and you'll find yourself in a very dangerous situation. One I don't recommend."

There was a twitch in the corner of his eye. Then he took a step backwards as I shoved the car into gear and sped away.

April was out there. I didn't feel any relief about that. But the dangers out there in the city were the same as the dangers back at that house. Maybe they were better.

"There's three of them."

I jerk my gaze beside me. For a moment I forgot he was here. Maybe it was hope.

"Stepbrothers."

"What would you like me to do about that?"

"I don't know." Jared scanned the file and shook his head.

"Where?"

"What?"

I jerked my gaze to his. "Tell me fucking where?"

He flinched, then turned his attention back to the pages. "Masterdom." He said, "Killivan road."

I gave a nod and hit the turn signal and turned the car east.

"We make contact, then go after them." Jared closed the file and lifted his gaze. "There's enough information in here to turn them against her."

And it started again...the same sick game. The same terrifying outcome. The only difference was, this time, it was for a trade. "Who is he?" I shifted gears and changed lanes, flying past cars like they stood still.

"What?"

"Who is he?" I repeated. "What purpose does he serve, Brontie?"

He opened the file once more, flicking through the pages. "Guns, money. Connections. Jesus this guy...he's fucking Mafia."

*Fucking Mafia?* That unnerved me. Cornering Jared and forcing him to serve his stepsister up to Brontie was one thing, but this was something totally different. I knew Jared, even if I didn't like him. I knew how hard I could push. Knew the ties he had with his family. This I was going in blind and that fucking terrified me.

Fear or not, this had to happen. I had to *make* it happen. "So she's the one Alex told us about. The one Brontie could take in exchange for the father's loyalty. One more fucking recording, one more fucking sister for Brontie to corrupt."

"Does it matter?" There was an edge of desperation in his tone. "It's either her or April."

"Yes." I shifted gears again. "It is."

We drove to Masterdom, the rich suburb east of the city. It was almost another world out here. Rich, affluent. Cut-off from the rest of the city. I did not know what kind of resistance we were up against. Three brothers…three brothers to manipulate. Three brothers to control…and one stepsister at the center of it all.

Jesus, I never imagined I'd end up here. No idea the kinds of things I'd do when I…

*When I…*

*When I fell in love.*

April's pain filled my head. That desperation rose inside me. She was out there, alone, trapped. Cornered between Brontie and pain. I had to get away from him, at any fucking cost.

I drove until I hit the off-ramp and took the south-east road all the way to where the houses matched Brontie's, hidden behind towering fence lines.

Killivan. A dead end road filled bankers, governors and dangerous men. Was that who this was, a dangerous man?

I scanned the houses, then pulled the car over, killed the lights and the engine. "Give me the file."

Jared reached over, handed me the folder. I hit the overhead lights and opened it, finding a young, dark-haired woman with wide, haunting eyes and full lips. She was beautiful, too beautiful. I glanced at the name printed underneath. *Maddie Alvarez.*

Alvarez. Not a common name. I searched my memory, trying to place it but I couldn't. I turned over the image, finding three more. The brothers. Calix, Aven and Brooks. One, not much older than her, Calix. The two others were twins. I stared at the images of those men. I just needed one. One I could track down. One I could break.

Just like I broke Jared.

I glanced across the seat and hit the overhead switch, plunging the car into darkness. "Sleep." I muttered, adjusting the seat and then closed my eyes. "We've got a lot of work to do."

---

THE GROWL of an engine wrenched me awake. I opened my eyes to find a sleek, black Audi as it tore past us and disappeared. Instinct made me sit upright. "Wake up, it's them."

There was a low moan next to me. I preferred to not look at him as I stabbed the button and started the engine before shoving the car into gear. Tires squealed as the Lamborghini shot forward. Jared let out a curse and clawed the seatbelt at his side, panic tearing through him as he screamed. *"Jesus fucking Christ!"*

I didn't care about the spineless piece of shit beside me. I only cared about that car, finding it and the person behind the wheel. As the Audi turned the corner and disappeared, I worked the gears and caught the flare of the brake lights.

I hunted him all the way into the city, where he pulled up outside some grungy brick building with no name out front. "What the fuck is this?"

I ignored him, pulled up three buildings away and killed the engine as he climbed out of his car and strode inside. Two more men disappeared through the door, wearing training shorts and shirts. It was a gym. I glanced at the store, the hardness of it, the quiet, unassuming front. No, not a gym. It was somewhere to train, like fighters.

I sat back, grabbed the folder once more. This time I shifted aside the images of our target and her kin, and instead looked at details Brontie had that would tear this family apart. There was a lot. An underground network of gunrunners and drug dealers.

The kind of criminal enterprise that'd see someone like Sebastian Lyons put away for life.

The man was worth billions, and he had connections. The kind of connections that would suit someone like Brontie...very...very *much*. Adrenaline coursed through me as I scanned the rest of the file. But we had time to kill. Two hours later and the two guys who walked in after the brother. I shoved open the door, catching Jared glance my way and follow suit.

We left the Maserati behind. *I* left Jared behind, striding slowly toward the black beast parked against the curb with the folder in my hand. I stopped at the passenger's door, turned and leaned against the car and waited. I didn't have to wait long.

"You're leaning on my car."

He looked just like his photograph. Tall, powerful. Thick shoulders, his skin still shining with sweat. I glanced behind him to the boxing ring and hung bags.

"Good work out?" I murmured.

He never answered. Ah, yes. Calix Lyons was the dark, stoic, dangerous brother. The one who'd force the others to do the unthinkable. *If I could break him...*

"Bank accounts." I murmured and opened the file. "Lots of them, it seems. Most in your father's name, some in yours too. But amounts too, along with images, warehouses full of guns and drugs. I wonder, did you know your name was all over your father's Mafia connections? Seems rather dangerous to me, you know, if this information say...fell into the wrong hands...you could take the father and the son."

Confusion smothered fear. He glanced at the file. "What the fuck?"

"This could ruin a man...and his family." I murmured, pulling out the last piece of evidence taped inside the file. "Take down the two strongest and then wipe out the rest of the family." I glanced at the USB. "I wonder what this is? Looks important."

He knew. Damn right, he knew. There was barely a heartbeat before he met my gaze. "What the fuck do you want?"

I gave a shrug. "Not much." I murmured. "Just a simple recording."

"A recording?" He glanced at the file. "What kind of recording?"

I gave a slow, bitter smile and pushed off the car. "Let's talk."

# Chapter Twenty-Nine

## MADDIE

"Squirt." Brooks muttered as I yawned, barely seeing anything, as I stumbled into the kitchen and flopped down on a breakfast barstool. "Coffee?" My stepbrother asked.

I just tilted my head, peered at him through the slits of my eyes. All I saw was a blur. "Is the Pope Catholic?"

He gave a chuckle and opened the door. Cups clattered before the hiss of perfection followed and the scent of cafe quality coffee filled the air.

"Oh, we have our own bitch today, do we?" I didn't even turn my head as Aven took the stool next to me. "A blonde with a pair." He snapped his fingers. "Now barista."

"Fuck you, Aven." His twin muttered.

God, I missed their banter. I was tired of bitchy girls. Exhausted from the back-stabbing antics of even my best friends, I flopped to the side, leaning all over my stepbrother. Hard muscles tensed under me as he caught my fall. "What time did you get in last night?" His deep voice resounded in my ear.

"Two." I muttered. "Goddamn roadworks."

I'd driven for six hours, having to take the long road back home from my Griffith University, dragging my sorry ass into my bedroom at some ungodly hour this morning. This was on top of classes all yesterday morning. The pressure of this goddamn law degree was overwhelming, and I wasn't even halfway into my first year. Christ, I wasn't going to survive this.

I was fried from non-stop lectures and studying, and so damn ready for four weeks of nothing but the sun, the pool, and having the house to myself. I cracked open my eyes as Brooks slid a cup along the counter my way—well, mostly to myself, anyway.

I doubt I'd hear them. Most of the time they stayed in their room, playing Xbox and watching porn...*so much damn porn.*

"You're smiling." Brooks muttered, drawing my focus to the present. "I don't like it when you smile like that, squirt."

I forced my eyes open, grab the steaming mug in front of me and lift it to my lips. "I was thinking about three damn weeks of doing absolutely nothing." As the sound of Calix's car came along the drive, I muttered and took a sip.

The hum of the garage door followed. I took a swallow of my coffee, my senses sharpening, tracking the thud as the garage door closed. I waited for his steps, my pulse kicking hard, knowing any moment Calix was about to walk through that door.

I purposely waited for him to leave before crawling out of bed. I needed coffee...and time before I saw him. The thud of his steps echoed and in an instant I was became acutely aware I was a damn mess. I lifted one hand, smoothing down the flyaway strands of my hair, hating how my eyes were gritty. I was sure I looked like Hell. Calix stepped around the corner of the hallway and into the kitchen without looking at me.

He yanked open the refrigerator, grabbed a bottle of electrolytes, twisted the cap and downed the contents without even turning around to face us. I caught the raised brow from Brooks as he glanced to Aven.

My stepbrother gave a shrug beside me. *Who the fuck knows?*

"Bad workout, Princess?" Brooks muttered carefully. Shit, he was game.

Calix drained the contents of the bottle, then threw it clean across the kitchen until it landed in the sink. He turned, striding out, heading for the hallway.

A pang of agony coursed across my chest. Not a *hello sister?* Not even a wince, something to acknowledge I was here...*and that he remembered what happened between us the last time.*

I almost didn't come home. But I was determined not to let my own stupid actions change our relationship. It was stupid...*so damn stupid*. But it happened. It happened, and it was real. And if he was angry at me, then so be it.

I might've made the stupid decision to crawl into his bed that night, seeking comfort from the endless screaming of our parents—but I wasn't the one who crossed the line. No. Calix did. And it was about time he owned up to it.

"Hey." Aven called as Calix strode out of the kitchen and across the foyer. "You not even going to say hi to your damn sister?"

Calix stopped dead. Powerful shoulders curled and that pang in my chest grew claws. I tried not to look at him...not like *that,* at least. But I couldn't stop myself. The floodgates had opened inside me when it came to my older stepbrother, and I didn't know how to close them again. Still, it didn't change the way he felt, which was plain to see.

He hated me.

No, *he loathed me.* "Welcome home, Maddie." His hard voice hit me in the chest hard like a blow.

I winced, watching him leave us behind.

My cheeks burned watching him walk away, leaving a gaping hole behind.

"Asshole." Brooks muttered.

I forced a smile. "It's fine."

"No, it's not." Avery snapped. "I'm sick of his pissy attitude. He was like this for three fucking weeks after you left the last time."

A surge of adrenaline coursed through me at the words. I glanced toward Avery. "He was?"

"Yeah." Brooks strode around the corner of the counter, draping his heavy arm across my shoulders. "He was. But don't let that worry you, little sister. You have us to annoy you every damn day."

"It's our specialty." Avery added for his twin brother. "It's what we're good at."

I gave a chuckle. "You got that right." I shoved Brooks' arm free and chuckled. "Pains in my ass, the two of you."

"Ouch." Avery muttered. "She even said it with a lawyerly tone."

I burst out laughing, drained my cup and rinsed it in the kitchen before stacking it in the dishwasher. Even the cleaner had time off, so it was just the four of us to cook and clean for ourselves. I glanced toward the opposite end of the house and the east wing where Calix's bedroom was. I thought we'd all be adults and act without getting our feelings hurt. Looked like I was wrong.

I made my way out of the kitchen and headed for the west wing, the one I shared with our parents. My room being closest, I could hear all their damn fights. It was a two-day barrage of accusations and arguments last time that drove me from my bedroom and into Calix's bed for comfort and support.

I hurried into my bedroom, scanned the darkened room, my bags still sitting there unpacked near the ruined bed. Maybe I should just leave? Just climb back into the car and head back to campus.

I can study back on campus. Maybe get a start on next semester's work...

I unleashed a sigh and felt heavy. The idea depressed me. Maybe I could just hide in my room. I didn't need to go near Calix if he was pissy, which he obviously was. I winced and strode for my bathroom, dragging my t-shirt over my head.

I undressed and showered, taking my time, using my favorite shampoo Mom always had waiting for me and dressed, tugging on black jeans and a mid-riff hot pink top. I dragged a brush through my hair and scrunched it on top of my head in a messy bun.

I felt better after a shower. Fuck Calix and his damn moods. I yanked open the blinds, wincing at the harsh glare of sunlight and set to work, unpacking my bags and making my bed. By the time I was done, I was quite content to forget Calix had existed.

I made my way out, headed to the kitchen, then made my way downstairs into the gloom to the state-of-the-art cinema. I grabbed a cola from the fridge downstairs, popped the top and flopped down on the soft sofa before searching for the remotes. Something dark and intense. Something sexy. I hit the button, flipped on the channels and searched for something I enjoyed... and stopped at *365 DNI*.

My pulse raced. I'd seen it before. Maybe a few too many times.

My fingers punched the volume, turning it low and pressed play.

Why the fuck not?

They wouldn't hear me, anyway. They'd be too busy in their rooms, doing whatever it is they do. *You know what they do. Dad's business...right?* Mafia business.

There was no way around it...my stepfather did bad things. I knew it...it was one reason I was at law school. Sooner or later, he was bound to get into trouble and there was no way I was letting that happen without me being there.

Gareth Lyons might not be the most stand-up guy, but he was a damn good father and a good husband when my high-strung mother wasn't nagging the hell out of him. I loved him...and I loved my brothers. Even the ones who couldn't stand to meet my gaze.

I tried to push that out of my head and focused on the movie, watching him overlooking the water, blood splatter all over his face.

"Really? You couldn't pick a better movie?"

My breath stilled, but I didn't turn my head as Calix stepped into the theatre room, those dark eyes moving from the screen to me. "If you want to watch a woman getting fucked hard, little sister, all you have to do is say. I got plenty of porn for you to watch."

Heat burned in my cheeks. Still, I said nothing, trying my best to ignore him.

"What, no response?" Calix came closer and leaned down on, placing one hand on the armrest at my side and the other on the cushion beside me. "You wanted me to greet you before. Now you're not going to look me in the eye."

*Move.*

That voice inside my head urged. But I didn't.

"You want the good bits?" Calix snarled, snatching the remote from my hand. "Then, by all means, let's skip to that."

On the screen, the moving raced forward, through the beginning of the movie until she was racing through the night... and was cornered. She fought, kicking him as he carried her over his shoulder. My pulse was pounding. The cola stale on my lips. I turned my head, meeting his gaze. "You have a problem with me watching the movie, Calix?"

His lips curled, eyes widening as our gaze collided. "Keep pushing me, little sister."

"Or what?" Anger punched through, driving me forward.

I was the one who crowded *him* this time. Making him backup as I rose from the sofa, leaving the cola on the drink holder. "What exactly are you going to do about it?"

He stumbled backwards...until he stopped. His chest rising with hard breaths. "Don't fucking push me, Maddie. Not today."

"Don't push you?" I hissed, my gaze moving to the doorway. "Don't push *you*? I wasn't the one who flat out ignores me just before. If you have something you want to say to me, *brother*. Then, by all means, *say it*."

I caught the tremor in his body...right before he lunged, grabbing me around the throat and driving me backwards. On the screen Massimo grabbed Laura in the exact hold, pushing her against the sofa...just like Calix did to me.

His hard body drove against me...God, he was fucking hard. His cock pushing into my thigh as he shoved me back over the armrest of the sofa, stretching my body underneath him. "You think I don't know what you're doing? You come into my goddamn bed, let me...*let me do those things to you*—then you fucking leave with not a goddamn word, Maddie. I fucked up...I fucked up big time. Now it's about time you pay the goddamn price, little sister."

"What the fuck is going on here?" Brooks snarled.

I couldn't move...couldn't tear my gaze away from the darkness in Calix's gaze. Couldn't do anything as Laura kicked and screamed, fighting Massimo's advances and all I knew...was *I wanted that done to me.*

# Chapter Thirty

*B*LOOD...

*It was blood.*

I stared at the mess on my fingers and stifled a moan. This can't be happening...it can't be happening. The *thud* of a door came from a room close to mine, tearing me from the slow slide of panic. I needed help. I needed someone. I shoved from the bed, cramps doubling me over as I made for the table and snatched the key before heading for the door.

Horns blared in the distance. The city frantic and mean as I stumbled out of the room, leaving the door open behind me...the reception—*get to the reception.*

Darkness blurred around me...the no vacancy light glowing neon blur in the dark. I shoved against the wall, stopping midway. A cramp tore through my belly, making me crumble against the wall. Hard breaths tearing through me before the pain eased enough for me to keep moving.

The lights were on inside, movement flickered behind the blinds. I shoved my hand against the glass and grabbed the door.

*Her name...what was her name?*

A tiny bell above the door gave a *ding* as I shoved through. I stumbled inside, unleashing a moan as a faint voice came through. "If you're after a refund, there's none given."

"Please..." I whimpered.

The counter blurred as I reached for it. My hand slipped, sending me crashing to the floor. *"My baby."*

Footsteps sounded before they stopped. "What the hell?"

"Please..." The word was a moan.

The thud of her steps came closer, that dark blur moving in above me. "My God, what happened?"

I lifted my fingers, the blood drying in the corners of my nails. "I think I'm losing my baby."

Her eyes widened as she knelt at my side. "You're pregnant?"

"Cramps in my belly." I whimpered. "I think I've—"

"We need to get you to a hospital." She grabbed my arm and pulled, forcing me to my feet.

But I shook my head. "No. Please, I can't. I yanked my hand from her hold. "I can't."

She stilled. Her confused gaze sharpened in an instant. "You can't."

"No." I moaned. "I can't."

She seemed to understand. Sadness and clarity sharpened in her eyes. "Okay then." She murmured. "So we won't take you. Come on." She tugged my arm once more and this time I was too exhausted and wracked with pain to fight her.

I let her drag me to my feet.

"Hold on to this." She wrapped my arms over the counter before she left, hurrying to the door. The lock snapped shut before she flicked off the light and then raced back to my side. "Come on. We're going to get you taken care of."

I doubled over when she pulled my arms free, leaning on her more than I wanted as I followed her out of the rear of the reception to a small Honda parked in the back. Lights flashed as the locks released. She yanked open the door. "Get in."

I did as she said, needing someone...*anyone* to take care of me. Kyle's face filled my mind. I wanted to call him, letting him come and make everything okay. But this was something personal, deeply personal. Something I could only share with a stranger.

The door closed. I reached for the seatbelt as she hurried around the rear of the car and climbed in behind the wheel. "You hanging in there, kid?"

"I nodded." Forcing a smile but it was more like a grimace. "Yeah."

She started the car and shoved it into reverse, backing out of the parking space and then shot forward. We hit the driveway with a jolt, then we were out into the street, mingling with the night traffic.

"No hospital." I urged.

"No, honey." She cast a careful smile my way and focused on the road. "No hospital. I've got someone who might be able to help."

She grabbed her cell, diving her attention between the road and the screen before she pressed the button and held it to her ears.

"Jess, honey, it's me." She cast a careful gaze my way. "I've got a bit of a problem. I'm hoping you can help me."

I stared out of the window as she spoke to whoever Jess was. But I had a sinking feeling that no matter who was on the other end of that call, that they were already too late.

Marion drove through the city to a quiet suburban estate and pulled up in front of a expensive looking house with a sign out front *Jesse McDonald OB/GYN/Women's Center.*

"Here?" I asked as Marion climbed out.

"Yes, honey. If there's anyone who can help your baby, it'll be Jess." She closed the door and hurried around to open my door and help me out.

The front door to the house opened and made down the driveway.

"What happened?" She asked.

Marion just looked at me as she helped me. "Tell her honey."

"I think I'm losing my baby."

A flicker of sadness crossed her face before she came closer, wrapping an arm around my shoulders. "Come on, let's see, okay?"

I followed her, and Marion inside, where the foyer was brightly lit, leading into the reception.

"Through there, honey." Jess motioned me forward, past the desk and along a hallway. "All the way to the end."

The memory of the other doctor filled me as I stepped through the doorway and into the darkened room.

"Here, let me get everything set up." Jess flicked on the light, and rushed around me to pat a hard bed at the end of the room. "Up here, sweetheart."

My body clenched as I lifted a foot to the step and rose.

"All the way down, honey." Jess murmured as she wheeled out some kind of machine with a monitor. "I'm going to use this to take a look, okay? Then we'll have a better understanding of what we're dealing with. When was your last period?"

"April." I answered. "And a couple of months ago."

She gave a nod, switched on the machine and typed in details before grabbing some kind of wand and a bottle of lubricant. "A little cold, sweetheart."

I lay there, trying to focus on anything else other than the news I'd lost my baby while she squeezed the jell on my belly and pressed the wand to my skin.

"Okay." She murmured.

I searched her face. She was younger than I expected, her features familiar to Marion, who stood at the other end of the room, biting her lip and twisting her fingers nervously. I looked at anywhere other than the grey blur on the monitor.

"You bled, you said?" Jess asked.

I couldn't answer. Just swallowed hard and nodded.

"And that's all?"

"Pain as well."

"Okay, what kind of pain?"

"Stabbing, terrible."

"Okay." Jess pressed harder.

I waited for the tears to come. I wanted them to come. My eyes were closed. "It's okay. I—"

"Still pregnant."

I froze, opened my eyes, finding hers. "What?"

"You're still pregnant. See that tiny dark blur there?" She pointed to a shadow on the monitor. "That's your baby."

"My baby?" I whispered.

"By this, it looks like you're about thirteen weeks along. Healthy, strong heartbeat. The blood could've been your body reacting to something. Have you been under stress lately, more than usual?"

Her face blurred under a shimmering sheen. I didn't care before, not like this...not like I almost lost what I had. I nodded. "Yeah."

"Then that will do it." Jess eased the pressure against my belly.

"So I haven't lost it?" I whispered, the tears sliding down my cheeks.

"No, honey. You haven't lost it. Not yet anyway. But you're not out of the woods. Consider this a warning. You need to put yourself first, honey. Reduce the stress and start to think more about this baby. That is, if you still want it?"

My breath caught. Did I still want it? My pulse sped with the question. I opened my mouth, and my heart answered for me. "Yes, yes, I want it."

"Then you need to look after yourself. No more stress, healthy eating, plenty of rest. I want to give you my card. I'm not sure of your—" she glanced toward Marion, then back to me. "Predicament, but I want to offer my services." She grabbed a card and a pen, scribbling down her number on the back of a card. "Call. Tell them you have a plan with me. I'll make sure to tell my receptionist that April to expect you." She stepped close, placing her hand on my arm. "I do hope you will."

I nodded, taking the card, while she grabbed a few tissues and handed them to me. "For the gel."

I wiped, then rose, stepping down to the floor.

"I'm going to give you some boxes of samples I have that will help stop the bleeding and relax you some." She moved to a cabinet, opened the door and grabbed out four small boxes of pills. "Take one a day for the next fourteen days. By then the bleeding should ease. If doesn't, I want you to call me straight away. If it does, I want to see you in a month's time."

She scribbled on the boxes, then handed them my way. "Marion will take care of you. But I hope to see you again, April, and soon."

I forced myself forward, took the pills she offered.

"Take care of yourself." Jess murmured before she turned to Marion. "Mom."

Marion stepped closer, smiling and gave her daughter a hug. "Thank you, honey. I knew you'd help."

"Just take her home, give her some of that nice chicken soup you make and send her to bed." She glanced my way. "Sleep, soup and if anyone calls you, pressuring you into anything I want you to hang up, deal?"

"Deal." I headed for the door, my hand moving to my belly as Marion spoke to her daughter behind me.

*Beep.*

My cell vibrated. The sound triggering, scattering my pulse. I didn't want to look down. Didn't want to read the message. But I did.

*Jared: I need to see you, April. I want to talk about this. If you don't let me be a part of your life. I'm going to tell Kyle about the baby. See if he wants you then.*

# Chapter Thirty-One

### BRONTIE

Where the fuck was she?

I paced the study as the desperation inside me moved into dangerous territory. The fucking bitch ran...she ran...*and someone blew up my goddamn car.* I winced as that thready thud in my chest became louder.

*Beep.*

I look down to my cell, finding a message from my head of security, Harley. *No sign of her.*

I pressed the call, waiting for him to answer. "Yes, Mr Brontie?"

"What do you mean, there's no sign of her?"

"We searched all the way up to Sixth Street. I have more men out looking now. But she seems to have disappeared. "

"She's in a ten thousand dollar gold dress and six-inch heels. How the fuck could she disappear?" I screamed into the phone.

Silence echoed down the line. But I knew he was there. Because I fucking paid him to be.

"I don't know." He said carefully. "But we'll find her."

I clenched the cell until the damn thing trembled. "Damn right you will. You'll stay out there until she's fucking found. Do you hear me?"

I didn't wait for him to answer, just yanked the phone away and hung up the call. No one ran for me. Not if they didn't want to keep running for the rest of their miserable life. But she did. She ran, and she fucking disappeared.

My pulse was thready. My breath caught in the back of my throat. The more she was determined to invade me, the more intense my feelings became. I wanted her more than I wanted anyone else. I glanced at my desk, to the stack of files. To the others I had on my radar. Other women like April, with fathers I could exploit.

Then I shifted my focus to the screen in front of me and stepped forward, hitting the button and waiting for the computer to come to life. The recording was already midway, stopped at my favourite spot.

April splayed out on the pool table, the glaring blue felt under her ass.

"Smile to the camera, little sister." Jared growled as he fucked her.

Her head was rolled back, her gaze unfocused as they rode her body one after another. They used her, because that's what I wanted. Exploited. Degraded...ruined. I dragged my teeth across my lip and leaned my hands on the desk.

But she wasn't ruined, was she? She wasn't degraded or broken, no matter what we threw at her. No, she stared me down, ate the food I paid for. Wore the dress and the heels I provided, then she ran.

*Let her go...she's nothing.* That nerve twitched in the corner of my eye.

I wanted to, but I couldn't. I was trapped in my hunger, bent on her destruction. My mind raced, trying to think of all the things I could do to bring her to her knees any way I could. I eased back in my seat, my mind drifting, before I grabbed my cell and hit the button once more, waiting for my call to be answered. And when it did ahead of my security was humble. "Mr Brontie?"

"I want you to track down her father and bring him in." That cold savage need rose inside me.

"Now?"

"Yes." I answered. "Now."

"I'm on it. We had a sighting of a young woman heading into some homeless kitchen—"

"Forget about it," I cut him off. "This is more important."

"Yes, Sir." He answered, and hung up the call.

I shifted my gaze back to the screen where Kyle and her stepbrother fucked her over and over again...and still it wasn't enough. It wasn't anywhere near enough.

---

"WHAT'S GOING ON?" Harmon Barnett glanced around the study as Harley escorted him in and hovered at the door. "Has something happened?"

God, you'd think having the kind of power this asshole had would've made him a stronger man. But it didn't. Instead, he glanced around the room like a terrified teenager.

"Have a seat." I motioned to the chair opposite. "It seems we have a situation."

He never moved. "What kind of situation?"

A twitch came from the corner of my eye. "April's missing."

"Missing?" He looked from me to Harley and back again. "What do you mean, missing?"

I leaned forward on the desk. "So, you're telling me she's not reached out to you?"

"No." There was a flare of panic in his eyes.

Harley moved from the door, walking around the back of his chair as I rose from my seat. He didn't know which one of us to watch, diving that scattered stare from my bodyguard to me as I rounded the desk and sat in front of him. "And you have no idea where she'd run to in the city?"

"She's never been here. She knows no one. You assured me she'd be safe here. *You* assured me that if I complied with your demands that my daughter would be unharmed."

"Unharmed." I repeated, leaning closer. "Such an interesting choice of words. I told you if she followed the rules, she'd be safe here. But as you can see," I motioned around the room as Harley moved closer. "She's not fucking here."

One nod and Harley grabbed him from behind. I rose from the desk and made the slow, purposeful act of rolling up my sleeves his sole focus. "She broke the rules, Harmon. She broke the fucking rules and this time, it's you who'll pay."

I clenched my fist and lashed out, hitting him in the nose. Blood spurted. So much blood, it gushed bright red, splashing against his white shirt. Flecks hit my hand as he screamed, yanking against my bodyguard's hold.

But it was no use now. All the screaming and wailing in the world wouldn't save him.

Maybe his daughter on her knees would.

*But then again...maybe not.*

I lashed out again and again until his screams turned to groans and whimpers. But by the time I was done, he was a bloody mess. I sucked in a hard breath and clenched my fist, feeling the ache. It was a good ache, a hungry ache. One I welcomed.

Harmon moaned and flopped forward, sliding from the seat until he fell to his knees.

"Call your daughter." I demanded, standing over him. "Call her and tell her to come home."

He cried. It was pathetic. Thick sobs wracked his shoulders. Jesus, why did all the men in her life have to be so pathetically weak? No wonder she was used. Look at what she came from...

"No." He whispered.

I leaned down, fisting his shirt and yanked, driving him to face me. "You'll call her, or the next time it won't be a fucking beating you'll get. Do you understand me? I'll empty your bank accounts, I'll take your goddamn friends, then I'll put a bullet in your goddamn head and fuck your daughter, anyway. I'll take her because that's what I do...*I take what I want.*" I shoved him away. Christ, he stank like piss. "Do you understand me?"

One pathetic nod.

"Call her." Harley shoved his cell into his hands. "Call her and tell her to come back or I'll be only too happy to get you out of my life for good. I'll hunt her down either way..."

His hands shook as he pressed the buttons, then lifted his cell to his ear. The phone rang...and rang...and rang. He lifted his head, his right eye bloody and bloodshot. "There's no answer."

I sucked in a hard breath, my rage pulsing like a heartbeat inside me. "Then you'll stay here and keep ringing until she does." I lifted my gaze. "Take him to the locked room and leave him there."

"Yes, sir." Harley grabbed him, hauling him to his feet.

"Make sure he'd given his cell every thirty minutes to call her and no one else. I want to be notified the moment she answers."

"Of course, Mr. Brontie." Harley dragged the whimpering, pathetic excuse for a man from the room.

She didn't answer...

*She didn't answer...*

I needed more, more men...more of those she trusts. Jared. *Kyle.* I could use them. I lifted my cell and rang their numbers, but each of them went to his message bank. Frustrated, I stabbed Alex's number, listening to it ring.

"Mr. Brontie." He answered, his voice muted and strange, and not like himself.

"Where are you?"

"At home. I've come down with some kind of stomach bug."

I stilled, my senses narrowing in on the lie. "Since when?"

"This afternoon, Sir. Is there anything you require?"

"No." The word was cold. "You're at home resting?" I walked back around the desk and sat in the chair, bringing up the tracking program on my computer.

"Yes, Sir. I think I'll just stay in bed."

The red dot blinked over his address. At least that part wasn't a lie.

"Please take care of yourself, Alexi." I murmured. "I'll see you at work when you return."

His words trembled with a hard exhale. "Yes, Sir." He murmured, then hung up the call.

Alexi had never been since a day in the past six years. He'd worked for me. I knew that because I checked all my employees constantly. So the fact he suddenly came down with some mystery illness on the night April went missing was too much of a co-incidence for me to ignore.

I rose from the desk, grabbed my handkerchief and wiped the blood from my knuckles before grabbing my cell. "Harley, I'll be going out."

"Yes, Sir." He answered. In the background, I could hear the low, guttural whimpers of a man in pain.

I headed to the garage and hit the button before grabbing the set of keys for the black four-wheel-drive Range Rover and climbed in behind the wheel. Alexi was lying. I knew that for a fact. Now I wanted to know why.

I pulled out of the garage and made my way through the city streets, pulling up thirty minutes later outside a quiet, darkened residential street. I knew which house was Alexi's. I've been here a few times before, some with him and some without. I wanted to know the ins and outs of those who worked for me. I needed to make sure each was loyal. And what better than to set up cameras and listening devices inside their homes?

But listening devices wouldn't tell me what I wanted to know. That I had to get from him.

I climbed out of the car and headed for the quiet, empty driveway. A dog howled in the distance, making me look over my shoulder before I headed to the front door. I gave a hard knock and waited. I didn't have to wait long.

The door was yanked open. "What?" My assistant snapped, before lifting his gaze.

When he did, his eyes widened. "Mr Brontie?" He gasped and looked behind me. Was he searching for Harley? "Is everything okay?"

"You mean apart from having my car blown up, and my visitor suddenly disappears in a city she doesn't know, I'm perfectly fine? The better question is, how are you?"

"I'm fine, Sir. There was no need for you to come all this way."

I glance at the door. "It was no bother. Are you going to at least invite me in?"

He didn't, not at first. I could see the panic building inside him as he shifted from one foot to the next. "Sure, of course." He opened the door, holding it wide for me to enter.

I knew exactly where I was going, making my way into the living room and looked around. There was a first aid kit on the counter in the kitchen. The top was open; the contents spilled out. "Has there been an accident?" I asked, turning to him.

He paled in front of me, and I could see that lie building in his eyes.

I took a step closer, meeting him face-to-face. "In five years you've never been sick, Alexi. And now tonight, of all nights, you're at home...with a first aid kit."

I scanned his body, finding one shoulder drooped lower than the other. There was something underneath it, a bandage that bulged under the sleeve of his shirt.

"Did you hurt yourself?" I yanked his sleeve down, exposing the white dressing. "Want to tell me what's going on?

He stumbled backwards, his eyes wide with fear. "I didn't want to do it, Mr Brontie. But they shot me and threatened to come back if I didn't do what they said."

I clenched my fist, feeling the ache once more. "They?"

"Kyle, and Jared." He whispered, his voice shaking.

"Take a seat, Alexi." My voice was icy. "Then I suggest you tell me exactly what happened...from the beginning."

# Chapter Thirty-Two

## KYLE

"WHAT THE FUCK IS WRONG WITH YOU?" I SNAPPED, jerking my gaze to Jared as he paced the room and stared at his damn cell. The bar was busy for a Thursday night. I grabbed my glass, took a sip of my scotch and placed it back on the table in front of me.

The fucker didn't even seem to care about finding out the information that was conveniently left out of the damn file. I stared at the pages and bought up the information on the underground network that the stepfather ran. But they were old names; Alvares, Salvatore, Rossi, to name just a few. I knew those names. They were Italian Mafia.

I pulled up the details. Five seconds was all I took for me to find information on Dominic Salvatore and his son, Finley. They were Cosa Nostra, a group of Italian mobsters. But it looked like the Rossis were Stidda. I sat back, a smirk spreading on my face. The Cosa Nostra and Stidda were enemies. Made things interesting.

But none of this helped me find the information I needed to turn the stepbrothers against Maddie. Not enough, at least. I bluffed him, giving enough information to rattle his cage.

I yanked the file closer, taking one last look. Alvares, Salvatore, Rossi...all Italian, all Mafia.

*All mafia.*

I stilled. They were all Mafia, *but not Lyons.* Sebastian Lyons wasn't the target. I placed the glass back down, slower this time. He wasn't the goddamn target. My mind raced as I tried to piece it together. I was looking at the step-father. But it wasn't the step-father at all. It was the mom.

This changed everything.

No wonder Brontie wanted her. But why not go after her? Why go after April instead?

I needed to figure that out...and fast.

*Thud.* The sound wrenched me out of my thought. I jerked my gaze to find this pathetic weasel muttering under his breath and staring at his cell.

"Got a problem?" I asked.

"No."

The icy touch of anger ripped through me as I shoved up from the table in the bar. It was bad enough I had to sit in the same fucking car as this spineless piece of shit, let alone spend any length of time with him. I could've overlooked both these things if the asshole actually fucking helped. "Then do you mind? One of us is trying to get April free of all this."

There was a scowl and then a mutter before he stood, adjusted his Armani jacket and headed outside. I stared at him, at his fucking jacket, remembering the gaunt, starved fucking woman I grabbed in the alley, and the way she barely ate, even when I bought her food. I clenched my jaw, staring as he stepped between a group of women, smiled and chatted to them before staring at his cell and heading for the door.

He pissed me off...

No, he more than pissed me off.

He made me feel dangerous.

I grabbed the file in front of me and downed the rest of my scotch, waiting for him to disappear before I followed. I wanted to know what was so damn important. I followed, ignoring the women when they turned, smiled and tried to engage me in conversation. I didn't care about them, not in the fucking slightest.

April occupied the space inside my head. Her hunger, need. The way she fought even in the face of someone like Brontie... *and me...let's not forget that.*

I was the who delivered her to him and the one who approached Jared in the beginning. But he was the one who wanted it, who craved it, who had the opportunity to release her, and he didn't. Just like he has the opportunity now, and still he plays the fucking game. I stepped out of the doorway of the busy bar, glanced around in the dark and spotted movement toward the carpark.

"You don't want to return my calls, don't want to fucking see me. What the hell am I supposed to do?"

Jared's voice carried the further I stepped away from the roar of the bar.

"I'll fucking make you. I'll fucking make you because it's my baby too, you hear me? It's my fucking baby too."

*My baby?*

*My fucking baby?*

I froze, my heart pounding, my mind screaming. I stared at Jared as he stood with his back to me. His cell was alight, his focus on the screen as he typed. He didn't see me and didn't hear me. But I heard him perfectly fine.

A baby...

April's baby.

I turned and headed back to the bar, not wanting him to see me. The same women still giggled and drank, scanning the bar like ravenous predators in the midst of a hunt. I clenched my jaw and cut a path through them, taking the same seat once more.

"Another?"

I lifted my head to the server and dropped the folder to the table. *My baby...my baby...my baby.* The words didn't stop; they kept coming and coming *and coming*. "Yes, and bring the bottle."

She just gave a nod and disappeared. I wanted to watch for him —I clenched my fist, I wanted to fucking kill him. My pulse sped at the thought as the loud group of women in front of me suddenly moved. There he was, sullen, moody, the father of April's baby.

*It should've been mine.*

Jared slumped down, jerked his head toward the folder. "Anything?"

A twitch came in the corner of my eye as the waitress slid a clean glass in front of me and placed the bottle at its side. Still, I stared at him, holding his gaze until he looked away. Was he embarrassed? No. The longer I stared at him, the clearer he was. He wasn't embarrassed. He was angry, rejected like some fucking teenage fuckboy. I clenched my fist, envisioning him dead. If he was dead, then she wouldn't want him.

If he was dead, then she wouldn't want me either.

It'd break her...especially now.

I grabbed the bottle and poured, making no offer to share. Fuck him. I flipped open the folder once more, staring at the information. Fuck...*him*. I stared at the image of Maddie Alvares. It would happen again. I'd make it happen. She'd fuck and fuck and fuck and we'd record it all for Brontie to use.

My pulse sped, my hand fucking shook. I lifted the glass to my lips and swallowed the heat.

*I can't do it.*

The scotch burned all the way to my stomach.

I couldn't fuck Maddie Alvares. I mean, I could...but I didn't want to.

I didn't want to because I didn't want to betray her—even if it meant to save her damn life.

My pulse raced as the words burned bright, drowning out the sound of Jared's voice in my head. I didn't care about the baby. No...I did. But I didn't care he was the father.

*I wanted to be.*

All I needed to do was to get him out of the picture. I lifted my gaze, looking at him.

"What?" He sneered.

"Nothing." The idea bloomed in my head and once it took hold, I couldn't let it go.

I needed him out of April's life and Maddie Alvares needed to be taped...riding as many guys as we could find. "If we don't deliver Brontie, then he'll find her, he'll drug her and he'll never let her go.

He scowled, his gaze growing darker. "That won't happen."

"No." I downed the scotch. "It won't. So we do what we have to do. We follow through with this no matter what. We get them drunk, do it, record it, then we use it to get April free."

There wasn't a hint of hesitation in his eyes, not a flicker of anything tortured in his soul. He just reached out, grabbed the bottle and drank from the damn thing. One swipe of his hand across his mouth and he nodded. "On one condition."

"Yeah?" I muttered. "What's that?"

He held my stare, those greedy fucking eyes cold as stone. "We never tell April any of this. She never knows, not about you or me. Deal?"

He thought he had a chance. This *fucker* thought he had a chance. We'd get Maddie Alvares drunk and fucked alright, but it wouldn't be by me...I'd be too busy...*making a recording of my own.* "Deal." I answered, grabbed my own drink and swallowed.

# Chapter Thirty-Three

## MADDIE

"C?" Brooks muttered, standing in the doorway behind me. "You going to answer me, brother?"

Calix shoved away, but the damage was already done. Our secret was out. My breaths were heavy, but they froze when Brooks spoke again. "What did he do to you, Maddie?"

I looked away, watching as Brooks came closer. "Nothing." I answered.

"Liar." Brooks snapped and stepped closer, glaring at Calix.

"Who's a liar?" Aven stepped into the media room behind him.

"Seems like our little sister and Calix have a secret." Brooks muttered. "And I want to know what it is."

Heat rushed to my cheeks. My heart was pounding as Massimo and Laura acted out my fantasy on full display.

"Well?" Aven stepped around his brother, looking at Calix, then where I lay on the sofa. "What the fuck is it?"

"Nothing." Calix forced the word through clenched teeth.

"I don't fucking believe you."

"He said something about coming into his bed, letting him do things to her." Brooks muttered. "I want to know what he did."

"C." Aven stepped in front of his brother, his brows creasing as a look of thunder. "What did you do?"

But there was no getting out of this. I pushed up, reaching out to stab the button on the remote, freezing the movie on the screen. God, if I wanted the sound of primal, carnal lust playing out on the screen in front of me.

"It was a fucking accident." Calix moved to step around his brother. But Aven moved, blocking his way, and Aven was there, standing beside his twin.

"What was?" Aven pushed.

"Calix, no." I whispered, wrapping my arms around my body.

I wanted to crawl into a hole and stay there.

"Yes, C." Aven countered my plea, stepping in between us. "Tell us...now."

I knew the moment Calix was going to break...no...not break —*expose me.* He lifted his head, those dark eyes glistening with hunger. A lick of his lips sent a surge of desire inside me as he spoke. "It was the night our parents were fighting."

"That week Maddie was here?" Brooks asked, but it was me he looked at for confirmation.

I just nodded, glaring at Calix as he betrayed me.

"She climbed into my bed. I was dead to the world, half drunk on scotch."

"The day you and Poppy broke up." Aven muttered.

Calix just dragged his fingers through his hair.

"You broke up with her?" I murmured, that thunder in my head growing louder. How did I miss that?

"Yeah." He answered, then clenched his jaw. I closed my eyes, inhaling hard as he kept talking. "I was drunk and Maddie was there, trying to hide from their fucking screaming, and I accidentally touched her."

"You...*accidentally touched her.*" Brooks repeated, looking from his brother to me, his voice growing husky. "Touch her how?"

My arms tightened around my body. "It doesn't matter." I shook my head, taking a step toward them. "Just go, all of you. Just leave it alone."

"Oh, I don't think so." Aven shook his head. "So this is why he was so fucking pissy when she left the last time."

"I wasn't pissy." Calix snapped.

"Oh yeah, you were. We couldn't even look your way for a fucking week, even then you were damn acid."

Calix sucked in a hard breath. I could see him fighting to not look at me. I hated I was so damn aware of him, every twitch of his body, every glance my way. It wasn't like this before...*before that night.*

We'd been brother and sister.

And then...

Then it became confusing and desperate.

"You touched her how?" Brooks' growl was husky and strange. "We want to know."

"I fucked her, okay?" Calix snapped, anger lashing his eyes. "I fucking fucked her."

"You fucked her?" Brooks whispered.

"I didn't know what I was doing. I was drunk and heartbroken and she was just there, so I fingered her. I fucking fingered our sister."

A sick surge of desire battled the heat in my cheeks. The door to the musty cellar was on the other side of the room, and I turned away from them. I'd walk through the darkness to get to the stairs of the house at that moment. I didn't care.

But I didn't make it. Brooks was fast, lunging around me to block my way. "Whoa." He held his hand up, his face dark and savage. "Where the fuck are you going?"

"Move out of my way, Brooks." I snapped, trying to step around him. But he refused to budge, blocking the door.

"I don't think so." He stepped forward, grabbed my chin and forced my gaze to his. "You let our brother slid his finger's inside you and you say nothing?"

Shame burned in my cheeks.

"He fingered you." Aven stepped closer to me. "Did you come, little sister?"

I jerked my gaze to him, shocked. "What?"

"Seems a simple question." Brooks answered for him. "Did you come?"

Oh, God...*oh God.* A pulse throbbed between my legs as that heat grew bolder.

"No need to be shy." Brooks murmured, holding my gaze to his when I tried to look away. "Tell us."

"No." I answered.

"No, you didn't come." Aven murmured. "Or no, you won't tell us?"

I jutted my chin up. They were playing with me, being crude, thinking I wouldn't answer. They were like this, more times than I admit. Thinking their dirty talk was shock value. I wouldn't let them shake me. *"No, I didn't come."*

"Didn't it feel good?" Brooks stepped closer. "Maybe the drunken fumbling of our brother missed the mark."

"Couldn't find the clit, Calix?" Aven smirked and glanced his older brother's way.

Calix's stare was savage, his lips curled, that hard gaze fixed on me. "I found the clit just fine."

That fire in my cheeks plunged all the way between my legs.

"Then, tell us." Aven came closer, moving to my side. "Tell us why you didn't come?"

He couldn't be serious? "He's my goddamn *brother.*" I snapped, jerking my head from his hold and stepped backwards. No way was I having this conversation with them.

"So, we're not blood." Brooks looked me up and down. "Don't tell me you've never thought about us like that, Maddie."

I swallowed and forced the lie out. "No. I've never thought about you like that."

Calix let out a chuckle. "Now you know that's a goddamn lie." He strode toward me, lifting his hand and in the blur of a second, tore his shirt over his head.

Hard muscles of his chest tightened as he rubbed his chest, drawing my focus to the red marks from the strapping tape he used at the boxing ring. "You don't look, don't think...don't fantasise about us at all?"

My breaths quickened before I looked away. "No, I don't."

Anger lashed as Calix reached down, grabbed the remote and pressed play, still he kept the remote in his hand. *Goddamn bastard.* They were damn sharks, turning from kind and protective in one minute to blood-thirsty hunters in the next second. Only one look in their eyes and I knew it wasn't blood that drive them. Massimo manhandled Laura on the screen, lifting her over his shoulder.

"So, absolutely nothing?" Calix reached down and cupped his cock.

His black trousers hugged the outline. I could see he was excited, semi-flaccid. Christ, there was potential. I hated that the thought rose. Hated more that the burn in my cheeks grew.

"You do, don't you?" Brooks murmured, searching my eyes. "You think about us?" He stepped closer. "It's okay, Maddie. You think we don't think about you too? Fuck, we're males in the prime of our life and you're right here, accessible."

Calix pressed skip on the movie, jumping all the way to the scene in the change room. Laura stood there dressed in a barely here black bra and panties.

*No...no, not this scene.*

My pulse raced as he grabbed her, driving her back against the mirror. My body tightened, that flutter between my legs grew bolder. I looked away. But I wasn't fast enough. My movement drew their gaze, they looked at the movie, then me.

"You like this?" Brooks moved, striding closer, grabbing me around the throat hard enough for me to catch my breath. "You want this...my hand around your throat?" He lowered his head. "My growl in your ear."

"You didn't come. Maybe it's not guys she's interested in." Aven glanced at the screen. "Maybe it's not Massimo she's looking at."

Calix lifted his hand and hit skip, cutting all the way to the scene in the bedroom. Her hands were shackled, feet splayed wide apart. I grew wet at the sight.

"Oh, fuck." Brooks muttered, glancing from the screen to me, his hand around my throat tightening. "It sure as hell isn't Laura. It's him, isn't it, Squirt? You want him, don't you? You want it hard, is that it? Tear your clothes, shove your legs wide. You want your pussy fingered and your nipples pinched, don't you? Teeth across your clit, I bet you'd come then."

He looked down, then grabbed my t-shirt, yanking it high, exposing my pink lace bra. His breaths were savage, heaving as he circled my nipple, then slipped his finger underneath the edge, yanking the cup low. My nipple bounced, tightening under his gaze.

I lashed out, slapping his hand away, but he grabbed my hand, driving it high against the wall. "Why didn't you come, Maddie?"

The room spun as he pressed my hand high on the wall over my head, then released my throat, driving my shirt up once more and looked down at my exposed breast. "Fuck you're so pink." He licked his lips. "I always wondered what you looked like. I bet your pussy is fucking tight, too." His calloused thumb danced around the peak, making me tighten. "Tell us...tell us why you didn't let yourself get there."

I jerked my gaze to his. "*Because...I don't know how. Is that what you want to know?*" I barked, bucking my hips until I slammed into him. "I don't fucking know. I'm broken, okay? I'm fucking broken."

One hard yank and I tore my hand from his hold. I stumbled from the release, tugging my shirt down as I stumbled around them.

Calix just scowled.

But I needed out of there...and far away from him. I lunged, tearing around the edge of the sofa and raced for the door, leaving all of them and Massimo behind. My steps thundered as I tore through the kitchen and barrelled through the house until I reached my bedroom, slamming the door closed behind me.

That didn't happen...

No, that didn't happen.

I closed my eyes, my heart thundered, the booming echoing... until I realised it wasn't just my heart making the sound.

"Maddie." Calix's husky voice came through the door. "Open the goddamn door."

"No." I gasped. *"Just fuck off, Calix."*

They were just playing, just trying to rile me up. And I played right into it, didn't I? I let them get to me... Jesus, what have I done? I closed my eyes, willing that ache between my legs away as the handle on my door shoved down.

"Open the goddamn door now, Maddie. Don't make me break it down."

I grabbed the handle, trying to stop it from moving, knowing Calix would do just that. I shouldn't have said that...shouldn't have told them the truth. Shouldn't have put that stupid movie on. What kind of idiot was I?

"I'm giving you to the count of three little sister, then I'm coming in, whether you want me too or not." The handle released...his voice shifting as he stepped backwards. "One... two...three—"

# Chapter Thirty-Four

I cracked open my eyes, yawned and reached for my cell. It was reflex, just one more thing I did without thinking. My mind was slow and scattered until the room came into view. And for a second I thought I was back there in the seedy motel rooms I shared with my brother until the silence swallowed me.

There were no snores beside me, and no sound of my grumbling belly. There was a flutter instead, a tremor of life in my abdomen. Then, in a rush, it all came back to me.

Kyle...

The drive...

Brontie...

And last, the baby. I dropped my hand to my stomach, touching the tiny swell as my pulse raced. My gaze moved to the screen as I re-read the message one more time.

*Jared: I need to see you, April. I want to talk about this. If you don't let me be a part of your life. I'm going to tell Kyle about the baby. See if he wants you then.*

See if he wants you then…

My hands shook as pain ripped through my chest. I tried to breathe. Tried to think. Even a day later and I still couldn't understand why he'd send something like this? I stared at the message, my fingers moving across the keypad:

*How dare you threaten me!*

Then a stab of pain tore through my abdomen, drawing me back to that desperate need to protect and provide. My baby. I glanced at my belly, then moved back to the message, backspacing all the way until there was no reply left. I wasn't doing this, wasn't going to hurt my baby, or give him the satisfaction. "No. You can go to Hell."

I dropped my cell onto the bed beside me and I rolled, kicking the bedding off to find the relief of the warmth and glanced down. There was a spot of blood on the sheets, reminding me of all the trauma that'd happened last night. *I almost lost my baby, that's what happened.*

A soft knock came at the door, drawing my focus. With a sigh, I climbed out of bed and padded barefoot to the door. I leaned closer, peering out of the spyhole. Marion stood there's holding two large coffee's and a brown paper bag. I slid the chain across and opened the door and the scent of bacon wafted in.

"Figured you'd be hungry." She muttered, stepping into the room and handing me a coffee. "Don't tell my kid I gave you this."

I lifted the cup and took a sip of the delicious brew. "I won't and thanks."

She nodded, glancing around the room like she didn't see the same thing day in and day out. "So, what's the plan?" She took a sip of her own coffee and glanced my way. "You're obviously on the run from some asshole. Now, I'm not one to pry, but if you're in trouble, then we need to get you somewhere safe."

"This is safe." I took another swallow and breathed deep. "For now."

"For now." She repeated. "Look, I have a friend who's a cop. I can ask him to come around and talk to you?"

A shudder tore through me with the words. The last time I turned to the police, it ended with me being raped in a damn interview room. "No, thank you. I have someone who's helping me."

"Oh, yeah?" She muttered, nailing me with a piercing stare. "He is the father of this baby?"

My pulse raced as I glanced at my cell phone on the bed. Jared's message still burning a hole in my mind. "No." I answered. "Not the father."

If Jared thought threatening me would get him back into my bed, then he had another thing coming.

"I don't want to play the role of your damn conscience or anything." She gave a shake of her head. "But what happens if this guy doesn't come through for you? People have a habit of doing that. Disappointing the people who need them the most. Why not protect yourself? That's all I'm saying. You can meet with Paul, talk to him, that's all I'm gonna say. If this asshole boyfriend of yours needs a talking to, maybe he can do that for you just to make sure you're safe."

I wanted to laugh. All I could see in my head was this poor rookie cop rocking up to Brontie's house to give him a talking to on my behalf...and finding himself in that dark room, the place I knew had seen its share of blood and pain. The smirk that threatened my lips faded in an instant.

Sending a cop to Brontie was like sending a lamb into the wolf's den.

"At least let him do that." Marion urged. "Let him talk to the asshole you're running from. He can report back to you. Let you know if there're any laws he's broken. You can make an informed decision then. Make plans for the future." She glanced at her belly. "For the two of us."

I wanted to pretend that this would be all it'd take, a simple conversation with the law and I'd be able to plan my future. But the truth was, this was way over my head. I gave her a small smile. "Thank you for the coffee, Marion. I appreciate it."

*Beep...*

Her gaze moved to my cell on the bed. "Well, you know where I am if you change your mind." She gave a sigh, and then nodded to the bag of food. "Enjoy."

I hated the shrug in her shoulders as she strode to the door and then left. But it was for her own safety. Brontie wouldn't just stop at a cop that started poking around his business. No, a man like that pushed and fractured, picking apart all the threads until it took him to the source of his problem. Marion didn't need a man like Brontie for an enemy.

She needed to be quiet and small. She needed to be safe and keep running her slightly run-down motel and occasionally provide coffee and safety to desperate women who stumble into her office.

*Beep.*

I waited for her to leave, walking over and locked the door before returning to the bed and picked up my cell.

*Kyle: I need to see you. If I send you the address, can you meet me tonight?*

He wanted to see me? My pulse sped at the words, so very different from the one my brother sent me. Then I looked at the second message.

*Kyle: I keep forgetting to ask, how are you feeling?*

My stomach sank and took that flicker of happiness with it. I stared at the message as the taste of coffee turned bitter. He wanted to know how I was feeling...right after my brother threatened to tell him about the baby.

Did Jared do it?

Did he tell Kyle I was pregnant? I re-read the message over and over again, slowly coming to the same conclusion. He had to. Because it was the kind of thing Jared would do. He'd hurt me, just like he hurt me before.

I tossed the cell to the bed. I'd ignore the message. Pretend that I didn't receive it.

I'd pretend it didn't exist, just like I pretended this baby didn't exist.

Until my body forced me to face the truth.

*The truth...*

What was the truth? That I was in a corner with my back to the wall. My asshole stepbrother on one side determined to blackmail his way back into my bed...or the bully turned savour who tried his best to protect me. My heart raced as I stared at the cell...

Then picked it up and opened the messages once more...typing.

*Yes, I'll meet you. I have something I need to tell you.*

Then I hit send and stumbled backwards until I hit the motel wall. Desperation screamed...*what have I just done?*

The only thing I could.

Now I just needed to pray Kyle forgave me.

# Chapter Thirty-Five

## CALIX

"Maddie." I snarled, before forcing the handle down on her door. The lock held, making me grit my teeth. "Open the goddamn door. Don't make me—" I heard her whimper inside. The sound only triggered that savage part of me. "I'm giving you to the count of three little sister, then I'm coming in, whether you want me too or not. One...two...three—"

I stepped backwards, dropped my shoulder and charged, hitting the door hard. The damn thing held, leaving me to unleash a bark, step backwards, and charge once more. The door flew backwards, slamming against the wall. I was inside in an instant, striding across the room to grab her.

"Stop, Calix!" She slapped me.

But I couldn't stop. I drove her backward, pushing her against the wall. "You fucking left...without a goddamn word and now you're what, *back?*"

"Yes!" She snapped, her eyes wild. "I'm *back!*" She tried to shove me away, but I wasn't moving, holding her there against the wall. "I'm back, so what are you gonna do about it?"

"What am I going to do about it?" I braced to one hand against the wall, and the other fisting her shirt. "How about, for starters, I'm not going to be bullied into handing over information about my father." I look down at my hand pressing against her breast. "No matter how tempting it is, to have you."

She just stared up at me without a hint of embarrassment. Or maybe she didn't care who he played with? Was that it? So she left pissed at me and now she's back and sent her fucking goons to what...*threaten me?*

"I don't play fucking games, little sister. So if you think that you're going to help me twisted around your finger, then you have another think coming. You can send your pathetic little fuckboys after me. That's one thing. But to threaten our father because of one stupid fucking night between us, now that's a new goddamn low."

Her breath caught. There was a tiny furrow in her goddamn brow that made her look so fucking cute. "Fuckboys? What the hell are you talking about?"

I shoved off the wall and released my hold on her shirt. "Don't play games with me."

"Threaten how?" She demanded.

I turned and paced the floor. "Don't bullshit me, Maddie."

But she came after me, grabbing my arm and trying her best to spin me around. "Threaten how, Calix?"

I just held that stare, searching her eyes, until my heart started racing. Heat raced, and that debased fucking desire rose with it. The one who dragged me back to that night over and over again. I can still feel her body shift under mine, still feel my fingers slipping inside her and the way she moaned. *Can't come, my fucking ass...*

She was goddamn close, and then she pulled away.

They say it's all mental with women, that they needed the fantasy in their head to get them there. But what I felt was no goddamn fantasy. She liked what I did...and now this was her payback. "You sent your fucking asshole frat boyfriends to threaten me."

"I don't have *any* frat boyfriends, Calix, and I have no idea what you're talking about."

Sure she didn't. How the fuck else did these two assholes know who the fuck we were, and why the hell would they come after our family? I stepped close to her and this time she didn't flinch or move away. "You really don't know what I'm talking about."

Movement came from the corner of my eye. Brooks and Aven stopped at the doorway until Brooks stepped forward. "What the fuck is going on?"

I jerked my gaze to them. "Payback, that's what."

They knew now anyway. They knew it all, why she left in a damn hurry the last time she came home, scurrying all the way back to her pathetic school. Now they knew how much I wanted her. But what none of us knew was what she was playing out.

She wanted to jerk me around thinking I could be damn well manipulated, then let's see how how that plays out when I fucking expose her. "Two assholes were waiting for me outside the gym today." I spoke to my brothers, but it was Maddie I watched carefully. "They had a file with them, and more than enough information to bury our family."

"What the fuck?" Aven muttered, stepping in to stand beside his twin. "What kind of information?"

"Banking details, a copy of our father's will."

"Our father's will?" Aven jerked his gaze to Maddie. "How the fuck did you get that?"

Her cheeks grew red. "How the hell should I know?" She glared at me, and then at her brothers. "I have no idea what you're talking about. I don't have any frat boyfriends, nor do I have any inclination to relieve what happened that night."

"You sure about that?" I stepped closer, staring down at her. "Because what they wanted in payment was exactly that."

Same paled in front of me, her skin turning a Ghostly white. "What are you talking about?"

But Maddie said nothing. Not a word...not a breath, for that matter. *Jesus...what the fuck?* Confusion flared inside me. "This was what you planned, right?" I urged, pushing her. "This was what you wanted. Payback, right? Payback from what I did."

There was a tiny shake of her head as though she tried to shove my words away. And then in a rush, she exhaled. Her chest rose and fell, the color returning to her cheeks with blazing fury. "You *think* I'd do something like this?"

I leaned down. "Didn't you?"

"I told you, no." She glanced at the others. "I have no idea about any of this."

"You think I want this?" I pulled her close. "These assholes have information on us. Shit, no one else knows, Maddie. Hell, shit, I'm not surprised to know."

"What do they want?" Aven asked, trying to work it all out.

"Fucking leverage." I snarled.

"Then give it to him."

I chuffed, my lips curling into a sneer. "You wouldn't be so fucking keen if you knew what they wanted."

"What. What is it what they want?"

"They want you to have sex with her?" Brooks growled. "Don't they?"

"No." I answered. "They want us *all* to have sex with her...and they want to record it."

"What the fuck?" Aven muttered.

"Leverage." I said once more. "So let me as you again, little sister. Have you spoken to anyone about what happened that night?"

She flinched and pulled away. "I told you, no."

"Then this is all a sick fucking coincidence?"

Something shifted in her eyes. "Coincidence, or something you planned for yourself." She jutted her chin upwards. "Maybe this is all a fucking game to you. Maybe this was the only way you could manipulate your way into my bed?"

"*Into your bed...*" I snarled. "You think that's what this is about?"

"Isn't it?" She whispered...*Jesus.* "Isn't that exactly what you want?"

*Yes,* the answer was instant. The lie was a little slower. "No. So if you didn't put anyone up to this, and I sure as hell didn't plan my morning trying to manipulate my little sister into my bed, then someone out there has some sick, fucking plan to ruin our family..."

"Or use us." Aven muttered. "The question is who...and why?"

"We could give them what they want." Brooks's tone was husky. "Lure them in, then beat the shit out of them until they tell us what we want to know."

"Give them what they want." I muttered. "Sounds like you're into this, brother."

"It's just sex, right?" He added.

I shot him a glare. "Just sex? With your sister."

"Stepsister." He added. The way he looked at her told me all I needed to know. He thought about her, probably more than I did. It looked like I wasn't the only one who wanted to fuck Maddie and by the way he stared at her, I was betting he'd envisioned it many times before.

"We can do it." Brooks stepped closer. "Aven and I."

"No, you can't." I snapped. "Not gonna fucking happen."

"Yeah, we can." Aven muttered and looked away. "We've done it before."

"What?" I glanced from him to Brooks. "Done *what* before?"

"Shared a girl."

*Fuck*...my pulse raced with the words.

"She's *not* just a girl, brother."

"Our parents are out of state." Brooks stepped closer and lifted his hand, dragging the back of a curled finger down her cheek. "They're gone for an entire week. They don't even need to know.

"Don't." She moaned and stumbled backwards until her foot caught on the edge of the mat and she fell.

Her arms windmilled, but Brooks was there, lashing out and grabbing her arm, catching her fall.

"What's the difference?" He urged. "It's not like you haven't had cock before."

Her face burned with the words, and she looked away.

"What the fuck?" I murmured, my mind racing. I didn't want to be here having this conversation, especially not in front of my little fucking brothers. But she had to have some fucking experience where sex was concerned, because if she didn't. If I'd been her first, then...

Brooks gripped her chin, forcing her gaze to his. "You *have* had cock before, right Maddie?"

# Chapter Thirty-Six

JARED

I LISTENED TO THE MOTEL DOOR NEXT TO ME OPEN, THEN close. The *bang* resounded along the hallway, drawing my focus. *He's leaving...*

I drained the last of the tiny bottle of scotch from the hotel's mini bar and rose from the couch. Footsteps resounded, slowing at my door as I walked to the hallway and stopped inside the door. I expected it to open and for Kyle to give me one of his holier than thou fucking stare before he berated me one more fucking time.

He was pissed about these Lyons assholes and their bitch stepsister. Hating that he was 'forced' to play the goddamn role he was good at...the manipulative piece of shit.

Only something had changed. He didn't want any part of this, not to coerce Calix Lyons into proving us a recording of his sister, one that we'd use to get April out of Brontie's grasp. The steps outside my door started again, only this time leaving.

He was going somewhere...

*Where?*

I waited for the sounds to fade and then cracked open the door, scanned the hallway before I followed. I wanted to keep an eye on this bastard, not trusting him at all. The hallway blurred for a second, leaving me to stumble. I'd already emptied the minibar of every small bottle of alcohol there was. Maybe I miscalculated? Still, my focus was on him. The bastard who wanted my fucking girlfriend.

I headed for the elevator, taking it all the way down to the foyer and stepped out, scanning the sleek, expensive lounges for him. But he wasn't here, leaving me to step out. My pulse sped as I made for the underground car park, catching the sight of familiar headlights flaring to life and my gut clenched in warning.

*Follow him...*

Desperation Filled me. I stepped out, lifted my hand, hailing a taxi and waited for it to pull over. "Follow that car." I demanded, my gaze fixed on the flaring headlights.

"You've gotta be fucking kidding me, right?" The taxi driver looked at the Maserati, and then at me.

I just held that stare and yanked the door shut behind me. One hard sigh and he shoved the car into gear and punched the accelerator. It threw me back against the seat as we raced to catch up. Heading through the city, Kyle pulled into a carpark where an all-night grocery store was alight.

*What the fuck was he doing?*

"Do you want me to pull in and park?" The taxi driver asked.

I'm nodded. "Yeah, over there." I pointed to the darkened area away from the car park lights.

Kyle climbed out and headed to the grocery store. I did the same, muttering over my shoulder as I shoved open the door. "Stay here. I'll be back."

I didn't even wait for an answer, just strode towards the automatic doors, scanning the inside of the store for the sneaky bastard. He could be just out for alcohol, but then again, he might not be. I couldn't take that chance...not where April was concerned.

"Hey." Some punk called out from the edge of the store. "Got a cigarette?"

"Fuck off." I snapped and moved towards the door, jumping backwards as their automatic doors opened, the grating sound of metal-on-metal screeching in the still night. "Shit."

I stepped away, sinking back into the darkness, catching Kyle from the corner of the store as he stood over the refrigerated shelf of fresh flowers. He picked up a bunch of red roses and stared at the damn thing before turning toward the front of the store. They were for April. I knew that without thinking. So the bastard was going to meet up with a woman who was mine?

"Yeah, let's fucking see about that." I clenched my fists as rage rippled through me and Turn to my attention to the punk. "Do you want to bum a cigarette from me?"

He's pissed off expression brightened instantly. "Yeah," he licked his lips and came closer. "You got any?"

I strode toward him, that rage desperate to be unleashed. "No." I grabbed him by the shirt, driving him backwards to slam his head against the wall. "But you better have something that I want." My mind raced, trying to think as I glanced over my shoulder at the Maserati parked behind me. I lowered with my gaze to the tyres and then turned back to the asshole in front of me. "You have a knife?"

"What?" His eyes widened.

I dragged him close, snarling in his face. "I said, do you have a knife?"

Fear bloomed in his eyes. The stench of stale cigarettes and desperation filled my nose. "Yeah, yeah, I have one."

"Give it to me."

He reached down, his hand shaking as he shoved his fingers into his pocket and pulled out a beaten switchblade. I shoved him backwards, snatching the knife from his hand and strode across the car park toward the Maserati. I had to be fast. Kyle would be out any second and there was no way I was letting him fuck my sister, not while I had breath in my lungs.

I flipped the switch, releasing the blade and neared the tyres. One hard thrust was all it took, and I punctured the rubber, listening to the air hiss. I made my way around the car, until all four tyres were slashed, before tossing the blade toward the punk once more. "Better make yourself scarce, or it looks like you're in for trouble."

His eyes widened at what I'd done. But I didn't wait around to see the fallout. I lengthened my stride, making for the taxi and climbed back in. "Take me back to the hotel."

"What the fuck did you do?" The driver stared at me.

"Protected what's mine." I answered. "Now drive."

# Chapter Thirty-Seven

KYLE

I clenched my grip around the roses and strode out of the grocery store, feeling a sting from a thorn cut deep. I hissed and slipped my thumb into my mouth. The metallic taste of blood bloomed as I headed for my car. Hurried footsteps caught my attention. I lifted my gaze to some punk, who glanced at me over his shoulder as he raced across the car park. I scowled. *What the fuck?*

The flare of brake lights caught my attention in the distance. I watched as a taxi turned the corner and disappeared. But it was the kid running away from me that drew me back, before I shifted my focus to the Maserati and the slashed front tire.

"Sonofabitch." I muttered, lifting my gaze to the rear tire and found the same destruction. Anger flared, quickly turning to rage as I moved around the other side of the car, finding all four tires slashed. *"Fuck!"*

The automatic doors to the grocery store opened behind me. One of the other customers stepped out, drawing my focus. He looked at me, then the car, before hurrying away.

"Goddamn bastard!" I jerked my gaze to the fading hurried steps of the punk as he disappeared into the darkness. The need to chase him down rose like a commanding wave. But I didn't have time, even if I caught the asshole and beat the shit out of him. Of all the fucking times for someone to take a goddamn blade to my tire...*no, not tire...tires.* All four of them.

This felt like more than a random act of violence. This felt *purposeful.* I lifted my cell, contemplating for a moment about calling April and telling her I couldn't come, until that desperation and savagery collided inside me. *Fuck no.* I wasn't about to let some asshole stop me from getting to her.

April's message rose inside me. I knew what she wanted to tell me. It was all I thought about since I overheard Jared in the bar's carpark. She was pregnant. I didn't need to think too hard to know who was the father. My pulse raced at the thought as I typed out a message:

*I'm coming, but I'm going to be late. Find a place that's quiet and careful, then send me the directions and I'll meet you there.*

I didn't wait for her reply, just scanned in the car park, searching the cars parked in the back in the empty lot and started forward. I clenched my jaw, the muscles tensing so tight I felt the crack in my teeth, and made for a dark blue sedan five spaces away.

I tossed the roses to the ground and worked the buttons of my shirt, yanking it free before winding it around my fist. Then I unleashed driving my fist through the window. Agony tore through my knuckles and sliced my palm. But I didn't care about that. I unwound my shirt, bleeding through the material as I yanked it back on, then reached through, yanked open the door and climbed in.

Ten panicked seconds was all it took for me to hot-wire the ignition and the Toyota roared to life. I backed out of the parking lot, punched the accelerator and glanced at the broken fuel gauge. "Of course." I snarled, hitting the street with a *thud.*

The metal underbelly scraped against the asphalt, sparks ignited in the rear-view mirror. My pulse thundered, ignited by the searing pain in my hand and the desperation that roared in my veins. Nothing on this night was goddamn easy.

My cell lit up with a message. I grabbed it, dividing my attention between the road and the message April sent. She was heading to an alley next to a diner near where she was staying. I pushed the vehicle harder, hovering over the speed limit as I headed back to the city.

This is the moment I'd been waiting for. The moment where she told me the truth. Because *she* needed to tell me the truth. I watched for cop cars in the rearview mirror, knowing that by the time whoever would report the sedan stolen, I'd already be in the city.

Four slashed tires. The image of my ruined Maserati grated on me. The footsteps still resounded in my head, along with the wide terrified eyes of the punk who ran for his life. Wide eyes. Filled with terror. Like he was scared of me. *But I didn't know him.*

It didn't make sense, and there was one thing I didn't like—it was something that didn't make sense. I grabbed my cell and dialled the number for my hotel and waited for it to be answered.

"Good evening, XX—"

I cut her off. "This is Kyle Blackburn. I'm staying there with a colleague of mine, Jared Scott. There's been an incident with my car and I'd like to be patched through to your security immediately."

"Oh, of course, Mr. Blackburn, right away."

I watched the rear-view mirror, scanning the headlights behind me while I waited for the guard to answer.

"Security, this is Alex."

"Kyle Blackburn." I commanded. "There's been substantial damage to my vehicle and I require some information for the police report. Jared Scott is staying with me. Can you confirm if he is currently in his room?"

"We don't have cameras in the suites, Mr. Blackburn."

A nerve twitch in the corner of my mouth. "I understand that. But you do in the hallways and the foyer." I checked the time on my cell. "Twenty minutes. Check the foyer for Jared Scott back in twenty minutes. I want to know if he left the hotel."

"I don't think I can—"

I yanked my cell close. "You can if you want to keep your goddamn job."

There was a second of silence before. "Jared Scott...room 345."

"Yes, room 345." I growled.

"Just looking at him now, Mr. Blackburn, back twenty minutes, just like you said. He's following someone out of his room... someone in room 346."

"Me." I answered, more for myself than the guard. "It's me."

"Let me follow him." The security guard muttered, his intrigue building in his tone. There was silence for a long time. I could only imagine what he was seeing. Jared stepping into the elevator, following me all the way down to the car park. "Yeah, yeah, Mr. Scott did leave the building. Hey...there's a taxi. He climbs into a taxi, Mr. Blackburn. So you say that there was damage to your vehicle?"

A taxi...

The memory of red brake lights pushed in. It wasn't in the goddamn kid...

My memory sharpened. It wasn't a goddamn kid at all. It was the fucking taxi. One that took off, roaring as it left the parking lot. The kid looked terrified, and it wasn't the kind of terror that was remorseful. It was the kind of terror that saw something you shouldn't, and wanted no part of it.

"Thank you." I answered. "That information is all I needed." I hung up the call and tossed my cell to the passenger seat.

It was Jared who slashed my tires. Jared, who followed me to the grocery store. Jared who stood outside watching as I bought his stepsister flowers. Jared who wanted to destroy any kind of relationship I had with April.

But he wasn't going to win, was he?

That dangerous hunger rose inside me. There was only one way around this now. One way that ended this once and for all. Jared had to die...

A plan hatched in my head. One that revolved around Brontie, Calix Lyons and Jared. Blood, death and danger swirled around in my mind like a tornado. One that built and built...and built.

One wrong move...

And it wasn't just my life in danger.

*It was April's.*

The sparkle of city lights drew closer as I thought about how I was going to do this. Jared wanted to take part in the destruction of Madison Alvarez. Then I'd let him. And I'd make sure April found out on her own. But that wasn't just the plan. I focused on Calix Lyons and his brothers. I'd make sure he hated Jared. I'd make sure he focus that desperation and rage on Jared first and then Brontie.

The Lyons family was mafia, there was no denying that.

So I'd let them do what mafia families did best—destroy anybody who harmed them.

I slowed with the traffic, reaching over and grab my cell phone to find directions April sent me and made my way to the diner. Excitement surged through me. I glanced down at my bloody open shirt and yanked the edges together, worried for the first time I'm my life about how I looked.

I glanced into the rear-view mirror and combed my fingers through my hair. The gash on my hand left a blood smear across my forehead. I cursed, leaned closer to the mirror and scrubbed the mark with the back of my hand.

I'd been so focused on trying to deal with Jared and the Lyon's family and not letting myself become sidetracked by April. But now that I left them all behind and focused on her, she was all I could think about.

The speedometer on the car crept higher, the more excited I became.

My pulse thundered as I turned the wheel, glancing at the directions on the map, then lifted my gaze to the diner. This was it. This was the place. I looked for the alley and pulled the stolen sedan into the gloom.

I was already scanning for movement before the car came to a stop, searching the shadows for her...

And through the murky light, April stepped forward. My heart slammed against my ribs at the sight of her. Dark shadows haunted her eyes. She looked pale and gaunt. I didn't like that. I yanked the wires apart and killed the Toyota's engine before climbing out.

I shoved the door behind me and closed the distance, lunging to grab her from the darkness and pulled her close. My fingers were in her hair in an instant. My lips were hard on hers. She was so warm, so alive, so...*safe*.

That's what she was. She was safe.

I kissed her, taking her mouth and drew in the scenes of her. She tasted like coffee and toothpaste, the faint stench of cigarettes lingering on her body. She was so small against me, so goddamn...*perfect*. I broke the kiss, realising for the first time with chilling clarity how deep my feelings were for her.

"God, I missed you." I stared into her eyes.

Fear echoed back at me. I forced a smile, brushing the corners of her mouth with my thumb. "You aren't glad to see me?"

She smiled, and but it was a sad, terrified sight. "Yes, and that might be the problem."

My thumb traced her bottom lip. "A problem that you care?" The words were so close to the truth, maybe too close...did she feel the same way about me that I did for her?

"Yes." She answered. "I do."

Excitement surged with her words. I smiled then, and it was probably the most honest smile that I've ever had in my entire life. I pulled her close. "I like that problem. I like that problem a lot."

She rose on the tip of her toes, chuckling softly before she kissed me. "You might not feel that way after tonight."

Christ, the truth weighed heavy on her. "I think you might be surprised."

Her brows narrowed, and confusion rose. "There's something I need to tell you. Something I've kept to myself, mostly because I didn't know how to deal with it. But now it's time for me to be honest. And I want to be honest with you, Kyle."

"I want to be honest with you, too." I brushed a strand of hair from her face.

She reached up, captured my hand and turned it to look at the gash. "You're hurt?"

I gave a shrug. "Let's just say tonight has been eventful."

She stilled, her fingers clenching around mine. "Kyle, I..." she started, her gaze moving from mine to somewhere behind me, before she froze. Fear shone in her eyes. Her breath caught, her body stiffened. She unleashed a moan. One sounded wounded and painful. She took a step backwards, away from me.

"April?" I murmured.

Heavy footsteps echoed in the alley behind me. I turned, catching sight of a man as he stepped into the mouth of the alley. A man dressed in a black suit. One that looked too fucking familiar. He glanced at me and shifted his gaze to April, and those eyes widened with surprise. "You?...April..."

She shook her head, stumbling backwards, deeper into the alley. I could hear her steps moving away from me.

"Don't fucking move." The bodyguard commanded, reaching into his jacket, "stop right there."

*No!* That desperation howled inside me.

I had to do something, had to save her *somehow*.

So I did the only thing I knew what to do.

I clenched my fist and lunged. Rage roaring inside me and tore from my lips as I screamed. "April, *RUN!*"

# Chapter Thirty-Eight

"April, *run!*" Kyle screamed.

I turned, finding the man lunging from the street toward Kyle. This man who saw me, who knew me...*who was sent to track me down.* Panic roared through me as I stood in the darkness, staring at Kyle as he strode forward. All I thought about was Brontie...Brontie who wanted to hurt me. Brontie, who wanted to control me...I searched the street behind the attacker, then I did exactly what Kyle said.

I stumbled backwards, then ran.

Agony roared through my chest as I left Kyle behind. My steps were frantic as I stumbled toward the alley in the dark, until desperation slammed into me, forcing me to stop.

I stared at the darkness, listening to grunts and groans behind me as Kyle met him head on. The thought of leaving him made my stomach clench, and my will weak. I couldn't leave him. I couldn't leave him...

I turned around, finding the man gripping Kyle around the throat and driving him backwards. "No!" I screamed and charged forward once more, only this time toward them.

I headed for the car Kyle drove, rounding the front and lunging at the man. I clawed at his face and yanked his hair. He jerked his gaze toward me, rage and desperation burning his eyes.

"Get the fuck off him!" I screamed, fighting harder than I've ever fought before.

"*No!*" Kyle roared. He looked at me, and I saw the desperation in Kyle's eyes. There was blood on his mouth. Blood where the man hit him. I had to stop this. I had to do *something*. Kyle saw this and drove his fist upward, punching the man in the chest.

I unleashed my fury, lunging once more as I sank into that cold bitter rage I held inside. They weren't going to take him from me. They weren't going to take him at all.

*"Leave him alone and I'll come with you!"* The words tore free of me in a rush.

The man stopped fighting. "What did you say?"

"I said, leave him alone," I sucked in a hard breath. "And I'll come with you." It was all I could do to save him. All I could think about. I stepped backwards, moving toward the street. "If you don't, I'll run. And you'll never see me again."

"*Stop.*" The man ordered.

But I kept moving, kept stepping towards the roar of the traffic in the street. *Please, please do this.*

He let Kyle go with the shove. One that sent him sprawling backwards.

"Come back here." The man demanded.

I glanced at Kyle, hoping he understood exactly what I was trying to do here. That I was trying to give him a second. Because I knew that a second was all he needed. His eyes were wide and dark. His face framed by the shadows and the streetlights behind me. I stepped backwards, listening to the cars roar, and the wind howl and called out. "It's me, or him. You choose."

I took another step to prove a point. The rush of tires and the growls of engines so close they made my pulse frantic. My hair scattered around my face, swept away by the rush of the buffering wind.

"*No!*" The attacker screamed and Kyle moved behind him, reaching around his back and pulled out a gun.

*Bang!*

The gunshot was loud, echoing along the street. I froze, staring at the attacker as he crumbled in front of Kyle and fell to his knees.

My breath was savage, burning in my chest. I took one look behind me, scanning the faces of those in the street. But no one looked our way. No one acknowledged they heard the sound at all. Instead, they hurried away from us, determined to ignore whatever was happening.

I hurried forward, away from the cars that went past me into the alley once more.

"Are you hurt?" Kyle grabbed me, pulling me into his arms. "*April, are you hurt?*" He repeated.

I shook my head. "No" And found his gaze, before looking at the dead man at our feet. "But we need to get him out of sight."

Kyle dropped his hands, staring at the body that spilled halfway into the light. He moved forward, grabbing the man's shirt and hauled him deeper into the alley, and toward the car.

"We need to dump the body before Brontie tracks him down" Kyle let the body go. It hit the ground with a thud as he looked at me with desperation, then unleashed a savage growl.

He straightened and turned. For a second, I thought he was going to leave me. My heart raced, slamming into my chest, before he stopped with his back to me. And in a quiet voice, he asked. "Will you come with me?"

"What?"

"His words were soft, but the impact they had on me was a roar. "Will you come?"

*Would I come?*

I knew what he was asking. Knew that if I went with him, there was no going back for us. That there was no going back for *me*. I'd have to leave the motel, and risk being found by more of Brontie's men. My fingers clenched, aching to rest against the flutter in my stomach.

"I'll find you a place to be safe." He continued. "One only I will know about. If you...if you want to be with me. If you...want me." His focus slowly sank to my stomach.

*Oh, God*...did he know about the baby? The panic thoughts raced through my head. I tried to remember what I said to him. I tried to remember if there was any way he could know. But there's no way he could, not unless Jared told him.

My heart raced at the thought. Surely he would've said something by now. Was this a setup? Was this some way of taking me back to Brontie? The thought crossed my mind and for a second, I couldn't think of anything else. Until I shoved it away. No. I had to believe Kyle cared about me. I had to believe the words he said were true.

I had to believe he...loved to me.

Hope waited for me in the darkness of his eyes and I answered. "Yes. Yes, I'll come."

Relief washed over him. His shoulder sank for a second until they straightened, and this time there was a newfound sense of excitement and determination in his eyes. "Then grab his legs. We need to get out of here now."

I rushed forward, grabbing the attacker's feet as Kyle yanked open the rear door of the sedan. Then he returned, grabbing him under the arms and lifted, hauling him toward the open door and slid him along the seat. "Jump in, April."

I did. Adrenaline hit me, now that I realised what we were doing. We were running. Running together.

I rushed around in the car and climbed in as Kyle shoved the body down low, hiding it as best as he could, then closed the door and climbed in behind the wheel.

"Look at me." He lifted a shaking hand, brushing the back of his knuckles against my cheek. "I'm so fucking glad, April. I'm so fucking glad you're coming with me. For a second there, I thought you were going to say no."

For a second, I thought I was going to say no.

I gave him a weak smile before he turned back, fumbling with the wires underneath ignition and start of the engine. Then we were backing out, tires squealing as we braked to a stop, then charged forward. We left it all behind. Jared, Brontie, my father. There was just us...us against the world.

We headed out of the city, and toward the forest that crowded west of the city. It felt like hours as we drove in silence with the body in the back, and the stench of blood that made me terrified. *Tell him...he has to know.*

The words were stuck in the back of my throat. Words that have taken far too long for me to say.

"Kyle...I..."

"We're almost there." He said his words were careful. "It's quiet here. I haven't been this way for years, ever since I was with my dad."

"Your dad?" Surprise filled me. "You lived here?"

He gave a nod. "Yeah, for a while."

The car bumped and bounced, leaving asphalt behind for the dirt road. He turned once more, taking us slowly along a narrow dark track until we left the road and the city behind us. There was nothing but darkness here, nothing that shadowed trees and stars that sparkled overhead. I didn't know where we were going, but I trusted him.

I trusted him with more than my life; I trusted him with my heart.

He braked, pulled the sedan into an empty car park, before he stopped the car. "I have to leave it running. "So we need to be quick."

I climbed out and rounded the back of the car as Kyle opened the door and hauled out the body. "Grab his legs."

I did, grabbing hold of his boots, and together we stumbled toward the trees, moving around the trees until finally he dropped the body, tearing the attacker's feet from my hold. He hit the ground hard and rolled. And it took me a second to realise we stood at the top of an embankment. "Step backwards, April." Kyle urged. "The ground here is soft. I don't want to risk you falling."

I took a step back, grabbing hold of a tree as Kyle lifted his boot and lashed out, kicking the body. It rolled, and then it kept on rolling and suddenly disappeared, falling into the darkness below us. I sucked in the cold night air, as what we done hit me like a blow.

We killed a man...

And got rid of his body.

Kyle turned toward me, striding close to pull me against him. "Are you okay?" It wasn't the first time he asked me that tonight.

"Yeah," I answered. "I'm okay."

He grabbed my hand, leading me back through the darkness to the car as it idled roughly, waiting. "Jump in."

I stopped, watching him walk toward the open driver's door before he realised I'd stopped. It was now or never. Now all keep hiding the truth. "Kyle, wait."

He turned, his brows furrowing. Panic waited in the glint of his eye as he shook his head. "April, we don't have to do this."

"Yes, we do." I answered. "Kyle, I'm pregnant. I'm pregnant and the father is—"

"It doesn't matter." He cut me off. "I want it...I want it and I want you."

He wants me...

He stepped closer. "I have somewhere you can stay, someone who can protect you. Someone I trust...with you, and with our baby."

*Our baby...*

The night shifted around me. My heart clenched with the words. "Who?"

"My sister."

# Chapter Thirty-Nine

## KYLE

"Your sister?" April stared up at me.

I smiled. "Yeah, my sister." I glanced at the car, the stolen goddamn car knowing what I was about to do. "Although, I'm not really sure she's going to be my sister after this. I think she's going to hand me my ass. If she doesn't kill me first. So let's find out how loyal she is. What do you say?"

I climbed into the driver's seat as she did the same climbing into the passenger seat. The car was already running, so I waited for April to climb in beside me before I shoved it into gear and headed back to the city.

The streets were familiar. Too damn familiar for liking. I thought I'd escaped this city with its damn ghosts. When I left years ago, I tried to make myself into somebody new. Somebody, somebody stronger than who I'd been. But seemed like the devil had a way of dragging me back.

And Brontie was the biggest devil of them all.

I pushed him from my mind and focused on the battle at hand...*my damn family*. I only hoped Hannah still cared. My sister was the only one who stood by my side when my father had me arrested and thrown in jail for some trumped up extortion charge. She saved me then, and I needed her to save me now. The only problem was I didn't know if she would turn me away as soon as she saw me or welcome me with open arms.

I hoped she'd welcome me I hoped she'd welcome *us*. Because hope was all I had.

"Kyle?"

I glanced April's way. "Yeah?"

"You haven't really heard anything I've said, have you?"

"Sorry, a little distracted. Tell me again." I urged, trying to force myself into this moment. April needed me, more now than ever before.

"I wanted to talk to you about...you know, the baby."

The baby...

*My baby.*

"Tell me again." I glanced her way. "Tell me anything you need."

I wanted to listen to her, but in my head, only one face rose in the darkness. That sonofabitch who used her. Who forced her to run when there was no good reason to keep hiding. Who claimed he loved her in one minute and then planned to fuck someone else the next.

Her brother, Jared.

"Do you want to know if it's a boy or a girl?" She asked carefully.

I flinched...*a boy or a girl...*

My pulse sped with the thought. I didn't need to know the sex of our baby, but I could tell that she wanted to tell me. "How about this?" I murmured. "When it is over, we leave? We take nothing with us, not even our damn names. I know someone who can get us fake identification. We can leave the city, leave the damn state if we need to. We'll find someplace safe. Someplace where we will make a whole new life. Then our baby." I glanced at her stomach and felt that surge of protection rise inside me. "Our baby will be protected, regardless if it's a boy or a girl. Who knows maybe...we can add another to our family?"

Her eyes widened. I surprised her. "Do you want to have a baby with me?"

I reached out, brushing my fingers against her cheek. "April, I *am* having a baby with you."

She smiled, and the sight of that was a blow to my chest. My heart hammered as I stared at her. I'd never seen anything more beautiful in my life. Anything more commanding...and this strong, determined woman was commanding. She commanded me.

I knew the moment I saw her months ago in her brother's arms that I wanted her. That the spark of fire inside her kindled something else in me. I tried to ignore it, tried to kill it. Tried to be the bastard I'd been because I thought I needed to be to survive...and become someone powerful like Brontie.

But that was before.

Before he took what was mine.

And April *was* mine.

"Yes." She answered, giving me a soft smile. "I guess you are."

I divided my focus between her and the road. I'd never wanted to pull a damn car over and fuck someone in my entire life. I wanted her more than anything I ever wanted before. More than this fake bullshit life I'd created. More than the family I once yearned for. Family I needed now.

She was quiet then, that smile lingering as I drove into the city, and headed east. My family wasn't rich, well, my sister wasn't at least. She lived on a meager cop's wage, from a bullshit job she spent far too long in. But I sent her money throughout the years. Money I hope she'd put to good use.

Her ugly damn Christmas cards stuck in my mind. I dragged up the memory of those hideous things. They were the only damn things I gave a shit about, especially at Christmas. Now I resurrected the address she wrote on the back and punched in the details into the map on my cell.

The street where she lived wasn't far away. I knew it had to be close to where we once lived. I kept on driving, following the red dot on the screen in front of me. The houses out here were neat and expensive. Surprise filled me as I drove, searching the street numbers and pulled up outside on my sister's modest stucco house.

"Maybe just stick with me, okay?" I murmured and yanked the twisted wires under the dash.

"You sure about this?" April asked as I reached for the handle.

"Yeah." I lied. I wasn't sure about anything. Not when it came to Hannah.

I closed the door behind me, waiting for April to round the front of the car, fully knowing I was about to walk up to my sister's house with a stolen car in her driveway.

The idea of that would've make me smile...if it wasn't for the fact I just killed a man...and disposed of his body.

And now I was about to confess it all...to my sister...*the cop.*

I grabbed April's hand and made my way along the drive to the front door. We had nowhere to go. Nowhere Brontie wouldn't find us...find her at least.

I glanced April's way and reached out, pressed the doorbell, and held my damn breath.

The piercing yap of some kind of small and annoying inconvenience came from inside.

But my sister didn't own a dog...not that I knew, at least.

God, don't tell me she actually turned into someone human? With real relationships and affection. The idea of that made me stiffen. What if she was married? Our relationship wasn't the kind where we talked about that kind of stuff...not like that.

I glanced at April, feeling that thunder in my chest once more as the faint growl of my sister's voice came from inside before locks clicked and the door was open.

Then there she was, the same Hannah and always known. Hard edges and the bloodless slash of a careful smile. Her brows narrowed, a flare of confusion widened her eyes. "Kyle? What the hell are you doing here?"

"Would you believe me if I told you I was in the neighbourhood?"

She opened the door, glancing at April. "No, I wouldn't."

I stepped past, striding into a neat foyer and glanced around. "Nice digs."

"Yeah, well, let's just say I put your money to good use, for once." She closed the door and hit the locks.

I turned around, unleashing a pent up breath and met my sister's stare. "April, this is my sister, Hannah. Han, this is...this is April. We wouldn't have come here if I had another choice, but we're in a bit of a situation."

My sister glanced at April. "Of course you are." She gave a jerk of her head toward the door. "Don't tell me the Maserati's in the shop?"

"Actually, it's not far from the truth." Annoyance cut through me. "Four slashed tires tonight left me with little option."

"Little option." She shook her head. "Now that doesn't sound like something I need to know about." She glanced to April, who stood quietly beside me. "How about you come inside? I just made a fresh pot of coffee."

But it wasn't me she spoke to. April gave a smile. "Thank you."

I followed her, trying to figure out how much to tell her. How much was going to keep her safe, and how much was going to keep her from tossing us out into the street? If there was one thing my sister was good at, it was detecting a lie. But the truth. The truth could get us killed.

We made our way into the kitchen, where my sister pulled out two mugs from a cabinet and placed them on the counter. "Coffee? It's hot."

"Sure." April answered.

My sister poured, then pushed creamer and sugar toward us, before grabbing her own, which was still half full. "The last time we spoke, you were cagey." She fixed that stare on me. "I didn't push, maybe I should've. Because whatever it is, it must be pretty bad if you're here." April's hands shook when she grabbed the mug and my sister noticed. "So you want to tell me what's going on here? Or do I have to suspect the worst?"

"How about we suspect the worst?" I answered. "It'll only go down from there."

"Really?" She lowered her mug to the counter and refilled it. "Then let's start somewhere." She glanced at April. "Let's start with you, April. Want to tell me how you got yourself mixed up with someone like my angelic brother, who I love to death...but wouldn't trust him as far as I could throw him."

My stomach tensed. I waited.

But April never flinched. She just met my sister's scrutiny and answered. "That's a long and ugly story. But let's just say that we moved past that...and ended up here." She lowered one hand to her stomach. "For him to be the father of my baby."

"Baby?" Hannah jerked her gaze my way. "Jesus..."

"That's not all." My tone hardened, praying to God this worked. "The car outside? Yeah, that's stolen...so I might need some help getting rid of it. Because tonight it was used to transport the death body of the man I just killed."

# Chapter Forty

## KYLE

"What the fuck, Kyle?" My sister barked and strode from the kitchen and made for the front door.

I followed her, knowing that this was inevitable. I expected it, almost welcomed it. Honesty, that's what Hannah craved, and that's what she's got. Because I needed her...more than I ever needed anyone else before.

April followed as we made our way toward the front door. Hannah brushed the curtains aside to stare out onto her driveway at the stolen car that was used to transport the body of the man I just killed. "Are you fucking serious?"

"Deadly serious."

She turned, glaring at me. "You're going to make a damn joke about this? Are you fucking crazy?"

I held her gaze. "More like desperate."

She stilled, her eyes whitening. "You're bullshitting me, aren't you?" The ghost of a smile tugged the corners of her mouth. "Of course you're joking."

She stopped, her eyes darkening as her brow furrowed.

"I wish I was." I turned my head, glancing at April over my shoulder. "I wish with everything I had that I was, Hannah. But I'm not, and there is so much more to tell you."

My sister unleashed a guttural moan. "You bought a stolen car used to transport a dead body to my house?"

I gave a nod and turn back to her. "If you'll only just listen."

She shook her head. "No... no, no, no." She took a step backwards and lifted a trembling hand, pointing to the door. "Get the fuck out, Kyle. Get the fuck out." She glanced at April.

But I didn't let her say the next word. I *couldn't* let her say the next words. Because this was my only option. I always knew it was going to come down to this. The plan grew in my head ever since I left to find that hotel tonight to come and find April. Just now it was a little rushed.

It was a risk.

One that I wouldn't have taken if I had any other choice.

But I was stuck. No, *we* were stuck...and here I was, about to risk it all.

To save her...

The woman I loved.

"Damien Brontie has blackmailed and forced us into this sick game. A game he's using against some of the most powerful men. All the players will be in his possession. The man will make all the moves. Hannah, he is going to be unstoppable. Do you understand what I'm trying to say?" I pierced my sister with a desperate gaze. "He's going to ruin us all."

"Brontie?" My sister whispered. She knew the name, of course she knew the name...everyone did.

"Blackmail, murder, and that's just the tip of the iceberg." I whispered.

"And you know this how?"

I caught April's flinch at the question and I steadied myself for the pain that was about to come. "Because I'm tied up in it all."

The breath left my sister's body, her shoulders sagged, there was a small shake of her head. "You've done some pretty stupid fucking things, Kyle. But this takes a goddamn cake."

She jerked her gaze to April. "And you're involved in this?"

April just wrapped her arms around her body and gave her a nod. But my sister sensed there was more she wasn't saying. She took a step away from the curtains. "I need coffee and the goddamn truth."

And she would get it all.

We followed her back to the kitchen, where she lifted a mug with shaking hands and took a slow draw of her coffee before she placed her cup back down. "Okay." She cut me with a cold, hard stare. "I want the entire story. Leave nothing out, understand me?"

I nodded. "I understand."

It all came down to this. My sister was a hard case. One who made her career upholding the law. And I was about to shatter everything she knew about me, and those she looked up to and respected.

Because Brontie' biggest supporters were the men she called, Sir.

I started talking, and I didn't stop. I laid it all out for her, telling her from the moment I started working for Brontie and the things that they forced me to do.

But there was no emotion for me in the beginning. Not until I came to April.

I froze...the words stuck in the back of my throat.

I had to tell my sister what I did to April. I had to tell her how I'm not only took part in what happened in April's pool room but that I was the one responsible for recording at all and handing the tape to Brontie, knowing what kind of man he was.

I watched as he obsessed over her. I watched him stare at the recording time after time with the kind of hunger that knew no bounds. When I finished telling my sister what I did to April, she glanced toward the woman who had my heart and whispered. "He did that to you?"

For a second April couldn't look at her. She looked at me instead. "It's okay. You can tell her the truth." I urged quietly.

I could see the torment on her face. The way her arms clasped either around her middle. "Yes, he did that."

April never answered, just winced and held my gaze.

"If he did that to me, he wouldn't be standing." Hannah muttered.

This was my sister. The only woman, apart from April, who ever gave a damn about me. And yet here she was, wondering how I was still left alive...

I was wondered that myself.

"Now Brontie is after someone else, a Maddie Alvarez. And they're going to use her stepbrother's getting what they need.

"Alvarez?" Hannah asked.

"Ties to the mafia. I suspect her mother is a mafia princess." I hadn't said the words out loud before. Yet here there were, as blinding as the truth. "They will hurt her, Han. They will use her, then they will destroy her."

"Jesus, Kyle." My sister exhaled hard, brace her hands against the counter.

"It's the truth, Hannah." I urged.

"I just don't get it." Anna shook her head, and lifted her gaze to April. "How are you still here? How are you still trusting him after all he's done, do you?"

This was the truth of the matter...

Because God knows, I didn't understand myself.

"Because I'm pregnant." April whispered.

I flinched with the words, my heart hammering.

"And my brother is the father?" Hannah asked, surprised.

"Yes." I answered for the both of us. "I am."

April's eyes were wide. Her chest strangely still like her breath and somehow locked inside her chest, and wouldn't come out.

"Jesus, Kyle." Hannah moaned. "This is a goddamn mess. I don't even know where to begin, how to unpack any of this."

"If you send April back out there, then you send her back to Brontie." I held April's focus. It wasn't me I cared about, it was her. "He has men all over the city hunting her."

"The man you killed." Hannah murmured.

I just found her stare and nodded.

One hard exhale and my sister nodded. "Fine, but better get rid of that goddamn car." My sister snapped, her voice softening as she gave April a small smile. "There's a pool house out back. Make yourself at home, use anything you need, okay?"

April's eyes widened. "Really?"

Hannah headed around the counter and stopped in front of her. She awkwardly took April in an embrace, pulling April gently against her. "As much as I hate my brother right now, I'm glad you came to me. I won't let anything happen to you, okay?"

I could tell April was close to breaking down. Her body trembled in my sister's arms. "Including my damn brother." She added, shooting me a glare. That said it all. *Hurt her again and I'll end you.*

I gave a slow nod.

"Thank you." April whispered and lifted her head. "The only reason I'm alive is because of Kyle. He saved me tonight. He's the only one who would." I could tell she was talking about Jared.

I hated him more in that moment than I ever had.

There was pain in her eyes, only she didn't know what he was planning to do.

Hannah dropped her arms and stepped away. "Well, I hope you enjoy staying here. Come to me if you need anything at all. Kyle will give you my number and if you text me, I'll store yours in my contacts and make sure I answer any time you call."

"Thank you." April whispered, tears shimmering in her eyes. "You're being so incredibly nice to me."

My sister just gave her shoulder a squeeze. "I think it's about time someone was, don't you?"

April just gave a smile, and my sister motioned toward the rear door of the house, giving me a jerk of her head. I followed, catching up to her as she switched on a light and slid open a glass sliding door.

"I think she's more vulnerable than she is leading on." My sister was always perceptive. "So I don't want you to upset her, okay?" She cut me a glare. "Kyle?"

"I understand."

"And I'll expect a call tomorrow from you. We need to come up with some kind of plan, someway to get you and April out of this." She muttered, leading us through the patio and around a massive in-ground pool.

"For now, let's get her settled." Hannah motioned to the pool house before she slowed. "I'll leave you two."

"Hannah, thank you." I meant the words.

My sister turned, levelling me with a stare. "Don't fuck this up, Kyle."

I waited for April and answered. "I'm going to try not to."

# Chapter Forty-One

### KYLE

Don't fuck it up. Hannah's words lingered as I opened the door to the pool house at the back of her house and waited for April to step inside.

The place was nice, warm and comforting. A king-sized bed commanded space in the middle of the room, and what looked like a small kitchenette was situated further in the back. She'd be comfortable here...warm, secure. I closed the door behind her, watching as April moved through the pool house, dragging her fingers along the soft beige comforter on the bed before she turned. "She's really going to let me stay here?"

I gave a nod. "Yes, she's really going to let you stay here."

But it was more than the plush furnishings in this secluded little hideaway. It was about protection. One my sister could provide. If only I could keep her onboard.

Fear moved through me. I *had* to keep Hannah onboard, because she was the only way I could see out of this. Bringing Brontie and his entire depraved fucking games out into the open...and exposing them all.

"She seems nice." April murmured as I stepped closer. There was a catch of her breath with the movement, her eyes widening as they lifted to mine.

"Yes," I brushed my finger along her cheek. "She is nice." But my sister wasn't the topic of conversation I wanted to have. "You're going to be safe here, okay? I'll make sure of it."

Christ, my pulse raced when I was near her. She was my secret obsession. The only one I'd risk everything for. I lowered my head, capturing her breath a second before I took her mouth. Everything was still in this moment, there was nothing but us and this...

My hands went around her, pressing her warmth against my chest. She trembled, and I didn't know if it was from the cold or from me.

I deepened the kiss, sliding my hands over her ass and yanked her against me hard. She unleashed a low moan that sound triggered the hunger inside me. I waited so long to be with her, and killed a man with these calloused, brutal hands for her. And yet all I wanted to do was touch her.

I picked her up. She wound her legs around my waist as I lifted her onto that massive bed in the middle of the room.

She was pregnant with my baby.

*My baby...*

It was all I could think of. Claiming her. Loving her. I broke the kiss to search her eyes. "Is this okay?"

She tethered that bastard in me, making me weak when it came to her. There was not one part of me that cared about the way she made me weak.

"Yes." She grabbed my shoulders, pulling me back down. "It's more than okay."

That was all the enticement I needed. With a growl, yanked her shirt until I exposed her breast. "Christ, I want to do this all goddamn night." I breathed the words into her skin, yanking down her bra until a peak of her nipple popped free. Her breath caught, and that tremble raced through her body.

I took her nipple in my mouth, grazing my teeth along the puckered flesh. She writhed underneath me, her hands sliding over my shoulders until her fingers speared through my hair. She didn't need to pull me harder against her. I was more than ready to take my fill.

That beast pushed to the surface. I pulled away long enough to slide my hands down her legs, taking off her shoes one by one before I moved to the button of her jeans. "It won't be like it was before, I promise." I slid the zipper down. "But I can't stop when it comes to you, April."

And that was the truth of it.

"I'm like a man obsessed. You're all I think about. All I hunger for."

She lifted her hips, giving me access to slide her jeans over the curve of her ass and down her thighs. My gaze went to her pussy as I tugged her jeans free.

"Kyle..." she started, and there was actual fear in her voice.

I lifted my gaze to hers.

She bit her lips, and with a shattered breath, whispered the words that plunged into my heart like a knife. "There was bleeding. I thought I was losing the baby."

*Bleeding?*

*Bleeding after that bastard Brontie abducted her?*

Anger plunged through me. The kind of uncontrollable rage then made me feel murderous. "But you're okay now?" I lifted my body, making sure she took none of my weight.

"Yes. There was a woman in the motel where I was staying. Her daughter was a gynaecologist. She ran some tests, checked the baby."

I pushed, rising on my arms. "Fuck, April. Why the hell didn't you tell me before?"

There was a flinch in her eyes. "There wasn't time, and I was scared. I didn't want to lose you."

She didn't want to lose me?

She didn't want to...fucking *lose me?*

As if I was worth anything. I was a piece of shit that put her in this position in the first place. The one that sent her to the fucking wolves and yet here she was, worried about my life. Christ, I didn't deserve her.

"I don't want you to stop." She whispered, pulling me back down. "I need this. I need *you,* Kyle."

"I wish you would've told me." I wanted to kill, I wanted to destroy, but more than anything, I wanted to keep her safe. Even if that meant from me...

But not right now.

Right now, I needed to touch her, feel her...fuck her. "I want you to tell me if you need me to stop, okay?" I met those beautiful, big brown eyes and reached down, unbuttoning my trousers. "I'll go slow, but I'm no bastard, April. Not when it comes to you, not anymore."

She swallowed hard and whispered. "Okay."

I needed to trust her, needed to trust that she wanted this baby as much as I did. I lowered my head, kissing my way down her breasts and then her stomach as I dragged the tip of my finger along her crease before I pressed in.

She closed her eyes, her hands dropping to the bed until she fisted the comforter. Took my time, pressing in deep, finding that tiny little nub that made her catch a breath. Slow, careful circles moved around her clit before I dipped lower, sliding inside. "So goddamn beautiful." I whispered and lowered my mouth, kissing the top of her crease.

"Oh, God." She moaned, opening her eyes, looking down.

I held her focus, sliding my tongue over her clit and then sucked, drawing her into my mouth. I wanted to take it slow, to burn this moment into my memory in case it carried me to my last moment.

Because in the end there was only her.

I said my fingers in deeper, working her until warps slid over me and my fingers came away slick. But I made sure there was no trace of blood. There was only her desire. "Open your legs for me, baby."

She did as I demanded, parting those creamy thighs. "That's a good girl." Christ, if I didn't enjoy praising her more than I enjoyed taking her hard. "That's a real good girl."

April gave a whimper and her slick came against my fingers as I slid two fingers in. My cock grew hard. That desire was a roar inside my head. I pushed upwards, shoved down my pants and moved between her legs.

"Eyes on me, princess." I demanded as I fisted my length. "I want to watch you."

I pressed against her entrance, holding her focus as she bent her lip, and I pushed inside.

She was like heaven...

No.

She was like home.

As I entered, I held her gaze. I etched my mind with the feel of her. I slowed my thrusts, making her eyes flutter. She bit her lip, dragging those teeth deep as I slowly thrust.

"April." The ground. "Talk to me."

"More." She whispered. "I need more."

I thrust deeper, making sure I kept my weight off her. "I need you to roll over." I slid out and dropped to her side.

Here I could adjust the depth and make sure she was safe. She dropped a hand, grasping my thigh as I slowly thrust, taking my fill of her. I kissed her shoulder, focused on the sensation of her body, and she grew bolder and more demanding.

I tried to keep myself held back, but she felt too fucking good. I closed my eyes, kissing her skin and drawing in her scent. "Come for me, baby." I urged.

My balls tightened, my cock twitched. The end rushed toward me.

*No...*

I ground my jaw, clenching tight as I kept the pace, driving her toward that edge. Her nails clawed my thighs. And I relished the sting, needing it to keep my focus. Her breaths became quicker until the sound of her pants filled my ears. "Oh, Kyle." She whimpered and lowered her head, her pussy pulsing around my cock as she came.

I unleashed a savage sound, filling her with warmth.

Until there was nothing left.

Just her...

Just *this*.

She held me close, still deep inside. This was where I wanted to be consumed by her.

"Did I hurt you?" I managed.

She shook her head, unable to speak.

The thought of that made me smile. And I never smiled.

I gently slid out, making sure I looked down. But there was only her come on my cock. I gripped her thigh and eased her leg back down. But I didn't leave her. I slid my arm around her and nestled against her body. "Just a little longer. Can you do that for me? Can you keep safe until we run?"

She turned her head. "We run?"

I nuzzled against her neck. "Yeah, baby, we run."

It was all I thought of.

All I wanted.

All we had to do was survive.

# Chapter Forty-Two

## KYLE

IT TORE ME APART TO LEAVE HER, STILL I HAD NO CHOICE. Kissing April on the forehead as I brushed strands of her hair from her face. "I'm going to be back just as soon as I can, okay?"

I hated the way she looked at me now. Those brown eyes were soft and filled with all the things she refused to say. But I knew... because I felt them too.

Maybe it would be better if she hated me. Maybe then she might've run and never look back. That might have been better than this...weakness.

Because Christ, loving her made both of us vulnerable.

I needed to change that...

I *had* to change that.

"Okay," she whispered.

It took all my strength to push off her and climb from that bed in the middle of my sister's pool house. I adjusted my pants, looking down at her, and a pang of agony tore through my chest. She looked so goddamn beautiful right now. Her skin flushed, her body bare...and spent. My gaze drifted to her belly, to the slight swell of her abdomen, and my pulse raced at the sight. My fingers curled, aching to trace that bump, to caress it with these bloodied, calloused hands. She deserved more than a man like me.

And I knew it.

 feel it under my hands too.

So this was what love felt like?

I both craved and hated it all at the same time.

"I'll call Hannah just as soon as I can." I forced myself to speak. "For now, stay here, stay quiet and stay safe. As soon as I can, I'll contact you.

She pushed off the bed the moment I turned from her.

"Kyle..."

I stopped, lowered my head, my shoulders curling. "Yeah?" My damn voice was husky, echoing the agony that moved through my chest. Right now, taking a bullet would be less painful than leaving her.

Her arms wrapped around me in an instant. I closed my eyes, etching the feel of her into my mind.

"Come back to me, okay?" She whispered, her arms tight around me.

Jesus...the woman was killing me here. "Not even Brontie could keep me away." I answered.

Her hold eased around me, then finally slipped away. I couldn't look at her. Instead, I forced my feet to move, striding from that pool house, and I walked out.

Because if I looked at her now, I'd never leave.

We'd be hunted for the rest of our lives, and the one opportunity I had to make sure she was safe would be lost forever. I couldn't let that happen.

So I left her behind, lifting my gaze to Hannah as she stood in the open door of the patio. But I didn't even say goodbye, just left...like I always did. I walked along the side of the house, finding the side gate to the front of the house open. The lock hung unlatched. It was almost like Hannah was expecting this. She knew I'd leave without saying goodbye. She also knew I was focused. I had to be.

There was a lot of work left to do.

I walked through the gate and headed for that stolen car.

By the time I climbed into the damn thing and fumbled with the wires, careful not to damage the immobiliser, Hannah stepped through the side door to watch me. The engine started with a grind. There was only one start in the engine left. But that's all I needed. I shoved the car into gear and spun the wheel.

My hands strangled the wheel as I forced myself to drive and not turn back. It took all my will, and every ounce of goddamn strength I had to drive out of that neighbourhood and head out of the city.

I stopped at a small all-night gas station twenty miles out of the city. Left the car running and parked out the back. I locked the doors and avoided the cameras, grabbed a plastic gas can and filled it, paying cash before I grabbed a disposable lighter and left once more.

I headed for the forest for the second time tonight, making sure I stayed far away from where we'd dumped the body and headed and pulled up in some ditch.

The car gave a sputter and then died for good this time. I doused the thing in gasoline, grabbed the lighter from my pocket before I flicked it once and tossed it inside.

Minutes. That's all it took for the car to turn into an inferno. I turned, pushed into a run as my eyes adjusted to the night, making my way back along the track to the highway.

By the time I hit the highway, my chest was on fire. Still, April's face drove me harder and faster. Her smile, her body...her love was all I thought of. I clung onto that, using it to drive me through every bone-jarring thud of my steps until the faint glint of headlights came up ahead.

I drove myself forward, spurred on by the desperate need for this to be over. By the time I left the gravel road behind and climbed out of the gully and back up onto the shoulder, I could barely breathe.

I sucked in exhaust fumes, lifted my hand and kept walking, praying someone might stop for a lone guy on the edge of the highway.

Someone did. A young guy in a hotted up Mustang pulled over in front of me. I yanked open the door, barely feeling my hands and more and climbed in. "Thanks for stopping." I glanced into the back, scanned the empty seats, then closed the door behind me. "My damn car got carjacked a few miles back, and they took my phone."

"Oh shit, that's hard. Jump in, man." The guy gave a nod. "I'll take you wherever you need to go."

I narrowed in on the guy, scanning his black t-shirt and ripped black jeans. He didn't look like one of Brontie's men, but I trusted no one at this stage. Not even a random guy who picked me up hiking on the side of the road.

We made little conversation as we drove back to Masterdom. If he smelled the gasoline on my hands, he said nothing. By the time he pulled over in front of the Hotel I almost liked the guy. I leaned over, grasping the guy's hand when he held it out. "Thanks, Iggy. I appreciate the ride, brother."

He gave a nod and a smile. "I hope you find the bastards who stole your car. If you do, make sure you leave them bleeding."

I gave a chuckle and climbed out. He had no fucking idea. I closed the door behind me and headed for the hotel. It felt like a week since I stepped through these doors. I gave a nod to the male behind the counter and dug out my room key, holding it to the elevator before I made my way upstairs.

My steps were slow, exhaustion weighing them down as I stepped out and headed back along the hallway. I glanced at Jared's door, slowing my steps and craned my head to listen for any movement inside. But there was only silence inside the room. The son of a bitch would probably be asleep, exhausted by all his tire slashing tonight. My fist clenched, aching to drive my knuckles into his face.

But I didn't charge into his room and beat him bloody. Instead, I swallowed that rage, channelling it to something more...*permanent*.

Smoke lingered in my clothes. The stench of gasoline was pungent, burning my hands. But I made my way into my room, closed the door behind me and made for the kitchen.

There was no time to shower...

No time to sleep.

I dug out the folders of Maddy Álvarez and her brothers and I made a plan. The only plan that mattered. One that ended up with April out of here and away from Brontie...and her goddamn step brother dead.

I splayed out the images in the information in front of me. I told Hannah the truth tonight. There was some nagging feeling telling me this was all to do with Maddie's mother, and not the wannabe gangster that was her stepfather.

I splayed the images of Calix Lyons and his two brothers across the table in front of me. I rose, grabbed the glass and a bottle of scotch from the cupboard, cracked open the lid and poured. Heat burned as I swallowed and returned to the file.

My cell vibrated, the screen alight with the incoming call. *April?* I snatched it from the table and looked at the caller ID. But it wasn't April.

It was Brontie.

Brontie calling because he fucking knew what I'd done...and why.

My pulse thundered at the sight of that name on the screen as my phone rang and rang and eventually went to voicemail.

He knew.

I was sure of it.

And Brontie and his men would come for me next.

I grabbed the glass and down the contents, forcing my attention back to the file in front of me. My cell rang once more. Only this time, it was Alex. I hated the fact I threw him under the damn bus. But I'd do it again in a heartbeat.

By now, Brontie would know that Alex betrayed him. And he'd know why. My damn hand shook as I gripped the bottle and poured once more, narrowing in on the information in front of me.

Calix Lyons.

I stared at his image, remembering our encounter.

He was a hot-head, just what I needed. Brontie would come, and he'd be coming fast. I needed Calix and his brothers to react. I needed them just as savage as I felt now.

And they needed a reason to be savage.

I dropped the black and white and picked up the one next to it.

The sultry, pouty image of his stepsister.

I needed Calix and his brothers to fucking love her, to want her...to fuck her.

Then...I needed them to kill for her.

*Kill them all...*

*Just like me.*

# Chapter Forty-Three

MADDIE

"I was wondering what took you so long, Maddie." Calix pushed away from the door, leaving it open behind him and strode into the darkness.

What the hell was I doing? Standing in my stepbrother's doorway, knowing one step would change everything.

My pulse was booming.

My knees were weak.

His shadow moved in the darkness, sliding between the sheets of his bed, and the movement drew me closer. I took a step, inhaling the scent of him and followed, closing the door behind me.

"Little sister..." his voice was husky in the gloom.

I trembled with the words and slid between the sheets. The bed was warm where he'd lain. Even from here, I could feel the heat radiating from his body.

"You need something from me, Maddie?" He leaned closer.

I flinched at the drag of his curled finger on my cheek before he hooked his finger around my chin and turned me toward him. "Christ, I've been desperate to do this for goddamn weeks. No man should want a woman as much as I want you. This is goddamn...unhealthy."

Warm lips met mine. He kissed me slowly, taking his time. I closed my eyes, consumed by the feel of his mouth and flinched as he cupped my breast. His hands were so big, swallowing the swell of my breast easily ...his fingers rolled over my nipple, making the peaks tighten. Electricity raced, shooting between my thighs as he broke the kiss to find me in the dark. The slow rolling of his fingers moved to lazy circles that teased and taunted until I moaned.

"So goddamn shy, aren't you, Squirt?"

I trembled when he called me that. It was a kid's name. "Not so shy anymore." I whispered.

"I guess not." He dropped his hand to the bottom of my shirt and tugged it upwards, leaving me bare.

One lick made me clench between my legs. I moaned as he took the tight nub of my breast into his mouth, making me shiver as he whispered."So goddamn beautiful."

"What is happening?" I whispered, blown apart by this building inferno.

"It's called sex, Maddie." My stepbrother answered, then licked, drawing my tight peak into his mouth.

I whimpered, shaking my head. "God, we can't do this. It's wrong, so goddamn wrong."

"Stopping now is wrong." He lifted his head, and in the wake of his warm mouth, my breast grew cold. "But we can stop if you want. All you have to do is say the word."

I should stop.

I *needed* to stop...

Desire mingled with desperation. My head screamed one thing and my body screamed another. I lifted my hand, spearing my fingers through his hair and inhaled that masculine scent of him. This was what I wanted. I wanted him. More than I wanted anyone else before. "No. I don't want to stop."

As my eyes adjusted to the gloom, I caught the hint of a smirk. "Good, because stopping this would be a goddamn crime. Now be a good girl and spread your legs."

That heat flared as he lowered his hand and cupped my pussy.

"Oh, God."

He shifted his body, dropping lower down on the bed. "God has nothing to do with this."

He worked the string of my pyjamas, tugging the tie until it unravelled.

"No one can ever know about this." I whispered. "Not Brooks or Aven."

"I think they'll be pretty pissed when they find out. But if you don't want them to know, then I won't say a word."

"Promise?"

He left his head, his gaze finding mine in the dark. "I promise, Maddie. Whatever we do is between us and no one else."

"Are you doing this because of what you told us tonight, because those men want you to...have sex with me?"

His hand stilled between my legs as he rose, bracing on his arm beside me. "This has nothing to do with the arseholes that are blackmailing us and *everything* to do with what you and I started before you left. I want this, I want you. I wanted you for a long goddamn time and I've been fighting these feelings, praying that they were something different. But I know now they're not. This is real, Maddie." He gripped my hand and pressed it against his chest. "This hunger I feel for you...is real."

The room spun because this was too perfect, and I didn't know what to do. Calix leaned in, gently gripped my jaw, and kissed me hard until I felt the soft bruise on my lips. I closed my eyes, consumed with the feel of him, until he slowly pulled away. "Now, let me give you the release you need."

He slid down the bed once more, hooking his fingers on the side of my pyjamas. I lifted my hips for him, letting him slide the garment free. He kissed the jutting bone of my hips, then my thighs as he moved down.

"When you said you couldn't bring yourself to orgasm, I almost took you down to the floor there in then." His words rumbled in the dark. "I haven't been able to get that night out of my head. You and me, huddled just like this in the dark."

He moved down the inside of my thighs and tugged my pyjamas from under my feet, leaving me in my panties and my shoved up t-shirt. "I always wondered what you looked like when you came."

He rose from the bed once more, his breath hot against my cheek. "Would it be okay if I switched on the light?"

My cheeks burned with the thought of him watching me. "Now?"

"Only if it's okay with you." He kissed my mouth. "I want to watch you, little sister."

Oh God...

"Okay." I whispered.

He shoved off the bed in one smooth move and strode toward his desk and flipped on the small light above his desk. The glare was instant, filling the room to blind me, until he angled the light down and the glare dimmed. White sparks danced behind my eyes. Still, I saw the hunger gleaming in his stare when he turned back to me. He slowly took me in, laying barely clothed in the middle of his bed. "Christ, you're beautiful. If you could see yourself now."

He came closer, standing over me. "I've dreamt of this moment, every single fucking day and night."

He climbed back onto the bed, straddling me. "I'm gonna make you feel so good you won't ever want to leave."

There was pain in his words. The sting reminded me of what had happened the last time. I hurt him when I left without saying a word. And this moment was the result of that.

He moved lower, sliding his finger under the elastic of my panties at my hips, dragging his finger down until he brushed my pussy. "I want to stare into your eyes while I finger you. Are you okay with that?"

God, I wanted to die, and stay in this moment forever all at the same time. My breath caught as he trailed my slit, then pushed in, dancing over my clit. I flinched with the sensation.

"Breathe, Maddie." Those dark eyes glinted. "Just relax, and breathe."

I tried to do exactly what he said, but the feel of his finger transfixed me as it circled and circled, sending shivers through my body. He leaned down, tugging the elastic aside to kiss the crease of my thighs and then over my mound. "Breathe, Princess."

His tongue followed the trail of his fingers. I froze as he licked deeper, spreading me apart with his fingers and sucked.

"Oh my God." I moaned.

That fire blaze to life, tearing through my middle. Agile fingers slid deeper, dancing around my entrance before they slowly thrust inside. "Fuck, you feel so good." He murmured, meeting my gaze. "Better than I could ever imagine."

His voice.

His words.

His fingers.

His gaze.

They consumed me, driving that heat deeper until I couldn't catch my breath.

"Calix." My body burned, yearning for something I'd never had before. I'd always been close to this moment, always to this point where I was gripped in the desperate need for more. But it never came, slipping away like sand through my fingers.

But this time, Calix lowered his head and nuzzled my legs aside. He lowered his head and licked, sliding his tongue inside. "You taste so fucking good."

I widened my legs for him and moved my hand to slide my fingers between the thick strands of his hair. Dark eyes met mine as he licked and sucked, his lips coming away glistening.

"I'm gonna eat this pussy every night." He promised. "There is no going back to school, Maddie. Not now."

I arched my back, and that feeling grew, building inside me like an inferno. The climax drew closer as I fisted his hair, driving his face harder against me.

He slid two fingers inside, slowly thrusting, sending shock waves through my body until I tightened. "That's it, Princess. Clench that pussy around me."

I shoved upwards onto my elbows and arched my back. My body moved on its own, driving lower to meet his fingers and his tongue. "Oh, God." I moaned and fucked him. "Calix, I..."

"That's it, Princess. Let yourself go."

My body trembled as that euphoric feeling slammed into me, tearing me from this bedroom, and I drifted in nothingness. Sparks ignited through my body. I was consumed with this feeling, overcome and desperate for more.

Shockwaves made me tremble.

I opened my eyes and looked down, watching my stepbrother lift his head, his lips glistening with my desire and slowly he slid his fingers from my body.

"Holy shit." I moaned, trying to catch my breath.

"Fuck, you look so beautiful right now. I want to see you like this forever."

I wanted more. I wanted him. "Calix, will you..."

"Will I do what, princess?" The corner of his mouth curled into a smile.

"Will you fuck me?" I whispered, my cheeks burning. "I want you..."

He gave me a slow chuckle. "Not tonight, Maddie. Tonight was all about you."

He pushed upwards to lie beside me. "How was it for your first time?"

I had no words to explain it.

How can you put into words that feeling of...everything. "Incredible." I whispered, staring at the wall. "Better than I ever thought possible."

"Come to my bed again and I'll give you more." He grinned.

I smiled, even though I burned with embarrassment. He slid his arms around me, pulling me against him. For the first time in a long time, I felt at peace. Like this was exactly where I wanted to be.

My thoughts returned to what he said. That he was going to find a way out of this for us. One that didn't involve me being videoed while I had sex with my brothers.

Aven and Brooks could never know about this.

Not now...

Not ever.

# Chapter Forty-Four

I woke with a damn headache, blinked and opened my eyes, and lifted my head from the dining table. Something stuck to my face. I tore it free and looked down to the image of Maddie Alvarez.

My thoughts were slow, returning to me one painstaking memory at a time. I winced with the memory of my car and the slashed tyres, and then in a rush the rest of the night slammed into me.

April and the attack in the alley, then us dumping the body and finally...my sister Hannah.

My pulse thundered as I remembered how fucking scared I'd been. I thought for sure Brontie had found her. If I hadn't been there, then he would've. And I would've lost her...for good.

But she was safe now, hidden in my sister's pool house. Still, it was only a matter of time before Brontie's men would track April down, and not even my sister's badge would save her.

I had to do something to keep her safe...and fast. I shoved up from the table and looked down at the splayed out folder, my gaze moving to Calix Lyons.

I'd use him.

I'd use them all.

I glanced at a half empty bottle of scotch and then turned away, making my way into the bedroom and then to the bathroom. The hiss of the shower made me wince and press my fingers against my throbbing head. I worked all night, catching the first traces of sunlight through the curtains before I crashed.

Now I felt like fucking Hell. I worked the buttons of my shirt and stepped out, making my way into the shower. The sting of the hot water on my shoulders made me close my eyes. But my thoughts were always filled with her...*April*.

The mother of my child.

Because it *was* my child. There was no other way the baby belonged to anyone else—I clenched my jaw as Jared's face pushed in—I'd make sure of it.

I scrubbed and shampooed before turning off the water and stepping out.

My thoughts were colder now. Cutting. Knowing exactly what I had to do as the plan that'd come to me in the early hours of the morning lingered. I sat there staring at the image of Maddie Alvarez and her stepbrothers, hating how I was forced to do this all over again.

Until it hit me.

I didn't have to.

I could save both Maddie and April...and take my enemies out of the equation. My thoughts turned to Jared. The son of a bitch thought he got away with slashing my tires last night, but he didn't know the half of it, and he wasn't going to either. The game had changed and from now on I'd make sure he stayed in the dark.

My phone beeped. I snatched it from the counter and looked at the message. It was a piece of shit himself.

*Jared: Where are you?*

I typed out a message: *On my way* and made my way out of the room...at the same he did. The bastard barely held back a smirk.

"You look like hell." He muttered. "Problem?"

"Not at all." I answered through clenched teeth. I wanted to shove my gun under the bastard's chin right here and blow his fucking brains out. He thought he'd gotten away standing between me and April. He was about to find out how wrong he was.

"So what's the plan?" He asked.

And that's why he was never in the running, because Jared was a weak piece of shit and a goddamn follower. He wasn't man enough to take care of April or his goddamn baby. But I was.

"I had car troubles last night." I muttered, stepping around him to head to the elevator. "So I'll be getting myself a ride. I need you to watch Maddie Alvarez. We need to know where she goes and who she talks to, then we can plan where and when this goes down.

He smiled at the words, liking the idea of forcing another woman into another blackmailing situation. He really was a piece of shit. I did not know what April ever saw in this schmuck.

"I can do that." He answered.

"Call me if you find anything." I turned and strode away, unable to stand the sight of him a second longer.

"And if I get the opportunity to force her?" He called out behind me.

"Do what you need to do, Jared." I kept on walking and added. "Because I'll be doing the same."

I made my way out of the hotel, lifted my hand, hailing a cab.

"Car rentals, please. Make it luxury." I closed the door behind me and yanked my seatbelt as the driver pulled out from the Hotel and drove me across the city.

Twenty minutes later and bit into my credit card and I drove out in a brand new Audi A8, testing the pick up speed from 0 to 60 and made my way through the city streets.

*Beep.*

I grabbed my cell, hoping it was from April but it wasn't. It was Jared, *again...*

The piece of shit couldn't even take a piss without checking in with me first.

*Jared: I'm sitting outside their gate and there's movement.*

"Good for you." I snarled and went to drop my phone back into the console beside me until I stopped. I could make this work for me, get Jared out of the way, at least until I narrowed down on the person I needed.

I quickly typed out a message: *Follow her, see where she leads you.*

Jared would be eager to hunt Maddie Alvarez. But I turned the wheel instead, making my way back to the boxing gym where I found Calix Lyons previously and pulled up outside the building.

I climbed out of the Audi and made my way inside, lowering my sunglasses and glancing around. Four guys worked the punching bags, two more were in the ring sparring. I glanced around, finding an older guy who wiped the sweat from his brow with a towel before throwing it over his shoulder and headed my way.

"You the owner?" I looked like someone interested in joining.

He held out his hand. "Dale Floyd."

I gave him a smile, shaking his hand. "I'm new in town, and interested in what you offer." I was interested in a lot more than that, more importantly, getting close to Calix.

"Look around." He gave a nod. "Fees are due first of every month. We are pretty relaxed around here. Most of the guys train professionally, but we take on a few outsiders. Get them into shape, if you know what I mean." He sized me up and down.

"That's just what I'm after." I answered. "I got your name from a buddy of mine, Calix Lyons."

"Yeah, I know Calix." The old man narrowed his gaze at mine. "He's a good kid."

The old man had a fatherly instinct around him. I needed to be careful. "He said he might come in today?"

The old man glanced at the wall behind me. "In the next half an hour, actually."

That's all I needed.

I gave him a smile. "I'll come back then."

I turned and strode away, heading for the door as the old man called out behind me. *"Hey! I didn't catch your name!"*

"That's because I didn't give it." I muttered and strode out, heading to the Audi.

I climbed inside, started the engine, and drove further away, parked ... And waited.

Thirty minutes, just like the old man said, Calix pulled up outside the gym and parked his car. He looked around, those dark eyes scanning me before he yanked open the rear seat and pulled out a gym bag.

I waited for him to enter before I followed, making my way across the street once more. But I didn't walk in through the front door, instead I made my way to the gate at the side of the building, opened it and made my way along the sidewalk to the parking lot at the rear.

Cars were parked in the back, a silver Hummer, along with a Mustang and a dark emerald green Ferrari. I paid them no mind. I was after one man and one man alone.

I stepped through the open rear door of the gym and headed along the narrow hallway to the change rooms in the back, inhaling the sharp scent of liniment and sweat.

*Clang.*

The sound rang out as I stepped inside and closed the door behind me. Movement came around the edge of the lockers. I stepped out, finding Calix Lyons standing with his back to me. He tugged off his shirt, revealing a hard, defined body. The guy worked out. That was easy to see. I only hoped to make it out of this in one damn piece.

"Your stepsister's beautiful." I muttered, watching him freeze. "She's the target Brontie will want to keep the moment he gets his hands on her."

Calix slowly turned to face me, those cold, dark eyes glinting with rage. "You?"

"I came here to—" I didn't even get the words out.

He lunged, closing the distance in a blur. But I was ready, muscles tensing, grasping his wrist with one hand as I ducked from the blow. Still, the bastard slammed into me, driving me back against the wall.

I hit the cold tiles with a *crack*.

Agony tore through my head with a fresh wave of pain. *"I come here to warn you!"* I roared. "I came here to help you...*protect her!*"

*"You came here to fucking threaten me and my family!"*

He swung again, and this time I wasn't so lucky. The blow cracked me on the side of the jaw, snapping my head to the side. Stars sparked behind my eyes as pain moved in.

*"I'm here to fucking help you!"*

"Why?" He screamed in my face. *"Tell me why I should listen to a fucking word you have to say!"*

"Because *he's after the woman I love!*"

He stopped, sucked in a breath and unclenched his fists from my shirt before taking a step backwards. I reached up, rubbing my jaw. The guy had a wicked right hook.

"What the fuck did you say?" He snarled.

"He's after the woman I love," I snapped, jerking my gaze to his. "Just like he's after your goddamn stepsister."

"You're lying." His lips curled, baring his teeth. "You're the one who is blackmailing us."

"No." I shook my head. It all came down to this moment. I had to make Calix believe me. "The man I was with reports directly to Brontie. I had to play along. I had to do exactly what he wanted. Because if I didn't, then there's nowhere we could run, nowhere I could hide her. That would be safe."

"That arsehole is the one who is orchestrating this?"

"Jared is, yes. He wants to coordinate the attack on your sister and deliver the recording of your sister to Brontie. Not only that, he wants to play a major role in it too."

I watched him stiffen, catching their tick near the corner of his eye. Holy shit. This guy had already fallen for her. I could see it now. All I had to do was let this play out. "He's going to come after her," I urged. "He'll use everything he can to force you and your brothers to record her, then he'll hand deliver the recording to Brontie for him to use to blackmail your stepmom."

"I can fucking try." The words weren't a warning, they were a threat.

He didn't flinch when I said it was his stepmom Brontie was after, so he knew about the Mafia ties...and he knew how dangerous this was as well.

"We need to be ready." I shoved from the wall. "When the time comes, you need to act, without hesitation."

His deadly stare nailed me to the spot. "Oh, don't you worry about that. I'll be fucking ready. The bastard won't see it coming."

It hurt when I smiled, still it felt good. "That's what I was hoping for."

# Chapter Forty-Five

## CALIX

I paced the kitchen, replaying the conversation over and over in my head. *He's after the woman I love...just like he's after your goddamn stepsister.* I ran my fingers through my hair. I couldn't trust the guy, no matter how it played out.

But somehow I had to.

As much as I dared, anyway.

The sound of the garage door rolling up dragged my attention from the panicked thoughts racing through my head. The throbbing engine of Brooks' Mercedes pulled into the garage and parked.

Car doors opened and closed with a *bang*. The heavy thud of footsteps resounded. I listened to their laughter and chiding as my brothers and Maddie opened the car doors and made their way around to the rear of the car.

"How many wardrobes did you say you needed?" Brooks laughed, feigning a grunt as he heaved an armful of shopping bags from the boot. I stepped into the doorway, watching as she gave him a playful punch to the shoulder, smiling.

Christ, she was beautiful when she smiled.

"Don't be such a sook." Maddie laughed. "You were the one who wanted to come shopping."

"Famous last words." Brooks turned to Aven.

The laughter trailed off the moment I stepped around the front of Dad's Alfa Romeo. Heads turned toward me. Maddie's eyes widened, and for a second, I couldn't move. The sight of her froze me. Those lips curled, and those cheeks flushed as she stared at me and then glanced away.

She was gone when I woke this morning I thought it'd all been a dream, but the flush in her cheeks and the ache in my cock at the sight of her said otherwise.

Brooks glanced from Maddy to me and back again. "What's going on?"

"Nothing." Maddie answered but my younger brother was like a dog with a bone, following a step behind her as she carried bags toward the house and past me.

"That look is not nothing, Maddie." He muttered. "Something happened after last night, didn't it?"

"Maddie?" Aven followed his brother carrying the last of the bags from the boot, leaving a few still on the rear seat. He shot me a look as he passed and called out, "You went to him, didn't you?"

"Holy shit." Brooks' voice carried as I strode to the open rear door of the car. I grabbed the bags and closed the door with a thud. This wasn't what I wanted to talk to them about, but I'd be damned if I let her face my brothers alone.

"Guys." I called out. "Leave it alone, will you!"

I could still hear them as I walked into the house and made for her bedroom.

"You went to Calix's room last night, didn't you?" Brooks' voice carried.

*Godamnit.*

"No." Maddie lied.

I ground my jaw and hurried my steps.

"You did." Aven sounded a little pissed. "You went to him after we left."

"*Enough.*" I carried the bags to the bed. "I said, leave it alone."

"Did you fuck her?" Brooks glared at me.

Maddie's cheeks burned bright red.

"No." I met my brother's stare.

"But something happened." Brooks added, glancing from me to her. "And you didn't say a damn thing all morning. I thought you were acting strange this morning."

"Brooks." I growled. "Stop."

Did I fuck her? *No.* But I wanted to. Christ, I wanted to. I wanted her to bury her face in my neck while I fingered her, listening to her guttural moans as she came against my fingers. I licked my lips, finding her once more.

That need consumed me as Aven dumped the bags in his arms on the bed. "So tell us what happened."

"It was nothing." She lied, because the truth was all over her face.

"So you'll fuck Calix but not us. Is that it?" Brooks muttered.

"Christ." I barked. "Do you actually hear yourself? What Maddie does is no concern of yours. You're acting like a jealous fucking asshole right now. So, get the fuck over it."

Maddie shook her head as she stared at Brooks and then at Aven. "That's not what this is about."

"Then what is it about, little sister?" Brooks stepped closer. "You don't want us, is that it?"

"Jesus, Brooks." I shook my head. But deep down, I wanted to know. I wanted to push her toward that moment where it changed between us.

She flinched with his words and shook her head, glancing to the floor. "That's not it."

"I promise I'll be good." Brooks moved closer to stand at her back as she stood beside her bed. The movement mesmerized me as he brushed the hair back from her neck and leaned close, kissing her shoulder. "If you don't want us, just say it. But if you do, then we could have all this together. That's all I'm saying. You can have Calix and Aven...and me."

Fuck. She hasn't even had a guy yet. How in the Hell would she want all three of us? My cock hardened at the thought.

She swallowed hard, her chest rising and falling. "I..."

She was thinking about it. I could see that now. Maybe book Brooks was right. Maybe she wanted all of us. I glanced at my brothers as a flare of jealousy rose.

If it came down to having all of us or having none, then I knew which one I'd prefer.

"What do you say?" Brooks murmured, sliding his hands down her waist to linger on her hips. "It can be just this one time, if that's what you want. Or any time you want it. Think of us as your private fuck toys. You can learn with us." He cupped her ass. "There's nothing wrong with having needs, Maddie. You can use us...until something more permanent comes along."

I flinched with the words. "More permanent?"

He meant a boyfriend. A *real* fucking boyfriend. That burn of jealousy turned into a damn inferno. I shook my head drawing Aven's gaze. I didn't like that at all. Her fucking my brothers was one thing. That I could handle, but a random guy? One who'd use her body and break her heart?

Fuck no.

"It doesn't need to be a thing, Maddie." Brooks urged, turning her around to face us. Her eyes were so damn wide, looking from me to Brooks in front of her. "It can just be...an experimentation. You can figure out what you want and what you like."

"It's just sex." Aven added, excited about it. His eyes glinted as he licked his lips. Was his heart racing the same as mine at the thought of having our stepsister to ourselves? I knew it was as he took a step closer to them, adding. "Until something more permanent comes along, right?"

"And then what?" She whispered. Her voice is so small and careful.

"Then we never have to speak about it again."

"And you do that?" She whispered, shifting her gaze from Aven to Brooks and then finally...to me.

"If that's what you want." I answered.

"Just sex." She whispered.

I gave a nod. "Just sex."

She opened her mouth to answer as my cell rang. Shit. I snatched it up, looking at the caller ID on the screen. *Kyle.* I put the bastard's number in my phone, hating that I even entertained his plea at all.

I press the button, answering. "Yeah?"

"It's happening." He growled into my ear. "Brontie found April, and you can be sure he'll be heading your way next."

I turned away from the others, feeling their gazes at my back. "You said we had more time."

"Yeah, well, it looks like I was wrong."

"I'm not ready for this. It's not safe for her." I made the mistake of glancing at Maddie.

"Not safe for her. Why?" Brooks asked.

But I was focused on the asshole on the other end of the line. "Ready or not, he's coming." Kyle answered. "This is me giving you a heads up like we agreed. It's up to you if you want to act on it. But if you don't, then you can expect your step stepsister will be owned by Brontie by the end of the week and there won't be a damn thing you can do about it."

*Not a damn thing?* I'll see about that.

"Consider me warned." I muttered and ended the call.

"Who the hell was that?" Brooks snapped, glancing at the phone in my hand.

"Kyle Blackburn." I answered.

"Kyle Blackburn?" Aven looked at Brooks, then turned to me. "The son of a bitch that cornered you in the gym? And the same arsehole who wants to expose our family?"

"Yes."

"How the hell did he get your number?" He stepped closer.

"I gave it to him today when he cornered me at the gym."

"He cornered you?" Brooks snapped. "And what the hell did he want?"

I told them everything that happened the moment Kyle cornered me against the lockers, until what he said about Brontie and a son of a bitch Jared, who would use our sister any sick way he could. "This is about more than blackmail. He wants her." I stared at Maddie. "Brontie wants him for himself, and he sent this piece of shit, Jared, to get her."

"He's going to abduct her?" Brooks growled, clenching his fist at his side.

"He's going to try." I answered. "But I will be ready."

"We need to call Dad." Aven said. "They took the security with them, but there are men still here."

"No." Maddy shook her head. "They don't need to know about any of this."

"I agree." I answered. "You involve them, and Brontie and Jared will deny everything. We have no proof of this. But we will always have to be watching. Is that what you want? Do you want our sister to live her life always looking over her shoulder?" I stepped closer, that desperation moving through me. "We do this, and we do it now. We do this once and for all."

"What are you saying?" Aven glared at me. "Are you talking about taking these fuckers out?"

"Yes." I answered. "That's exactly what I'm talking about."

"You trust this asshole?"

"No. I don't." My focus was on Maddie. "But I know what's at stake if I don't listen to what he says and take action."

"There are guns in the basement." Brooks glances toward the doorway. "If we do this, we want to be armed to the teeth."

"And what about the security?" Aven asked.

"I shake my head. "You really want our parents involved in this?"

Both Brooks and even close to Maddy. "No."

"Good," I answered. "Because neither do I."

# Chapter Forty-Six

APRIL

I STOOD INSIDE THE SAFE ROOM WATCHING THE CAMERAS AS Hannah parked in the garage hours after she left. I'd spent the entire time in turmoil, waiting for Brontie's men to attack the house.

But they hadn't, and now Kyle's sister was back. I only hoped she came with a plan. The sound of the garage door rumbled, drawing my focus toward the front of the house.

Still, I didn't move, making sure they did not hold her at gunpoint and force her inside. I leaned closer, my attention fixed on the cameras as Hannah climbed out of the car and closed the door behind her before striding toward the house.

Movement came behind the car as the garage door closed. I left the safe room behind and headed for the front of the house.

"Everything okay?" I murmured as she stepped into view.

She shook her head, the muscles of her jaw flaring in anger. "The bastards will not help us. They won't even touch the case, not with Brontie's name involved."

"They're not going to help us?" I whispered.

"Not even remotely. That's not all." She met my gaze. "I'm pretty sure I was being followed the entire way there and home."

A chill tore along my spine.

"You have to leave," she stepped closer. "It's not safe for you here, not anymore."

"Leave?" I whispered. "Where am I supposed to go?"

"There's really only one option now. You need to go to Kyle. It's not safe for you to be alone and, to be honest, it's not safe for him either. Together, you can protect each other. Together you can run."

"Run?" I shook my head. I'd been there before, spending months in filthy motel rooms with no food and no fucking hope. Look where that got me—dragged back and thrown to the wolves.

"You have to, April." Hannah lowered her focus to my belly. "You have no choice now. You have a child that you need to think about."

"There is somewhere else I can go. Somewhere that's safe. A motel in the city."

She shook her head. "If it's the same motel Kyle told me about, then it's not safe. It's also not there. Brontie had his men burn it to the ground last night with people inside."

"No." I whispered.

Hannah dragged her cell out of her pocket. Her fingers moved across the screen before the sound of a news report came through.

I moved closer, my focus fixed on the screen. I stood there, watching it all play out. The camera was focused on the reporter as she stood outside what had been the motel's reception hours ago. Now it was nothing more than a pile of ash.

And burned bodies...

Yellow tarpaulins covered the ground behind the reporter. My stomach tightened like a clenched fist. "Oh God, Marion."

"They're closing in April." Hannah's voice pierced the void. "Nowhere is safe for you right now." She moved closer, grasping my arm, forcing my attention to hers. "The safest place you can be right now is with Kyle."

She was right. I knew she was right, but I was terrified...

"They'll come here. I'm almost surprised that they haven't already been. So you need to protect yourself. Get as far away from here as possible."

"And what will you do?"

She gave me a soft, sad smile. "Don't you worry about me. I'm used to making a few waves. Right now, my focus is on you and my pain in the ass, little brother. I'm going to pack you a bag with some clothes and then some food, enough to last you a few days, okay? At least I can do that."

She left me then, heading to her bedroom and disappeared inside. I wrapped my arms tight around my body and closed my eyes. All I could see in my head were the charred remains of that motel and the people who helped me.

Marion...I did this to her, I did this to all of them.

A tremble cut through my body. Brontie would never stop.

I know that now.

He'd burn and destroy everyone and everything that stood between me and him. So how could running stop that? How could Kyle prevent a man like that? Because he wasn't just a man, was he? *He was a result, and that result ended with me.*

The thud of steps echoed inside the bedroom.

I should just go to Brontie and end this once and for all. I could save those I cared about. Those who were willing to put their lives on the line for me.

*I could save Kyle.*

Hannah stepped out of the doorway, her focus moved to mine. And there was a flicker of fear and desperation. She shook her head. "No. I know that look and that's the kind that will get you killed."

"You don't even know what I'm thinking." I whispered.

She gave a hard bark of laughter. "Oh, don't I? Let me get this straight. You're thinking of going to Brontie, right? Thinking you're going to stop all this. But let me tell you this now, April. Brontie is not a man that will stop at one person or one thing. He will consume and destroy because that's all he knows what to do. You are just one small part of his plan and if you think it ends with you, then you're more naïve than I thought. A man like Brontie doesn't care about loyalty or trust or any kind of human emotion other than greed." She stepped closer, dropping a bag at my feet. "Now it's time to think about yourself and this baby. Kyle has done things to protect you. And he *will* do them again. So it's lose yourself to a sick son of a bitch or give yourself a chance, and right now that's your only option. You need to make a choice. Lose yourself or fight like Hell for freedom."

Desperation rose inside me. She was right; I knew that. Nothing else mattered but this baby. That's where my loyalties had to lie. "Then I'll run."

"Good girl." She gave a smile and stepped around to head for the safe room.

I followed, watching as she grabbed a gun from a rack on the wall and grabbed two fresh clips of ammunition. "Take this. Use it if you have to. My car has a full tank of gas, and Kyle knows that you're on your way. I'll pack you some food and then you need to go."

I grabbed the gun when she handed it to me and stared at the weapon. This whole thing seemed...*surreal*.

"April."

I glanced over my shoulder as Hannah stood outside her bedroom. "Yeah?"

"You can do this." She said, "I *know* you can do this."

Then she left, disappearing inside. I followed, listening to her pull out drawers in the bedroom and returned minutes later with a small overnight bag of clothes.

"Here." She handed me the bag. "Let me get the food."

I grabbed the handles, leaving her to step around me and slowly made my way to the garage. "You need to drive straight there." She made for the car, stepping through the garage. "Do not detour and whatever you do, don't stop for anyone."

I gave a hug and climbed behind the wheel. My hands shook as I turned the key and started the car. I lifted my gaze to Hannah as she leaned down and gave me a hug.

"Good luck." She said and pulled away.

The driver's door closed with a *thud*. I could barely breathe as I yanked the seatbelt down and snapped it closed around me. A heartbeat later, my hand closed around the gears.

Hannah stepped to the entrance to the house, her finger poised over the garage door. One press and it rose behind me. I checked the rear-view mirror and punched the accelerator, launching the car backwards.

Tires squealed as I tore down her driveway and braked hard. I was driving away from her house before I knew it. My hands clenched around the wheel, drove like a madwoman.

Still, I kept the speed, my focus divided between the road ahead behind. By the time I pulled onto the freeway, I was sure that I was being followed.

Panic rose inside through me as I watched the rear-view mirror, tracking a dark sedan as it wove in and out of the steady moving stream of cars behind me, following me with every turn I made.

I yanked my cell phone out of my pocket, hitting the button and calling the one person who could help me. The man I loved...

Kyle

MY CELL RANG BESIDE ME. I glanced at the caller ID and my heart lunged as I answered it instantly. "April?"

"I think I'm being followed." She sounded terrified.

"Where are you now?" I pulled into the parking lot and lifted my gaze to the parked cars in front of me.

Jared stood outside his hotted-up Toyota Supra with his arms crossed and a scowl on his face.

"I'm on the freeway heading to you."

"Just keep coming," that desperation rose inside me. "And whatever you do, don't fucking stop."

"I'm scared."

Those words were a punch to the chest. "I know, baby. I know. Just keep coming, okay? I'm right here." As I pulled up, I fixed on him. I'm right here."

"Okay." she whispered. "I'll see you soon."

"I love you." I answered and killed the engine before reaching over to the passenger's seat before I climbed out.

"Took your sweet fucking time." Jared snapped when I slammed the door closed behind me and headed his way.

But the mouthy fucker didn't stop. Just pushed off his car. "I'm sick of being your fucking errand boy, Kyle. So it—"

I shoved out my hand, driving the camera against his chest.

He looked down. "What's this?"

"It's time."

He lifted his gaze. "Time?"

"Head out to the house, Jared. They're waiting."

His eyes widened, crammed full of surprise and *exhilaration*. Christ, he was into this. He was so fucking into it that he didn't even see the danger around him.

And I needed it to stay that way.

"The sister?" He murmured.

"Is all yours." I answered, nodding to the camera now in his hands. "As long as you get it on camera...and her brothers, too."

He smiled, and that smile turned into a grin. "Fuck yeah."

I watched as he yanked the handle on the driver's door and stepped away when he climbed behind the wheel and started the engine and all I thought of was...April.

# Chapter Forty-Seven

JARED

I CLIMBED INTO THE SUPRA AND YANKED THE DRIVER'S door closed behind me. One punch to the button and the engine started with a purr. In a heartbeat, I was backing out of the parking lot and leaving Kyle far behind.

Fuck him.

Fuck them all.

Excitement burned inside me as I glanced at the rear-view mirror, catching the sight of that shopping center slipping away. I clung to that feeling, shifted gears and punched the accelerator. Tires spun as I skidded. I gripped the wheel and yanked hard, heading back out of the city...heading to the Alvarez estate.

And the further I drove, the more that feeling seemed to invade me. That feeling of excitement...of purpose, and *hunger*.

My fingers tapped against the steering wheel, my foot bounced against the floor. This was what I wanted...no, this was what *I* needed.

The idea of owning another woman consumed me. It was the same high I felt that day Kyle and the others came for April. The same high I craved as a drug.

The hunger had me in its grip... strangling me until it was all I thought of, all I needed. My grin faltered at this moment.

That same sense of excitement faltering, stealing the curl of my lips and the excited thrum of my heart. Cold slipped in, the feeling fleeting, like an icy caress.

I didn't like it...

*Not at all.*

I focused on the road ahead and clenched the wheel. Something was changing inside me—somehow slipping away. And in the wake of a shudder, her face rose inside my mind.

My feisty little stepsister...

*April.*

I winced as her face grew bolder, taking up far too much space. I was snatched from this moment and slammed headlong into the truth. I thought I loved her. Hell, I wanted to love her. I thought I could pretend while we hid out in seedy motels and lived on nothing but scraps. But I was only lying. To myself and to her.

I didn't love her.

Not really.

I wanted to use her, her energy, the love in her heart. I wanted to burn through her goodness like a comet burning through itself. I was filled with fuel and a hunger that hadn't been sated since the day we took my stepsister into the poolroom and had our fun.

Instead, the hunger only grew worse until it consumed me.

I didn't care about her, not really. I ate the food we scourged. My fill of water was the first thing I drank, and I fucked her every night and day, desperate to relive that moment we had with the others. Only I couldn't....

Because she wasn't the fuel I needed.

She wasn't even close.

I didn't love her. I have a hard chuff—I barely even liked her most times. And now I felt that excitement return once more. I'd try again...with Maddie Alvarez and maybe this time...this time, that excitement would stay.

Still April's face lingered as I drove the accelerator hard against the floor, making the Supra's engine snarl. "I wanted to love you, April. I really did...but you just weren't what I needed."

I turned along the country road, heading past the lookout where Kyle and I had watched them days ago and geared down, slowing the Toyota. The gates to the Alvarez estate loomed up ahead. I braked, peppering the underbelly of the car and turned the wheel, pulling up at the gates in the driveway.

I pressed the button for the window and leaned out when the gates opened. I smiled. They knew I was here.

As the gates opened and I drove forward, it felt like that day all over again...the day in the pool house. Only Kyle wasn't supposed to arrive early, and he wasn't supposed to take a liking to my damn stepsister.

But he did...*didn't he?*

Only this time, the tables were turned...and I was the bad guy.

I braked, coming to a stop outside the house as the front door opened and the older brother, Calix, stepped out.

The engine ticked as I killed it and reached across the seat for the camera and froze. My fingers trembled, closing around the device. A faint voice deep inside my head whispered, *is this really who I am?*

I stared at that camera as movement came from the doorway. I turned my gaze, watching Calix Lyons heading toward me with his sister not far behind.

I shoved that fear from my mind, closed my fingers around the camera and climbed out of the car. Calix strode toward me, cutting across the glare of the sun. "Are you here for Maddie?"

I closed the driver's door and smiled, wincing as I looked into the sun. "Yeah, I'm here for her."

From the corner of my eye, I caught movement as he lifted the gun and took aim.

The world seemed to stutter and slow. His finger tightening...

*Boom!*

I stumbled backwards and slammed against the car with the impact. The thunderous sound rang in my ears as I slowly looked down, finding blood spilling across the front of my brand-new white shirt.

"You think you can come here and touch what's ours?" Calix stepped closer.

I lifted my head, finding him standing in the glare.

Shadows clung to his eyes, making him look dangerous.

A cough tore free, blood splattered the air, falling fast. That salty, metallic tang filled me. This was bad...*real fucking bad.* And as that red stain on my shirt grew, my knees trembled, then gave way, leaving me falling to the ground.

"You'll get nowhere near her, you hear me?" Calix came closer until he stood over me. "Not while we're alive. We are her brothers, we protect what's ours. You sick fucks can stay the Hell away...or die, either way you don't get to lay a finger on her. Do you understand me?"

I wanted to nod...to tell him I understood.

But I didn't. Instead, that face haunted me...*her face.*

"April." I whispered.

Calix kneeled down, the gun still in his hand. "What did you say?"

In my head, I replayed that moment when Kyle climbed out of his car and headed toward me, pushing the camera against my chest. He knew...of course he knew. He organized it all to protect my sister, because that's what a man in love does, right?

I stared at Calix...

They protected what was theirs.

Warmth slipped from me and the cold closed in. But I didn't shake and tremble...I was strangely calm.

"It's my baby." I whispered.

Calix leaned closer. "What did you say?"

But it didn't matter. Not anymore.

My body slipped, my head hit the ground.

It was my baby in her belly.

I was that child's dad...

*Not anymore...*

Darkness stole the sunlight from my world.

I closed my eyes as a shudder tore through me.

And as that darkness swept around me, I had one last thing to say...

One last plea to a woman I once thought I loved.

The words rose in my head...I hoped somehow they found her... and she understood.

*April...*

*I'm sorry.*

ONE

## Mine

---

I hope you enjoyed Stepbrother Games. If you want more dark, hot as fuck stepbrother romance I have more for you...

Flames reached high into the night, consuming the room on the second floor of our house with a roar. The room that had until moments ago been mine. I blinked, trying to dislodge my tears, and shivered.

*"Is anyone else in there?"* an officer screamed as he raced toward our home and others followed.

But mom didn't answer. She just stared blankly at what remained of our life as it went up in flames. I coughed and spluttered as I stumbled toward him as he ran to the open front door. I wanted to tell him it was useless...wanted to tell him there was nothing inside to save...*not anymore.*

Our things were already gone. Our cars, the TV's, even my laptop with all my assignments for school. All taken, even before the first lick of flames had started.

Taken by the feds for 'evidence'. Evidence of what, I didn't know.

I looked at the few clothes in my hands, clothes that were all I had left. I hadn't even grabbed my cell phone that was lying on my dresser charging. They were all I'd had time to grab as I stumbled from the shower, threw on some jeans and a t-shirt, grabbed a handful of clothes off the bed, and raced from the house. Two shirts and a pair of ripped jeans were clutched in my hands, along with one change of panties, but no bra. Tears welled in my eyes. *What was I supposed to do with no bra?*

Movement drew my gaze to the street behind me. A black sedan with heavily tinted windows rolled past. The red and blue flashing lights from the official vehicles splashed against the gleaming paint. I'd seen cars like that, knew who drove them.

*The Rossis...*

"Mom?" I stared as the black car cruised past, red brake lights flaring as it drove down our street.

Her wide eyes shone with panic. She hadn't spoken to me, not said a goddamn word, even when the cops had slapped cuffs on dad and taken him away.

"What the hell happened?"

She flinched when I stepped closer and touched her arm. "Did...*did the Rossis do this?*"

Her breath caught and her eyes closed. That was all the answer I needed. *Jesus.* I wrapped my arms around my body. First they'd come for him, now they'd taken out our home, leaving us with nothing.

"Elle," a woman's voice came behind us.

Red and blue lights flashed in the dark, illuminating Stacey Cromwell's face as she stumbled over the hedge dividing our properties and came closer. She was dressed in her nightie, a satin wrap covering her modesty. A display for the emergency services, no doubt, as she headed toward us with a black plastic bag in her hand, one she held out to my mom. "For your clothes, honey."

"Go away." Mom just stared at our home without turning as it burned to the ground.

But Mrs. Cromwell didn't move, she just stared at my mom until she jerked her gaze toward our neighbor and screamed *"GET THE FUCK AWAY FROM ME!"*

She flinched and stumbled backwards, throwing the garbage bag to the ground before fleeing as fast as she could.

"You didn't need to do that," I said as her cell lit up with a message.

The same first responder who'd run into our house now coughed and spluttered as he stumbled from the door. The piercing wail of sirens filled the air as two more fire trucks pulled up to our house. But the officer just pulled his mask free and shook his head, meeting my mom's gaze. *"There's nothing... nothing we can do. It's all gone. All—"*

*Boom!* Something inside the house exploded. I flung myself backwards, dropping my clothes and grabbing mom, dragging her with me as the second floor of our house collapsed. But mom didn't even flinch, just looked at her cell as it lit up with a message.

"What is it?" I picked up the plastic bag and shoved our clothes inside.

*God, please don't let it be dad.*

"We have to leave," she announced.

"Leave to where?" I straightened and motioned to our burning house as it spewed thick smoke. "We have nowhere to go."

Headlights splashed against the living room window as it shattered. I glanced behind us to a taxi as it pulled up in our drive and stared as my mom walked toward it.

"Mom, what the hell's going on?" I followed her, thick tears sliding down my cheeks.

"Just get in the taxi, Ryth." Mom yanked open the back door and climbed in.

I caught the reflection in the back window of the taxi, my still-damp hair, my t-shirt sticking to my skin. I reached up, touching the mark on my cheek as I shivered. I'd been in the middle of a shower after straightening up the destruction the feds had left behind when mom tore into the bathroom screaming the place was on fire.

*It's him!* she'd screamed as I lunged from the shower and yanked on some clothes before stumbling down the stairs after her. *He knows what your father's done!*

*Crack!* Something in our house collapsed, flinging embers into the sky. I stared at the reflection of the inferno in the taxi window before climbing in. It was gone...*everything*. Tears filled my eyes, blurring the inside of the vehicle as I yanked the door closed behind me. We carried the stench with us, staining the already foul air. The driver rolled down his window before he shoved the car into gear and pulled out of our driveway.

"Where are we going?" I glanced toward her.

"Somewhere safe," she muttered, staring out the window.

"Safe?" The Rossis' dark sedan filled my head. "Where's safe?"

We had nowhere to go, all our friends were dad's friends, and right now they were...*dangerous*.

The word resounded as we left our world behind and headed toward the city.

"Are they going to hurt him?"

"No," she answered quietly. "They need him."

They might need him, but that didn't mean they needed us. "But that won't stop them from coming after *us*, will it?"

Silence.

That was the answer I was afraid of.

I leaned back against the seat. *Jesus, dad. What the hell have you done?* The last two days were a blur. First the argument and the sound of one of my parents' all too frequent shouting matches, before chaos...and then, the feds.

The ache in the back of my throat felt like a fist. I swallowed, watching the city lights brighten in the distance before we took the exit ramp and headed east toward the place where million-dollar homes lined the streets and where rich kids raced expensive cars for slips...and we didn't know anyone there.

Ten-foot wrought iron fences and CCTV cameras were all I saw before the driver pulled into a driveway where the black gates were open.

"Thank you." Mom reached out and handed him a fifty-dollar bill, pulled from a purse I hadn't noticed until now.

"Mom?" I murmured as she pulled back to the seat. "Where are we?"

But she didn't answer, just shoved open the door and climbed out.

I followed, finding a three-story house partially hidden from the street. A midnight Shelby Mustang sat outside, a dark blue Lamborghini beside it, leaving one other parking space empty. What kind of people had cars like that?

I stopped walking.

"It's just for a few days, honey." Mom never once looked my way. "Just until I figure this out."

A man stepped out of the door. Tall and intense, his gaze was fixed on my mom.

"Elle." He strode toward her and pulled her into a hug. "*Jesus,* I was so damn worried." He glanced my way and forced a smile. "Thank God you're both okay."

"I'm sorry, Creed." Mom looked away, discreetly brushing her tears away. "I had no one else to call."

"Sorry?" He seemed confused. "You don't need to be sorry, Elle. That's what friends are for. Come on, let's get you both inside, you're shaking like a damn leaf."

He slid his arm around mom's waist, pulling her toward the front door. But it was that empty car space that nagged me, enough to make me glance over my shoulder before I followed.

Footsteps thudded upstairs before a door closed with a bang. I flinched and jerked my gaze upwards.

"Don't worry." Creed said as he met my gaze. "You won't hear a damn thing inside. Double glazed windows."

Like everyone else, his gaze drifted to the mark on my cheek. The ugly, disgusting strawberry disfiguration I hated. Heat flared as I tugged my hair across to hide it.

"It's just for the night," Mom assured. "So I can think."

"For as long as you need a place, this is yours," he replied. "Come on, I bet you're exhausted."

I carried the plastic bag of clothes inside, acutely aware as I stepped into a stranger's house in nothing more than a damp t-shirt and dirty jeans.

"Let me get you settled," he called to me, and headed for the stairs. "Then your mom and I can have a drink and try to figure out a way out of this."

"How did you know my dad?" I asked as I followed.

His steps faltered for a second as he glanced over his shoulder. "Your dad? I don't, not really." He glanced toward mom. "Your mom and I knew each other in college."

I looked back as I climbed the stairs. She looked so lost in that moment, so utterly lost. I followed him up to the third floor and stepped forward, listening to the drone of a TV coming from a room further along the hall. "You have a son?"

"Sons..." he answered with a smile. "Three of the pains in the ass, unfortunately. But don't worry, two will be gone before long." He said as he moved ahead of me. "God knows, my damn wallet could use a break. They eat like horses."

He opened a bedroom door and flicked on the light. "The room's a bit cluttered, I'm sorry. We mostly use it as a storage room, but there's clean sheets on the bed."

At first glance, he'd looked younger in the outside lights, but standing here in the brighter glare, I caught flecks of gray amongst the black. He held my gaze, and in the connection, goosebumps raced along my arms.

"I hope you'll like it here," he murmured as I stepped into the room, automatically whispered "thank you," and closed the door behind me.

The heavy thud of his steps echoed as he left. *Like it here?* I scowled. "For the night, sure."

By morning, we'd have a plan. Mom, me, and our lawyers to figure out a way to get my dad free.

The faint sound of an engine drew my focus to the window. I rounded the bed, squeezed between some kind of machine covered with a sheet, and looked out the window as a black Jeep Cherokee drove through the open gate and pulled into the empty parking spot.

*Sons...the word resounded. Older sons...older than me, at least.* I leaned closer to the glass, trying to get a glimpse as he climbed out of the four-wheel drive and closed the door. But he was hidden, leaving me to stare at his shadow before even that disappeared.

Downstairs, the front door closed with a *thud*. I glanced toward the doorway, then moved around the machine, stubbing my damn toe as I went. *"Shit!"* I cried, shoving against the damn thing.

The sheet slipped, revealing stainless steel...a machine...a breathing machine.

I'd seen these things...*respirators*. That's right. "High five to my constant reruns of Grey's Anatomy," I muttered.

But why was it here?

I tugged at the covering, revealing more and more of the room crammed with medical equipment. New equipment, at that. There was an ID sticker on the side of one machine. Unable to help myself, I peered closer.

"Naomi Banks." I glanced at the doorway and moved around the bed, finding a pile of bereavement cards stacked in a pile and shoved underneath a stack of paperwork.

A flare of sadness moved through me as I bent and pulled them free. I knew I shouldn't be looking at something so personal. I wasn't that kind of person, not one who invaded. But I was unable to help myself as I opened the first one and started reading...

*Creed,*

*I'm so sorry for your loss. Naomi was a breathtaking woman, alive and vibrant, especially when she spoke about you and the boys. The world will be a sadder place without her. Call me if you need anything at all.*

*Aulla Goldsmith.*

"Aulla Goldsmith?" I whispered. "I know that name."

Then it hit me. Senator Aulla Goldsmith had been all over the news and social media, pimping his new campaign for the next electoral term, triggering a whole new wave of name mocking as he stood outside Popeye's and scarfed down a piece of chicken, like he was just one of the community. *Aulla the beluga!* The chants filled my head. It was a name no one'd forget in a hurry.

"A senator?" I opened the next card and kept reading. There was one from Sting...yeah, *that Sting.*

"Holy shit," I mumbled, and glanced at the doorway again. "This guy's kind of a big deal."

But they were all the same, all cards from very influential people...dated a month ago and all saying the same things about how his wife was loved, and how much she'd be missed.

Here I was being bitchy to the guy for helping us. "Nice one, Ry," I muttered, and leaned back against the end of the bed.

The heavy thud of footsteps stopped at the landing.

My pulse pounded harder, sending a pang across my chest, until those resounding steps started once more, only this time they came closer. I shoved the cards back together, gathered them into a pile, and pushed them back where they'd been hidden.

I didn't need to be a genius to put two and two together.

This wasn't just a bedroom, or a storeroom, for that matter, no matter how much Creed Banks wanted it to be. This room was a purgatory of grief. The last memories of a wife—I glanced at the doorway, and a mother.

Read here on Amazon
Grab the signed paperback here from my store